THE PATIENT MAN

A gripping crime thriller full of stunning twists

JOY ELLIS

DI Jackman & DS Evans Book 6

JOFFE BOOKS

First published in paperback 2020
by Joffe Books, London
www.joffebooks.com

ISBN 978-1-78931-440-3

CHAPTER ONE

It was a long time since DI Rowan Jackman and DS Marie Evans had left work this early. It was early May and the sunny afternoon showed every sign of continuing well into the evening.

Marie was grinning broadly, like a truant schoolgirl. 'I can't believe I'm finally doing this.'

'If you don't, my mother will never stop nagging me. She's tenacious, always has been.' Jackman smiled. He had a great deal of love for his mother who, after all, was the one responsible for his enduring fascination with horses.

As long as a year ago, Harriet Jackman had asked Marie if she would like to try horse riding. Marie, an inveterate motorcyclist, had jumped at the idea — it offered the chance of a different kind of exhilarating ride. But life in the Fenland Constabulary was pretty frenetic and it had got in the way.

Now they were strolling down a dappled, tree-lined avenue, heading for the Jackman livery stables. Jackman noted the sun dancing on the pale green foliage of the silver birches and oaks. It gleamed and dazzled with an almost magical brilliance. How come he had never noticed this before? Was he just too busy? He was about to mention it to Marie, when he saw her give a wave.

Ahead of them, waiting at the gate, stood his mother, delight written over her face. 'You made it! At last!'

Marie stepped up her pace, calling out a greeting.

Jackman watched her, the sun lighting up her long chestnut-brown hair.

He followed with a rare sense of contentment. It was quiet and warm and two of his favourite people were happy to see each other. He let out a sigh. Peace was not something you often experienced at Saltern-le-Fen police station.

'Hi, Mum! Hope you've got some really feisty beast saddled up and ready. Mind you, if Marie rides a horse anywhere near as well as she rides that bike of hers, you'll never get rid of her.'

'She'll be very welcome. Get rid of her indeed.' Harriet beamed at him. 'Hello, son. Are you ready for a nice evening ride?'

'Try and stop me.'

Marie turned towards him, 'I'm so looking forward to thi—'

A loud crack reverberated around the stable yard.

Marie stopped mid-sentence, a look of utter shock on her face.

'Marie!' For a few seconds Jackman stood paralysed, watching in horror as a scarlet stain spread across Marie's blouse. Then she slowly started to collapse. Galvanised, he caught her before she hit the ground and gently laid her down. 'Marie! No! Marie! Dear God!'

He was vaguely aware of his mother on her knees next to them, hands at her face, eyes wide in horror. 'Call 999! Mum! Now! Ambulance!'

He held Marie, begging her to please be alright, but he'd seen that strange empty look before. He knew what it meant.

As his mother shouted directions to the emergency services, Marie's body went limp, her head drooped to the side. He howled her name, over and over, but she lay still.

His eyes filled but then, through the blur of tears he saw her stir, very slightly.

He looked up. At the far side of the stables he saw a shape, the figure of a man. As he stared, the man held up a hand, waved at Jackman in a kind of salute and melted away into the trees that surrounded the stables. The sun glinted for a moment on the dull metal of a rifle barrel. Jackman recognised him immediately.

Still cradling Marie in his arms, he screamed out, 'Ashcroft, you bastard, I'll kill you for this.' He looked back at her pale face. 'Marie! Marie!'

* * *

'Darling! Wake up! You're having a nightmare!' Laura pulled him towards her, held him tightly and whispered, 'It's all right, it's alright.'

Sweat coated his face and stained his T-shirt. 'Laura? Oh, Laura, was I dreaming?'

'I should say! And shouting your head off. Lucky we have no near neighbours.'

All he could see was the hole in Marie's chest, the red blood spreading across her white shirt. Jackman began to shiver.

'Can you tell me what it was about?'

He told Laura what he recalled, though it was already beginning to fade. What remained was the feeling of peace, the light dancing through the trees, and then Marie dying in his arms. The sight of that blood creeping insidiously across her white shirt would probably haunt him for years. 'I wonder what caused that,' he murmured, leaning back against the pillows.

'You know perfectly well.' Laura relaxed her hold on him but kept his hand in hers. 'Alistair Ashcroft. The elephant in the room. He's always present, day or night, awake or asleep. And what was the last report that landed on your desk before you left last night?'

'An attempted break-in at the Fenside Gun Club. Now I'm seeing the connection.' He shook his head, amazed at what the mind will do.

'Add to that the fact that Ashcroft threatened all those closest to you and it's all too clear where that nightmare came from.'

'I thought those dancing lights were a bit weird. I've seen beautiful sunlight before, but what I saw on the lane to the stables was more like fairy dust from a Disney movie. Blimey.' He gave a short, humourless laugh. 'I find dreams a bit scary. I mean, they are so real.'

'I know, but the science behind them is interesting. I did a bit of research on them a few years back.' Laura yawned. 'We can talk about it another time. Right now, do try to get another couple of hours' sleep. It's only three thirty, you know. You'll be shattered in the morning.'

She slid down beneath the duvet and turned on her side. Jackman put an arm around her waist, seeking comfort. He closed his eyes and then opened them, afraid of the nightmare's return. The minutes ticked by.

This was stupid. He'd had bad dreams often enough. They were inevitable in his line of work, but none had affected him as this one had. It was the shock he'd felt. It was so real. He watched the numbers on the bedside clock until, at five, he slid out of bed and crept from the room, while Laura slept on.

In the pre-dawn silence, he made a pot of tea and sat down at the kitchen table. He kept telling himself that he was a rational person, someone who didn't believe in premonitions. If he hadn't felt so shaken, he would have laughed at himself but right now not even the sun, just starting to rise above the fen, could dispel the feeling of doom. Something bad was about to happen. With an impatient sigh he stood up. He might as well grab a shower, have some breakfast and go in to work early. Sitting here staring into space wouldn't help anything. What he needed now was noise, the hubbub of the CID room. Hopefully that would sort out his head.

Jackman poured Laura a cup of tea and took it up to her. He left it on her bedside cabinet and quietly took some clothes from his wardrobe. The noise of the shower would probably wake her, but he didn't have the heart to do it himself. He stared down at her sleeping form and smiled. They had wondered if their living together would work. It was early days yet, but so far it seemed just right.

His house at Mill Corner was a comfortable, old-world conversion of the buildings attached to a disused windmill. Although the mill itself still stood, albeit now without its sails and distinctive onion-shaped top, it had been disused for years. Since Laura had moved in, Jackman had enlisted the expertise of an architect to design and renovate the tower, creating an office, consulting room and storage space for her to work from. For years now, he had wanted to make something of the mill. It was an obligation. He was responsible for a heritage piece and should not leave it to rot. Even if it didn't work out between them, the mill would be a usable building again, rather than a desolate hulk towering over his home. The renovation work had been costly, but it was almost finished and he knew it would be worth it.

'What time is it?' Laura said, still sleepy.

'Around five thirty, sweetheart. I didn't want to wake you, but I'm going in early today.' He stroked her hair, 'There's tea here but you don't have to be up yet, okay?'

Laura smiled, mouthed 'I love you' and drifted back into sleep.

Jackman turned his thoughts to the day ahead. They had no big cases on the go, but his desk was groaning under a mountain of paperwork and he needed to make a start on clearing it. Something major might suddenly hit them. He grunted in annoyance, knowing very well that "something major" meant Alistair Ashcroft coming back into their lives. Laura had said that Ashcroft was the elephant in the room. It was true. He was out there somewhere, biding his time before he struck again. The one that got away.

The face of the wanted killer was everywhere. Every officer in the Fenland Constabulary knew that face like the back of their hand. Ashcroft had not cared whether they saw him or not. In fact, he wanted them to know him. He was cleverer than they were — or so he thought. But one day he would take a wrong step, just one, and Jackman and the team would be waiting for him. Well, not waiting. They weren't sitting on their hands — they were actively hunting him. Apart from flooding the county with his likeness, they had notified estate agents, letting agents and landlords, hotels, B&Bs, solicitors, local banks and the post office, to stop him slipping back into the area unnoticed. They couldn't block all the holes, but they could make it as difficult as possible for him to move around freely.

Jackman had heard a number of officers say these efforts were a waste of police time and money. After all, there was no guarantee that Ashcroft would ever set foot in the county again. Jackman and Marie knew differently. He had vowed to come back, and he would. Alistair Ashcroft was a man of infinite patience. He would return. They just did not know when.

Jackman got dressed, looked in on the still sleeping Laura, and tiptoed downstairs. He made some toast and, eating it, stepped out into a new day.

Today, he intended to break the back of the remaining minor cases and finish those reports. For some reason, it was imperative that he do this without fail. Was it that awful dream, or just a general impatience? Despite his earlier dismissal of premonitions, he couldn't shake the feeling that soon they were going to be very busy indeed.

CHAPTER TWO

Marie walked into his office wearing a deep turquoise silk shirt. Jackman felt relief flooding through him. So much for his dream.

'Good grief!' Marie exclaimed. 'How long have you been in?' She stared at the pile of paperwork in his out tray.

'Oh, a while.'

'You've been reading up on feng shui again, haven't you, sir? Clear your clutter and promote a tidy mind.' Marie grinned at him. 'Or is the super breathing down your neck for results?'

'Neither, actually. Just couldn't sleep. And this lot,' he pointed to the paperwork, 'was haunting me.' He returned her grin. 'How was the day off yesterday?'

'Brilliant, boss. I took the new bike for a spin. She handles amazingly.'

'Ah, this one's a girl, is it? How come?'

'Well, after Harvey was annihilated, I decided I'd try a new line, if you know what I mean. We went to Cromer, had the best crab lunch ever, and drove back before the traffic got too bad. It was the perfect day.'

'And her name?' asked Jackman.

'Not sure yet, sir. But she'll tell me when she's ready. So, I'm all refreshed and raring to get to work. What's first?'

'After a strong coffee and the morning meeting, you and I are going to visit a certain Mr Kenneth Harcourt, at a house named Wits' End. How does that sound?'

'Wits' End? Is he some kind of nutter? The coffee sounds good but I'm not too sure about someone who calls their house that.'

'Well, I hope he's no nutter, because he owns that private gun club out on Bartlett's Fen. Someone attempted to break into it yesterday.'

'What? The Fenside Gun Club? That's pretty snobby.' Marie raised her eyebrows. 'Actually, very snobby indeed. So, what happened?'

'Last night there was a break-in at his home. Most likely it was the same bunch of villains who'd failed to get into the club earlier that day.'

'Okay, I'll go and get those coffees and you can fill me in on what we know so far.'

Jackman watched her leave, wishing he could shake off the remnants of his nightmare. That feeling of doom. It was like a film clip played on a loop in his head. It just wasn't like him to be so unsettled by a stupid dream.

He stacked the final reports in his out tray and heaved a sigh of relief. At least they were done. Now they could concentrate on the petty crimes and, hopefully, in a couple of days they would see daylight.

Marie returned with coffee and he told her what uniform had reported following their visit to the gun club and Kenneth Harcourt's home. 'Whoever tried to get into the gun club underestimated the security they have there. The CCTV images showed a couple of rough-looking scrotes who obviously had little previous experience of breaking and entering. It's thought they were chancers who bit off more than they could chew. We've got some pretty good pictures, but no faces. As you can imagine, they were wearing the usual hoodies.'

Marie frowned. 'But we have to assume that they were pretty desperate to get hold of a gun if they then turned their attention to Harcourt's private address. That doesn't sound like chancers to me. How did they get hold of his home address in the first place?'

'He's well known, has fingers in all sorts of pies apparently. If I were after his address, I'd just follow him home when he left the club, no sweat.'

'Mmm.' Marie stared into her coffee, swirling it around like a fortune teller about to read the tea leaves. 'So, did they get away with a gun?'

'Two, according to uniform. Both have valid licences. They've circulated the type, calibre and serial numbers to all forces.' Just for a second, the final scene of the dream flashed through Jackman's mind, Alistair Ashcroft waving to him from across his mother's stable yard, rifle in hand. 'I don't like the thought of firearms here in Saltern-le-Fen.'

'Me neither, boss,' said Marie. 'Especially not in the hands of a couple of low-lives. Although they were probably stolen to order and are a hundred miles away by now. Firearms fetch a high price on the black market.'

'That's what I'm hoping.' He glanced at his watch. 'Let's get daily orders out of the way and then go and talk to Mr Harcourt. As a shooting man, he should know better than to leave his guns where they can be stolen so easily. Doesn't he keep them in locked gun cabinets?'

He had seen it far too often, the casual attitude to guns displayed by people who used them regularly, especially among the upper classes. He'd found them in wardrobes, in umbrella stands, propped up behind doors, in the downstairs toilet and numerous other insecure places. Time after time, people had said to him, "What's the use of a gun if you can't lay your hands on it quickly?"

Jackman's father had taught both his sons to shoot at an early age but although Jackman was a natural and far better than his brother, he'd never taken to it, especially hunting. Target shooting was fine, but as soon as he got a living creature in his sights, he faltered. But at least it had taught him a healthy respect for guns, even air rifles, which were religiously locked away after every use. The laws were in place for a very good reason.

Jackman stood up. 'Right, let's go. The quicker we get the morning meeting done, the sooner we can go.'

* * *

They turned into the long, straight driveway of Wits' End. Situated on the outskirts of Saltern-le-Fen, it stood alone among miles of arable fields, which were now a sea of acid-yellow rape, almost too bright to take in. The grounds covered perhaps two acres, part walled and part fenced, filled with all manner of trees and shrubs and carpeted with extensive lawns. Marie saw a small stable block and a greenhouse of Victorian design. The perfect country residence.

'No comments about the house name, please, Evans. Not the slightest giggle.' Jackman tried to look serious, but his eyes let him down.

'As if, sir!' she said, all innocence.

The house rose up in front of them, tall and elegant. The front door had a white columned portico and Marie could see heavy, lustrous drapes through the windows. The whole place reeked of money. 'It should be called something classy, not Wits' bloody End,' she muttered.

'I totally agree,' said Jackman. 'It should be a Regency Lodge or perhaps an Enderby. Well, let's see what kind of man the owner of Wits' End is.'

They climbed out of the car and mounted the steps to the front door. Jackman rang the bell. They heard dogs barking and someone shouting.

'Well, at least they are home,' Marie whispered to Jackman. 'Sounds like he's rounding up the hounds.'

The man who answered the door was tall and straight-backed with a full head of greying hair and looked every inch the county "squire."

'Ah, good, the detectives. Come in, come in.'

Marie and Jackman entered a spacious hall, sparsely but tastefully furnished, the walls adorned with a collection of beautifully framed hunting scenes that were definitely not prints.

Harcourt led them through to a large airy sitting room where Marie got a closer look at those impressive drapes. The room had a lived-in feel. It was used, not merely kept as a showplace.

Marie took a seat in a comfortable armchair and had a proper look at Harcourt. He looked familiar somehow, although she couldn't imagine where she might have seen him before. She was good at recalling faces, but she was struggling with this one.

Jackman asked him exactly what had happened, 'From the beginning, sir.'

'As I told the uniformed officers, we were all out, the whole family. I have a brother visiting from South Africa, and we went to the Red Lion for a celebratory dinner. The little bastards took an axe to the kitchen door, hacked off the lock. Wrecked the blasted door.' Harcourt glowered at them. 'And before you ask, no, we didn't set the alarm before we left. We rarely use the alarm. The damn thing is so sensitive a breath of wind sets it off.'

'You have dogs, sir. We heard them when we arrived. Didn't they bark?'

'Probably barked their heads off, but who's to hear them? As you can see, we have no nearby neighbours.'

'The intruders didn't harm them?' Jackman asked.

'No, and they weren't put off by them either. The dogs were shut in the family room and the thieves didn't go in there.'

'So, where were the guns taken from, sir?' Marie asked.

'My study. I have a couple of gun cabinets, one a steel shotgun safe with a digital keypad and one that belonged to my father, an antique carved wooden one. That's the one they trashed. Used the bloody axe on it. Beautiful piece, irreplaceable both in design and personal value. Now it's matchwood. Your officers have already photographed it and gone over it for prints — what's left of it.'

'So they were all locked away?' asked Jackman.

'All bar one air pistol that my son uses. That's in a drawer beneath my desk. It's still there. It would have taken brains to work out the catch that releases the drawer and these savages were evidently not well endowed in that department. It's an old desk, and the drawer has a secret compartment especially made to house a service revolver, not that we have one.'

'Perhaps you'd be kind enough to show us later, sir?' asked Jackman, more sympathetic now that he knew the guns had been locked away.

'Certainly, Detective Inspector.' Harcourt suddenly looked tired. 'I'm assuming you won't get them back?'

'It's highly unlikely, Mr Harcourt.' Jackman said. 'Stolen firearms are usually moved on very quickly.' He glanced down at his notebook. 'I see the guns stolen were a target shooting rifle and a shotgun.'

'Yes, the shotgun is a Dickson & Son boxlock ejector made in the 1930s, a family heirloom like the cabinet, and the target shooter is an Anschutz Super Match bolt action rifle.'

Marie frowned. 'You had other guns in the cabinet, but they left those?'

Harcourt nodded. 'Yes, funny that. They could have had another couple, and that's apart from those in the main steel cabinet. Not that an axe would be any match for that gun safe. But they just took those two, and some ammunition.'

'Anything else taken or damaged, sir?'

'Nothing, so I suppose I should be thankful for that. At least they didn't draw pictures on the walls in excrement.'

'Very true, sir. Sounds like they knew exactly what they wanted.' Jackman paused. 'The other two guns, the ones they left behind, what were they?'

'Air rifles. Varmint guns.'

'Sorry?' Marie said, puzzled by the unfamiliar expression.

'An American term. They are used to keep rodents and rabbits down. Basically, they are reliable small calibre guns for pest control.'

'So, they only took a valuable shotgun and an expensive target rifle?' She was trying to work out why they would have been so selective. 'Surely even the "varmint" guns would have had some value?'

'Not really. They come in at around five hundred pounds each.'

Marie considered that plenty to spend on pest control. 'And the others?'

It took Harcourt a moment to respond. 'Well, my father's shotgun isn't worth a great deal. It had more sentimental value. I had it valued for insurance purposes about a year ago and they said two and a half thousand. The Anschutz is around two thousand.'

She let out a low whistle. 'And that's not a great deal?'

Harcourt laughed. 'If they'd been able to get into the other cabinet it would have been a different matter.'

'A Purdey?' asked Jackman.

Harcourt laughed louder. 'Spot on. It's the jewel in the crown. But apart from that, I have my best target rifles in there, Walthers, and they are worth four and a half each.'

'So how many guns do you own, sir?' Marie asked, having lost count.

'Well, personal guns would be nine, including the pistol. We also have a small collection for general use in the armoury at the gun club.'

'And every single one is legal and licensed?' she asked.

'Check for yourself, Detective Sergeant. You'll find all my guns are properly registered. And my gun club is hot as hell when issuing club firearms to members. The armourer is present at all times. They never leave his sight. Most of our members prefer to use their own firearms. We only offer ours if requested, usually to give visitors a feel for the club prior to joining.' Harcourt turned a hard gaze on her. 'I take both the ownership and handling of weapons extremely seriously,

DS Evans, I always have. I spent my early life in the military, so I know my guns. I also know what they can do.' Without taking his eyes off her, he rolled up his left sleeve and showed her an ugly scarred area on his forearm. 'That wasn't the enemy, Detective, it was a friend of mine whose mind wasn't fully focused when he was cleaning his weapon. Something like that would instil a lifelong respect for lethal weapons, wouldn't you say?'

Chastened, Marie nodded. 'Absolutely, sir.' Clearly there would be no Uzis in *his* umbrella stand. 'Could we see the damage the thieves did, Mr Harcourt? Both to the door and the gun cabinet?'

Harcourt stood up. 'Of course. Come this way.'

They followed him through the house to the kitchen door at the rear.

'Not much finesse used on that, was there?' Jackman shook his head.

Marie stared at the deep ragged gouges and the splintered wood around the lock. It looked almost frenzied. A few well-placed blows could have done the job with far less damage.

'A man is coming to fit a new door,' Harcourt said. 'But the damage to the gun cabinet is irreparable.' He marched off back through the house, calling out over his shoulder. 'Come. I'll show you.'

Marie took careful stock of the house as they moved through it. It was a real family home, obviously well loved. She passed several doors with brightly painted plaques on them — the children's rooms. *Jack's Room, Keep Out! Kirstie's Room.*

They entered a spacious study with double-aspect windows that looked out over the extensive gardens. The room was centred around a massive antique banker's desk that put Jackman's beloved office desk to shame. Marie almost laughed.

'Wow! That's a statement piece!' he whispered, reverently. Jackman had obviously fallen totally in love with that desk.

'So was that.' Harcourt pointed angrily to what remained of the gun cabinet.

Even Marie could appreciate why he was so upset. The ornately carved wood had been hacked at and chopped up like kindling. As with the kitchen door, a huge amount of force had been used. 'Using a sledgehammer to crack a nut,' she murmured.

'Precisely,' growled Harcourt. 'And I'd like to use some of the same tactics on them, the bastards.'

Jackman said nothing and just stared at the wreckage that had once been an elegant piece of furniture.

Marie found it almost embarrassing to see this man so distraught about losing his father's precious belongings. She felt like she was intruding.

She gazed at the rest of the room. Nice stuff, classy, but once again, well used. There was dog hair on the seat of a winged armchair by one of the windows, and a closer look showed dust and the odd stain on the carpet that looked suspiciously like the remnants of children's wax crayons. Then she looked at the glorious desk again, saw the leather letter racks and matching pen holders. It wasn't all museum pieces, though. At one end stood a laptop and a dock for a mobile phone. And a rather lovely modern woodblock photo frame.

Marie almost gasped.

One look at the picture instantly brought realisation of why she recognised Kenneth Harcourt.

The photo showed a young girl, wearing the red-and-yellow football strip of Saltern-le-Fen Juniors Football Club. She was clasping a ball under her arm and looking directly at the camera lens. Kirstie Harcourt, eleven-year-old girl, killed in a hit-and-run the year before. The car had been stolen and the driver had got away. There had been suspects, but no evidence that would hold up in court, and the coroner had found an open verdict. Not the kind of thing that gave closure to a grieving family. "Kirstie's Room." The plaque was still on the door.

Marie backed away from the desk, hoping that Harcourt hadn't noticed her staring at the photo. 'I think we need to get back and get some enquiries underway, sir, don't you?'

Evidently puzzled by her sudden desire to leave, Jackman said, 'Er, yes, we do. Thank you for your time, sir. We'll keep in touch.'

Outside in the car, she told Jackman what she had seen.

'Of course! Why didn't we recognise that surname?' Jackman exclaimed. 'It was all over the papers for weeks.'

'They always just referred to her as Kirstie, didn't they?' Marie said. 'Kirstie the whizz-kid footballer.'

'And it didn't happen on our patch, either. She had been at a friend's place over Greenborough way, hadn't she?'

Marie nodded. 'That's right. DI Nikki Galena handled it. It wasn't our case.'

Jackman looked pensive. 'Not that this break-in will be connected, but I wish I'd realised before we spoke to the poor guy.'

Marie felt the same. She hoped Harcourt hadn't thought she and Jackman not mentioning it showed insensitivity, that they were dismissive of his family's tragedy. She turned on the engine but didn't yet pull away. 'Sir? Did you notice that Harcourt hesitated when I asked him how many guns he owned?'

Jackman shrugged. 'Not especially. He does have a lot of them. It's not surprising that he had to think about it.'

'I guess so, but . . . forget it, you're probably right. I just had an odd feeling that he was being, well, very careful as to how he answered.'

Jackman smiled at her. 'Hold that thought, Marie. You and your intuition. It's rarely wrong.'

'We'll see. Tell me, Mister Knowledgeable, how much is a Purdey worth?'

Jackman rolled his eyes at her. 'My father told me this. Would you believe over a hundred and thirty grand?'

'What?' Marie exclaimed. 'How much?'

'And Purdeys aside, a Peter Hofer sidelock can cost a cool million.'

'For a bloody gun?' She tried to imagine what she would do with a million pounds. Buying a shotgun certainly didn't feature.

'They *are* works of art, Marie. They have the most intricate engraving on the handle. Some take years to make.'

'I guess so. But it's still a gun, isn't it, not a life support machine or a cancer research laboratory. A million pounds could save hundreds of lives by supplying clean water to African villages. All a gun does is kill things.'

'I gather you won't be purchasing one if you win on EuroMillions?' said Jackman.

'Dead bloody right I won't. I hate the things. I've seen what they can do to people.' Marie glanced across to Jackman and saw an odd look on his face. She was about to ask him what was wrong, but when she looked again, he seemed his normal self. Maybe she'd imagined it. No doubt, Jackman was recalling a particularly bad case he'd dealt with, where someone got shot or, more likely, he was reliving the time he was shot himself.

Sometimes Marie wished she wasn't so sensitive to tiny nuances in people's demeanour. Like that hesitation of Harcourt's when he was telling her about his guns. Yes, maybe it was simple hesitation, but Marie had seen cogs turning and sensed a tension emanate from the man. As soon as she got back to the station, she would check out those guns and their licences. Otherwise it would keep bugging her.

Jackman was staring out of the window. They were only minutes from town, but the fenland farming area swept right up to the outskirts of Saltern itself. 'I wonder why such force was used?' he mused. 'You hit the nail on the head when you described it as using a sledgehammer to crack a nut. What was all that about?'

'That bothers me too, boss. I mean, if they did it because they hated the Harcourts and wanted to wreak mega damage, they wouldn't stop with just those two items, would they? They'd have smashed the whole place up.'

'Exactly.'

Marie slowed as they entered Saltern-le-Fen. 'One thing is for sure: they aren't professional thieves.'

'And they aren't crackheads looking for something to sell for drug money or they'd have taken anything they could lay their hands on,' Jackman added.

'So what are they?' she said.

'I have no idea, Marie, and that bothers me. I like simple and straightforward, not convoluted and tortuous.'

'If I knew what that meant I'd probably agree with you.' She stopped at a red light. 'What's clear is this. They wanted guns or they would never have tried to get into Fenside Gun Club and then when that failed, Harcourt's home.'

'But they only took two. Why leave those other two? Even decent air rifles are worth something. Why not just take all four?' Jackman asked.

'I thought this was a simple break-in. Now I'm well confused,' Marie said.

'And you're not alone.' Jackman scratched his head. 'Let's just get back and see how the others are doing with the petty crime cases, then maybe we can have a campfire. See what they think of our baffling theft.'

'Good idea, boss.' They drove the rest of the way in silence, each lost in thoughts of lethal weapons.

CHAPTER THREE

Robbie Melton opened the boot of his car and took out a pair of Wellington boots. He'd been caught out wearing inadequate footwear when called to investigations in farmyards before. As he pulled them on, he saw the farmer hurrying towards him. 'Frank Beaton? I'm DC Robbie Melton.'

'Thanks for coming out, Officer.' Tall and thin, the man was dressed in many-pocketed brown work trousers and an old faded jumper under a worn and weathered gilet. 'Let me show you where the pigs were stolen from.'

'How many did you say were taken?' asked Robbie, looking around at the rather ramshackle farm buildings. The farmer and his small estate looked to be in the same condition — tired and overworked.

'Six, and the rest of them were left wandering about the enclosure. I reckon they drove something pretty big at the fencing and just crashed through it.' Frank Beaton rubbed the back of his hand across his forehead. 'Funny, though: they tried to drag the damaged fencing back into place before they left. I can't think why.'

'Were you here when it happened, sir?' asked Robbie.

'No, it was our night for going to the Comrades.' He must have noticed Robbie's blank expression and added, 'The

Old Comrades is a Social Club in the town. I takes the wife out and we have a bit of supper there once a week. That night both my sons came too, for a darts match, so there was no one here.'

'Meaning they knew the place would be empty?'

'Seems that way. We've been going to the Comrades on a Friday night for years. It's no secret.'

Robbie made a few notes in his book. 'Were the pigs valuable, sir?'

'Depends what you mean by valuable. They weren't fancy breeds, just good wholesome stock. Four boars, one sow and one gilt.'

'Gilt?'

'Female pig that hasn't had any piglets yet.' Frank smiled at Robbie. 'City boy, are you?'

'Not really, just not well up on pigs. Call me pig ignorant, if you like.'

Frank laughed. 'I see. Well, I suppose they were worth around five hundred for the six of them. They were all ear tagged with our herd number.'

Robbie had a feeling DEFRA's compulsory tags wouldn't be of too much use. He was pretty sure that these pigs had not been stolen to be sold on but to stock a freezer. 'Has anything like this ever happened before, Mr Beaton?'

'Never in all the years we've been here, and that's quite a few, I can tell you. My kids were born here, and now they work alongside me.' He frowned. 'Leaves a bad taste in your mouth, this sort of thing.'

Robbie agreed. He tried to match the farmer's stride as he headed for the pig enclosure. Unlike the rest of the place, this area was well looked after. The animals had a large pasture with several farrowing arcs and field shelters, and a smaller enclosure with a low barn-like structure as well. There were big water troughs and sectioned feed troughs, and some very happy pigs rooting and wallowing in the field.

'Over here, look.' Frank Beaton pointed to some hastily repaired fencing. 'I reckon they drove it down, then turned around and backed a trailer in.'

On closer inspection, Robbie was inclined to agree. 'A 4x4 or a Land Rover, with a small livestock trailer, I'd guess.' He pulled out his phone and took a couple of close-ups of the tyre tracks. This kind of theft didn't warrant forensics, but if he could get an identification of the vehicle used, it would help a lot.

Frank glowered at the damage. 'I hope this isn't the start of a spate of this kind of thing, Officer. I'm sure to some it's just a few head of livestock, but we reared those pigs and we really try to do a good job with their welfare, sometimes to our own detriment. This kind of thieving is bloody unkind.'

'I'm hoping this was a one-off, sir. I can see how you care for these pigs; they look really contented. But if anything else does happen, ring us immediately. Now you are on our radar, we'll do our best to keep a look out, but to be honest . . .'

Frank finished off the sentence, 'You've got bigger fish to fry.'

'It's the cutbacks and the size of our budget, sir, but as I say,' Robbie handed the man his card, 'ring me direct. I'll be sure to get a car out to you.' He felt for the man. This was no wealthy landowner or gentleman farmer. Frank Beaton was just a family man, a grafter who cared about his beasts. 'Perhaps you'd ring me if you hear of this happening to anyone else in the area? Not everyone reports this sort of thing.'

Frank Beaton nodded. 'And I'll make sure the news gets around to the other small farmers in the area.'

'Good idea.'

Robbie changed back into his shoes and packed his boots away, wondering about the theft. Even the smallest livestock trailer would safely carry far more than six pigs. Why stop there? He didn't think they had been disturbed. Apparently the Beatons hadn't got home until some time after the theft took place. So why just take six?

All the way back to the station he couldn't shake off the idea that this figure was in some way significant.

* * *

DC Charlie Button had been to some odd shouts in his short time as a detective, but this one took the biscuit. The theft of oil in farming communities was nothing new. Even in the villages, domestic heating oil tanks were regularly being targeted. Because they are pretty unsightly, many homes off the mains gas grid tried to hide their tanks away from the house and out of sight. Perfect for thieves. Cases of oil theft were on the rise.

This was different though. This was red diesel.

On the edge of the yard at Dewsbury End Farm was a large oxide oil tank painted red. It was used to store the diesel for the tractors and other farm vehicles. Charlie knew the law regarding this low-tax oil. It was called "red" because of the dye put in it to prevent it being used in road-going vehicles.

'Flippin' heck!' Charlie stood with his hands on his hips and surveyed the mess. 'What on earth happened here?'

Len Dewsbury shook his head. 'Bloody idiots!' He looked down. 'And careful where you walk. My lads have done their best to clean it up but get it on your shoes and you'll stink for days.'

Charlie surveyed the large pool of sludge surrounding the base of the tank.

'When we saw what had happened, we dug a trench to stop the spill spreading into the water course.' The farmer gestured towards a deep ditch that ran alongside the entrance to the yard. 'Then we covered what was on the concrete in sand and soil to try to absorb it. We need to leave it overnight, then hopefully we can sweep it up.'

'What do you think happened?' asked Charlie.

'A bungled attempt to steal diesel. We found a discarded hose, so they must have syphoned a fair bit off into cans, then the silly sods couldn't stop the flow. If my son hadn't heard something and come out here, the whole bloody tank would have drained out. This storage tank holds five hundred gallons when it's full. Can you imagine the damage that would have done?' Len Dewsbury shook his head and let out an exasperated sigh. 'Whoever did this was no pro, just an incompetent prat.'

Charlie nodded. 'Have you got that hose, sir?'

'It's over by the gate, but if you're thinking of saliva or prints, it was left floating in the oil, so you'll get nothing from that, Detective.'

Charlie was starting to feel nauseous from the smell of diesel and was rather glad that he wouldn't have to bag the hose and take it with him. He took down as many details as he could, then beat a hasty retreat to his car. No way would he find any other evidence. The whole scene had been trashed, first by the thieves and then the farm workers who had prevented the leakage contaminating the ditches. It was very doubtful that they would catch the thieves, and anyway, since they had made such a glorious cock-up of this job, it was doubtful they'd try that sort of theft again.

Then the thought of that syphoning hose began to bother him. Like it or not, it was evidence, and as such he should bag it and tag it and take it back with him. If they did find a suspect, a piece of hose from his garage or garden could be matched up quite easily. With a resigned sigh, Charlie got out of the car and took an evidence bag from the boot. He pulled on a pair of nitrile gloves and went back to retrieve the hosepipe. Oh well, the stink was already up his nose, what was another fifteen minutes breathing in the cloying stench of diesel?

Back at the station, Charlie told Jackman about the bodged job at Dewsbury End Farm. 'I've suggested security cameras, sir. If they'd had them last night, I'm pretty certain they would have got some interesting pictures, probably like something from a Laurel and Hardy film.'

Jackman listened, frowning. 'What is it with all these petty crimes being carried out by blundering amateurs?' The frown deepened. 'Kids?'

'Or maybe a gang of wannabe crooks, learning the ropes the hard way?' Charlie suggested. 'Whatever, they made a right dog's dinner of this little caper.'

'Red diesel, you say?' asked Jackman thoughtfully. 'Would they dare use it in a road vehicle, I wonder? If they got pulled over, they'd get their collars felt for that.'

'I checked it out, sir. They could have their vehicle seized and they'd have to pay a fee for its release, plus the duty owed.'

'And if we proved they nicked it, a fine and a prison sentence of up to two years. Hardly worth it, is it?' Jackman added.

'It can be used for machinery, as well as tractors and diggers and the like, so maybe they live on a farm?' Charlie suggested.

'Good point. Bear that in mind if we get anything else along these lines.' The boss grinned at him. 'And by the way, Charlie — you stink!'

'Thanks for that, sir. I had noticed.'

* * *

As soon as everyone was back at base, Jackman called the team together to tell them what they knew about the gun theft. This was an unofficial "campfire" discussion so they gathered in his office.

There they all were — Marie, Robbie and Charlie, along with PC Gary Pritchard and DC Rosie Cohen. He smiled to himself. He still wanted to call her Rosie McElderry and he struggled to get his head around the fact that the young detective was now married to the one absent member of his team, Max Cohen. Max and Rosie were taking responsibility for their baby twins seriously and so far, had just about managed to juggle their shifts, leave and days off satisfactorily. It was an arrangement full of compromises. Both were dedicated police officers and neither wanted a lesser role in the team, but their children came first and somehow, with the help of their combined families, they had made it work.

'I hate to feel perplexed by the small stuff,' Jackman grumbled, 'and right now I can't help worrying about the theft of those guns. It's just not straightforward.'

'Me too,' Robbie said, 'over six bloody pigs.'

'And I still can't stop thinking about Kenneth Harcourt's manner when I asked him how many guns he owned. Stupid, but it's doing my head in. Oh, sorry, sir.' Marie pulled her phone from her pocket and stared at it. 'A text. Can I check it, boss?'

Jackman nodded, still wondering if he were making something out of nothing.

'Sir.'

Marie's voice shook. He took the phone from her outstretched hand and looked at the message: *Forever in my thoughts.*

He stared at the attached photograph. His mouth went dry. It was a shot of himself with Marie at his side, on the steps of the police station.

He closed his eyes for a second.

'Alistair Ashcroft?' asked Robbie softly. 'That is his favourite method of communicating, isn't it?'

Jackman looked at Marie, and they nodded. They had known he would be back, but receiving actual confirmation made Jackman's blood turn to ice.

'He was here, right here, outside the station, watching us,' Marie whispered.

'CCTV?' asked Charlie immediately.

Jackman stared at the picture. From what they were wearing, it was taken some time ago. 'I'm thinking this was taken maybe eight or ten weeks ago. We only keep the footage for twenty-eight days. I'm afraid he's cleverer than that, Charlie.'

Marie had begun to pace around, 'Why haven't we had a single sighting of him if he's been hanging around for months? He's never been shy of smiling for the camera. Uniform have his face etched into their memory banks, but no one has seen hide nor hair of him.' She glared at Jackman, her expression a mix of anger and trepidation. 'We are in his sights again, aren't we?'

With a calmness he didn't feel, Jackman said, 'We were never out of them.'

Alistair Ashcroft had always professed to be a patient man. He had taken that photograph but waited two months before showing his hand. Jackman wondered how long he had been watching them from the shadows and why he had chosen this particular moment to bring himself to their attention.

'I guess checking out the sender's phone will be a complete waste of time, but I suppose I should do it anyway,' said Robbie. He held out his hand to Marie, who handed him her mobile.

'As you say, it will be pointless, but nevertheless . . .' Marie flopped down into a chair and watched Robbie leave the room. 'Here we go again. Cat-and-mouse games.'

She was right. Privately Jackman wondered at the man's audacity in walking among them unnoticed. Now they were all in a state of high alert, but Ashcroft would have known this when he sent the photograph. He could well melt away again for another month, leaving them to stew. Ashcroft might have the patience of Job, but Jackman did not.

'What more can we do to find him?' asked Gary helplessly. 'I'm no pessimist but it seems to me that we've exhausted every avenue. We've had the whole town looking out for him for months, resulting in sweet Fanny Adams.'

'I hate to say it,' chipped in Rosie, 'but unless we get a stroke of good fortune — which is very unlikely — we are going to have to let him make the first move.'

'Which could mean someone losing their life,' Jackman concluded. 'Not an option.'

He had to act. It was time they got out on the streets themselves. Someone out there knew something about Ashcroft. Maybe that person was hiding him. He knew he might be making the team into sitting targets, but that was a risk they were going to have to take. 'Look, guys, I can't dither around waiting for the hammer to fall. Let's tie up these annoying petty crimes and get out there ourselves.' He turned his attention to Rosie. 'With the exception of you, Flower. I want you to run the show from here.'

Rosie opened her mouth to protest, but then closed it again. She had two new lives to consider. Her priorities had to be different now, and Jackman recognised that. 'I know it's not what you want to hear, but I need a solid anchor in the office, collating and chasing up anything and everything that we might uncover, no matter how small. You can do that standing on your head — and bloody well.'

'You don't have to over-egg the pudding, boss. I get the drift.' Rosie pulled a face. 'But don't forget I'm still a police officer, not just a new mum. We all have to face danger every day that we show up for work. Both Max and I are fully aware of that.'

'So am I, Rosie, but can we run with this for a while? I won't wrap you in cotton wool, I promise, but right now I'd like to know the ship is in safe hands while I'm running around like a headless chicken, okay?'

Her expression softened. 'You're the boss, sir. But somehow I can't see you doing the chicken bit, you're far too organised.'

He wished he felt organised. Right now he had no idea where to start.

'What about the gun theft?' asked Marie. 'Life goes on, even if Ashcroft has started playing silly buggers again.'

He was pleased to hear a little of the old Marie. Receiving that text must have been one huge shock. 'You and I will get straight onto that, although by now those guns are probably long gone from the county.' He glanced at Charlie. 'Get the report done on your oil spill and pass it down the line. We have more important things to worry about than idiots nicking diesel and trying to ruin the ecology of Dewsbury End Farm.'

He looked up as a glum Robbie came back in.

'As we guessed, unregistered phone and sim. Ron in IT said he reckoned it was a proper burner phone — bought anonymously, used once, wiped free of prints and then thrown away.' He handed Marie back her mobile. 'End of story.'

'Okay, Robbie. No more than we expected. I was just saying that we'll tie up all the loose ends and go hunting. So can you sort out the paperwork on your piggy thefts, then report to me, okay?' Jackman looked at the worried faces surrounding him. 'Think of it this way. This is day one of the investigation that will see an end to Alistair Ashcroft, so cheer up and let's get on with what we do best. He won't win. He's had his moment of glory, but it won't happen again. This time we bring him down.'

It wasn't exactly a rallying cry, but he did see determination on the faces of his team. It would do for now.

CHAPTER FOUR

He was so deep in thought that he didn't notice the priest until he spoke.

'You look troubled, my son.'

Troubled? Hardly. It was all Alistair Ashcroft could do to stifle a laugh. 'No, Father, my heart is full of joy.'

'Then I'm happy for you. I'm afraid very few of my congregation could say the same.'

Ashcroft shrugged. 'Then maybe they are not following the right path.'

'And you believe that you are?'

'Oh yes. I know what path I have to tread.'

He wished the man would go away. He was here for peace and solitude, not for a bloody sermon. What was that quotation? "Who will rid me of this turbulent priest?" Maybe a modern-day William de Tracy would arrive and slay this troublesome cleric. Sadly, he failed to materialise.

'I was just on my way to the confessional. Maybe you . . . ?' The priest looked at him expectantly.

'No thank you, Father. I confessed my sins this morning. In St Barnabas in Greenborough.'

The priest stepped back. 'Then I'll leave you to your reveries. God bless you, my son.'

He bowed his head as if in prayer, waiting for the man to take the hint and leave him alone. After a while he heard his footsteps fade away and the sound of a door closing.

He wondered what the holy man would have thought if he had made his confession and told him what was really on his mind. A small chuckle escaped his lips.

He needed these "safe" places, quiet refuges from the chaos of the world. It might be a church, or sometimes he visited the lonelier spots out on the marsh at night. He sought them out at times when he needed to calm the inner voices when they threatened to overwhelm him. There were times when they screamed at him like banshees, demanding to be heard, urging him to act, goading him on to right past wrongs.

He breathed in, slowly. Slowly exhaled.

To right wrongs. To seek justice for the ones who had no voice of their own. Those who had gone before, and one in particular.

He stared up into the high vaulted ceiling, breathed again. He had indeed found justice, brought restitution for the dead. He had accused, tried and executed. But he found it hadn't been enough. The path continued to unfold before him. What had he said to that priest? *I know what path I have to tread.*

No longer was he driven by a desire for vengeance, a need to bring about justice. His crusade was over, but it had left him with the certain knowledge that he was like no other killer on earth. No one else could have achieved what he had done. Now he could relax and indulge himself. It was time to play.

Had he played games as a child? He couldn't remember. Well, now he was about to embark on the game of his life. The board was set out, the opponents chosen. Did they have any idea what was at stake?

Alistair Ashcroft stood up.

Let the fun begin.

* * *

'Sarge?' Gary stood beside Marie's desk and looked down at her. 'I've been thinking.'

'Careful, Gary.' Marie winked at him.

'Seriously, I was wondering if you'd like your old lodger back for a while?'

Marie sat back in her chair. 'Have your curtain-twitching neighbours finally got too much for you?'

He shook his head. 'The neighbours are no problem. But, with a certain psycho on the loose, your being alone *is* a problem.'

A while back, Gary had stayed in Marie's guest room in order to avoid a long commute while he looked for a new place in Saltern-le-Fen. They had both enjoyed the experience, largely because of Gary's love of cooking and Marie's enjoyment of the results.

'That's thoughtful of you, Gary, but I'm fine, really, and you love your home in the village. We aren't far away from each other, and if anything happens, I'll ring you like a shot, believe me.' After all, their patient man could leave it months before he contacted them again.

'Well, the offer's there, and I suggest that if we have the slightest suspicion that he's about to make a move, you think seriously about it.' Gary gave her a look of such concern that Marie felt a rush of affection for him.

'I will, my friend. Don't you worry about that.'

He hesitated a moment before returning to his desk. 'To be honest, Sarge, I'm with the boss on this. I think Ashcroft's finally ready to roll.'

Marie sighed. Deep down, she agreed but was reluctant to admit it. Ashcroft had hurt her, physically and mentally, and even though she was recovered, she wasn't exactly enthusiastic about a repeat performance. 'Me too,' she said softly. 'But I'm not going to curl up in my shell or quake in my boots. As the boss said, if he shows himself, we'll get him. We must. If he starts again, no one will be safe.'

'Too right.' Gary straightened up. 'Now, can I help you with your gun theft? I've tied up what I was doing and I'm free to lend a hand if you like.'

'Perfect.' She handed him a sheaf of papers. 'Would you check out our Mr Harcourt's gun licences for me? Make sure his collection is all kosher and accounted for?'

'Consider it done.'

Watching him return to his workstation, Marie was struck by a sudden emotion. This team meant so much to her. She would be devastated if something happened to any one of them. And while Ashcroft remained at large, their safety was constantly under threat.

Somehow, Marie felt that it was her responsibility to stop him. This was personal, of course. She wanted payback for what Ashcroft had done to her and her fellow team members. Part of her almost wanted him to make a move. She needed this whole Ashcroft thing to be over. To breathe freely, wake up in the morning knowing that he was not coming back. Ever.

Suddenly she knew that it was going to be down to her to finish it. Even if she had to use herself as bait to draw him out, she'd do it. Jackman was right. This time they'd take him down.

* * *

'Marie?' Jackman came over to her desk and sat down next to her. 'I've just been talking to a friend of mine at HQ. He's heading up a new unit that specialises in tracking and tracing the illegal movement of firearms and other weapons across the country. I've given him the details of Harcourt's missing guns and he's going to let us know if he gets a whisper about them.'

'Good, and Gary's checking out Harcourt's licences for me, so—'

At that moment a PC hurried into the CID room. 'DI Jackman, sir! Sergeant said to tell you there's been a shooting.'

'Where?' barked Jackman, leaping to his feet.

'In the theatre car park down Ferry Lane, sir. Will you attend?'

'On our way.'

Marie was already heading for the door. 'I'll grab a car. See you downstairs.'

Jackman called across to Robbie, 'Go and tell the super that we are attending a shooting in Ferry Street, in the car park at the Saltern Playhouse. I'll keep her updated from the scene.'

Jackman knew the Playhouse well. In the past, he and his sister-in-law Sarah used to take his nephews to the pantomime there. It had been an après-Christmas ritual, one the kids were not alone in enjoying.

He conjured up a picture of the car park in his head. Secluded, it was tucked around the back of the old Jacobean-style building with the walls of the theatre on two of its sides. Few people used it during the week, as it was somewhat out of the way and only catered for around fifty cars.

He saw Marie waving to him from one of the pool vehicles and he hurried over and jumped in. It would take only a few minutes to get there and Marie had already activated the blue lights.

'Do you think we've found the reason for Harcourt's guns being stolen, sir?' she asked, pulling fast into the main road.

'Bit of a coincidence if it's unrelated,' he murmured. 'I wonder just how serious it is.'

'Grapevine says it's a fatality, sir. Unconfirmed of course.'

Jackman's heart sank. Knife crime was bad enough, but the thought of people using guns on the streets of Saltern-le-Fen sickened him.

As they arrived at the entrance to the lane that led down to the theatre, they saw a whole collection of emergency vehicles. 'Park it here and we'll go on foot.' Jackman released his seat belt.

The whole area was cordoned off, every inch of it flashing with blue lights. Jackman saw a black van and a team of armed officers pouring out of it. 'I see they've scrambled the ARV.'

They hurried over to where uniform were manning the cordon.

'What have we got, Kevin?' Jackman asked.

PC Kevin Stoner lifted the blue-and-white tape for them to enter. 'IC1 male, sir, probably early twenties, shot as he went to access his car. Key is still in his hand. Single shot to the head from long range. We are waiting for the medics to confirm life extinct but from the look of the wound, he died instantly.'

'Any ID on him?'

'We haven't touched him, sir. We sealed the area immediately and have prohibited access until the photographer gets here.' He looked across to where the paramedics were about to leave the body. 'We do know that the vehicle is registered to a Christopher Keyes of Baltimore Gardens, but I guess we don't know for sure that it's his car, do we?'

Jackman nodded. The scene had to be protected from contamination, but as senior officer he needed to know who this young man was. He'd probably get a bollocking from the scene-of-crime guys, but he'd risk that. He took a protective suit from the pile close to where Kevin was standing and slipped on the necessary shoe covers and gloves.

'You wait here, Marie. The fewer of us trampling the scene, the better. Not that I think there will be too much in the way of incriminating evidence if he was shot from a distance.'

'Problem?' She hadn't responded.

'Christopher Keyes, sir. He was one of the suspects in the hit-and-run where Kirstie Harcourt was killed, wasn't he?'

Jackman let out a small groan. 'I think you're right, Marie. Oh hell.'

'And what if it's Harcourt's gun that killed him?' Marie said.

'Let's not get ahead of ourselves. I'll check the body first.' Jackman's head was racing. He didn't like the way this was shaping up at all.

The paramedic gave a resigned shrug. 'Already dead when we arrived, sir. We've verified life extinct. The shot entered his brain through his temple, exited through the back of his head.'

Jackman approached the body. He had never seen Keyes, so identifying him would be down to finding a driving licence or credit card on his person. He stood for a moment staring down at the still form. The lad was pale and fair haired and was wearing jeans, a T-shirt with a slogan on it and a sleeveless hoodie. He could see the key fob clutched in his hand.

There was very little blood from the entrance wound, just a neat hole in his right temple that had oozed a tiny scarlet rivulet that ran in a thin stream towards the young man's ear. Jackman couldn't see the exit wound because he was lying on his back, but he could see the blood that had pooled beneath his head. He could have been asleep. He didn't even look surprised. This young man hadn't seen death coming for him.

Jackman knelt, said a few words that seemed appropriate, and felt in the pockets of the hoodie. He found what he was looking for almost at once. He opened the wallet and took out a driving licence. Christopher Keyes.

Jackman let out a soft groan. This was going to be difficult and would have to be handled with extreme care. It could cause the Harcourt family a great deal of pain — unless, of course, Harcourt was behind it.

He stood up. Time to call Superintendent Ruth Crooke, and he wasn't looking forward to it.

* * *

While Jackman made the call to Ruth Crooke, Marie walked slowly around the perimeter of the crime scene, accompanied by Kevin Stoner.

'Was it you that found him, Kev?' she asked.

'Someone reported hearing a gunshot and when I got here, I saw the poor guy lying beside his car.'

Marie looked across to where the body of Christopher Keyes still lay on the concrete. 'Was he in exactly the same position as he is now?'

'Pretty much, yes. The medics didn't disturb him much.' He looked at Marie. 'Why, Sarge?'

'I was trying to work out the trajectory of the bullet, but I guess we need forensics to calculate that. They'll be accurate, I'd only be guessing.'

Kevin looked at the body and then the surrounding buildings. 'I would guess from there.' He pointed to an old warehouse to the left of the theatre. It was a crumbling red brick affair with a series of tiny windows in rows. 'It's empty. Apparently there's been a bit of a bunfight going on between landowners and developers. They want to convert it into swanky flats but there are problems.'

Kevin was probably right. If the building was empty, that made it all the more likely. It corresponded to the location of the wound, unless the guy had spun around with the impact. 'How about CCTV coverage?' she asked.

'We've already put in a request for it,' Kevin said. 'There were two private security cameras operated from the theatre. They had a bit of bother a while back with drug dealers in the car park, so they upgraded the system. Hopefully we should get some good footage.' He looked around the car park. 'This is the work of a sniper, isn't it, Sarge? A single-kill shot.'

'And Christopher Keyes was the suspected hit-and-run driver in the Kirstie Harcourt enquiry.'

Kevin gave a low whistle. 'And her father owns a gun club. Jeez! This is looking nasty.'

'You can say that again. We have to keep an open mind, I suppose, but even so, I'm not looking forward to talking to Kenneth Harcourt.'

'Rather you than me,' Kevin said, fervently.

'Ah, but it'll be you soon, eh?' Marie smiled at him. 'I believe congratulations are in order. You've passed your entry examinations to join CID.'

Besides being good-looking and with a ready smile, Kevin Stoner was also compassionate. Marie had worked with him on several occasions and had been impressed by his aptitude. For years now, Jackman had been pressing him to try for CID, but Kevin had insisted that he wanted to get more experience on the streets first. Now it seemed he was finally ready.

'Yes, Sarge. I'm starting as a pool detective next week. Hope I'm up to it. It will seem really weird ditching the uniform.' He looked almost apologetic.

'You'll get used to it, Kev. Just remember that warrant card in your pocket. You're still a policeman, uniform or not.'

'It will be like starting all over again. Doing all the crap jobs to begin with, just like a rookie PC.'

'You'll love it, Kevin. You've got what it takes, both Jackman and I are sure of that.'

Marie was amused to see Kevin Stoner blush.

'Uh, thanks, Sarge. That means a lot. I'll do my very best, I promise.' He looked up. 'But there's your boss calling you.' He pointed in Jackman's direction.

Marie hurried off, calling back, 'Will you let me know directly about the CCTV?'

'Will do, Sarge.'

'Ruth Crooke is not a happy bunny.' Jackman looked harassed.

Marie raised an eyebrow. 'Did you expect her to be?'

'No, but she's particularly vitriolic this time.'

'Considering you're her favourite officer, that's worrying.' Marie pulled a face.

'She kept hammering home the warning to tread very, very carefully with Harcourt. He may have been polite to us, but he is no lover of the police. He lost his only daughter and we couldn't find anyone to put in the dock for it.'

'Understandable. So, what's the plan now? How do we proceed?' Marie asked.

Jackman was watching a group of officers in protective suits erecting a tent over the victim and his car. 'Forensics first. We need to know what make of gun was used here. If it was an Anschutz Super Match bolt action rifle, then the shit will hit the fan with considerable force. And soon.'

'I'll remember to duck. Could a target rifle kill, sir? I don't know a thing about firearms, as you've probably guessed by now.'

Jackman smiled. 'If you were hit in something vital, even a BB rifle could kill. All guns, even air pistols, have lethal potential.'

'I always knew I hated them,' Marie growled.

'Me too.' Jackman absent-mindedly massaged the scar where he'd been shot. 'Yep, me too.'

'With very good reason.' Marie touched his arm gently. 'Let's change the subject. Scene-of-crime officers are here.' She raised a hand and waved. 'I can see Ella Jarvis unloading her camera and equipment.'

'And our favourite pathologist has turned out as well. Professor Rory Wilkinson's Citroen has just arrived.'

'I'm amazed that old thing is still roadworthy!' Marie exclaimed.

'Are you talking about Rory, or Dolly the Lime Green Mean Machine?'

Jackman was lightening up a bit. Good. Marie grinned at him. 'Don't let Rory hear you talking like that. He'll get an even bigger complex about losing his boyish good looks.'

'He's got Spike with him too,' Jackman commented. 'He doesn't often let that young man out in public.'

It was true. Rory usually worked alone, leaving Spike, his number one technician, in charge of the mortuary.

'Hello, cherubs!' The Home Office pathologist greeted them with an angelic smile. 'This makes a refreshing change! Mind you, having just returned from a gruelling fortnight with DI Nikki Galena in Greenborough, I'm starting to wonder if you lot aren't in some kind of local derby — you know, who can notch up the most deaths.' He peered at them over his wire-rimmed glasses. 'If you are, then I'm sorry to say that my money is on Nikki this month.'

Jackman smiled at their friend. 'She's welcome, and long may we be the losers.' He glanced at Spike. 'What did you do to get a taste of freedom? Is it your birthday?'

Rory smiled benignly. 'Dear boy was looking so pasty. He doesn't get out much, you know. I thought a bit of a treat was called for.'

'Very funny. Now tell them the truth, Prof.' Spike stared at him pointedly.

'If I must. Actually, dear Spike is moving ahead, forensically speaking. He's making a study of ballistic trauma and gunshot wound trajectory analysis, using forensic animation to establish the relative positions of both shooter and victim.' He took a deep breath. 'Did I get that right, Spike?'

'To perfection, Prof. Now can we go and look at the crime scene?'

'It's all yours, dear boy. I'm but a humble spectator today.'

Rory watched his protégé march confidently up to the cordon and pull on his zoot suit. 'He's turned into a damned good technician and it's time he moved on. I'll miss him, but that's life, isn't it? Nothing stays the same forever.' He gave a little sigh, then added, 'But tell him that and you could finish up on my dissecting table.'

Marie grinned. 'As if we'd dare.'

Rory turned to the matter at hand. 'Anything special you need from us regarding this unfortunate victim?'

'First and foremost, the type of gun used.' Jackman went on to mention the recent gun thefts.

'Ah, you are looking for a connection?'

'It's vital, Rory,' Jackman said softly. 'We need either to rule out one particular gun or start making very difficult and delicate enquiries.'

'Well, at least your request is a simple one this time. I'll put you out of your misery just as soon as we remove the bullet. Assuming of course that it's still in situ.' He gave a little laugh. 'Bullets do the strangest things sometimes. Do you know they can even ricochet off the skull and leave the body entirely?'

'There was an exit wound, Rory. I saw the blood pooling beneath him,' said Jackman. 'So, we'll need to find the bullet.'

'Fear not, dear heart. Spike is on the case, and he's as happy as a pig in chiffon. I'm sure we'll get the answers you need very quickly.'

'Will you ring me as soon as you have any news?' Jackman glanced at his watch. 'We'd better get back.'

'Of course. Now I have Billy the Kid working the case with me, we should be in touch by later this afternoon. Now run along, you two. Your young victim is safe with me.'

They walked back up the lane. 'I hate this bit,' said Marie, 'the waiting for forensic reports.'

'You should be used to it by now,' said Jackman. He climbed in and did up his safety belt. 'At least this took place off the beaten track, and was a single death, not some drug-crazed kid with a scrambled brain prowling down the High Street with an automatic weapon.'

'Thank God for our gun laws,' Marie added, getting into the car. 'Sure, there have been massacres like Dunblane and Hungerford, but thankfully otherwise they're rare in the UK.' She started the car. 'The press didn't take long to turn up, did they?'

'I don't want some smart young hack making the connection between Keyes and Harcourt before we are ready with some answers.' Jackman drew his brow together in a worried frown. 'We have to keep a lid on the victim's identity, at least until we know about the type of gun used.'

Marie pulled out into the main road. 'We'll cope, sir, and hopefully, with Billy the Kid on the case, we won't have to wait too long.'

CHAPTER FIVE

'It's a what?' Jackman said.

'Well, from the kind of bullet and the distance between sniper and target, I reckon we are looking at something like an L115A3 sniper rifle, which is used by the British Army, Royal Air Force and the Royal Marines, DI Jackman.' Spike sounded very sure of himself.

This raised a whole lot of further questions, but at least it wasn't one of the guns stolen from Kenneth Harcourt.

'A military weapon,' murmured Jackman.

'Absolutely, sir, a long-range bolt action rifle used by British Special Forces.' Spike confirmed. 'The longest-recorded kill shot was made using one of those, when a British Army sniper took out two Taliban machine gunners from a distance of over two thousand seven hundred yards.'

'That's over one and a half miles!'

'Impressive, isn't it?'

'How on earth would someone get hold of one of those?' Jackman said.

'Oh, they are not just military. You can purchase them for hunting, and some civilian long-distance competition target shooters like to use them. And it's British,' Spike added proudly. 'A Portsmouth based company produce them — the firm was started by an Olympic gold medallist in shooting.'

'Okay, so what would one of those set me back?' asked Jackman.

Spike didn't take a breath. 'Twenty-three thousand quid.'

Jackman whistled. 'That much?'

'They are the bee's knees, sir. If I was into shooting, I'd be very happy to own one of those.'

Jackman's brain was going into overdrive. For some reason, he had been certain that the stolen target rifle was going to be the culprit. Now he knew otherwise, he was still concerned that Harcourt was connected to the killing. He owned a gun club, ergo he had access to all sorts of weapons, so why not a sniper rifle? 'Spike? Do you have an idea of where the shooter was standing when he fired the shot?'

'Certainly have, DI Jackman. I notified uniform immediately. They are checking it out right now. From the angle of the entry wound, the trajectory was pretty clear. It was from the roof of the department store just beyond that derelict warehouse. It has a customer car park up there, connected to the multi-storey council one next door.'

Jackman knew the place. The top floor of the car park was only used on busy market days when traffic was heavy. It was some distance away, but made the perfect spot for a marksman, having an unobstructed view of the theatre car park. 'I guess a sharpshooter would have no trouble at all.'

'Especially with the telescopic lenses they have on them,' Spike added. 'It would have been child's play for a crack shot.'

'Thanks, Spike. I really appreciate your expertise on this.'

'Tell that to the prof when you've got a minute, will you, sir?' Spike laughed. 'Anything else we come up with, we'll contact you.'

Jackman hung up and beckoned to Marie. While he waited for her to join him, he closed his eyes and tried to think.

Marie hurried in and shut the door behind her. 'Can we sum up where we are, sir? I need to get my head around all this.'

'One dead male, name of Christopher Keyes, executed by a sniper using a military weapon, from some distance away. On the roof of Burridge's Department Store to be exact. Keyes was suspected of driving the car that killed Kirstie Harcourt. Her father, Kenneth, owns guns and runs a gun club. Plus, he is known to be angry and resentful that no one was made to pay for his daughter's death.'

Marie grunted. 'Looks like we are going to have to have that difficult conversation after all.'

'Ah well. I suggest we grab a coffee, see what uniform have found up on the car park roof, then go and visit Harcourt again. At very least he has to be notified about Keyes's death,' Jackman said.

'What about Chris Keyes's family, sir? Have they been notified yet?' Marie asked.

'Robbie and Rosie have already gone to speak to them. We need his next of kin to formally identify him, and then we can proceed.' He checked the time. 'They've been gone a while so we should hear from them soon.'

Marie left to get their drinks and Jackman realised that over two hours had passed without his having a single thought of Alistair Ashcroft. All their plans of getting out there and making inquiries about him were suddenly on hold. Naturally the shooting came first, but Jackman was very aware that Ashcroft would really enjoy making a move while they were trying to deal with a murder.

Robbie phoned. 'It's him, boss. It's Christopher Keyes. His father came to the morgue with us and made the ID.'

'How are the family holding up?' Jackman asked.

'We've left them with a family liaison officer, sir. We had no one immediately available so Greenborough have sent us Sergeant Lucy Wells, and she is looking after them. They are all in shock, as you can imagine. The mother is devastated.' Robbie sounded pretty strung out himself. Notifying relatives was one of the more harrowing aspects of police work.

'Get yourselves back here, Robbie.'

'Yes, sir. Oh, before I go, we asked if they knew why Christopher was in that particular car park. His father said he always parked there on a Thursday. He had a part-time job at the theatre. His killer obviously knew that.'

'Okay. Good work, Robbie. Now you and Rosie come back, get yourselves some strong coffee and take a break.'

'We have a positive ID?' Marie placed a steaming mug of coffee on his desk.

'Confirmed. It is Keyes.'

His phone rang again and he heard the deep voice of the desk sergeant. 'No evidence found up on the car park roof, sir, but the cameras have been tampered with. One was turned aside and another was covered in some kind of sticky-backed plastic. We've spoken to the security staff at Burridge's and they say no one drove onto the roof at the time of the incident.'

'The area you mentioned, the one where the cameras were tampered with, does it give a view of the theatre, Sergeant?'

'Oh yes, sir. Clear view.'

'Then he most likely parked on one of the lower levels with all the other cars and walked up.'

'That's what we thought, sir, so we are going over the CCTV for the whole car park from the time it opened to the approximate time of the attack.'

'Thanks, Sergeant. Keep me posted.'

'Will do.'

Jackman stared into his coffee. 'Marie. Do you honestly believe that Kenneth Harcourt is the kind of person who would have a young man executed in cold blood?'

Marie drew in a long breath. 'Well, sir, we don't know the family, do we? If he was the kind of father who idolised his only daughter, maybe it's possible. But my problem with that scenario is that there were two suspects. If Keyes was indisputably the driver, and we simply hadn't got enough concrete evidence to put him away, I'd understand it, but that wasn't the case.' She sipped her coffee. 'Or maybe if Keyes had been heard bragging about getting away with it, in the pub or somewhere, that would also cause Harcourt to want to kill him. But Keyes always denied being the driver.' She shrugged. 'We need to know more about the Harcourt family and their relationships with each other. But on the surface, I'd say no, I don't think he is.'

'I'm of the same opinion,' Jackman said. 'The act was premeditated. Whoever killed Keyes was cold and callous and Harcourt doesn't come across like that. Even so, I'll be interested to know where he was at the time of the shooting. We mustn't forget the man is an expert shot.'

'Plus, he's ex-army, which means that he mixes with like-minded people,' said Marie. 'He didn't have to pull the trigger himself, did he? He's a well-off bloke. He could have hired an assassin to do his dirty work for him.'

Jackman knew it would not be the first time that a grieving parent or loved one had taken the law into their own hands. 'Maybe.'

'I'm still uneasy about three crimes all happening one after the other and all being connected to Harcourt in some way.' Marie screwed her face up in concentration. 'The gun club break-in, then Harcourt has his own house broken into and guns stolen. Now a man connected to the death of Kirstie his daughter, is shot and killed.' She shook her head. 'There has to be something linking all three.'

Jackman took a long swallow of his coffee. 'I think we are going to have to take a close look into the life of Christopher Keyes. I want a clear picture of that young man — what he was like, whether he was trouble or a little saint, everything about him. He was the target, no question. If it has nothing to do with Kirstie Harcourt, then what on earth did he do to get himself murdered?'

'Good question.' Marie drained her mug. 'Okay, ready when you are, boss. Wits' End. The name sounds about right this time, doesn't it?'

* * *

Charlie Button couldn't wait for the day to end so he could get home and spend an hour in the bath. He still smelt of diesel. The odd thing was, even though there had been a serious crime committed that day, his mind kept wandering back to the balls-up of a job at Dewsbury End Farm. If *he* still stank of diesel, and he'd only been in contact with the hose they had used to syphon off the fuel, what the hell did they smell like? They must have been covered in the stuff. He wished he had a list of offenders known to commit that kind of crime. A quick visit and a cursory sniff could be quite illuminating.

The problem was, all the villains specialising in fuel theft were either banged up or far too good at it to have made such a mess of a job. There were a couple of lads from one of the fen villages who he suspected might be heading for a life of crime, but it couldn't be them, they were too young to drive and they would hardly be carrying oil cans on the handlebars of their bikes.

As soon as Jackman got back, there would be far more important things to deal with, but all Charlie could think about was the damage done to the environment. If he could only find a few names to call on, he'd even collar the scrotes in his own time. The stink of diesel would hang around the perpetrators for days, a dead give-away. He wasn't being a lone avenger, or looking for kudos, he just kept thinking that if the farmer and his lads hadn't acted so quickly, the foul stuff would have contaminated the dykes and ditches and caused untold damage to the wildlife there. Plus, it would have been the devil's own job to clean it up. The stupid little shits needed to be told, and he'd happily be the one to do it — if only he could work out who they were.

Then it dawned on him. PC Kevin Stoner! If anyone would know the likely suspects, it was him. Kev knew everyone. He was still at the crime scene in town but he would be back before Charlie's shift ended. He'd have a quiet word.

Charlie Button returned to his reports, doing his best to ignore his mates' comments about the smell.

* * *

On the way to Wits' End, Jackman and Marie formulated a strategy for interviewing Kenneth Harcourt. It wasn't exactly good cop/bad cop, but Jackman was going to take a harsher approach, while Marie would be rather more conciliatory. Yet as they stood under the elegant portico waiting for someone to answer the door, Marie found her resolve faltering.

This was not going to be easy. He was a possible suspect in a murder investigation, but at the same time he was a grieving dad whose only daughter had died needlessly, with no one made to pay for it.

Kenneth Harcourt answered the door himself. His expression told them he already knew the reason for their visit. He looked grey, drained.

'It's all over the local news. A man was shot in a Saltern car park. And my gun was probably the weapon used. Is that what you are thinking? Because *I* certainly am.' He held the door open for them.

They sat in the same seats, in the same room, as before, but this was going to be a very different kind of interview.

'I'm afraid it's a little more complex than that, Mr Harcourt,' Jackman began. 'The media do not have all the facts. We are here to make you aware of some of them before they become public.'

If anything, Harcourt turned even paler. Marie tried hard to look at him dispassionately. After all, he could be this pasty colour because he had killed someone or been instrumental in that death. Her empathy was threatening to cloud her judgement.

Luckily, Jackman seemed very much in control. Marie took a deep breath and listened.

'Sir, the young man who was murdered was called Christopher Keyes.' He stopped to allow the name to register, watching Harcourt closely.

'Keyes? Are you sure?' Harcourt's face was a picture of disbelief and confusion.

'No doubt at all, sir. He's been formally identified by his father.'

'My God.' Marie saw his Adam's apple move jerkily up and down as he swallowed. 'Was it my gun? Oh, dear Lord, was it my target rifle?'

'No, sir,' Jackman said flatly. 'We can't say for certain yet, but it appears that it was something with the calibre of an L115A3 sniper rifle.'

Marie had difficulty trying to disentangle the confusion of mixed emotions that passed across Harcourt's face on hearing this.

'An assault rifle? But . . .'

'I'm asking you this, sir, because of your expertise with weaponry. Do you know of anyone who might own such a gun? I understand there are competitions for long-distance target shooting. Someone who belongs to your club maybe?'

'Impossible. We don't hold that kind of weapon. Weapons like that are either for the use of the military or elite target competitors who are aiming for medals, not the kind of amateurs that belong to our club. Apart from which, an L115A3 would cost a small fortune.' He paused, stared at Jackman. 'Oh Lord. I'm a suspect, aren't I? Because I can shoot and because I always believed Keyes was the driver who killed my Kirstie.'

Without answering his question, Marie asked, 'Did you have any specific reason to believe that Keyes was the driver, sir?' She kept her voice soft and as non-judgemental as she could.

'Nothing we could prove.' He sighed. 'But a friend of Kirstie's told us that they had seen Keyes driving that particular car earlier, when they were on their way to football practice.'

'We are very sorry for your loss, sir, but you can understand why we have to ask you these questions, don't you?' She managed to keep her voice calm.

'I'm not a fool, Detective,' Harcourt said. 'And if you want to know where I was when this murder took place, ask away.'

Marie raised an eyebrow. 'So, where were you this afternoon at fourteen-thirty hours?'

'Right here, waiting in for the mower company to come and collect my ride-on mower. They picked it up at two forty-five exactly. The driver and my wife will verify that.'

Jackman made a note of the name of the mower repair company. 'So, that gun is completely unknown to you?' asked Jackman.

'Damn it, man! I've told you that already.' His face coloured briefly.

Marie found this interesting but wasn't sure why. Had he been too quick in his denial? 'I'm sorry we have to ask these questions, Mr Harcourt. Can we rely on your assistance regarding this matter? This is a murder enquiry and we're going to need to interview members of your club. We'll be as discreet as possible, but anyone with a knowledge of guns or their use will have to be spoken to.'

'Yes, yes,' Harcourt said. 'I'll cooperate as much as I can, but, please, do be discreet. It's taken years to build up that club. Decent people don't like the thought of being suspected of something so dreadful as murder.'

'Decent, innocent people have nothing to fear,' Jackman added.

Harcourt said nothing.

'Can I ask you about Kirstie, sir?' Here we go, Marie said to herself. 'If it's not too painful?'

Harcourt's expression softened. 'She was a handful alright, no denying it. Full of life, and headstrong. But she was a great kid!' He swallowed. 'I know every parent thinks the same of their kids, but Kirstie would have gone places, I know it. She was destined to have a full, exciting life, and it was cut short. I don't think I'll ever get my head around it. The fact that it only takes a split second for a life to change, to be extinguished.'

'And it changed for the whole family, didn't it?' Marie considered how the sudden death of her own husband had changed everything for many people, not just her.

'Her brother's character altered, almost overnight, DS Evans. I hadn't fully appreciated the bond between them but when she died it was as if someone had thrown a switch and Jack's lights dimmed. He was several years older than Kirstie, but they were very close.'

'You had just the two children, sir?' Jackman asked.

'No. The eldest, Aran, is away on a gap year, somewhere in the Middle Kingdom, so he says.' His eyes had a distant look. 'He doesn't contact us much. It pains his mother, but,' he shrugged, 'I can't force him to talk to us. We hope the travel will sort his head out, then maybe we'll get him back.'

Jackman coughed. 'Going back to Keyes, sir. Had you known him before the accident? Only you mentioned that Kirstie's friend recognised him.'

'It was no accident, DI Jackman, it was manslaughter at the very least. But, no, we didn't actually know him, other than by sight. It was Kirstie's friend who knew him. He lived a few doors away from her.'

'I see.' Jackman closed his notebook and stood up. 'I think that's all for now, sir. Here's my card. If you hear the slightest whisper about that gun, please phone me immediately.'

Harcourt took the card and stared at it. 'You aren't related to Lawrence Jackman, are you?'

'My father, Mr Harcourt.'

'Give him my best, won't you? We go back a long way.'

Jackman gave him a tight smile, 'I'll be sure to do that, sir.'

As soon as the door closed behind them, Jackman sighed loudly. 'Is there anyone my father doesn't know?'

Marie laughed. 'That's what comes of being a toff, boss. You know all the best people.'

'And murder suspects.'

'Seriously, sir. You really think Harcourt might have done it?'

'There's something about him that is ringing alarm bells, Marie. At the very least, there's something he's not telling us. Or else he knows a hell of a lot more than he's letting on.'

'Body language?'

Jackman frowned. 'Not exactly. I need to think about it.'

'And I had that odd thing about his gun collection yesterday. If we both feel there's something not quite right about him, we should dig deeper.'

Jackman was silent on the drive back to town. Marie guessed his thoughts were on Harcourt. Marie, on the other hand, had turned her mind to Alistair Ashcroft.

Forever in my thoughts. What an odd choice of words. Well, he was certainly in hers. More than anything, she wanted to hear her voice reading him his rights. The photograph of Jackman and herself outside the nick troubled her. All that time he had been spying on them, and they had never known. It made her shiver.

Superintendent Ruth Crooke had taken Ashcroft's threat extremely seriously. She certainly didn't need reminding of the hell his last reign of terror had put them through. Security at the police station had been beefed up, the CCTV cameras checked several times a day and the dog handler with Stan, his furry Exocet, patrolled the perimeters. People going in and out of the busy station were being vetted carefully and just driving back through the security gates, Marie sensed the heightened tension in the air.

Strangely, Jackman seemed oblivious to it. He was spending a lot of time in his head today and not sharing his thoughts with Marie. This was unlike him and it unsettled her. Once or twice she had caught him staring at her with a peculiar, rather haunted look on his face. After everything they had been through together, she and Jackman were close, sharing an unspoken affinity and a bond that went beyond mere camaraderie. This meant that each was very sensitive to the other's moods and states of mind.

'Everything okay, boss?' Marie asked tentatively.

Jackman, closing the car door, stared at her. 'Sorry? I was miles away then.'

'I'll say. So, is it Harcourt, or Ashcroft?'

He gave her a sheepish smile. 'Both, actually.'

'Then let's get inside, and Auntie Marie will make you a nice coffee— er, the nearest the Fenland Constabulary can get to one anyway.'

'I'll take you up on that, Auntie. Extra sugar today, please.'

But Jackman's attempt at a smile was unconvincing. Marie guessed it was the thought of Ashcroft's return. Jackman was frightened for her and the team, and probably their families.

It was understandable, but worrying too. If they were to catch Ashcroft, they had to have a strong and inspiring leader. Jackman was the perfect man for the job, but these fears of his would undermine him. If it came to a struggle between a man who cared too much versus a man who cared about nothing, the former would lose.

CHAPTER SIX

Jackman and Marie had missed the four o'clock meeting, but the whole team was still in the CID room. Gary Pritchard, who had gone to talk to Chris Keyes's parents, looked preoccupied.

'Fill us in, Gary,' said Jackman, taking a spare chair next to Marie.

'Not the happiest experience, as you can imagine, sir. I'm not sure how officers like Lucy Wells can do that sort of thing all day, every day. He sighed. 'Basically, Christopher, age twenty-four, was one of three siblings, two boys and a girl. All were living at home. He'd never been in trouble prior to the incident involving Kirstie Harcourt. He had a decent job with a local double-glazing company until it closed a few months ago, and recently he had been doing several part-time jobs, including working at the theatre.'

'Happy family life?' asked Jackman.

'Pretty average, I'd say, boss. Not well-off but they were managing. The Harcourt investigation obviously caused them a great deal of distress. Oh, and the teenage girl has some sort of developmental problems, which is another source of worry.'

'Did the family give an indication of what they believed had happened when Kirstie died?' asked Marie.

'We didn't get into too much detail, Sarge. They were well cut up and it was all pretty fraught. The mother swears he was not even in the car at the time, but then I suppose she would. He never came up with a proper alibi, so . . .' Gary shrugged. 'We'll most likely never know. Lucy mentioned to me that the little sister did say something rather odd.'

Jackman looked at him. 'Oh?'

'Lucy suspects she has a form of autism. She lacks certain social skills — she has no consideration for others' sensibilities, you know, can't tell a white lie.'

'What, like if someone asked her, "Does my bum look big in this?" she'd probably answer, "Yes, bloody massive"?' asked Charlie Button.

'Nicely put, Charlie. Lucy managed to talk to the girl and her older brother and asked them about Chris and the accident. Apparently, she said, "How should I know when I wasn't there? But he was driving the car a lot that day because his best friend had been ditched by his girlfriend and was drunk. Do you think they'll let me have Chris's room now he's gone? It's bigger than mine."'

'Phew.' Marie let out a breath. 'Plain-speaking like that must be hard to live with.'

'And it rather indicates that his mate might have been the hit-and-run driver and Chris was protecting him by not speaking up,' said Jackman thoughtfully. Still, as Gary had said, they might never know for sure. 'Thanks, Gary. Now, anything else before we call it a day?' He looked around. No response. 'Then I suggest you all head off home. We'll start early tomorrow — and I don't have to tell you all to be vigilant. Anything out of the ordinary, anything bothering any of you, please shout. Ashcroft is here somewhere, so be on your guard, and stay safe.' He stood up. 'Now, bugger off home.'

* * *

Charlie Button collected his things but instead of leaving, made his way downstairs to the back office.

'Is Kev around?' he asked the gathered officers.

'Saw his car pulling in a few moments ago,' one of them said.

Charlie went out to the reception and saw Kevin talking to his sergeant. He waited until they had finished and called to him. 'Kev. I need a favour.'

Kevin Stoner grinned at him. 'Better be quick because I'm coming upstairs next week. Joining you lot.'

'I heard. That's really great.' Charlie clapped him on the shoulder, 'Well done.'

'Thanks, mate. So, what's the problem?' asked Kevin.

Charlie explained his dilemma.

Kevin had a think about it. 'I know a couple of idiots that are more than capable of messing up a caper like that. I'll pay them a call and let you know, okay?'

* * *

Jackman watched them all leave, and the anxiety began to build again. He knew what Ashcroft was capable of. He and those he loved had been on the receiving end of Ashcroft's evil tactics in the past, and now he had all the more reason to worry. For the first time, he had a personal life, and it was precious to him. He had come to realise that he wasn't quite the loner he had believed he was. He had always considered himself to be a solitary soul, living for his work, and destined to end his days alone in Mill Corner with a horse and a couple of dogs. Now he had Laura. He was happy. He had plans, one of them being the renovation of the old mill.

His only regret was that Marie was still alone. She had once told him that she was still married to Bill, her husband who had died, and she would have felt she was being unfaithful if she formed a relationship with anyone else. That was sad. If only his friend would allow herself to be happy again.

Jackman wondered if he should go and check in with Ruth Crooke before he left, then decided that he'd leave it till morning. Mrs Maynard, his daily help, had promised to leave them one of her special cottage pies, and after this awful day, all he wanted was to eat some home-cooked food, drink a glass of wine with Laura and shut out the world.

* * *

Marie coasted into her driveway, killed the engine and patted the tank of her lovely new bike. This beauty was the most expensive and exciting motorcycle she'd ever owned, and Marie was proud of her.

After Ashcroft's attack on her in which Harvey had been trashed, she had considered lighter, sportier models. But after she'd recovered from her injuries, she made up her mind to treat herself. She had chosen an adventure bike, built for both off- and on-road riding. She had finally opted for a Triumph — a Tiger 12XRt, in scarlet and black — and she could not have been happier with it.

She pulled off her helmet and shook out her long dark brown hair. Should she take advantage of the beautiful evening and go for a ride? After a hard day, the speed and freedom were a tonic, the exhilaration cleared her mind. Leaving the bike on the drive, she went inside to check for messages, make herself a quick cup of tea, and then decide whether to go back out or not.

A message from her mother. Marie smiled. She always looked forward to talking with her mother. She took her favourite mug, the one bearing the motto, *Only bikers understand why dogs stick their heads out of car windows*, made her tea and took it through to her conservatory.

Her mother answered almost immediately. 'Hello, darling, I've been thinking about you all day. How is everything?' She always knew when Marie was worried or having a bad day.

'We've had a murder here in town. A man was shot.'

'And are you working the case?'

Marie always found her mother's attempts at police speak amusing. 'Yes, Mum. Jackman is SIO. Our team is investigating.'

There was a slight pause. Marie knew exactly what was coming next.

'There's something else too, isn't there?' Her mum always knew.

'Yes, Mum. We've had a message from Alistair Ashcroft. Nothing specific, he's just letting us know he's still around.'

'I see. Marie, should I come up for a few days?'

'There's nothing I'd like more, but not now. I'd be terrified all the time about you being here alone.'

'Ah, but I wouldn't be alone. You see, I now have Lloyd.'

Marie screwed her forehead up in puzzlement. 'Lloyd? Lloyd who?'

'Doesn't have a surname. Lloyd is a German shepherd dog, darling. His owner had to go into a nursing home after a long illness, and he had no one to take him in.'

Besides working tirelessly for a dozen charities, her mother made time for anyone who needed her. Despite all she did, her mother spent a lot of time alone and if not, in the company of the homeless and the addicted, and Marie worried about how vulnerable she was. A large dog was a very good thing to have by your side. 'Good for you, Mum.'

'So, what about that visit? I think it's about time, don't you?'

'I'd love to say yes, Mum, but if you had the dog *and* an SAS team surrounding you, I'd still be shit scared of letting you out of my sight. Let's make a date for as soon as we've nailed this psycho.'

'Consider me unconvinced, but I'll let it go for tonight.' She paused. 'Just ring me every day. I haven't forgotten what happened to you last time. You are my only daughter and I need to know you are safe.'

'I promise. Although I can't say what time it'll be, I'm afraid.'

'Of course. No problem. I just need to hear your voice. And your voice, Marie, none of those text thingies.'

'Received and understood, Mum.'

'Good, now I'm off to feed my new baby. Night night, my darling.'

As Marie set the phone back into its cradle, something dropped through the letter box. Junk mail probably. She went to the front door and saw a plain white envelope lying on the mat.

The warm feeling that her mother's call had given her was instantly replaced with disquiet.

Her chest tightened. She bent down and opened it. Another photo, again of her and Jackman, this time sitting in a car in town. There was no message.

Marie dropped the picture and flung the door open. There, legging it up the road, was the lanky figure of a youth. She ran after him.

He turned the corner at the bottom of the road and headed for a lane that led to the village green. Marie was in good shape, but he was young and remarkably fast. Even so, after a few minutes she began to gain on him.

All at once he veered to the side and headed straight for a high fence. As he leapt, Marie grabbed at his jacket. For a moment she thought she had him, but he slipped out of her grasp, leaving her holding a grubby sleeveless hoodie, while he scrambled over the fence and was gone.

Out of breath, Marie trudged slowly back to her house. At least he hadn't damaged her new bike. Then she noticed something that hadn't been there before.

Dangling from the handgrip was a small wreath of artificial flowers. She peered at it without touching it. A hand-written card was attached. It read, 'Lest we forget.'

Marie heaved in a deep breath. It would probably be a waste of time and money, but she called in and asked for SOCO to be dispatched to her address. It was the second communication from Ashcroft in one day. She couldn't ignore it. It would appear the bastard really meant business this time.

She stood outside her home, staring at that silly, sinister, plastic wreath and made another call.

'Gary? Remember what you asked me this afternoon? Well, I've had a change of heart.'

CHAPTER SEVEN

Gary hung up, went straight to his bedroom and took a small suitcase from the top of his wardrobe. He filled it with enough off-duty clothes to tide him over for a couple of nights, plus a few personal bits, and checked that all his windows were shut.

He was ready to go in twenty minutes. He could sort out what to take for a longer stay after he'd talked to Marie.

He had gathered from her call that she was more angry than frightened. The two of them together would have had a better chance of catching Ashcroft's messenger boy. No matter what her reason, Gary was glad she had turned to him. He had hated thinking of her alone in her house with that murdering psycho in the neighbourhood.

He locked up and put his things in his car. Marie only lived five minutes away on the other side of Sutterthorpe Village, so rather than drive straight to her house, he decided to cruise around the village keeping a look out for fugitive youths. The bus shelter and the churchyard, both favourite haunts, were empty. Seeing no one suspicious, he headed for Marie's place.

When he arrived, he found a lone SOCO, a new lad called Thomas Keene, carefully dusting her front door for prints. The motorcycle was still on the drive, the garland of artificial flowers decorating the handlebars.

Marie came out to meet him. 'I appreciate this, Gary.'

'Rubbish. You only asked me because you've got fed up of your own cooking.' He grinned at her, then added, 'You okay though? Really?'

'I'm just so mad at that son of a bitch! The thought of him watching Jackman and me, snapping pictures of us. It's an intrusion.'

'Journalists do it for a living.'

'*They* aren't planning on killing anyone,' she retorted. 'Come on in. Thomas has got a bit to do yet. I suddenly realised that the letter box is quite stiff and my postie always has to lift the flap to get my mail through. Thomas said there's a nice big thumb print on the underside, so hopefully our delivery boy will be known to us.'

They went through to the kitchen and Marie made tea.

'I gave the village a quick recce on the way over, but there were no suspicious-looking little beggars around.'

'I'm betting he's long gone. He was like a whippet, went over that bloody great fence like a rat up a drainpipe. I stood no chance.'

'But you got his jacket. That's brilliant,' Gary said.

'Thomas has it all bagged up. He'll take it back to the lab with his samples. If we've ever collared that lad before, we should get a match.'

Gary nodded. 'If we get him in an interview room and put the frighteners on him, he might be a lead to Ashcroft.'

Marie looked doubtful. 'I'm not so sure about that. Ashcroft's clever. He'll get some street kid to do his dirty work, pay him, and move on to the next hard-up teenager. I doubt they see him more than twice. And don't forget, Ashcroft loves his disguises.'

'I suppose so. But that jacket could be important.'

Marie handed him a mug of tea. 'I think I must have always known this day would come because I've kept your room made up and ready. You can take your stuff up any time you like. Have you eaten yet?'

He shook his head. 'Hadn't got that far.'

'Fish and chips? When Thomas has finished?' she asked.

'Smashing. I'll go and pick some up.' The village didn't have much by way of amenities, but like so many Lincolnshire villages and small towns, it had a cracking chippie.

'I've got a better idea, we'll go and eat there,' Marie said. 'My treat.'

It wasn't a big shop, but it did have a small café out the back where a fish supper with mushy peas, scraps and bread and butter, plus a giant mug of tea, cost little more than a takeaway.

'I need to do something normal, something ordinary, like eating a big plate of haddock and chips with a good friend. Something that has nothing to do with crime, subterfuge or death,' Marie declared.

'Sounds perfect,' Gary said. 'Talking to the Keyes family earlier fair wrung me out. I could do with a large helping of the commonplace too.'

'You have to order plaice in advance,' Marie said.

'Very droll.' He sipped his tea, suddenly pensive. 'How do we cope, Marie? I wonder sometimes. It can be a shitty job.'

'If you could go back to the start, knowing what you know now, would you do it all again?' Marie asked.

He didn't answer immediately. After a while he said, 'I would, because I'd never believe that the bad bits could be so awful! But I definitely wouldn't go to Harlan Marsh. That place, and some of the people who worked there, drains your very soul. You and Jackman were the saving of me. I was just about to throw it all in when you turned up and got me transferred to Saltern.'

'You're a good copper, Gary. Jackman appreciates that. Our team wouldn't be the same without you.'

He flushed with pride. 'How about you?'

'Without a doubt. It's in my blood,' Marie said. 'I've always known this was what I was cut out for, and I've never had the slightest doubt that I'm in the right job.'

They sat drinking tea, each lost in their own thoughts. Then Gary said, 'Did that lad look familiar? Like one of our regular troublemakers?'

'I only saw the back of him, but no, I can't say I recognised him at all.' Marie paused, thinking. 'He was just a scruffy kid, with slightly straggly dark hair, faded jeans, battered trainers and a sweaty, stained camouflage T-shirt.'

'Pretty good description. Shall I circulate it?' he asked.

'Already done. After I rang you, I called it in to uniform. Not that I'm expecting them to find him. He'll have gone to ground. And I nearly had him, the little toerag!'

'Have you phoned Jackman, Marie?'

She bit her lip. 'Uh, no, not yet.'

'Marie! Why? He'll skin you alive if he finds out about this from someone else.'

It wasn't like the sarge. She and Jackman operated in tandem, always. What was up? He leaned forward. 'Okay, lady. Spill the beans.'

Marie put down her mug with a groan. 'I will ring him, but . . . oh, he seems so over-anxious about our safety, I wanted to spare him more worry, let him have a night's sleep without imagining all sorts of horrifying scenarios.'

'I think he has every right to be anxious, don't you? He's the one with the responsibility. We are his team, and if anything happens to any of us, the blame will fall on his shoulders.'

'It's not just that, Gary, but all day he's been acting oddly, even before Ashcroft raised his head. I've caught him looking at me as if he'd been told I had a terminal illness. Frankly, it unnerved me.'

'I wouldn't know about that, but you really should talk to him, Marie. Play it down, by all means, and tell him I'm here with you, but fill him in for heaven's sake.' He looked towards the house phone. 'Go on. Do it now, and then we can have our supper in peace.'

'Okay, but only if you do me a favour and watch him tomorrow, will you? I'd value your opinion in case I've turned neurotic all of a sudden.'

'It's a deal.'

Gary couldn't help hearing Marie inform Jackman of what had happened. She kept it as light as possible, assuring him that Gary was with her and apologising for not contacting him sooner. She listened awhile and put the receiver down.

'That was tricky, Gary.'

'But it's done now. I never knew you were such a good liar, Sarge.'

'I should be, I've mixed with some class acts over the past two decades, haven't I?' she said dryly.

'Sergeant Evans! I'm just about through here,' Thomas called from the hallway. 'You might want to put that awesome bike somewhere safe for the night.'

'Dead right! She's going under lock and key, don't you worry.' She went to the door. 'Did you get anything useful, Thomas?'

'Oh, there's a fair bit of stuff there, but that thumb print is a corker. I'll get the lab to ring you tomorrow.' He gathered up his aluminium cases and carried them to his car. 'We'll pay especial attention to that hoodie, Sarge. There may be a hair with a follicle on it that could give us DNA.'

'Thanks, Thomas, much appreciated.' Marie watched him go, and then turned back to Gary. 'Right. I'll put the bike away, then we can act like ordinary people for a bit.'

'Perfect.'

* * *

Kevin Stoner, now in civvies, walked slowly along Water Lane, a wide pathway running alongside a straight, deep drain. To a stranger, this might have looked like a well-kept river, but the fens were criss-crossed with waterways like this one, most manmade. Water Lane led from the outskirts of Saltern town to a large expanse of waste ground. There had been great excitement when it was rumoured that a major player was buying this piece of land to build a supermarket, but the project had fallen through and it had been left to become overgrown and desolate. The walls between the open space and the railway track were now daubed with graffiti, and the place served as a sort of park where teenagers and kids on BMXs could gather. They had even tried to set up part of it for skateboards, though this looked a bit hazardous to Kevin.

Not a place to visit alone at night, it was also fast becoming a haunt of dropouts and drug dealers.

Kevin was hoping to see a guy named William. He wasn't exactly a snout, but he was often open to supplying a little information for the price of a bottle of cider. All Kevin needed were a few names of people who might have cooked up the bungled fuel theft job. He liked Charlie Button and was keen to give the lad a hand to track the diesel thieves.

He found William sitting with a couple of other rough sleepers outside the ruins of an old storehouse close to the railway line.

He knew most of them by name, or at least recognised them, but tonight he noticed a new face in their ranks.

Kevin had come prepared with a pocketful of chocolate bars. The stranger, a guy of around forty Kevin supposed, snatched the chocolate from him, ripped the foil wrapper off and pushed the lot into his mouth. Kevin took careful note of his appearance for future reference. He was of medium build, stocky, with brown wavy hair, a dark complexion and a single earring in his left earlobe. From the state of his clothes he had not been on the streets long. Kevin noted the grey and red rucksack that he kept very close to him.

William nodded in the man's direction. 'Calls himself Barney.' Addressing the newcomer, he said, 'Kevin's okay, understand? He's alright.'

Barney's brown eyes were frightened, distrustful. Another sign that he was no seasoned street dweller. Kevin stuck out his hand, but the man shrank back.

'William? Got five minutes?'

'Got all the time in the world, guv'nor.' He stood up. 'Want to take a walk around my country estate?'

They sauntered across to where a group of youngsters were gathered round their bikes listening to hip-hop on a mobile phone.

Kevin took a fiver from his pocket and handed it surreptitiously to William. 'Wondered if you'd heard any rumours on the street about someone nicking red diesel and getting a blow-back from the tank. Real mess apparently, total car crash of a job. Sort of thing the pros would have a right laugh over.'

William pocketed the money and gave a short laugh. 'There's an art to carrying off that kind of racket. All the guys that I've come across are smarter than that. They can drain a tank and be away before you even know they were there.'

'Ask around for me, Will. I'll come back tomorrow evening.'

'With another fiver?' William asked.

'Find me a name, and it'll be more than that.'

'I'll see what I can do.'

For a while they watched the kids scorching around the waste ground on their bikes, doing wheelies and yelling to each other, then Kevin asked, 'How long has Barney been here? He looks like a rabbit caught in the headlights.'

'Three days, Kev, but he's told us nothing about himself.' William stared across the scrubby area at the slowly setting sun. 'Lovely, ain't it? Even over a dump like this, it's still beautiful.'

Kevin knew that William was a bit of a street poet. Circumstances had made him homeless, but he had kept his dignity and often showed a very sensitive side, especially where the natural world was concerned.

Then he abruptly added, 'But he's scared shitless about something, I know that much.'

His words called a halt to Kevin's musings over William's virtues. 'I thought that too, but it must be pretty daunting landing here if you aren't used to it.'

William shook his head. 'No, it's not that. It's something else. I'll find out soon enough though, I always do. Now, Officer, anything else I can do for you?'

'Just stay safe, Will, that's all.'

They walked back to the old store, where the little group were pulling sleeping bags and blankets together into temporary beds for the night. Kevin observed that Barney was still clutching his rucksack to him. Poor guy. It's bad enough finding yourself homeless, but to be terrified as well . . .

Shadows were starting to form. The music had fallen silent. The young bikers were leaving their makeshift park. Kevin could hear a blackbird somewhere.

'Night, guys, see you again,' he called out. 'Night, Barney, good to meet you.'

The man stood straighter, tentatively lifted a hand in a wave or a salute. As he did so there was a sharp crack.

Everyone froze, looking around in confusion. The man who called himself Barney went over backwards, hit the ground and lay still.

Kevin leapt forward, yelling to the others to get down and out of the line of fire.

He threw himself down next to Barney and saw instantly that there would be no saving him. A bullet had torn a ragged hole in his head.

Immediately he was on his phone and calling for assistance. By the time he'd finished the frantic call, he was alone with the dead man. The others had melted away into the gathering darkness. Suddenly the waste ground was no longer a place where a beautiful sunset could still be appreciated but was full of threat and menace.

His fear began to mount. Was the sniper still out there? Was Kevin in his sights?

Throat dry and palms sweaty, Kevin inched back into the ruined store and took cover. In the distance the noise of two-tones ripped the twilight apart. The station was only minutes away, but those minutes were very long.

He found that he was shaking. Shock. It had happened so fast. The gesture the man had made was etched indelibly in his mind. Every time he closed his eyes, he saw the hand half raised. It looked like a farewell.

Two deaths, two shootings, both discovered by him, and one had happened right in front of his eyes. Was this what he'd signed up for?

Blue lights were approaching, sirens wailing. Kevin blinked back tears of relief. He crept away from the ruined building and crouched over poor homeless Barney.

Automatically he started to raise his hand to his fellow officers, then recalled that final gesture of Barney's. He brought his hand down quickly and called out, 'Over here!'

Now men and women were running towards him. He saw faces he recognised and then someone was throwing a foil blanket around his shoulders.

'Come on, mate, let's get you out of here. I think you've had enough for one day.' His sergeant propelled him towards an ambulance that was joining the other emergency vehicles. 'Let these guys look after you and we'll talk later.'

Kevin opened his mouth, but no sound came out. All he could see was Barney's lifted hand and all he could hear was a blackbird singing and the crack of a sniper rifle.

CHAPTER EIGHT

Laura Archer looked out of the kitchen window. Jackman, silhouetted, stood motionless beneath the imposing hulk of the old mill tower.

He'd said he wanted to check on something the builders had mentioned, but she knew he just needed to be alone for a while.

Like everyone else who had been involved during Ashcroft's initial murder spree, Laura was feeling the strain of being constantly on guard. No one with a connection to Rowan Jackman or Marie Evans was safe.

Her heart went out to the tall brooding figure in the twilight. No one felt the gravity of the situation more than her darling Jackman. Added to this was a further problem that police work wouldn't fix. In her time as a force psychologist she had occasionally come across this complication, an irrational fear but no less serious for that. She needed to nip it in the bud before it escalated, but for once she didn't know how. She was too close to Jackman, and it's impossible to be impartial where someone you love is concerned.

Laura let out a soft sigh. She had to do something. Of course! She'd do what she always did when a tough case or an unusual client bothered her. She'd consult with Sam

Page, her old tutor and dear friend. Sam would know how to proceed.

While she pondered all this, she saw Jackman take his phone from his pocket and hold it to his ear. He suddenly stiffened. After a few moments he ran back to the house and burst in through the door.

'There's been another shooting, Laura, in town. I have to go.' He paused, looked anxiously at her. 'Lock up immediately after I've gone. Don't answer the door to anyone and ring me if there's the slightest hint of something not being right.'

'Darling, please! I'll be careful, I promise. Now go.'

He was already pulling on his jacket and snatching the car keys from their hook. 'I'll be back as soon as I can but I'll ring first, so you know that it's me coming in.'

A hasty kiss and he was gone.

Laura locked the door, made sure the windows were all fastened and sat down at the kitchen table to call Sam Page.

* * *

Marie and Gary had managed to enjoy three-quarters of an hour of being "ordinary" before the call came.

Marie paid for their meal and they jogged back to the house to pick up Gary's car. They were at the crime scene in twenty minutes.

'Who would shoot a homeless guy?' asked Marie incredulously.

Jackman narrowed his eyes. 'I'm beginning to formulate a theory but it's too vague to share just yet. The main thing is to identify him.' He glanced over to the ambulance, standing with its blue lights intermittently illuminating patches of the darkened waste ground. 'Kevin says the others reckon that the man hadn't been homeless for long, and that he was terrified of something.'

'Does he have a name yet?' Marie asked.

'Barney,' said Jackman shortly. 'And Kevin who, by the way, is very cut up over this, said that he had a rucksack with him, and he kept hold of it as if it contained the crown jewels.' He pointed to a blood-spattered bag, still clasped in the dead man's hand. 'I had a sneaky look before forensics arrived, and I made a surprising find.'

'Yes? And?' Marie asked impatiently.

'A gun.'

'What?' she exclaimed. 'What kind of a gun?'

'A Ruger Speed Six revolver.'

Why did that sound familiar? Marie screwed up her eyes, trying to remember, and then it came to her. 'They were what we used, before they were phased out and replaced by the Glock 17 pistol.'

'Well remembered, Marie. But it wasn't only the police, the military used them too. The question is, what was Barney here doing with a loaded gun?' Jackman stared down at the body.

Marie exhaled. 'No wonder he was hanging onto that bag!'

Gary came across to join them. 'I've been talking to Kevin Stoner. Apparently, it happened while he was talking to the guy. He's well shaken up, boss.'

'I know. I've spoken to him myself. I've suggested he takes a few days' leave, but knowing him, he'll go home, down a couple of vodkas and be back in tomorrow.'

'What was he doing, off-duty, in this godforsaken place, Gary?' asked Marie.

'Trying to help out Charlie Button. He was looking for street gossip on the red diesel theft. There's a homeless guy hangs out here that he talks to regularly. It was pure fluke that Barney was shot while he was with him.'

Or was it? Marie glanced at Jackman and knew he was asking himself the same question.

'I suppose the shot was intended for Barney, and not for Kevin?'

'I'd say this marksman is a crack shot and he wouldn't have taken out the wrong target. No, Marie, I'm certain he got the right guy. And then there is that revolver.' Jackman nodded at the rucksack.

Uniform had brought in some halogen lamps and set them up in the area around the body. The very bright lights threw the rest of the scene into total blackness. It was strangely otherworldly, almost dreamlike.

Gary nodded to where the emergency vehicles were parked. 'Forensics are here.'

Spike, equipment bags in both hands, was hurrying towards them.

'Sorry, you've got me again. Prof Wilkinson says we have another of our sniper's victims, sir.' He looked towards the blood-soaked body. 'Oh my. He's not wrong, is he?'

'Afraid not, Spike. We could use your expertise again. I need to know where the shooter was standing, and whether the same weapon was used. It seems obvious, but I have to have it confirmed,' said Jackman.

Spike knelt, then looked closely at the wound. 'Well, if it is the same gun, he's changed his ammo. The damage is far greater here than with Christopher Keyes.'

Jackman grunted. 'That's what I thought. Which is yet another puzzle.' He looked around. 'No Ella Jarvis tonight?'

'Sorry, sir. I'm the only one who was free to attend. She's already committed to another incident in Greenborough. We're thin on the ground this evening, so I'm photographer, SOCO and pathologist.'

'That sounds like the deep end, Spike,' said Marie.

'I'm not complaining, Sergeant. I like the variety.' He looked up at Jackman. 'I won't be able to tell you much until first light, I'm afraid. Especially where the shot came from, but I'll make it my priority.'

'One favour?' asked Jackman. 'The bag. Could you check it to see if there's any ID in it? And his pockets too. We need to know who this man is.'

'Give me a minute to photograph the body in situ, then I'll check it out, no problem.'

His minute seemed to take forever. While they waited, Marie mulled over the possible reasons for the man having a gun in his possession. It could have been a souvenir, or he was going to sell it. In which case, why was it loaded? Protection seemed most likely. But protection from what? Or rather, who?

Gary had gone back to sit with Kevin. Marie and Jackman remained, waiting for Spike to open the rucksack. Marie noted with amusement that Jackman had omitted to tell Spike about his premature glance into the bag. He had said nothing about the handgun. Crime scene contamination was a massive source of dispute between forensics officers and detectives. She herself had witnessed even high-ranking officers receive a tongue-lashing from an exasperated SOCO.

Finally, Spike turned his attention to the bag. He felt around inside it. 'Oh! I was expecting a few precious items from his previous life, fags and maybe a bottle of cider, but not this.' Spike drew out the gun and placed it straight into an evidence bag.

'Is it loaded?' asked Jackman, all innocence.

'It is. As I'm sure you know, sir.' Spike threw Jackman a wry smile. 'The flap on this bag has been lifted — after the blood had sprayed across it. The spatter pattern is slightly out of alignment. Nice try, but the prof warned me about what might happen if you got here first.'

Jackman threw up his hands. 'Good old Rory! Okay, I'll cough. But I only glanced inside, so I do need to know about anything that could ID him.'

Spike checked through the contents and shook his head. 'Sorry, sir, there's nothing. The gun will be the first place to start. If it's licensed, you can trace the owner, and even if it isn't, you can check back to its original provenance. I'll ring you with the serial number as soon as I get it back to the lab.'

Jackman stared down at the unfortunate victim. 'Pockets? Can you check them too, Spike?'

Marie expected nothing, and that was exactly what Spike found. 'The fact that gun is still loaded is a bit disconcerting, Spike. Is there a safety catch?'

'Not on one of these.' He smiled at her, 'But don't worry, they have built in safety features to stop the gun accidentally discharging, even if it's dropped. It's perfectly safe — in the right hands.'

The right hands. Marie wondered about Barney. Did he have the right hands? Was it his gun, or had he stolen it? They'd already had one theft of a gun, only hours ago. This could have been obtained in the same way.

Jackman's voice reached her as if from a distance. 'We should leave Spike to work.'

As they walked towards the ambulance, Marie could not help looking around to try and ascertain where the sniper had concealed himself. Spike had been right. That would have to wait until after daybreak. Uniform had already established a large perimeter area, excluding anyone other than emergency service personnel and extending beyond the waste ground.

'I'm thinking another trip to our local gun expert, Kenneth Harcourt, should be lined up for tomorrow,' said Marie.

'First thing, never fear, and if this gun has the slightest connection to that man, I'm bringing him in for questioning,' Jackman assured her. 'I'd call on him tonight, but I think we need to run the checks on the serial number first. I have to know who the dead man is.'

'It might come down to dental records if all else fails. I did notice his teeth were good, so he must have been receiving regular treatment, at least until recently.' She looked across to the ambulance. 'Kevin looks like shit, sir. Has he got anybody at home, or does he still live alone?'

'I believe he's in a relationship, but I get the feeling they don't live together.' Jackman moved ahead of her. 'I'll check. It's not a good idea for him to go home to an empty house after what he just witnessed.'

Kevin said he had phoned his friend, Alan, who was coming to pick him up. 'He'll stay with me tonight, sir. I'll be fine after a hot shower and a large drink. It was just the shock of it. One moment William and I were chatting, then . . .' his voice trailed off and he shook his head as if trying to rid himself of the memory. 'You'll want a full statement, sir. Shall we go to the station before going home?'

'Tomorrow, Kevin. As soon as your friend gets here, off you go, understand? The statement can wait.' Jackman squeezed Kevin's shoulder. 'And try to get some sleep.'

Marie saw someone waving from the other side of the cordon. 'I think Alan is here, Kevin.'

Kevin stood up, unwrapped the foil blanket and gave them a faint smile. 'I'll get off then. See you tomorrow.'

Marie watched him join a tall, slim man with blond, almost white hair and an anxious expression. Not the best way to bow out from his time as a uniformed officer. As from next week he would be helping them track the sniper as a detective constable.

'We should get away too,' Jackman said. 'Uniform have got this all under control and the Sorcerer's Apprentice is revelling in his new role as ballistics trauma specialist. There's nothing more we can do here. We are going to need our wits about us tomorrow, so try and grab some rest. We can't keep this one out of the press, unfortunately. The cack is really going to hit the fan when the public hears about it and armed officers appear on the streets'

'Ruth is going to have to give one of her famous tight-lipped speeches to the media, where she talks a lot and says nothing,' Marie said.

'Damned if I could do it,' muttered Jackman.

'So far the press has been told that we're dealing with an "incident,"' said Gary. 'No details as yet. What scares me is the speed our shooter is working at. Two deaths in one day. Does he have a list? Is he picking off specific targets? Or maybe they were just like little ducks on a fence, random victims who walked into the cross-hairs.'

They had reached their cars. 'We have a lot of work to do to find out, Gary.' Jackman paused, looking at them intently. 'Guys, don't let this blind you to the fact that Alistair Ashcroft is still waiting in the wings. Don't drop your guard for a second, and, please, watch each other's backs.'

Marie smiled at him. 'Believe me, I'm not about to forget Ashcroft. And the warning goes for you too, sir. You take care of yourself.'

Marie watched the taillights of Jackman's car disappear. He was looking gaunt again, older, exactly like the last time Ashcroft appeared on the scene. Where was that trademark steely look in his eyes?

'Come on, Sarge,' Gary said. 'Let's go home and get ourselves a nightcap. I brought a bottle of Jameson's Irish whiskey with me. It was my late sister's favourite tipple and I'm beginning to understand why.'

'Good idea. I've had enough of today.'

* * *

In a narrow layby on the outskirts of one of the Saltern villages, two shadowy figures stepped down from an old Land Rover. They had not exactly covered themselves in glory on their last two exploits, so tonight they were determined to get it right. It shouldn't be difficult, really.

'Okay? Ready?' Noah asked his brother.

'Suppose,' Jacob mumbled.

They climbed over a low fence and, keeping close to the edge of the field, arrived at a five-bar gate. They stopped and listened.

All was quiet in the yard beyond. They knew there were a couple of sensor lights around the stables, but they had been observing the place and knew there were several areas these didn't cover.

'Good luck, bro.' Noah pushed him forward. 'This is your thing, so get on with it'

Jacob looked a lot less confident than his older brother.

Noah slowly swung the gate open and wedged it back. Once he was through, Jacob moved along the block of stables until he found the one he was looking for. He raised a hand to Noah and slipped in through the half door.

Noah held his breath, hoping the horse wouldn't get spooked.

It seemed to take forever until Jacob emerged from the stall, leading the animal across the yard towards him. He had placed a soft bridle over his head and the magnificent horse was ambling behind him like a favourite pony.

Once they were through the gate, Noah secured it again and followed his brother and the horse back across the fields.

'There's an entrance a bit further down. I'm not risking jumping that fence we came over,' whispered Jacob. 'Go back to the car and get home. We'll see you there.'

Noah nodded and watched as his brother swung easily onto the horse's back and, with a click, urged it forward. He allowed himself a sigh of relief. Apart from the odd whinny and a few snorts, the handsome beast had been as docile as a lamb. Barring any accidents before they reached home, it looked like they had actually pulled something off for once.

Noah, too, was hoping the family would be pleased this time. He was fed up with being labelled a clueless moron. He felt even worse for Jacob. Okay, his brother had struggled with schoolwork but he had other talents, like his way with horses.

Noah started the Land Rover and pulled away, smiling. Jacob had been awesome tonight. Just so long as nothing happened in the next fifteen minutes.

CHAPTER NINE

Dawn was a glorious affair. Across the fens, the trees and the vast fields of rape took on a green-gold hue as if they glowed from within. Jackman immersed himself in the moment, absorbing the peace of it. He took several deep breaths.

Reluctantly, he turned his back on the vista, walked back to the car port and unlocked his car. It was no good mooning over a sunrise. He needed a clear head, a strategy, and a loyal and focused team. Well, he had the team. Now he must take care of the rest.

The closer he got to Saltern-le-Fen, the darker his mood became. One dreadful case was enough to contend with, especially since it revolved around psychotic Alistair Ashcroft. But two, both involving killers, was almost too much.

As he neared the station, Jackman realised he couldn't continue in his present frame of mind. This was no time to feel sorry for himself. The team needed a tough, decisive leader, not a self-pitying wimp. Suddenly he remembered a detail from Ashcroft's file, something concerning his history. At one point in his younger life he refused to talk. He remained mute and unreachable until someone had the idea of getting him up on stage. Acting, he became a different person altogether — articulate, animated and assertive. Maybe the killer Ashcroft had something to teach the policeman.

He parked in his usual place and sat in his car to think.

It was an amusing thought, but was it so crazy? He couldn't continue as he was, that was for sure. But could he push aside all his fears, doubts, restless nights and terrible dreams, paint on a new face and become the leader his team deserved? If nothing else, he owed it to them to try. He tried to think of a character to base this new persona on, and in the end decided on Jackman. The old Jackman, the man who had risen to detective inspector.

Jackman stepped from the car.

Curtain up.

* * *

Light was streaming through his bedroom window and Kevin gently disentangled himself from Alan's arms. Remarkably, he had managed to sleep for a few hours. A couple of strong drinks, a few tears and the strong arms of his patient lover had all worked their magic. The incident was still fresh in his memory, but it had lost its power to frighten him. He was now able to detach himself from the experience, view it like a scene from a movie.

Alan stirred. Yawned. 'What's the time, babe?'

'Almost seven thirty. What time do you have to be in this morning?' Kevin said.

'I'm doing a late shift to cover for Tim. I'll finish at ten tonight. Will you be okay till I get home?'

"Home." It suddenly sounded so good to Kevin. 'I could be late myself, so no problem, but keep in touch, yeah?'

Alan smiled. 'Course I will, you donkey! I'm not likely to forget about you, am I?' He paused. 'Actually, I'm going to be worrying myself sick about you all day. So you ring me too, any time you want, and definitely if you feel a bit shaky.'

'Thank you. And thanks for being here for me last night. I'm not sure what I'd have done without you.' He sat on the edge of the bed and ran his fingers through Alan's short fair hair.

'I know what you'd have done. You'd have drunk far too many vodkas and passed out.'

'And felt like garbage this morning. Now, I feel okay, and that's down to you.' He reached for Alan's hand. 'You are good for me, you know.'

'Ditto, Kev. We are good for each other.'

Recently Kevin had noticed a shift in their relationship. Their initial passionate lust for each other had levelled out and settled into a comfortable companionship. It felt like a permanent thing. He wanted to talk to Alan about moving in together but wasn't exactly sure if Alan felt the same.

However, now was not the time. He stood up. 'I'll make you a coffee. You get back to sleep while I grab a shower and get off, okay? Got your key?'

Alan nodded sleepily. 'I've always got my key.'

Kevin bent down and kissed Alan's forehead. 'See you tonight,' he whispered, but Alan was already asleep.

As he showered, he wondered what it would be like to live with someone again. He had been alone for so long.

Kevin found a clean white uniform shirt and clipped on his black tie. Next week it would be civvies. He'd already bought two new suits. So, big changes at work. Maybe his private life was also on the brink of a new beginning.

Kevin stepped out into a bright new day.

* * *

Marie and Gary travelled to work separately. There was no way Marie was going to leave her new Tiger in the garage on a morning like this. The journey was short, but it promised to be a delight.

Jackman's car was already in the car park. No surprise there. She doubted he'd slept any better than she had. She realised that she was almost dreading seeing his troubled face this morning. She pulled off her helmet and marched into the building, where she bought herself a bit more time changing out of her leathers. She checked her face in the mirror and took a deep breath.

She pushed open his door. 'Morning, boss.'

'Ah, Marie. Glad you got here early, I thought we'd hit Harcourt before his Weetabix starts working. What'd you say?'

Marie realised her mouth was open. She closed it and nodded.

Jackman wasn't slouched over his desk looking at reports or staring vaguely at his monitor screen. He was pacing the room, notebook and pen in hand.

'Then, when we are back and the others are in, I want someone to chase up the military medics, see if any of the local regiments have anyone on file who could be a danger to himself or others. Then we'll do the same with our own people, see if we have a firearms officer in one of the tactical units, maybe SCO19 or an armed response vehicle officer, who has been stood down for stress reasons or was giving cause for concern. Then—'

'Whoa! Sir! Can we take this one step at a time? I'm still with Harcourt and his Weetabix.'

'Oh, sorry.' He didn't look too apologetic. 'I just want to make the most of every minute.'

'Then let's go and interrupt the Harcourt breakfast, shall we?'

Jackman's phone rang. While he listened to the caller Marie saw a slightly puzzled expression cross his face. He told whoever it was that they would be down directly.

'Well, that's convenient. Harcourt is downstairs, asking for us.'

'No kidding?' She opened the door. 'Well, we'd better not keep him waiting.'

Harcourt was sitting in an interview room. But this was a different man to the one they had met yesterday. He looked terrible — haggard, unkempt. His hair stood on end and his clothes were creased, as if he'd slept in them. He hadn't shaved.

Without so much as a greeting, Harcourt launched straight in. 'That incident last night. It's all over the bloody television. You have to tell me, was it another shooting?'

'Why do you ask, Mr Harcourt?' said Jackman, calmly.

'Just answer my question, Detective Inspector. Was it a shooting?' Harcourt was almost shouting. His hands were shaking.

'Why are you here, Mr Harcourt?' Beneath the calm, Jackman's voice had a slight edge to it. 'Because I'm the one who asks the questions in this room.'

Now Harcourt sounded almost pleading. 'Please, I need to know. Does it have some connection to either me or the gun club?'

'Marie, would you be kind enough to ask one of the officers outside to get Mr Harcourt a cup of coffee?' Jackman said.

Marie opened the door and asked a young constable outside if he would organise a drink for their interviewee.

When this had been done, Jackman sat back in his seat. 'Okay, sir. What is this all about? From the beginning, if you don't mind.'

'I lied to you,' Harcourt said softly. 'On both occasions you came to Wits' End.'

'The gun that was used to kill Keyes. I suspect it was mine. I own a L115A3 and it was stolen during the break-in.' His voice was almost a whisper.

'I see.' Jackman frowned. 'And you chose to hide this fact because you don't have a firearms certificate for it.'

Harcourt nodded. 'It was a souvenir.'

'Spoils of war?' asked Jackman.

'A lot of us had memorabilia, mostly taken from the Americans. Some of the men brought back AK-47s just to hang on the wall. In theory we and our shipping containers were supposed to be checked by the military police, but in reality it rarely happened. We kind of felt entitled.' Harcourt shrugged. 'Some of our elite SAS boys brought back bazookas and quad bikes from Afghanistan. All stolen from the US military.'

Marie recalled an amnesty some years before that had resulted in all manner of weapons being handed in, from rocket launchers to handguns.

'So, tell us about your weapon, sir,' she said.

An officer entered carrying three mugs of coffee. 'Got you and the DI one as well, Sarge,' said the constable, placing them on the table.

Marie thanked him and waited for him to leave. 'Your gun, sir?'

'I should have had it decommissioned and proofed but I just never got around to it. I didn't tell anyone about it. It was personal, a part of my old life. I never used it at the club. I did look after it. I cleaned it regularly and I did shoot it on my own land but as far as I knew, apart from my immediate family, no one was aware of its existence.' Harcourt slumped in his chair. 'Then when you said Keyes had been killed with an L115A3, I panicked.'

Marie nodded. Just as she thought. *But you gave it away when you hesitated over the number of guns you owned.*

'It was another shooting last night, wasn't it?' Harcourt asked softly.

Jackman gave a little shrug. 'I'm not at liberty to discuss the incident, sir, but,' he picked up his mug of coffee and stared into it, 'there was another death.'

Harcourt closed his eyes and murmured something under his breath. An oath, or a prayer? 'Who was it, DI Jackman?'

'We haven't identified him yet. He was living rough.' Jackman glanced across to Marie, clearly unsure as to how much to divulge.

Marie guessed he was deliberating about whether to mention the handgun in the rucksack. She still couldn't see Kenneth Harcourt as a killer. He was an ex-military man who had illegally brought back a gun as a souvenir, end of story. She returned Jackman's look and nodded.

'We have something of a dilemma, sir, and you might be able to help us.' Jackman looked at Harcourt thoughtfully. 'Our dead man had a gun in his possession, a handgun.'

Harcourt's forehead creased in a frown. 'What kind of a handgun?'

'It was a Ruger Speed Six revolver.'

Harcourt blew a breath. 'Law enforcement and the military carried those until they were phased out.'

'We know,' Marie interjected. 'Which means there must be one hell of a lot of them floating around. We wondered if you knew of anyone, maybe through your club, who owned a Ruger?'

'There are collectors who use the club regularly, though I really wouldn't know exactly what each one owned.' He paused. 'Could you describe the victim?'

She did so, as fully as she could, omitting the massive exit wound.

Harcourt started. He looked aghast.

'Do you know someone of that description, sir?' asked Jackman.

'Well, it sounds like Arthur Barnes, our old armourer at the club, but . . .' Harcourt faltered. 'On the streets, you say?'

'That's right,' said Marie. 'He was hanging out with the homeless on the waste ground where the incident happened.'

'The constable at the scene said his street name was Barney,' stated Jackman, a new light in his eyes. 'So it could well be him. We need all the information you have on Arthur Barnes, Mr Harcourt.' He pushed a pad and a pen across to him. 'Starting with his address.'

Harcourt took out his smartphone and scrolled through the contacts. After a while he said, 'Got it, but he hasn't lived there for a while.' He hesitated, looked up. 'Arthur was accused of domestic violence, Detectives. I couldn't see it myself. I liked the man. I'd known him since we were teenagers. I trusted him with our guns, for heaven's sake! But mud sticks, and I suppose none of us knows what goes on behind closed doors. Even so, I was shocked to hear he had been hounded out of his home. Last I heard he had been planning to go up north where his family originally came from.'

'Looks like he never made it,' said Marie grimly.

'Would you be up to looking at our dead man, Mr Harcourt?' asked Jackman. 'But I'm warning you, it's not a pretty sight.'

Harcourt gave a weak laugh. 'I'm an ex-soldier, Detective. Yes, I'll look at your man.'

Jackman stood up. 'I'll ring the mortuary. We'll take you there now.' He paused, 'And we appreciate your honesty regarding the gun, even if it was a little belated.'

'I have no idea why I behaved like that, and I'm truly sorry.' He rubbed his forehead. 'I've not functioned well since my daughter was killed. I'm not making excuses for myself, but I lose my temper easily and I'm angry — angry all the time.'

'It's grief, sir. You have every right to be angry.' Jackman stopped in the doorway and smiled understandingly. 'And don't concern yourself about not notifying us about the gun. We won't be making too much of that.'

Marie was left alone with Harcourt. 'Can you tell me anything else about Arthur Barnes, sir?'

'He was military — SBS. A brave man but he didn't make the best of marriages.'

'Ah, Special Boat Services. They are an elite force, aren't they?'

'Yes, the Royal Navy's SAS,' said Harcourt. 'Pretty fearless lot.'

So why was he frightened? Surely, he would've survived the streets more easily than most.

That was one for later. 'Tell me about his marriage.'

'Brenda hooked him in because she wanted to be seen with a hunk in a uniform. He was a handsome guy back then. I knew Brenda from childhood. Even as a kid she was a schemer, set great store by looks and possessions. What she didn't bargain for was that Arthur would get injured and be retired out. Like a lot of military personnel, civvy street didn't suit him, and things went downhill from then on.' He sighed. 'He was out of work and couldn't find anything that suited him, until I gave him a job at the gun club. He settled with us really well.'

Marie made a mental note to follow up the domestic violence aspect as soon as possible. 'Sir,' she said, 'can you think of anyone who would want him dead? Maybe another military man?'

'The man who stole my guns, you mean?'

Marie narrowed her eyes. 'Possibly, sir. Although the thief could have stolen them to order, and a different party is using them to kill people.'

Harcourt closed his eyes. 'DS Evans, I spent all night going over that question. I have no idea.'

Jackman entered the room. 'Rory is preparing the body for a viewing. We can go straight to the morgue.' He looked at Harcourt. 'Are you still okay with it?'

Harcourt stood up. 'I must know if it's Arthur. I don't know what this all means or what it's about, but I seem to be in the middle of it and I want some answers.'

You and me both, thought Marie with feeling. She looked at her watch. It was not yet eight thirty and they could soon have their dead man identified. Today was turning out to be full of surprises. A strangely re-invigorated Jackman *and* an identification that could have taken them days to uncover. What next?

CHAPTER TEN

Alistair Ashcroft had seen the news. An incident, they said. Police have not yet released the details. Well, well. On top of that death in the car park, pal Jackman would be a busy man. He bared his perfect teeth in a vulpine smile. Poor old Jackman.

He looked out of his window. Below, a group of children were playing tag. He could hear their squeals of laughter. He wondered what it must be like to play games like that. The games he remembered from his own childhood hadn't been a great deal of fun.

He shook his head. He disliked thinking about the past, although there were times when the memories came creeping back of their own accord. He turned away from the window. The present was so much more enjoyable.

It was a new day and he had a lot to do. First, a substantial breakfast, and he knew exactly where to get one. He had people around him now, people who cared about him, this man they thought they knew. He was liked and respected. Things were going well — for Alistair Ashcroft at least.

* * *

Pigs. Six of them, to be precise.

Why, wondered Robbie, when there'd been two fatal shootings, did he keep thinking about farmer Beaton's missing pigs? He sensed it was significant somehow, but he couldn't for the life of him think why.

His desk phone rang.

'Detective Melton? It's Frank Beaton. I did like you said and spread the word to my friends and the other farms around. I was told there's been another animal theft. This time it was a stallion.'

'What? A horse?' Robbie said, rather densely. 'Where from, sir?'

'Appleyard Farm Stables, just outside Ferndyke Village. Belongs to a Mr Clay Bullimore. And he is well pissed off, I can tell you. Besides being his best breeding stallion, it's his favourite too.'

'When was this, Mr Beaton?'

'Last night. He's not sure what time exactly.'

'Can you let me have his number, sir? I'll try to get hold of him as soon as I can, but we are snowed under at present.'

'Ah, yes. I heard the news, bad business that. But . . . ?'

Robbie understood. 'It's still a serious theft, sir, and it will be dealt with, I promise you.' He scribbled down the number in his notebook. 'Thanks, Mr Beaton.'

Robbie wondered what Jackman would say. Most likely uniform would pay a call, give the owner an incident number and it would be shoved on the back burner.

Robbie wondered what a breeding horse would cost. Thousands? He really had no idea.

Marie hurried into the office. 'Success! Positive ID for Barney.' She went to the whiteboard and wrote the name Arthur James Barnes next to the post-mortem photograph of their latest victim.

'Excellent', said Robbie. 'Don't often get that lucky so soon.' He looked towards the door. 'Is the boss with you?'

'In his office.' She grinned at him. 'I think I deserve a coffee. Want one?'

He shook his head. 'No thanks, Marie. I need a word with Jackman.'

He went over and tapped on Jackman's door. 'Sorry to bother you, sir, but there's been a horse theft reported.'

Jackman's head snapped up. 'Where from?

'Uh, Appleyard Farm, Ferndyke Village.'

'Clay Bullimore's place! He's a friend of my mother's. He has a breeding stable there. Nice bloke, great horses. What happened?'

'One stallion stolen, sir. Er, what would you like me to do about it?'

'Go and see him, of course! Do it now. We've got a lot on today.' Jackman practically shoved him out of the office. 'And tell him we'll do all we can to get it back. Oh, and Robbie, I want to know the horse's name, okay?'

Outside the office, Robbie stood and stared back at the closed door in bewilderment.

'You have the look of a startled gazelle, Robbie.' Marie came up behind him with a coffee in either hand.

'Er, well, I . . . The boss, he . . .'

'Oh, that. Yeah, caught me unawares too. Well, don't worry too much. I don't think he's on anything. His pupils aren't dilated.'

Robbie gawped at her.

'I had considered the possibility of a changeling, but that usually applies to babies.'

He saw the merriment in her eyes but wasn't quite sure how to respond. 'Er, I think I'd better go and do as I was told.'

'And that is?' she asked.

'Catch me some rustlers. Bye!'

* * *

After daily orders, Kevin Stoner went to look for William. He wanted to know if he and the others who'd been with him the previous night were alright.

He found William in a small café tucked away down a back alley in Saltern town. He sat alone, staring into an untouched cup of coffee.

'You eaten?' Kevin asked softly.

William shook his head slowly. Kevin went to the counter and ordered two bacon butties, a Danish and two coffees.

Kevin took the drinks and the pastry back to the table. 'I was worried about you and the others. That was a terrible thing to happen. It really shook me up, so I guess you guys are feeling the same.'

William finally looked up. 'I've been on the streets a long time, Kev, but I've never seen anything like that. You'd have thought we were in Afghanistan, not Saltern, the way that sniper took him out. Just for one horrible moment I thought I was back in Northern—' He stopped abruptly.

The realisation suddenly struck Kevin. He knew absolutely nothing about William's past. He had no idea why or how he became homeless, who he really was, or even where he came from. Asking had always seemed like an invasion of privacy. So, William was ex-military, just like Barney had been.

He looked up as a young waitress placed their food on the table.

'Ketchup or brown sauce?' She sounded Eastern European.

'Brown sauce, please,' Kevin said.

William nodded. 'Same for me.'

Kevin waited until the sauce was on the table before continuing.

'We have a name for him, William, so at least he won't finish up as a John Doe in the mortuary. His name was Arthur, and I'm told he was ex-SBS.'

William sat up straight. 'No shit? Those guys are tough cookies.'

Kevin wasn't going to mention the gun, but he did pose a question. 'So, why would one of those tough cookies be so scared at being on the streets?'

William gave him a somewhat patronising smile. 'Think about it, Kev. He was off his meds, wasn't he? Now you tell me he's a veteran, well . . . Neurosis, most likely. I've seen battle fatigue reduce a seasoned fighting machine to a gibbering wreck, crying like a baby and frightened of the dark.' He doused his sandwich in brown sauce and chewed contentedly.

Kevin watched him eat. That butty, for which he'd paid some insignificant amount, was making a big difference to William's whole day. Then he told himself not to feel guilty. It was William's choice to live this way. William had told him it was preferable to the life he'd left behind. 'You and the others disappeared pretty fast last night,' Kevin said.

'Doesn't do for us street dwellers to hang around when the police are about to turn up. No disrespect to you, Kev, but some of your lot aren't exactly sweetness and light where the homeless are concerned.' He took a gulp of coffee. 'Something bad happens and no one to pin it on and it's, "Oh, this guy's a homeless drunk, he'll do, stick it on him."'

Kevin couldn't argue with this. He'd seen how some of his colleagues behaved towards the homeless. He stared at his half-eaten sandwich. William had consumed his and was now eyeing the pastry. He pushed his own plate and the pastry towards him. 'Go on. You have this. I've got to get back.'

William didn't hesitate. He grabbed the pastry, saying, 'Before you go, last night you asked about the oil theft, didn't you? I couldn't sleep after what happened, so I spoke to a few people. Do you know a family called Lorimer?'

'Doesn't ring a bell. Should it?' Kevin asked.

'They're not villains, so you might not have had call to meet them, but they are, er . . .' William tapped his temple. 'A bit barmy. Unorthodox like.' He lowered his voice. 'You know what happens with old fenland families, cousins marry cousins . . .' He raised an eyebrow. 'Let's say you probably won't see any of them on *Mastermind*.'

Kevin took out his notebook and scribbled down the name. 'You don't know where they live, do you?'

'Somewhere over Hawkers Fen way. They have an old rundown smallholding. They're sort of self-sufficient, or so I'm told.'

'And it's them who are responsible for the bodged theft?'

'No idea. It might pay to look in their direction,' William looked innocently at him, 'but you never heard it from me.'

Kevin closed his notebook. 'Thanks, William.' He took a fiver from his pocket. 'If it turns out to be a viable lead, I'll add another.' He stood up and pushed his chair back. 'It's unlikely you will, but if you hear anything at all about the shootings, will you ring me?'

'No can do, mate.'

Kevin started to protest, then realised. 'Ah, what an idiot. A mobile wouldn't last five minutes on the streets, would it?'

'Dead right. Kids have been killed for their phones. I can get a message to you though. But as you say, that kind of shit is serious stuff and I'm not likely to hear too much about it.' William wiped his mouth with the back of his hand. 'Appreciate the breakfast, Kev. See you around.'

On his way back through the town, Kevin thought about inbreeding. Surely, it doesn't still go on today? He'd come across a few old Lincolnshire people who had told him that prior to the Second World War they had lived in isolated villages with no transport services. They had no cars back then, so where did you go to meet a likely spouse? As far as a bicycle or horse-ride would take you. And what happened when the neighbouring families were all spoken for? What then? Cousins married cousins.

It was a different world now, of course, but in some lonely backwater hamlets the legacy lingered, and you could see the results in the children.

Kevin was eager to see the Lorimers for himself, but it was Charlie Button's case. He'd give the kid the tipoff, let him take the credit, but he'd ask Charlie if he could go along too.

* * *

Rosie Cohen had spent the last two hours trying to find details of military personnel who'd been relieved of their duties due to stress or disability. It had not been easy. No one had been prepared to talk to her, doctors declared themselves unable to discuss the people under their care, so she kept hitting brick walls. Luckily for her, one or two had engaged in anti-social behaviour that had brought them to public notice. Two men and one woman, to be specific, had presented serious cause for concern in recent years.

She had copies of the records of these three "possibles" and read them through again. They were Jeremy Freeman, former marine, Lewis Smith, ex-army rifleman, and Bethany Gadd, one-time police officer. All had been expert marksmen. All were damaged in some way.

Now she could hand the records to Jackman for him to deal with. Thank God that was done. It was hard to concentrate when she had come to work this morning leaving Tim and Jessica, her beloved twins, with ear infections.

The symptoms were relatively mild, so Max was keeping an eye on them. She didn't need to worry. Max had gone from being a nervous wreck to "Super Dad" almost overnight and had thrown himself wholeheartedly into the task of parenthood. This was helped by the fact that he had a magic touch with a crying baby, and in fact was much better at it than she was. Still, it was a constant struggle to balance policing and parenting. When they were at work, they wanted to be at home with the twins and vice versa. Here, too, Max seemed to do better than she did.

It wasn't helping that they now had a sniper on the loose, as well as the sinister figure of Alistair Ashcroft waiting to strike.

Rosie yawned. It was all a bit too much.

* * *

Marie and Gary were busy investigating the married life of Arthur James Barnes, an elite naval commando who had once lived according to the motto, "By Strength and Guile."

Gary knew a great deal more about the Special Boat Service than her, and Marie had learnt that apart from their extraordinary prowess as swimmers, divers and canoeists, they were highly skilled at engaging in underwater demolitions and maritime counter-terrorism.

'He deserves a proper investigation,' stated Gary, 'no matter what we dig up. The mere thought of a man like that being on the streets and scared is simply unthinkable.'

Privately, Marie wondered how many others were in the same state. Not everyone received the level of care that they deserved, even if they were heroes. Even so, she agreed with Gary. She handed him a sheet of paper. 'That's all I know so far. You see what you can find out about the wife herself. I'll run a check on the report of domestic violence and see if the police were involved.'

It didn't take Marie long to discover that they had been called on several occasions. Each time no one was prepared to press charges, so no further police action was taken. She noticed a comment made by one of the attending uniformed constables, that the domestic set up seemed a bit odd. In her opinion, the wife seemed more like the aggressor than the husband. Marie read the name of the officer concerned and remembered that she had seen her at the crime scene of the shooting the night before.

Marie rang down to the back office. Luckily, PC Hazel Stewart was on shift that morning, out in the yard cleaning her vehicle.

Marie headed off to find her.

Hazel thought for a while. 'Yes, I do remember it. Very weird, that particular shout. I actually got the feeling that it had all been staged, you know, like play-acting.' She paused, frowning. 'All except the husband, and I got the feeling he was on something. He seemed spaced out. He definitely didn't come across as if he'd just behaved as aggressively as the wife and her friend had said he did.'

'Her friend?'

'Yes, this other woman was there, and giving it plenty of mouth too.' Hazel pulled a face. 'Between the two of them I finished up feeling quite sorry for Arthur Barnes. He looked more like the victim than the wife.'

'That's interesting,' said Marie. 'A close friend of his said he wasn't the type to go in for that kind of violence.'

'As I said, it all looked like a set-up, and no one wanted to take things further, so we just walked away in the end. Puzzled me, though.' Hazel wrung out the cloth she'd been using and hung it over the side of the bucket. 'I was shocked to hear he'd finished up on the streets, and then got murdered like that. I can only think it had something to do with drugs. I did think he was on something when we went to his house.'

'He was ex-military, so maybe after coming out of the services, he just never settled,' suggested Marie.

'Why don't you talk to Kevin Stoner about that, Sarge? He's been talking to a snout about Barnes.'

She found Kevin by the vending machine, muttering threats and curses. 'Bloody thing! It's just swallowed another pound coin. It should have an ASBO slapped on it.'

Marie walked round the machine and gave it a hefty thump. There was an immediate whirring noise, and a small handful of cash and a chocolate bar fell into the drawer.

Kevin looked at her in awe. 'Respect, Sarge. Nice one!'

She smiled sweetly at him. 'In return, you can fill me in on what your snout told you about Arthur Barnes.'

'Snout? Oh, you mean William? Well, not much, other than his thoughts on why he might be on the streets and in the state he was.'

'And that was what?'

'Well, Sarge, like a lot of veterans, especially injured or traumatised ones, they finish up on serious medication. He was pretty certain that Barney was off his meds and suffering from paranoia. That would account for his excessive fear, and his belief that he was being threatened.'

'Very true, except for the fact that someone really was out to kill him, and they succeeded.'

'Good point.' Kevin sighed. 'But I'll bet meds show up in the post-mortem.' He pocketed his change. 'Is Charlie Button in the CID room, Sarge?'

'He was when I left.'

'Then I'll come back with you, if you don't mind. I'd like a word with him.'

Kevin fell into step with her. 'I wonder what we are looking at with these shootings. This sniper doesn't seem like anything I've read about in old cases. Shootings are usually mayhem, aren't they, Sarge? Mass killings, or else a clear target, as in the assassination of a spy.'

Marie nodded. 'I agree, and we can't think of a thing that might link Christopher Keyes and Arthur Barnes. Other than being shot on the head by our sniper.'

For a moment, Kevin's step faltered.

'Sorry, Kev, that was really thoughtless of me. I've not even asked how you are today. What a callous cow I am. My mother would give me hell.'

Kevin laughed. 'I'm good, honestly. It was simply shock, and that's wearing off all the time.'

'Charlie's over at the photocopier.' Marie pointed across the office. 'See you later.'

Marie watched him go. It was going to be no bad thing to have Kevin Stoner as part of their CID complement.

'Sarge? Got a minute?' Gary called to her.

She went over to his desk, pulled up a spare chair, and sat down. 'What have you got?'

'Quite a bit of hearsay and a load of supposition, but beneath all the smoke and mirrors, I think Brenda Barnes was having an affair and was using her new lover's sister to back up her allegations that Arthur was violent towards her.' Gary stared at his screen. 'I reckon she drove Arthur out just so that she could be with her new man.'

'Poor sod! After all he went through. He had no luck at all, did he?' She paused. 'Hang on. Where did you get all that from, Gary? Sounds more like *Coronation Street* than the Police National Computer.'

'My sister's best friend, Julie, still lives a few doors away from the Barnes's house. I rang her and got the lowdown from the neighbours. Neat, huh?'

'Very. So, can you tell me what he did to get assassinated?'

Gary looked apologetic. 'Sorry, Neighbourhood Watch doesn't go that far.'

Marie leaned back in her chair, 'You know something? I think we're wasting our time. I'm beginning to wonder if the victims are just red herrings to keep us occupied when we should really be looking for the shooter.'

'Rosie's on that,' said Gary. 'She's checking out sharpshooters who have been decommissioned because of mental health problems.'

'Well, I don't envy her. The military are notoriously tight-lipped when it comes to discussing their failures. But maybe that's another red herring. My money is on the gun club.'

'You could be right,' Gary said. 'Uniform are on the ground, gathering up names and taking statements from members. They were onto it immediately after you had your visit from Mr Harcourt. They've promised to flag up anything of interest.'

'Keep an eye on that, Gary. Anything even the slightest bit interesting, and we'll go ourselves, okay?'

Gary nodded. 'I'll keep you updated.'

Marie stood up. 'Just going to check in with the boss.' She stopped and added, 'Have you spoken to him this morning, Gary?'

'Not yet, why?'

'Oh, nothing, just wondered.'

CHAPTER ELEVEN

After leaving Mill Corner, Laura Archer had gone directly to Greenborough Police Station to help assess a prisoner in custody, a woman who was exhibiting signs of mental distress. It hadn't taken her long to discover that the whole thing was a scam.

It was around ten thirty when she finally got to her consulting room. The place was no longer home, it was just where she worked. She belonged at Mill Corner now. It gave her a comfortable feeling.

She went first to her apartment to check everything was OK. She hadn't been in for several days and was wondering if she'd left any milk in the fridge. Her consulting rooms on the ground floor were completely self-contained with a tiny galley kitchenette and a separate toilet.

She wondered whether she should rent the flat out. It was well cared for and modern and in a good location, so it could fetch top money. But would she be pushing Jackman into committing himself when he might not be ready? She didn't want to tempt fate, then find herself with nowhere to go. 'Don't rush things, Laura,' she whispered, and then laughed. Ever the counsellor.

The key to her consulting room door refused to turn. She pulled it out and looked at it. Yes, it was the right one. She tried again, and this time it worked.

'Must get that oiled,' she muttered, opening the inner door to her office.

Her main consulting room was designed to foster a sense of calm. It smelled of aromatherapy oils and had a clever colour-change system of lighting that relaxed the mind.

Her desk was in one corner of the room, the centre of which was occupied by two comfortable leather recliners, and this was where she conducted her sessions with her clients. Laura went to her desk to get the case file that she required, then stopped mid-stride. In the centre of the desk, in a china pot, was a pure white orchid. Jackman. 'What a lovely thought,' she murmured, smiling. He was the only other person with a key, so it had to be him. Then she saw the card and opened it eagerly.

My dear Laura, Such a lovely room! I'm in awe. Go to your computer and open Videos, and I'll tell you more. Alistair.

Laura saw that her hand was shaking. She dropped the card as if it were covered in acid and stared at it. Alistair Ashcroft? Here?

She pulled her phone from her pocket, found Jackman's number, then cancelled the call. Hesitantly, she lifted the lid of her laptop. Before she touched the keys, she looked closely. The whole thing had been carefully wiped with an astringent-smelling cleanser. It looked as good as new.

She switched it on and waited for it to load. She needed to see this before she spoke to Jackman. She clicked Videos, and a new MOV file was waiting for her. Laura swallowed. *Here goes.*

A man was seated in a high-backed chair, his face in shadow. Laura adjusted the volume and listened.

'Laura Archer, I really must congratulate you! You have a wonderful room. I've been in many consulting rooms in my time, but yours . . .' Alistair Ashcroft gave a small, controlled laugh. 'Even I might be persuaded to share some of my secrets with you in a room such as this. I am sorry that we aren't speaking face to face, but maybe another time? Yes, another time, very soon, we will talk frankly.' He shifted slightly and light caught the arm of the chair he was sitting on.

Laura paused the footage and stared at the image frozen on the screen.

It was her chair. He was filming this right here in her room. She was overcome with fear and outrage. The mere thought that he had been here, contaminating her sanctuary, made her want to vomit.

She started the video again, forcing herself to listen to his insidious voice.

'Now, I know you will be itching to ring Jackman and tell him about this, but . . . perhaps you might reconsider. You're an intelligent woman and will know more than anyone, except possibly Marie Evans, just how what is happening has affected him. You will think . . . *do I want to be the one to cause him to fall apart*? If he knows for certain that you're being watched by Alistair Ashcroft, it will send him into freefall. Do you want to do that to the man you love?'

He shifted again. The darkness hid his face, but he was gloating. 'I'm right, am I not? He is suffering, Laura. Last night for instance, standing there by the old mill tower, brooding and troubled, a dark silhouette against the even darker night sky.'

Laura's mouth went dry. She paused the video again. He'd been out there, watching Jackman! He could have killed him. And had he been there when Jackman left to go to the shooting incident and she was alone? Her legs trembled, grew weak. She sank into her office chair and stared in horror at the screen. Where was this going?

'Now, if I'd been that sniper he is chasing, he would have been right in the crosshairs, wouldn't he? He really shouldn't make himself into a target like that.' He stopped. 'Enough of this. Enjoy your orchid. We'll meet properly when things are less hectic. And, Laura? Do think carefully, won't you?'

The screen went black. Laura closed her eyes and exhaled.

Ashcroft was right. Her initial reaction had been to tell Jackman and show him the video. Get a SOCO in and dust the whole office, and especially that lock. But could she do it?

She remembered that nightmare. Jackman hadn't needed to tell her that it visited him regularly. He saw Marie die in front of him, probably several times a day. Then there was the stress he was under, his constant anxiety about the people he loved and cared for. He knew that all those connected to him were in immediate danger until he could catch and incarcerate Ashcroft. Where Ashcroft was concerned, Jackman was as vulnerable as a child.

The competent and compassionate psychotherapist was suddenly at a loss. She took hold of the china pot with the orchid in it and hurled it against the wall. And howled in rage.

* * *

'Thought I'd ring in person, just in case you were missing my sparkling wit and mordant humour,' Rory said.

Marie smiled. 'Who is this, please?' she replied, trying to sound officious.

'Titania, Queen of the Fairies.'

'Thought so.' Marie chuckled, 'So, what have you got for us, Prof?'

'I have absolutely nothing, dear heart, but my very able assistant has worked out where the sniper was and some information on the gun and ammunition. I shall hand you over to him forthwith.'

The Spike who took the phone sounded very different to the funky, spiky-haired young mortuary assistant who'd gone to work with Rory all that time ago. Seemed Rory had been right to keep him on.

'Sergeant Evans, there are identical marks on the casing of the bullets, which confirms that it was the same gun that fired the shot at Christopher Keyes. But as I suspected from the damage done to Arthur Barnes, he used a different bullet, a hollow point, often referred to as a dumdum.'

'Why would he do that?' asked Marie.

'They are mainly used for their stopping power. They expand on impact, hence the bigger wound, but because they slow down as they travel through soft tissue, they are less like to pass through the target and hit something or someone else.' Spike paused. 'But I think he used it because it's pretty lethal.'

'Rory said you've calculated the location of the shooter?' Marie said.

'Once we had daylight it was simple,' Spike said confidently. 'He had taken up position on the footbridge over the drain. It's rarely used, as the land on the other side of the water is fenced off. They're about to begin a new housing project. It gave him the height, and a perfect view of the old storeroom. I took a telescopic lens over there and looked for myself, and it was a clear line of sight.'

'And the SOCOs have gone over the spot, I assume?'

'Thoroughly, but nothing was found. It seems he's very careful,' Spike said.

'Isn't he just,' murmured Marie. 'Thank you, Spike.'

'The prof wants another word, Sergeant.'

Rory was speaking again.

'Dumdums. You're dying to ask why they are called that, are you not? And don't lie now, I know you are.'

'You got me. I admit it. As far as I'm concerned, it's one of life's great mysteries. Go on, Rory, educate me.'

'Because the inventor, Lt Col Neville Sneyd Bertie-Clay was the superintendent of the British Arsenal at Dumdum in Bengal, and that's where they were first produced. Now isn't that interesting?'

'Riveting. You've made my day, Rory. Now, please can I go and catch some bad guys?'

'That's what they pay you for. Off you toddle, dear lady. Ta-ta for now.'

Marie had worked with numerous pathologists in her time. Some talked down to you, some seemed to speak another language it was so technical, and others were plain creepy. Some never talked at all. Rory Wilkinson and his humour were a panacea for the sorrow, the horror of death. Apart from which, he was the best pathologist she'd ever come across.

'Marie? Got a minute, please?' Jackman beckoned her into his office.

Inside, she found Charlie Button already there.

'Charlie has a lead on the diesel theft, and considering it wasn't a textbook heist, to say the least, we are thinking that it could be linked to Robbie's pig-stealing gang.' Jackman flopped down into his captain's chair, 'Both efforts were rough around the edges, to say the least.'

'As was the gun theft,' added Marie, remembering the axed-off door lock and the shattered gun cabinet. 'Could it be the same gang?'

Jackman shrugged. 'I wouldn't rule it out. Those guys were heavy handed in the extreme.'

Marie looked at Charlie. 'Anyone we know in the spotlight?'

'Well, I've made a few discreet enquiries. This lot aren't known to us, but they are an odd bunch.' Charlie looked at her. 'An old fen family, name of Lorimer.'

Marie laughed. 'Lorimer? Rachel Lorimer's boys? Oh my! Now if anyone was going to embark on a life of crime and balls it up, it would be the Lorimers.'

Jackman and Charlie glanced at each other, 'You seem to know them rather well,' said Jackman.

'My dad knew the grandfather, Caleb Lorimer. He was a blacksmith and a farrier, and he used to make all sorts of stuff in metal — wrought-iron and the like. He was a talented man, but uneducated. They hailed from right out on Hawker's Fen, miles from anywhere.'

'That's right, Hawker's Fen.' Charlie nodded. 'Not somewhere I've ever been.'

'Very few have,' said Marie. 'It's at the bottom of a long straight drove that goes on for miles and miles and ends nowhere. The only place close to it is Thatcher's Fen village, and all that has is a church and a village hall. No other amenities at all.'

'Are the family trouble?' asked Jackman.

'Not trouble in the criminal sense, other than poaching and generally doing things their way.' Marie tried to remember their names. 'Rachel was Caleb's eldest daughter. She married a second cousin and has four sons and one daughter. All have biblical names.'

Jackman grinned. 'Please don't tell me they are Matthew, Mark, Luke and John.'

This was another Jackman, a relaxed and almost chirpy one. It was rather disconcerting, but it was a hell of a lot better than the other version. 'I remember one was called Noah, and another Levi, but I don't recall the rest. And every one of Caleb's grandchildren had a disability of one sort or another, mainly learning difficulties. The tiny village school couldn't cope with the disruption they caused and getting them to a bigger school wasn't possible because they had been barred from using the school bus, so they lost out completely on an education.' Marie could hear her father now. "That poor Caleb has his work cut out with his children, all bar Rachel, she's got her head screwed on, but the others . . . The original wild bunch. God help us if they ever have kids of their own!" And of course they did.

'I was about to send Charlie,' Jackman said. 'Since you have some knowledge of the family, Marie, would you go with him?'

'Sure. At least I know where they live. No offence, Charlie, but you could be driving around until nightfall looking for their place.' She turned to Jackman. 'Should we go now?'

'Absolutely. If we can dig up something to work on and get this small stuff cleared, then we'll be free to concentrate on the serious issues.'

'Ah, talking of serious issues, boss . . .' Marie quickly filled him in on what Spike had told her — omitting Rory's contribution.

'Okay. Well, I've pulled in a couple of pool detectives to help out with following up the gun club members and any other locals with firearms licences. I'll keep them beavering away on that while you try to get us a lead on these botched jobs, alright?'

Marie threw Charlie an amused smile. 'Okay, Button, prepare to meet the Fenland's answer to *Shameless*.'

'Sounds interesting.'

'That's one way of putting it.'

They left Jackman's office and made their way down to pick up the keys to a CID car.

'Sarge? Is it alright with you if we take Kevin Stoner with us? To tell you the truth, it was him that found this lead for me, and he said he'd like to get a look at the Lorimers. He's never come across the family before, and he's quite interested.'

So that was what Kevin had been talking to his snout William about. 'I would say no problem, but I don't want to put Rachel Lorimer on the defensive by bringing a big crowd. She can be very protective of her boys, and I'm not sure how she'll react to seeing a police uniform.'

'No worry, Sarge. I'll just tell him that before we go, if that's okay?' Charlie asked.

'Oh, damn it, let him come, Charlie. Rachel Lorimer will at least take us seriously if there's a uniform with us, and it could scare one of her boys into giving something away. Go and see if he's free while I get hold of a vehicle. I'll see you in the car park.'

CHAPTER TWELVE

Sam Page had always known that retiring wouldn't mean giving up. You didn't spend your entire working life trying to assuage the anguish of damaged minds, only to switch off completely when a certain date on the calendar came around.

Initially he had tried to do just that. He had bought his lovely little cottage next to the marsh and had devoted every waking hour to his beloved hobby of nature watching. His garden was a glorious wilderness of plants and flowers and provided a haven for all manner of birds and animals, and he loved it. He also made plans to do all the things he had never found time for when working. Recently, however, he'd found his thoughts increasingly returning to psychology.

It could have had something to do with Laura Archer. She had been his star pupil and throughout her subsequent career had continued to stay in touch with him. She could have been a real high-flyer, rising to the position of senior lecturer at one of the best universities. She could have made a fortune as a private consultant. Instead, Laura had turned her back on all that and continued to work at grassroots level. She was now the Fenland Constabulary's on-call psychologist. Though slightly uncomprehending, Sam was pleased. He had moved to the fens, close to the marsh, so that he could spend time studying the migrant water birds that fascinated him so much. It also meant he was able to see her regularly.

Laura had become the daughter he'd never had, and he couldn't have been more delighted when she and Rowan Jackman finally decided to make a go of it. He just wished that there was no dark shadow over their happiness, but until they caught Jackman's old nemesis, they would have no peace.

Sam sat on his patio, sipping tea and watching for birds out on the marsh. It seemed inconceivable that one man could evade an entire police force, all of whom were focused on bringing him down. Most worrying to him was that both his precious Laura and DI Jackman were clearly in the killer's sights.

His mobile rang, startling him from his reverie.

'Laura!' Staring unseeing across the marsh, Sam listened. 'Okay, so what is easiest? Shall I come to you? Or would you prefer to come here?' He stood up. 'On my way. I'll see you in half an hour.'

He drove far too fast to her consulting room and skidded to a halt outside her door.

'Sam! Thank you so much for coming. I've just been trying to keep my cool while dealing with a new client who's suffering with major difficulties. I'm drained. Come on in.'

Indeed, Laura looked grey. Exhausted. 'Let's go up to my apartment, Sam,' she said. 'I need to get out of here.'

Puzzled by this last remark, he allowed her to usher him out again, lock the door, and lead the way upstairs to her living area. He made them tea and they sat in the lounge.

'Tell me what's happened,' Sam said gently. 'From the beginning.' Laura took a deep breath. 'Well, it started a couple of nights ago . . .'

As she spoke, all her fears for Jackman and the state he was in poured out of her in a torrent. Her story began with a nightmare and ended with her sweeping shards of china and crushed white petals from the floor.

'I can barely face going into my rooms anymore. He's taken what was beautiful and peaceful and poisoned it. He's like a terrible virus, contaminating everything he touches.'

Just as he'd intended, Ashcroft had planted in Laura's mind the insidious notion that she might turn out to be responsible for pushing Jackman over the edge.

'He's a master manipulator, Laura,' Sam said, 'as we know from before. You must tell Jackman everything, now. You are not protecting him by keeping this awful violation to yourself, you are bowing to Ashcroft's will, playing into his hands. If you say nothing, you are handing control to Ashcroft, and he'll have won.' He took a sip of his tea. 'And we change the locks on this place. He clearly had no trouble picking this one, but there are better systems. I know it's a bit like bolting the stable door, but even so . . .'

Laura nodded. 'I'll do it as soon as I've talked to Jackman.' She let out a long breath. 'You are right, Sam. I knew what I ought to do the minute it happened, but he puts such believable doubts in your head. It's like mind control.'

'It *is* mind control, Laura. And he's very good at it.' Sam could see what lay behind Ashcroft's actions. He craved power. As a child he had been helpless. Now, as an adult, he was taking his revenge.

Sam badly wanted to see that video, but he wasn't about to ask Laura to sit through it a second time. He'd wait until Jackman got here.

'Okay, I've procrastinated long enough.' Laura stood up and went to find her phone. 'Here goes.'

Sam listened. She did remarkably well, considering the state she had been in. Her tone was even, she sounded perfectly calm. Ending the call, she turned to Sam. 'He's on his way.' The corners of her mouth lifted. 'You know, I actually feel as though a weight has been taken off my shoulders.'

Sam returned the smile. 'You've seized back control. You've told the truth. You won't have to struggle to keep it from Jackman. In any case, he'd have guessed there was something wrong.'

'Thank you, Sam. I don't know what I'd do without you.' Laura looked close to tears. 'Not everyone is lucky enough to have a friend like you, someone to pick them up and explain that they aren't as barking mad as they think they are.'

'Barking mad? Is that accepted psychiatric terminology?' Sam smiled.

* * *

Like Sam Page, Jackman drove too fast along the fen lanes. As he went, he fought to retain his new persona, but the image of scarlet blood spreading across a white blouse kept going through his mind.

By the time he arrived at Laura's, the determined, energetic Jackman was back in control.

He hugged Laura, long and hard, and then he and Sam went downstairs to the consulting room. Jackman went to her computer and found the video Ashcroft had left. 'Ready for this, Sam?'

'Oh yes. I'm going to be very interested to see how he works.'

Jackman opened the file. When he finally closed it again, he realised that his jaw had been clamped tight throughout.

'I wonder why, when we all know what he looks like, he has chosen to use the darkened silhouette effect?' said Sam ruminatively.

'I wondered that too,' said Jackman.

'Maybe he's changed his appearance and doesn't want to be recognised,' Sam suggested.

That could be the case, but Jackman knew Ashcroft. It could have been done purely for dramatic effect.

'He's good,' Sam said sombrely. 'For a while there, he had Laura wondering. He put the thought in her head knowing it would drive a wedge between you.'

'My poor Laura,' Jackman whispered. Unconsciously, he had clenched his hands into fists. 'Where the hell is the bastard? He's everywhere and nowhere.' He turned to Sam. 'You know, I wasn't going to get the SOCOs in. After all, we know he was here, we have a video to prove it. We also know who he is and a lot about him, there seemed no point. Now I'm thinking differently.'

Sam looked at him with interest. 'Go on.'

'That plant. He had to buy it somewhere. If we can trace where it came from, we could discover if he has changed his appearance and you never know, maybe he left some small trace of himself behind. Forensics might pick up something that would give us a clue as to where he is staying. You know, like plant material, soil or fibres. It's a long shot, but I think it's worth a try.'

'Laura said she's had very few clients here recently. Most of her work has been in hospitals, prisons or the like.' Sam pointed to the door. 'In which case, shall we . . . ?'

Jackman nodded. 'I'll ring this in and get a sweep done. The more I think about it, the more I realise we have to grab any opportunity to nail him.'

After he'd made the call, he went back upstairs. Laura was wondering how she might cleanse the apartment of all traces of Ashcroft's presence.

Jackman paused in the doorway. Maybe this was the moment he'd been waiting for.

He took a breath and went in.

Laura and Sam looked up. 'All arranged?' asked Sam.

'They are organising to get someone out ASAP.' He looked at Laura. 'We have to hang on until they get here. Do you have a lot of work on today?'

'I've rescheduled the lot. After that first consultation, I knew I wasn't capable of doing any more today.' Jackman saw how tired and drawn she looked, and his heart went out to her. Ashcroft's deadly mind game had obviously taken its toll. 'Er, I know you won't mind Sam hearing this, Laura, but there's something I want to say to you.'

She tilted her head to one side.

'I overheard what you said about the way Ashcroft's ruined this place for you. The thing is, you don't have to worry. The renovations at the mill are all but complete. We can get it decorated, kit it out and get carpeting down in no time. Sell the apartment, get it on the market immediately. I want you to come and live with me permanently, as my partner. I won't throw the word marriage at you just yet, but damn Ashcroft, he's not going to stop us moving on.'

Laura was staring at him as if he'd suddenly sprouted wings. He knew what she was thinking and couldn't suppress a smile. Where was the careworn, haunted man of a few days ago and what had brought about this transformation? Sam, meanwhile, was watching the two of them, his slightly bewildered expression slowly clearing.

'You really mean that?' Laura said.

'Of course I mean it!' Jackman turned to Sam. 'What do you think?'

'Best thing I've heard all day. I shall treat myself to a little something with dinner tonight and raise a glass to you. Congratulations!'

'I think we can do better than that, Sam. Join us. I was going to take Laura to Johnnie Bull's when we finish work. Mrs Maynard is having a day off today and we'll be too tired to cook. I think we all deserve a meal out.'

'It's kind of you to ask but you don't want some old fogey cramping your style,' Sam said.

'Rubbish! Please come,' Laura added. 'Without you, I'd still be paralysed by indecision, trying to find ways of keeping what happened here from Jackman. You saved us from disaster. Besides which, Johnnie Bull's does the best home-cooked meals in the county. You can't turn that down.'

Sam beamed. 'Well, if you're sure?'

Jackman clapped him on the shoulder. 'Certain! Seven thirty. We'll meet you there.' He looked at his watch. He really should get back, and he had no idea when forensics would arrive.

Sam read his thoughts. 'If you need to get away, I'm happy to wait here with Laura.'

'I'm going to take you up on that. We're in an uproar over this sniper and the two deaths.' He gave Laura a hug. 'Ring me and let me know about the SOCOs, alright?'

She held him tight, extra warmth in her embrace, and he didn't want to let go. Reluctantly, he loosened his hold.

Then he was driving away. His new, resolute self was holding out, but how long would it last? His jaw jutted. It would damn well hold out until Ashcroft and the bastard sniper were both under lock and key.

CHAPTER THIRTEEN

The day was fine and sunny, and Marie badly wished that she was on her bike and not inside a 4x4. It would have been great to drive the half hour or so to Hawker's Fen with the warm breeze in her face and the smells of the countryside all around her.

'What crop is that?' asked Charlie, looking out at acres of blueish green plants with white and purple flowers.

'Field beans,' said Marie. 'Almost identical to broad beans, only they are grown for animal feed. They both have the same Latin name.'

'Blimey,' Charlie said. 'The sarge has gone all agricultural on us, Kev.'

She laughed. 'Just a useless bit of fen information, courtesy of long evening dog walks with my Dad.'

'How much further is Hawker's Fen?' asked Charlie. 'There seems to be no end to this road, or that ditch beside it.'

Charlie was right. Their route lay along one of several stretches of perfectly straight road, called "droves" in the fenland, with nothing but fields and the occasional dilapidated barn to break the monotony. Here and there were a few scattered dwellings — the sort that estate agents list as "rural setting, no near neighbours."

'Just a few minutes. You'll see a flat bridge over the drain that runs directly into the Lorimers' property.'

Soon Marie was crossing the bridge into a scrubby, tarmacked area that served as a parking bay. She turned off the engine and looked around. The place had changed little over the years, except for the addition of a couple of shabby static caravans and a few more sheds. It had never been tidy, but now it resembled a junkyard. The house itself was a small weathered farm dwelling with rundown outbuildings attached to it. Bits of the yard had been fenced off into pens, some for chickens, some with ducks, and others, left unused, were overgrown and choked with weeds.

'Self-sufficient, huh?' Kevin looked disappointed. 'I thought it was going to be more, well, like a proper small-holding — nice organic veg and a sign outside saying, "Free Range Eggs for Sale."'

'Sorry, Kevin, but this is it. And the only sign you are likely to see is one that says, "Keep Out."' Marie made sure the 4x4 was locked. 'Come on, let's go and say hello to Rachel Lorimer.'

The front door opened, and a cat streaked out past them.

'Damn and blast! Taken me an hour to get that thing in here for its flea treatment. Now the bugger's done a runner! What do you lot want anyway?'

Rachel Lorimer stood with her hands on her hips and glared at them.

She had a wild mane of prematurely grey hair and small, shrewd pale eyes set in a weathered face. She was dressed in men's cord trousers, a check shirt, a half jacket and tan leather boots.

'I'm DS Marie Evans, and this is DC Charlie Button and PC Kevin Stoner. Could we have a word, please, Mrs Lorimer?' They all held up their warrant cards.

'Must be at least a murder to drag three of you out here.' She gave them a disparaging look. 'Or are you frightened of going out on your own?'

'Neither, actually.' Marie smiled at her. 'Don't you remember me, Rachel? My dad and your dad were friends.'

Rachel Lorimer peered at her. 'Little Marie! Well, stone me! A policewoman! A detective, no less. Wonders will never cease.'

'Can we come in, Rachel? We won't take long.'

'I suppose.' She threw the door fully open and stepped back. 'Come through to the sitting room. It's a bit of a mess but I don't get a lot of time for housekeeping.'

As a matter of fact, compared to the outside, the interior wasn't too bad at all. It was a typical old-style fen home. An open fireplace dominated the room with a faded picture in a worn gilt frame hanging above it, depicting a blacksmith shoeing a horse. There was an ancient, well-used sofa and three armchairs, a sideboard, a gate-leg table and a coffee table. Apart from several straggly houseplants and a lot of ornaments, that was it.

Rachel Lorimer pointed to the chairs. 'I suppose you'll be wanting tea?'

'We won't trouble you, Rachel. I know you're busy, so we'll just ask you a few questions and be on our way.' Marie sat down and decided to plunge straight in. 'There have been one or two petty crimes committed in the area recently, all involving rural village farms. We have been warning the owners of small farms and other properties like yours to keep vigilant.'

'What kind of crimes?' The shrewd eyes had narrowed to slits.

'Theft of animals, and diesel, among other things.' Marie stared at her. 'And someone told me your family might know something about it.'

'Marie Evans! How dare you!' Rachel Lorimer was incandescent. 'We might not be well-off or brainy, but my lads are good boys, every one of them! They've never been in trouble with you lot, as well you know.'

'I'm sorry, Rachel, but I have to follow up all statements and leads. You can appreciate that, surely? It's not personal, I promise.'

Rachel thought for a while. 'Alright, and it's just because I liked your father, mind. Ask what you need to. Then you can go.'

'Could you tell us, Mrs Lorimer, are all of your sons still living at home?' Charlie asked politely.

'Each and every one, even Levi, who's married now. They have my bedroom, as is only right and proper being wed and all.'

'So, there is Levi, Noah . . . and who else?' Charlie asked.

'Jacob, Esther and Paul.'

'And that is everyone that lives here?' asked Kevin. 'Only I saw that the static vans have curtains and a gas bottle, and there's an old motorhome parked up in the yard.'

'Esther has the smaller static, to give her some privacy, and Noah and Jacob have the bigger one. This house only has three bedrooms and it got too cramped for us all.' Her expression darkened. 'Anyway, what the hell has that got to do with anything? And who pointed the finger at us?'

'We can't say, Rachel, but we have to talk to everyone here. Maybe one of them has heard someone talking about the thefts?'

Marie's softly spoken response obviously hadn't placated Rachel Lorimer. She continued to glower at them.

'And the motorhome?' asked Kevin, 'Who does that belong to?'

'My cousin Ezra,' growled Rachel. 'He's down from north of the county for a while, catching up with the family, and I'd be grateful if you don't give him the impression that we're a brood of thieves and ne'er-do-wells.'

Following Marie's lead, Charlie spoke gently. 'That's not our intention, I assure you, Mrs Lorimer. But two of your sons work locally and they might well have heard something that could assist us.'

Before anyone could say anymore, a loud crack interrupted them.

Kevin jumped.

'Never heard an air gun before, have yer? That will be Noah, shooting rats. They're everywhere when there's poultry feed and a dyke close at hand.'

Marie knew that was true, you didn't live in a wet area like this without rats being a problem, but she was reminded of the last time Kevin had heard a gun fired. 'Is it just air guns you own, Rachel?'

She nodded. 'Caleb had a shotgun when I was young, but he sold it when times got hard. The children all have air guns, except for Jacob. He doesn't hold with hurting or killing any living thing. Funny ways he has, but that's our Jacob.'

There was a distinct softening of her manner when she spoke about Jacob. Marie had noticed that she constantly referred to them as children, though they were all adults or at least in their late teens.

There was another shot. This time Kevin didn't jump. 'Are they good shots?' he asked, casually.

'Fair enough. The best by far is Esther. She can knock spots off the boys. Bit like me really. Caleb taught me well, and my mother cooked the best rabbit pie in the world.' The dreamy look in her eyes was soon replaced by one of irritation. 'Look, you don't want my family history. Go talk to whoever's here but I promise you, you're wasting your time. And go easy with Jacob, you hear? He's sensitive.' She stood up and pointed to the door.

Marie ushered the others outside, then turned to Rachel. 'Thank you, Rachel. It's good to see you again. I'm just sorry it's an official visit.'

'I liked your father. He was a good man.'

'He was,' Marie said. 'I still miss him.'

'As I miss Caleb. You felt safe with him around. Now I have to fill those big shoes of his. It feels a bit lonely sometimes.'

'I think you are doing an amazing job, Rachel. It can't be easy, living out here, having to take care of the family. They have their problems, don't they?' Marie hoped she didn't sound patronising.

'I have my cross to bear, but I love my children, no matter how God chose to make them.' A hint of the hardness returned. 'So tell those two whippersnappers of yours to tread careful, or they'll have me to answer to.' Rachel Lorimer went back inside and closed the door.

Marie caught up with the others. 'We'll start with Noah, shall we?' She pointed at a young man who was levelling his air rifle at the far bank of the ditch.

They heard a crack, followed by a squeal and a small splash.

'Yesss!' Noah lowered the gun and looked across the water with a satisfied expression, then he saw them and his expression changed.

Marie introduced Charlie and Kevin and asked if they could see where he lived.

'I suppose. If Ma said it was alright.'

Noah must have been around nineteen, and was gangly, with long straggly hair. He seemed defensive.

'You don't work, Noah?' asked Kevin.

'I work bloody hard! Here's where I work. Me and Jacob look after the animals and the farm.' He paused. 'And I look after Jacob too.'

Marie nodded. 'We just meant did you go to work for anyone else, that's all. There's been some thefts in the area, and we were wondering if you'd heard anything about them.'

'Why would I? I never leave here, 'less it's to shop, or fetch feed for the beasts.'

'What about friends?' asked Charlie.

'Don't have any. Ma says that's for the best. We got each other. We stick together here.' He spoke the words as if he were reciting some oft-repeated slogan.

Marie changed tack. 'Where does Levi work, Noah?'

'In the abattoir over at Leedyke. He's good at his job, or so he tells us.'

Marie shivered. It wasn't something people usually boasted of being good at. 'How does Jacob cope with that?'

'He doesn't. He hates Levi. He hasn't spoken to him since he took that job.'

'How long ago was that?' she asked.

'Five years ago.'

'Do *you* like Levi?' she asked suddenly.

Yet again, Noah shrugged. 'He's my big brother, isn't he?'

'But do you like him?'

'I love Jacob. I don't like it when people upset him.'

'That must be really difficult when you say you all stick together,' Charlie said.

Another shrug. 'It's just the way it is.'

Marie looked around the caravan. She had expected it to be a tip, but it was oddly tidy. No piles of dirty clothes or stacks of unwashed dishes, and there was no technology. No television, no PlayStation, no laptop and no chargers plugged in ready for a mobile phone.

Instead there were pictures of wild animals — deer, badgers and foxes — and birds too — owls and hawks. Not a football hero in sight. Marie saw crude wooden carvings, clearly the work of one of the boys, again all animals. There was a kingfisher, a long-haired dog and a sleeping cat. There were jigsaws and books, most intended for children.

'Where is Jacob now?' asked Charlie.

'With the chickens. One has got mites and he's treating it. And don't ask him anything about whatever it is you want to know, because he don't know nothing. He only knows his animals and birds, so leave him alone.' He sounded more fearful than anything, afraid for his brother. 'Talk to Levi and Paul if you want answers.'

Noah flopped down on an old sofa and stared at the floor. They'd get nothing from him now.

Marie nodded to the others and they left. Outside, she led them a short distance away. 'Two things. One, what did you smell in that caravan?'

'Oil. Fuel,' Charlie said immediately. 'Faintly. It wasn't strong, but it smelt like I did after my trip to Dewsbury End Farm.'

'Exactly. And, two . . .' She sighed. 'Two. Did you notice a sleeveless hoodie hanging on the back of the door?'

Kevin nodded. 'Grey, with an orange logo, something-stars, on it?'

'Falling Stars.' Marie nodded. 'It may be a coincidence, and you know how much we hate those, but that hoodie is identical to the one I snatched off the kid who put that wreath on my motorbike. Ashcroft's little messenger.'

Neither of the others spoke for a while, and then Charlie said, 'You think one of the Lorimer boys is working for Ashcroft?'

'I have no idea what I think yet but seeing that hoodie gave me the heebie-jeebies. I checked it out last night, and it's a fairly common supermarket own brand, but that style hasn't been around for ages. What's the likelihood of two turning up so close to each other?'

'If it was cheap, it's possible,' said Kevin. 'And if they're available at the supermarkets. Shall I go back and have a word?'

'Go and ask him about that fuel smell. Then just mention the jacket, ask if it's his or his brothers. Don't make a big thing of it,' Marie said. 'We should have the forensic report regarding the one I grabbed hold of soon enough.'

Kevin wasn't long. 'He said he always smells of fuel, as he's the one who looks after the tractor and the digger. He wasn't fazed by the question either. And the jacket is his. He said his Ma bought it for him, she buys all their clothes. Again, he wasn't nervous or spooked when I asked him.'

'Mm, feasible I guess, but I still don't like coincidences.' She looked around. 'Thanks for that, now you two find Jacob. Go carefully, mind. We've been told he's sensitive. I'll see if Esther is at home.'

Esther was not in her caravan. Marie decided to take a wander around and see if she came across her.

She didn't remember ever having met any of the Lorimer family apart from Rachel. They had a reputation for being anti-social. They were no respecters of land boundaries, and they did a little poaching, but none of them had ever crossed the line into outright criminality. For them to do so now would not only be wildly out of character but she suspected that mother Rachel would heartily disapprove. But then there had been that stink in the static caravan. She wondered if Noah was lying.

'What are you doing here? This is private property.'

Startled, Marie looked up and saw a young woman staring accusingly at her. She noted the light brown hair cut in a rather untidy boyish style, the worn, faded jeans and open-neck denim shirt. What made her look twice was the grey sleeveless hoodie with the Falling Stars logo.

'Esther?'

'Who wants to know?'

Marie held out her warrant card. 'I'm Marie. I knew your grandfather. Can we talk?'

'What about?'

'Your brothers. I'd like to know whether you think they are capable of theft, among other things.'

'Oh. I see. You'd better come back to my caravan.' She turned on her heel and marched across the yard.

Marie followed.

She wasn't sure what she was expecting to see in that caravan, but it wasn't this. It wasn't filthy, nor was it piled to the ceiling with old newspapers and magazines. She didn't have to wade through junk, cat litter and food cartons to find a seat, but even so, the amount of stuff packed into the small space was overpowering. Esther collected things. Keepsakes, souvenirs, ornaments and, surprisingly, books. Not children's books either. Marie ran her eyes over some of the spines — Steinbeck, Atwood, Hemingway, Capote. No chick lit here.

'Okay. Has someone been accusing my brothers of something?' She had a lot of her mother's attitude. 'If so, I'd like to know who.'

Marie sidestepped the question. 'Esther, do you think your brothers could possibly have been talked into doing something they shouldn't?'

'No way! Our mother would kill them. They'd be too scared to even think of it.' She snorted. 'Apart from the fact that they aren't bright enough to pull it off, whatever it is. Jacob's useless, Noah's a wimp, Levi's too savvy and Paul, well, Paul does what he wants, not what other people tell him to.'

'The thefts I'm talking about were definitely not carried out by experts, believe me.' Marie watched Esther. What kind of young woman was she dealing with here? People said that all the children had problems, but she couldn't see too much wrong with Esther.

'We've spoken to Noah, and my colleagues are chatting to Jacob, and yes, before you mention it, we do know he's sensitive, okay? But what about Paul? He has a job, hasn't he?'

'Seasonal work on the fields mainly, but he's good with engines, so he's always got work.'

'And you, Esther, what do you do?'

'I help Ma with the house and I'm good with figures, so I do the accounts and manage the money — what there is of it.' She pulled a face. 'I did have a job in retail but they let me go a couple of months ago. Ma said I was needed here, so here I am.'

'Don't you get lonely?' asked Marie.

'Lonely?' Esther looked puzzled. 'With all my family around me? How would I get lonely?'

'Don't you miss having friends?' Marie went on. 'A boyfriend maybe? Other young women of your own age to talk to?'

'Most girls are stupid. If I want to talk, I have Gillian, that's Levi's wife. She's nice. Anyway, I prefer to talk to my brothers, or Ezra. Especially Ezra. He's different. He was lucky, he got an education.' She uttered the last words reverently.

'That's your mother's cousin?' Marie asked.

'Yes. I wish he'd stay with us, but he'll move on soon. He doesn't hang around too long in one place.'

'Is he here now? I'd like to meet him,' Marie said.

'No, sorry. He's taken Ma's car and gone to do a big shop for her. Ezra pays his way, makes sure we all eat well.' Esther had a rather haunted expression. 'He's come down from Hull to visit, says he didn't want to lose touch. Says family is the most important thing.'

'Your hoodie, Esther? Where did you buy it?'

Esther looked down. 'What? This old thing? Ma got us all one about a year back. The local supermarket was selling them off for next to nothing. She reckoned every trolley in the store had at least one or two in it. Why?'

'Nothing, just thought a sleeveless hoodie was a good idea in the warmer weather.'

'Wouldn't suit you. You're too posh.'

Marie laughed. 'I've been called a lot of things, Esther, but posh isn't one of them!'

'Compared to us you are.'

Again, that fleeting, rather sad expression. Marie had a feeling that for all her brave words about family, Esther Lorimer would like to sprout wings and fly away to another life, a million miles from Hawker's Fen.

CHAPTER FOURTEEN

Having listened to Jackman's story, Superintendent Ruth Crooke sat back and folded her arms. 'So, he actually gained access to your, er,' she paused for a moment, unsure of what to call Laura Archer. She knew that she and Jackman were in a relationship but how serious were they? 'Gained access to Laura's apartment and her consulting rooms? As in, he forced an entry?'

'He did, ma'am. He picked the lock, then proceeded to video himself and download the file onto Laura's laptop.'

'Is there any way IT can assist with that, Rowan? Could the file be traced back to his phone, or am I being naïve?'

'Ashcroft is too clever for that, ma'am. He used a camera, not his mobile, and downloaded the clip directly from a SDHC card.'

'Thought I was clutching at straws. Tracing his phone would have been far too easy.' Ruth was starting to feel the pressure. Apart from drafting in several armed units from other forces to help with the threat from the sniper, the chief was already suggesting they request the help of a Serious Crimes Squad from HQ, but she was reluctant to do that. She had been here before with Ashcroft and dearly wanted to see those he had targeted and intimidated for so long have the satisfaction of bringing him down themselves. 'I can assign someone to watch Laura if you think it appropriate, Rowan?'

Jackman drew in a long breath. 'He did say they would soon meet face to face, but I don't think it's Laura who is really in his sights. Yes, by getting to her he gets to me, but for some reason I believe that in destroying her sanctuary, he has achieved what he set out to do. He has invaded her personal space and infected it with his evil presence. I reckon he'll consider that enough of a victory and will move on.'

'Suppose Ashcroft becomes angry that she ignored his warning and told you what he'd done,' she suggested.

'To be honest, Ruth, I think that could earn her his respect. He preys on people's weaknesses, as we well know, and Laura has shown strength in going against him. I believe he'll admire that.'

'So? Shall I get someone to keep an eye on her or not?'

'I want to say yes, for obvious reasons, but I'm certain he'll move on to someone else now. And uniform are keeping a close eye on all police personnel.'

'Well, if you're really sure, Jackman . . .' Ruth made a mental note to make everyone aware that Laura Archer had been singled out for attention by the killer. It wouldn't hurt to have a few more eyes watching her.

'And the shooter, Rowan? Are you any further forward regarding him?' Ruth watched him, noting his apparent reluctance to answer.

Hesitantly, he said, 'As you know, we are checking all ex-military and police personnel who have known psychological disorders along with expertise with rifles of that sort, but . . .'

Ruth was beginning to grow impatient.

'That gun club keeps haunting me — the Fenside Gun Club belonging to Mr Kenneth Harcourt, whose own guns were stolen. The second victim was the armourer there for several years. He was killed by the same make of gun that he would have used when he was in the armed forces.' Jackman sighed. 'I don't understand the links, but they do exist, I'm sure of it.' He hesitated again. 'Am I being paranoid, or is it just too much of a coincidence that all this is happening at the exact same time as Ashcroft chooses to suddenly reappear?'

Ruth gave him a tight-lipped smile. 'Not at all. That's what I've been thinking since day one.'

Jackman exhaled. 'That's a relief. I was beginning to think I was becoming obsessed with him, believing him to be responsible for every single thing that happens.'

'I believe he might have orchestrated all these events to coincide with his return. Don't forget, he's a manipulator. He loves to pull the strings. Planting a sniper in our midst and throwing us into turmoil is just the type of scenario he would revel in.' Ruth was gratified that Jackman had considered the possibility, it justified her faith in him. 'If he used a gofer to deliver that photograph and wreath to Marie's address, he could just as easily hire an assassin, don't you think? We know he's got the money.'

'I agree, and if it's all right with you, we'll pursue that line of enquiry. If we can track the kid Marie nearly caught and lean on him, we might get some information on where Ashcroft is operating from, and maybe what he looks like now. He could well have changed his appearance, which is why he's been able to move around the town undetected.'

'Go with that,' Ruth said, 'and keep me updated every inch of the way.'

She watched Jackman leave, relieved that he seemed more positive than of late. Ashcroft had the power to destroy those who came under his influence, and she didn't want that happening to Rowan Jackman, or any of those under her command for that matter. She didn't always show it — in fact she rarely showed any form of emotion — but she was fiercely proud of her officers. It was just not like them to be doing their jobs while looking over their shoulders, fearful of the slightest movement.

* * *

'Bugger!' Marie cursed. They were on their way back to Saltern-le-Fen. 'It's just dawned on me that I forgot to take a look at Jacob, check whether it was him that hung the wreath on my Tiger. I got so caught up in talking to Esther.'

Kevin shrugged. 'He looked like any other late teen — scrawny, scruffy hair, kind of fairish, light brown, and bad skin.'

'Pity I never got to check his complexion while I was chasing his butt for half a mile,' grumbled Marie.

'Can't see it being him, Sarge.' Charlie said. 'He's too . . . well, too simple even to get your address right. All he cares about are animals. I'm betting Ashcroft chose a street kid, one of the streetwise ones.'

'Charlie's right, Sarge,' said Kevin. 'If you'd talked to him, you'd have seen what we meant.'

'I will. We have to go back to see Paul and Levi.' Marie had become quite fascinated by this family.

'And I want to meet Cousin Ezra, the "clever" one,' said Charlie.

'Actually, I rang in and had them run a background check on Ezra Lorimer,' said Kevin. 'I don't think he's that bright, because he's been hauled in for questioning several times by the Hull police. No convictions, but he's definitely considered one to watch.'

'What kind of crime?' asked Marie.

'Mainly handling stolen goods, and one suggestion of being connected to a small-time fraud scam. Nothing heavy and nothing conclusive.' Kevin stared out of the window at the never-ending fields. 'But if the Lorimers are squeaky clean, they could do without visitations from dubious family members.'

'Dead right,' said Marie. 'Those boys are vulnerable and seem easily open to suggestion I'd reckon, wouldn't you?' She scowled. 'Esther mentioned that Ezra always had money and paid his way, so where did he get it from? Ill-gotten gains?'

'Wouldn't surprise me,' said Kevin. 'By the way, did you guys get the impression that the family were rather in awe of him?'

Charlie nodded, Marie too. 'Esther looked quite wistful when she spoke about him, she said she loved talking to him. Maybe we ought to go back at close of play today, what do you think? We should catch the rest of the family if we call around tea-time.'

'I'm going to have to pass on that, Sarge.' Kevin pulled a face. 'I've got a whole load of reports to write up before I leave tonight.'

'I'm free, Sarge,' Charlie said. 'And I'm more than happy to meet the rest of the family.'

'Okay, we'll report our findings to Jackman, and aim to get back out there around six.' They were now in Saltern. Part of her was scared they were wasting time. Ashcroft was on the loose, along with a gunman. But another part told her she should persist with the Lorimers.

'Can you drop me at the end of the High Street, Sarge?' Kevin asked. 'I'll walk the rest of the way in. There's someone I'd like a word with, and he's generally hanging around that area.'

'Of course, but watch your back, Kevin. The super has asked all officers to move around in pairs, for safety's sake.'

'It's alright, Sarge, I'll be careful.'

She pulled into a parking space just before the High Street to let Kevin out. 'Remember, eyes wide open.'

He gave her a mock salute, then loped off towards the main shopping area.

'I'm looking forward to him joining us in CID,' said Charlie. 'He's a good bloke. I like him, don't you, Sarge?'

'I do.' She glanced across at Charlie. 'I'm guessing you're missing having Max around all the time. You two were like Batman and Robin.'

Charlie nodded. 'Don't tell him, will you? I wish Max was back full-time. We bounced off each other perfectly and I feel a bit at a loss when he's not here.'

Marie smiled. 'I won't say a word, Charlie, and I understand what you mean. Life moves on, I guess, and now he's a dad, he has different priorities.'

'I understand. I'm just being selfish really.'

'Maybe Kevin will fill the gap,' said Marie. 'I get the feeling he'll fit in a treat.'

Marie drew in to the police station, still mulling over their visit to Rachel Lorimer. She kept hearing Noah say that their mother told them they didn't need friends, they had each other, then, almost in the same breath, that Jacob hated Levi and didn't speak to him. She thought about her own mother and father, estranged, yes, but still filling her life with love and happiness. And they had encouraged her to make friends. Why would Rachel not want her children to socialise? Was she hiding something in that tiny kingdom of hers?

* * *

Robbie Melton had been going out with Ella Jarvis for over a year now. It was not too serious — neither demanded much of the other, they just had fun. Ella was a forensic photographer in the SOCO team and a favourite of Professor Wilkinson. Of late, Robbie had been wondering where the relationship was going. Would it ever get more serious? He wasn't exactly sure what he wanted. He was fond of Ella, but did he feel more than that? And if not, what then?

'Any chance of getting an answer any time soon?'

Robbie looked up to see Gary Pritchard staring at him curiously.

'You were well away with the fairies, Robbie. Anything I can help with?'

Robbie grinned at his friend. 'Daydreaming, mate, and trying to answer the unanswerable.'

'Sounds a bit weird, if you don't mind me saying,' Gary said. 'Now, back to my question. Would you like a coffee?'

'I fancy a tea, actually.' Robbie felt in his pocket. 'And it's my turn. You bought the last round.' He passed a handful of change across his desk. 'And a packet of crisps, please. Any flavour.'

Marie and Charlie walked in while Gary was putting their drinks on the desk. Marie went straight to Jackman's office, and Charlie flopped into his chair.

'Charlie-boy! How did your trip to the twilight zone go?' Robbie called out.

'Interesting. There's this old crow of a matriarch lording it over a rundown farm, her brood of oddballs, who incidentally all own rifles — well, with one exception — and a visiting cousin who is under the watchful eye of the Hull police for possible handling of stolen goods. How's that for starters?'

'Anything else?' Gary asked, smiling.

'As if that's not enough, two of the sons live in their own static, there was a distinct whiff of diesel floating around and they all own sleeveless hoodies like the one the sarge ripped off her running man the other night.'

'Blimey!' Gary's eyes widened.

Robbie frowned. 'They didn't have pigs on this farm, did they, by any chance?'

'Oh, yes: pigs, sheep, a couple of cows, chicken, ducks, a donkey, and a beautiful horse. That was the nicest thing I saw in the whole visit.'

'What?' Robbie jumped up. 'Hang on. What kind of horse?'

Charlie shrugged. 'I dunno, it was just a big, handsome horse. Why?'

'There was a horse theft, didn't you hear? A guy called Bullimore had his best breeding horse stolen last night. I've just got back from talking to him.' He rifled around on his desk and found a photograph. 'Did it look like this?' He held the picture up.

'Could be,' Charlie squinted at the photo. 'I only caught a glimpse of it and I don't know a thing about horses. Come to think of it, I don't think that lad Jacob wanted me to see it. He closed the stable door really fast when he saw me taking a butcher's inside.'

'I bet he bloody did,' Robbie growled. 'That horse is worth thousands.' He made for the door. 'I have to tell the boss about this. Coming?'

Charlie got up. 'The sarge and I were going to go back when the shift finishes. Looks like we have a good reason to now, doesn't it?'

'And I'm coming too. I have a vested interest in getting that horse back to his owner. Bullimore is a friend of Jackman's mother.'

They went to Jackman's office. On hearing their story, Jackman said, 'Too much of a coincidence to ignore. I can't see a family like the Lorimers owning a horse of that calibre. Take a picture of it on your phone, Robbie, and send it to Clay Bullimore. If he confirms that it is his, then we'll organise a horsebox and get it collected. Have you got his number?'

'Yes, boss.'

'Marie, go now. If it is Bullimore's horse — what did you call it? Nimbus? — and that boy Jacob realised Charlie had clocked him, they could be moving him out as we speak.'

Marie jumped up. 'Charlie, Robbie. With me. Animal Farm, here we come.'

As they left his office, Robbie was sure he heard Jackman muttering something about all animals being equal . . .

CHAPTER FIFTEEN

Rosie was just winding up her search for army personnel who had been retired out on mental health grounds. Not one could be placed in Saltern or the surrounding area at the time of the shootings. She was now concentrating on Bethany Gadd, a female sharpshooter who had been one of the police force's shining stars.

Rosie found the report to be particularly disturbing. Bethany had been a CTSFO — an elite counterterrorist firearms officer — highly trained and dedicated. She became involved in a controversial police shooting and saw her life and her precious career disintegrate, simply for doing her job. The ensuing court case destroyed her. She spent months in and out of psychiatric hospitals and then dropped off the radar. She was the only one of the possible suspects that Rosie just could not locate.

Her mobile buzzed. A message from Max. The twins had not improved, in fact they were worse, and Max had made an appointment to see the GP. Thoughts of Bethany Gadd evaporated, and all Rosie could think about was Tim and Jessica. She checked the clock. She had an hour before her shift ended. Rosie chewed on her thumbnail. Could she ask to leave early? It would be the third time she'd done so recently and it wouldn't look good. Sooner or later she was going to have to choose between her children and her job, and she had no idea what to do.

Rosie texted Max and said she'd meet him at the surgery.

She stood up and slowly made her way to Jackman's office. He'd understand, she was sure, but for how much longer? He needed reliable team members, which did not include one who wasn't pulling her weight.

She had to decide.

* * *

Kenneth Harcourt paced up and down the foyer at the Fenside Gun Club. He had made this club into what it was today, a very successful business. From a single range, he had extended to three, with 100 metre and 50 metre ranges, and also a clay shooting layout. He hosted regular competitions in all disciplines and even had facilities for private companies wishing to showcase their products. Along with the social club, it was now a very popular venue. But now, haunted by the ghost of his old armourer, Arthur Barnes, the place that had once been his hobby, where he could indulge his love of guns, was suddenly full of dark secrets. Barnes had been assassinated, there was no other word for it. But why? Surely, that scheming, adulterous witch of a wife of his wouldn't have gone so far as to have him murdered? Would she?

Harcourt paced. Worse still, it could be his old gun that had been used to kill his friend. Why the hell hadn't he just deactivated it and hung it on the bloody wall?

Suddenly, guns had taken on a whole new meaning for Kenneth Harcourt. Every member of his exclusive club had become a potential suspect. Was he a good enough shot? Was she ruthless enough to shoot a human being? Wasn't that man ex-Army? Isn't he training to shoot with the British team? What do I really know about that guy?

This sniper had to be connected to either him or his club in some way, so perhaps he was the one who could discover who it was.

Harcourt called the number the detective had given him. He would offer his help — and mean it. He would do it for the sake of his old friend, Arthur Barnes, and his own peace of mind.

* * *

They were on their way to Hawker's Fen. This time Charlie drove, while Marie and Robbie discussed the possibility that the Lorimers were responsible for all the recent thefts.

'It all depends on Nimbus, doesn't it?' said Robbie. 'If they stole the horse, then ten-to-one they nicked the pigs, the diesel as well.'

'And the guns?' asked Marie doubtfully.

'They all know how to handle them. Plus, they'd have an axe like the one that was used on Harcourt's door and gun cabinet.'

Marie pictured the massive woodpile she had seen in the corner of the yard. 'Good point, Robbie. But I'm still convinced that Rachel would never condone theft. If they are responsible, I'm betting they'll be far more scared of her than whatever the law might dish out. Prison might actually seem like the better option.'

'Then we are forced to look at one of the working sons or the dubious cousin, Ezra,' added Charlie.

'Which is why we are here.' If only they hadn't left the grotty farm when they did. The horse was essential to their enquiry, and by now the Lorimer boys would have had plenty of time to make it disappear. Marie leaned forward. 'Foot down, Charlie.'

As soon as they arrived, Marie and Robbie went to the front door and informed Rachel Lorimer of what they intended to do. 'I can get a warrant, Rachel, but I don't want to go that route. It would be better if you'd just allow us to walk around your property and chat to the family members we missed earlier.'

Rachel Lorimer finally agreed, although not without treating them to some colourful language and a few barely veiled threats.

'Charlie! The stable. Show us where you saw the horse,' Marie barked.

They ran over to where Charlie and Kevin had seen Jacob tending to the chickens. 'Over there, Sarge. That old barn. That's where I saw him.'

Stepping over horse muck, Marie and Robbie followed Charlie towards the barn.

It was empty.

'What do you want?' They'd been indulging in some colourful language of their own. 'Ma don't like to hear words like that. She'll make you wash your mouth out with soap and water.'

There stood Jacob, a heavy sack of feed draped over his arm as casually if it were made of tissue paper.

'Hello, Jacob,' Marie said. 'We were looking for the horse that was here earlier. Where is it?'

His eyes narrowed. 'Who wants to know?'

She sighed. This was not going to be easy. 'We do, Jacob. We are the police. Look.' She held out her warrant card, and the others followed suit. 'I'm DS Marie Evans. I knew your grandad, Caleb.'

Jacob eyed the ID cards suspiciously. 'I can't read what they say. They could be anything.'

Robbie smiled at him. 'We really are coppers, but we're just in plain clothes.'

'Show me your whistle and your truncheon then.'

Marie took a different approach. 'Your ma said you were to help us.'

'Ah. Okay. I moved him to another barn, a nicer one. I wanted him to be happy. He's a lovely animal.'

'Good lad! Ma said you'd show him to us,' Marie said. 'Can we see him, please, Jacob?'

He turned on his heel and walked towards a smaller, newer structure a little further away.

A massive chestnut horse stood with its head over the half door. Immediately it saw Jacob, it gave a little whinny and nuzzled him gently.

'Well, I'm damned,' muttered Robbie. 'Will you look at that?'

'Is it Nimbus?' asked Marie.

'Without a doubt. Here, look at the photo.' He showed her. The markings and the shape were identical.

'Get a picture, Rob, and do as Jackman asked, send it to Bullimore.'

They went into the barn and, while Robbie photographed the horse, Marie turned to Jacob. 'He likes you, doesn't he?'

'I like him too. We're friends.'

'What's his name?'

'Trigger.'

Trigger. 'Did you name him, Jacob?'

'No. He's Uncle Ezra's horse.'

Marie tried not to react. 'So, did Uncle Ezra bring him with him when he came? Did Trigger gallop along behind the motorhome, or sit inside? I can't imagine that, can you?'

Jacob giggled. 'Of course he didn't! A man stole Trigger, so Noah and me went and got him back.'

'Oh, right! I see. Well, that's fair enough.' She stared at the horse. 'You're looking after him nicely, aren't you?'

He gave her a scathing look.

'Where did you learn how to care for horses, Jacob?'

'Didn't learn. They tell you what they need, you just have to look and listen.'

Great, thought Marie, a horse whisperer as well. Before she could say anything more, the barn door flew open and Noah crashed in. 'Get away from my brother! Don't listen to him! He's not right in the head. Go away!'

'Calm down, Noah. We're only talking, and your ma gave us permission,' Marie said. 'We're not upsetting him, alright?'

Noah looked almost hysterical. 'You don't understand! You can't believe what Jacob says, you can't!'

'Oh, I think we understand all too well,' said Robbie quietly. 'Now, before you scare the horse, I suggest you and I go and have a nice little chat. Outside.'

Before he could protest, Robbie had frog-marched him back into the yard.

'Is Noah in trouble?' Jacob didn't look particularly worried, just interested.

Marie smiled at him. 'Maybe. It depends on whether he tells the truth or not, doesn't it?'

'I always tell the truth,' Jacob stated flatly.

'Then you won't be in trouble.'

He nodded slowly. 'That's what Ma says. Tell the truth and shame the Devil.'

'She's right. Now, about the six pigs you took from Mr Beaton's farm. Was that something to do with Uncle Ezra too?'

'Sort of.' Jacob screwed his face up into a frown, 'Uncle heard that they were being ill-treated, so we rescued them. It was for their own good, and now they're really happy. Want to see them?'

'Later, Jacob. Right now, I'd rather see your uncle.'

'He's not home yet.' The giant youth's face lit up in a broad smile. 'He brings me presents from the town. Yesterday he bought me some sweets that looked like spaceships! They tasted fizzy and I really liked them. Maybe he'll bring me something else tonight.'

'Maybe,' said Marie, wondering how to tell him that his friend Trigger would not be in his new home for much longer. Most likely, Clay Bullimore was already preparing his horsebox to fetch his beautiful Nimbus home.

'Sarge?' Robbie stuck his head back through the door. 'I've got a sort of confession to all three thefts — horse, sheep and diesel — but not the guns. And you were right, Rachel knows nothing about it. Noah is shitting himself about what she's going to say.'

'What the hell is this Ezra playing at?' asked Marie. 'Supposedly family means everything to him and he wants to keep in touch, then he turns the kids into young offenders!'

'Sarge,' Charlie Button said, 'I suggest we talk to Ezra before we confront Rachel Lorimer. He's obviously fed these two young guys a whole stack of lies and I'm wondering why. Maybe there's a valid reason for it.'

'If there is, I'll be damned if I can think of one,' Marie grumbled. 'But you're right. No good lighting the blue touch paper under Rachel before we know the facts.'

Robbie's phone buzzed. 'Message from Bullimore. He'll be here in half an hour.'

Marie gave a sigh. There was no avoiding it, Jacob had to be told. 'Jacob? Come and sit down with me for a minute.'

She led him over to a couple of bales of hay and sat down facing him. 'Listen, Jacob. Your lovely horse doesn't really belong to your uncle. The real owner is a man who has lots of horses. He loves his animals very much and takes good care of them. And the horse's name is Nimbus, not Trigger. I don't know why your uncle lied about it, but I'm afraid he did, and Nimbus has to go home to his real owner. He's on his way here now. Do you understand?'

Jacob stared at the horse. 'He was in good condition, I suppose. He hadn't been badly treated. And the place we took him from was clean. It smelt nice — fresh hay and leather.' He looked from the horse to her. 'Why did Uncle lie?'

'I don't know, but I'm going to find out, and I'll make sure to let you know, I promise.'

'Do you think I could visit him? Trigger — I mean, er, Nimbus? Will the man let me, do you think?'

Oh boy. How to answer this? You steal his favourite horse, and then want visiting rights? 'I'll ask him, Jacob, but no promises, okay?'

The boy nodded and got to his feet. 'I'll get him ready, then, and say goodbye.'

'Good lad.' Marie heaved another sigh, of relief this time. 'As a matter of interest, Jacob, wasn't your ma surprised to see a horse here? What did you tell her?'

'Nothing. Uncle Ezra told her we found it running loose and brought it here for safe keeping while he looked for the owner.'

'Thank you, Jacob.' Thank heavens for that. At least the sudden arrival of a horse box wouldn't come as too much of a surprise.

Leaving Jacob to sort out Nimbus, Marie went back into the yard. When was Ezra coming back? One horse, six pigs and a couple of cans of diesel. What in hell's name was the man playing at? Well, while they waited, there were two more Lorimer sons to talk to — Levi and Paul.

CHAPTER SIXTEEN

Kevin Stoner didn't find the man he was looking for, so he made his way back to the station. He had a mountain of paperwork to tie up before the move to CID and Alan was working late tonight.

After a couple of hours, Alan called. 'How's it going?' Kevin asked. 'Busy night?' Alan was a senior radiographer who, until he met Kevin, had been perfectly happy to work nights. How things change.

'Pretty steady, which is good, it makes the time go quicker. Miss you, babe.'

'Miss you too. And if it's any consolation, I'm working as well.'

They chatted for a while, until Alan was called away.

Kevin put his phone on the desk beside him and pulled the last report towards him.

Just as he was about to close the file, his phone beeped. Kevin smiled. Alan must be really missing him tonight. He stared at the message on the screen.

Kev, can you meet me? I have something for you. And it's big. Please don't tell anyone or bring anyone. Half an hour at the place Barney died? William.

It's big. But what William was asking of him was a big thing too. A directive had gone out to all personnel ordering that while the shooter remained at large, they were not to go out on the streets alone and must always inform Control of their whereabouts. By going to the meeting, Kevin would be breaking the rules, big time. But if he didn't go, or even if he took a mate, he wouldn't get the info William had for him.

Kevin put his jacket on, closed his computer and left the office.

No moon tonight. The waste ground was in darkness. He'd walked past earlier today and the place had been deserted. No kids, no bikes, no skateboards and no street dwellers. Following Barney's death, this piece of ground had become truly desolate.

A movement.

A black cat slunk out from a pile of debris, stared at him for a moment, then sloped off. Kevin began to feel distinctly nervous. He picked his way over to the old storehouse.

He was about two hundred metres away when the headlights of a car suddenly illuminated the front of the old building. Kevin stood, caught in the light and frozen in place like a rabbit.

After a few moments his heart stopped racing and his vision cleared. A strange scene unfolded, dreamlike, before his eyes.

An old fence post, maybe six-foot high, a leftover from an earlier fenced-off area belonging to the railway. A figure tied to it, wrists and feet secured with thick rope and a white hood over its head.

Kevin started forward.

'Stay where you are! Move and he dies.'

A trap! What an idiot he'd been.

He saw the figure moving, trying to get free of its bonds, but there was nothing he could do. 'What do you want?' he shouted.

'I have a message for DI Jackman,' the voice called back.

Kevin swallowed.

'Tell him not to get side-tracked with his old adversary, because I'm just as dangerous, believe me.'

Kevin went cold.

'And in case you don't, here's the proof!'

The crack of a rifle-shot, and the man tied to the post slumped forward, held in place by the ropes. In the glare of the headlights, Kevin saw a dark stain spread across the white hood.

He dashed forward, filled with a terrible foreboding and careless of his own life. He stopped in front of the still figure. Slowly he raised a shaking hand and removed the hood.

'William. Oh no. Not you, my friend.'

He turned and screamed into the black, 'You bastard! I'll see you in hell for this!'

The lights went out, the waste ground was plunged into darkness, and Kevin heard laughter, followed by an engine starting up, revving and driving away.

'You bastard.' This time it came out as a sob.

He gently touched the side of William's neck, though he knew his friend had gone. Slowly he pulled out his phone and rang the station.

* * *

Levi Lorimer looked steadily at Marie, who returned his gaze. Levi was the first to look away. Nevertheless, he made her feel uneasy. The others were oddballs but at least also open books. Levi's blank expression gave nothing away. She pictured him heaving whole carcasses of meat up onto his muscular shoulders, those small narrow eyes registering nothing.

She had engineered it so as to speak with Levi alone. For one thing, she didn't want Rachel hearing what she had to say and another, Levi was now — nominally — the head of the household. Everyone knew that Rachel was the real power in the family, but Levi was a man.

'Your brothers Noah and Jacob could be in serious trouble, Levi. Did you know what they were up to?'

Levi shook his head, still impassive. 'We might all live here but we have our own lives. I have no idea what you're talking about.'

'Theft, Levi. And if a certain horse breeder chooses to press charges, they'll probably be arrested. Now,' she intensified her stare, 'I wonder how your mother will feel about that?'

The expression flickered for a moment, although Marie couldn't tell what it meant.

'Idiots. Morons, the pair of them, but they've never done anything this stupid before.' The eyes hardened. 'You've got proof it was my brothers?'

'We have confessions, plus the stolen goods, which are right here on the farm.'

'Ma will kill them.' He spoke through gritted teeth. 'If I don't get to them first.'

'Before you do that, Levi, it seems your cousin Ezra lied to them in order to get them to commit these crimes.'

Now the expression was easy to read — utter bewilderment. 'Ezra? Why?'

'When he gets home, we'll ask him.' Marie stood up.

Towering over her, Levi took hold of her arm. 'Please, Sergeant Evans, don't tell Ma until you know what's going on. She'll . . .' He didn't finish the sentence. He released his grip. 'This is terrible for the family. We have to sort it ourselves. My brothers are fools, but they're not bad. If Ezra has corrupted them, I'll wring his damned neck.'

'I suggest you leave the punishment side of it to us, Levi. We can do it legally. I'd hate to have to cart you away in handcuffs.' Her opinion of him had shifted slightly. Maybe he really did have no idea what was going on? Who knew? He would make a bloody good poker player. 'Is Paul home yet?

'I saw his car drive in a few minutes ago.' He hesitated, grunted. 'Look, Paul is, well, he's unpredictable. Flares up without warning, if you know what I mean. Tread carefully with him. He has no respect for the law, nor people either.'

Marie shrugged. 'I've been told he's volatile.'

'Ma says he lacks social graces, whatever that means.'

'Thanks for the warning. I'd better go and see him now.'

Out in the hall, she found Charlie Button in animated conversation with Paul Lorimer. They were talking about engines. Charlie introduced her, and Paul stuck out a hand.

'Paul Lorimer. Hello.'

She shook the proffered hand. 'Pleased to meet you, Paul.' Could this lad be the skinny little git that she had chased down her road? She looked again. Maybe not. He had to be older than that one. Still . . .

'Why are the police here?' asked Paul bluntly.

'Let's talk out of your ma's earshot, shall we?' She ushered him out through the front door. 'Noah and Jacob are in trouble, Paul. Do you know why?'

He looked both suspicious and concerned. 'No, I don't.'

She told him briefly what had happened. When she mentioned Ezra, he erupted. A torrent of words poured from him like lava.

'You can't accuse Uncle Ezra! He hasn't done anything! He loves this family. He'd do anything for us. He's our rock now Dad's gone. I want him to stay here forever! You mustn't upset him. I don't want him to go because of you. Why don't you just piss off and leave us alone?'

'Hey.' Charlie touched Paul's shoulder. 'No one is sending him away. We just need to hear his version of why certain things have happened, that's all. Then we can sort it all out and be on our way. Simple.'

Marie looked at Charlie with new respect. She hadn't known he could be so understanding. His calming voice seemed to do the trick and Paul's sudden burst of rage dissipated almost as quickly as it had begun.

Marie decided to back off and allow him to turn the conversation back to engines. Charlie knew what she needed to get from Paul and she was sure he'd do his best to elicit some answers. She left the house and went to look for Robbie. It was completely dark now, and she wanted to finish up here and get away.

'I've checked the pigs' ear tags — not that I needed to, as Jacob has told me exactly where they came from. Poor little sod, he thought he was helping the animals.' Robbie's eyes grew hard. 'Couldn't you cheerfully swing for people who manipulate the vulnerable?'

'Couldn't I just,' Marie growled. 'And where the hell is bloody Ezra?'

'Dunno about him, but I think Bullimore is here to collect Nimbus.' Robbie pointed to a big horse box that was carefully negotiating the bridge over the dyke.

'Right. Let's tell him to go easy on Jacob.'

Robbie too looked apprehensive. 'Let's hope he's so pleased to get his nag back that he doesn't look any further. It's not Jacob's fault he was hoodwinked.'

They hurried over to where the vehicle was parking up. Marie turned a big smile on Clay Bullimore. 'He's safe, sir, and he's been very well looked after. When I think what kind of outcome we could have had, it's a massive relief.'

Clay Bullimore was a tall, well-built man, his fair hair just greying at the temples. He was dressed in similar style to Jackman's mother — cord trousers, check shirt and a Barbour gilet with a dozen pockets. 'Jackman called. He didn't give me the full story, said you'd fill me in. The main thing is, Nimbus is safe.' He looked around. 'What a dump. I'd really like to know how he finished up here, but I need to see my horse first.' He looked enquiringly at Marie.

'I'll tell you everything, sir, but as you say, let's start with Nimbus.' She hesitated. 'Er, there's something you need to know, and then I'm going to ask something rather odd of you.' She quickly explained Jacob's limitations and his extraordinary talent with horses.

Looking rather taken aback at her request, Bullimore said, 'I'll see for myself, DS Evans, before I commit to anything.'

'Fair enough, but I think you'll be surprised,' Marie said.

When they opened the barn door, they saw, in the light of a single bulb, Jacob gently brushing the big horse's mane and talking it to it like an old and trusted friend. For a long moment, Bullimore stood and watched. Marie glanced at his face and knew that they had nothing to worry about.

'Jacob,' Marie said gently. 'This is Mr Bullimore. He's come to take Nimbus home.'

Both horse and groom looked up. Neither moved.

'Nimbus? Here, boy.' The horse gave a soft snuffle of greeting but stayed beside Jacob. 'Well, there's a nice welcome!' Bullimore turned to Marie. 'He's usually an excitable boy. They haven't drugged him, have they?'

'No, sir, you can check. He's just contented, I promise you.' Robbie stood behind them.

Bullimore went over to his horse and patted him, then addressed Jacob. 'You really have a way with him, lad.'

'He's special,' said Jacob, quietly.

'That he is. Have you ridden him?'

'Yes, sir, and he handles beautifully. He's the best horse I've ever seen.'

Marie nudged Robbie and nodded towards the door. 'Let's leave them to it for a while.'

Robbie grinned. 'All's well that ends well?'

'Let's not count our chickens, Robbie, or our pigs either. I'm pretty sure that Bullimore won't take this further, but the Lorimers are mercurial, they can change in the blink of an eye — think of Paul. I'll only be really happy when I see that Nimbus is on his way home.'

She stared down the lane, hoping to see headlights announcing the arrival of Ezra, but there was only darkness. Her phone rang. She listened to what Jackman had to say and the colour drained from her face. She ended the call and turned to Robbie. 'I have to go. Can you take over here? There's been another shooting, and Kevin Stoner was there again. He saw it happen.'

'Oh, my God! That poor guy. Who was shot?'

'His snout, William.' Marie shivered. 'A car with a crew of uniforms has been dispatched to help you and Charlie, and to get you home again. Can you manage everything — and Ezra, if he finally materialises?'

'Don't worry, Sarge, and Ezra will be all mine if he turns up. I'll make sure of that.'

'You'll not knock seven bells out of him, will you?'

He gave her a faint smile. 'I'll try.'

'Keep me up to speed, Robbie.'

'Will do. Just watch those fen lanes in the dark, won't you?'

Actually, Marie loved driving at night, heading to nowhere along those long, dark roads. Of course, it was far more exhilarating on her motorbike but a car was good enough. 'I'll be careful. And you look out for yourselves.'

CHAPTER SEVENTEEN

Like in some nightmare Groundhog Day, Kevin Stoner sat wrapped in a foil blanket at the back of an ambulance with blue lights flashing across the waste ground. Once again, a cordon had been set up, and as before, they awaited the arrival of the forensic team.

Kevin was far too calm. Jackman didn't like it at all. The paramedics had told him that he'd been frantic when they arrived but had suddenly lapsed into silence. Now he was talking again, but they were concerned that he was suffering from shock and wanted to take him to hospital for a check-up.

Kevin refused. 'I'd rather be with people I know, sir, really. I want my friends around me right now.'

Jackman could understand that.

'This was my fault, sir. William was a good man and now he's dead because he tried to help me.'

Jackman laid a hand on his shoulder. 'That's not true, Kevin, and you know it. There's only one person to blame here and that's the man with the gun.'

'But I should've realised. William didn't have a mobile phone, so the message sent to me couldn't have been from him. How could I have been so stupid?'

'He told you he'd contact you, didn't he?' Jackman said.

'Yes,' muttered Kevin. 'I thought he'd borrowed a phone to send the text.'

'Well then. That's fair enough. Show me the text again, Kevin.'

Kevin took his phone from his pocket and handed it to Jackman. His hand shook.

'I'd have believed it,' Jackman said. 'It sounds perfectly reasonable. By the way, even though you were totally out of order in going off alone, I do understand why you did. We can all be wise after the event. Just so you understand that, alright?'

'Thank you, sir. And, sir, he knew our names, the sniper. How did he know them?'

Jackman shrugged. 'Quite easy to find out, I should think. Mine would be dead simple. Every time we are quoted in the news, my name is emblazoned across the bottom of the screen. And you're well known on the streets of Saltern. He'd only have to ask one of the homeless who that "nice young copper" was and he'd have got your name in seconds.'

As they spoke, Jackman noticed Marie standing close to William's body, which still sagged from the post. She was staring intently at the lifeless form and he wondered what she was thinking. After a few more words with Kevin, he went and joined her.

'Anything of interest catch your eye, Marie?' he asked.

'Only the accuracy of the shot, sir. It was dark. Okay, Kevin said there were headlights shining on him, but they would have caused distorting shadows, and the man was moving, trying to get free. Even so, it was a perfect shot. This sniper is first class.'

'And all just to deliver a message to me.' Jackman felt sick at the thought.

'Back off worrying about Ashcroft and concentrate on the sniper. I can't believe it, sir. What are the chances of a power struggle between killers in a small county town like Saltern?'

'I can't help thinking about one of our past cases, Marie. One that affected you badly, as it happened.' He knew this was painful for her, as it had involved a dear friend, but nevertheless he was struck by the similarity. 'Do you remember when someone hired another man to carry out a dirty job for him, but he picked a wrong 'un and everything went tits up?'

'As if I'd forget, sir! You're thinking Ashcroft might have hired this shooter as a distraction from his own work, but accidentally chose another psycho?'

'One who believes he can compete with his employer. I'm trying to remember what I learned as a student. I believe it's a recognised fact that when copycat killers reach a certain point, they suddenly want to become even more notorious than the one they were obsessed with.'

'Oh, just great. So we are caught in the middle of a killing competition. Bloody marvellous!'

Jackman couldn't help smiling. He loved the way her Welsh accent always came to the fore in such outbursts. But this was a very real possibility. 'Not a good place to be, I'll admit that.'

They both stared at William.

'But not nearly as bad as where he is right now,' said Marie softly. 'I'm dreading what happens next, aren't you, sir?'

'I'm terrified that this could turn into a tit-for-tat contest, Marie. It's like a damned great knot in my stomach.'

He'd put his fear into words. Dammit. Was he about to revert to the frightened man of the days following his nightmare? It seemed not. 'There's one ray of light in this whole scenario, Marie. If either of them gets hurried or angry, they could easily make a mistake.'

'If I were Ashcroft,' Marie said, 'I'd be very angry indeed, wouldn't you? Not only is someone trying to steal my thunder, but they are disrupting my carefully laid plans and ruining my game.'

'Meanwhile, I'm paying them good money to do it! Oh yes, I'd be beside myself,' Jackman said.

Marie pointed to William. 'And this poor soul is a casualty.'

Jackman turned and looked over to where the huddled form of Kevin Stoner still sat, wrapped in a blanket. 'And William's not the only one, unless I'm very much mistaken.'

Jackman's gaze moved to the white hood lying at the dead man's feet, which Kevin had removed in order to identify the victim. Clearly defined in the bright glow of a police halogen lamp was the hole made by the bullet. William's blood had seeped through around its edges, forming a scarlet stain.

Suddenly his nightmare came back to him. Marie's white shirt, the blood from the gunshot wound oozing from her chest. He almost reached out to touch her arm and reassure himself that she was still warm, still alive.

'Boss? Whatever's the matter? You look like you've seen a ghost.'

'Nothing, really.' He shook himself. 'It just struck me what this sniper is capable of.' It sounded feeble even to him, but he could hardly tell her the truth. 'And I'm thinking that by tomorrow Saltern will be emblazoned over the front of every newspaper and on every TV channel. Ruth is already organising armed units and specialist snipers of our own. We are going to be operating in a war zone, Marie, and heaven help us!'

* * *

Robbie, with Charlie alongside him, watched Ezra Lorimer step out of Rachel's old Mitsubishi Shogun. Robbie wasn't sure what he was expecting, but it wasn't this almost biblical figure with long grizzly hair and a full beard. Looking for all the world like Moses, albeit without the flowing robes.

Robbie held out his warrant card. 'DC Robbie Melton and DC Charlie Button, sir. We'd like a word, please.'

If Ezra was surprised, he didn't show it. He merely nodded towards his mobile home. 'Then you'd better come with me, gentlemen.'

The educated voice, so at odds with his appearance, confused Robbie even further.

The interior of the mobile home was spartan, to say the least. The only item of interest was a small cabinet packed with books. The rest was entirely functional.

Ezra indicated for them to sit on a padded bench seat while he swung the driver's seat around and sat facing them.

Robbie explained that both Jacob and Noah had admitted to stealing diesel, pigs and a valuable breeding horse. They had stated that they committed those crimes on his say-so.

'What's your response to these allegations, sir?' Robbie asked.

Ezra leaned back in his seat and stared at them thoughtfully. 'It wasn't supposed to happen like this.'

'If you could just explain, sir,' Charlie added. 'The horse, for starters. According to the boys you said that the horse was yours and that Bullimore had stolen it from you. You'd asked them to get it back for you. Is this correct?'

Ezra rubbed his eyes. 'Yes, that's the story I gave them.'

'But why? It's a valuable horse. Did you have a buyer for it?' Robbie asked.

'Oh no. Nothing like that. As with the other thefts, I sold the boys a line and they believed me. But it's not what you think.'

Robbie watched him. He looked straight back at them from dark, almond-shaped eyes. A scar on his right cheek extended from his cheekbone down into his beard. It looked old. Somehow, he didn't look like a conman or a thief, but more like a character from *The Lord of the Rings*.

'Please explain, sir,' said Robbie, getting out his notebook. 'From the beginning. But first, your home address and your reason for being here.'

The man rattled off an address, which sounded like a caravan park. 'I'm here because I heard that my cousin Rachel was struggling. They are my family and I wanted to offer some support, both emotionally and financially.'

Robbie was baffled. It was a funny way to offer support, getting two of her kids in trouble with the police.

'I know what you're thinking, Detective, but believe it or not, I did it to help them.' He leaned forward. 'Let me explain.' He let out a long, low sigh. 'I was accosted by a man in a Saltern pub. He had a proposition for me, one that could have been very lucrative indeed. He told me a story about losing his livelihood because of three local men — two farmers and a stable owner. He said that he wanted them to taste a little of the anguish they'd caused him. He said he was well-known locally, so it would be difficult to find anyone willing to carry out the jobs he had in mind without someone knowing it was him behind it.' Ezra pulled a face. 'And that's where I came in. He offered me a large amount of money to organise the whole thing. Hire a couple of lads to carry out the thefts, see that they did it properly, and to take care of the stolen goods for a short time.'

'Have you done this sort of thing before, sir?' asked Robbie. 'And why did he ask you in particular? Did you know him?'

'I'd never met him before, Detective. He said he'd been watching me for a week or two before he approached me. He knew I wasn't local.' He added, 'I admit I'd been talking to one or two dubious characters who were trying to offload black market gear. That must have decided him that I was the kind of man he was looking for.' He sniffed. 'And, no, I've never done anything like this before.'

'Did he give you a name?' asked Charlie.

A sardonic laugh. 'Of course not.'

Robbie looked up from his notebook. 'What pub did you meet him in? Can you describe him?'

'Let me think. The Duke of York — small pub on the outskirts of the town. He was about my height, that's around five foot ten, brown wavy hair, average build, stocky but not overweight, smart clothes, and well spoken.'

'You said he was going to pay you well?'

'He *did* pay me well, in cash. I collected it this evening. And it was all going to Rachel.' He thrust a hand into his inside pocket and laid a bulky envelope on the table. 'This would have kept her afloat for a good long while.' He sighed again. 'Now she'll get nothing and her boys are in trouble, all because of me.'

'Probably not your smartest move, sir,' Charlie said wryly.

'I take full responsibility for this, Officers. I deceived the boys, knowing they would fall for the line about cruelty to animals. It's not their fault.'

'Maybe so, but what about the diesel? Cruelty to fuel? They made a right balls-up of that one. If the diesel had spilled into the water in the dyke they would have been putting animals in danger.'

Ezra grimaced. 'I admit I didn't realise how limited Jacob was. Apparently, he began to syphon and couldn't stop it running.'

'Why use them at all, Mr Lorimer?' asked Robbie. 'Two young men with learning difficulties and no criminal record. I'd call that pretty low myself.'

'Call it what you want.' There was an edge to his voice. 'Noah said he wanted to do something to help his mother and make things easier for her. So I told him about my plans to get "my" horse back, saying I was going to hire someone to do the job. That's when he jumped in and said he'd do it with Jacob, anything to put some money in the family coffers.'

It all sounded like a load of cobblers to Robbie and from the look on Charlie's face, he was thinking the same. 'And how were you going to explain this "windfall" to Rachel?' He pointed to the fat envelope. 'She'd throw you out on your ear if she knew the truth. And we're still waiting for your explanation about the diesel. You haven't said what you told the boys about that.'

Ezra stared at him balefully. 'I've a reputation as a gambler, which Rachel knows. I thought I'd say it was a big win on a horse. It did have a grain of truth in it.'

Robbie suppressed a snort. Ezra Lorimer wouldn't know the truth if it bit him on the arse.

'If you must know, I gave them a sob story regarding the diesel. I said their ma couldn't afford to top up the diesel in the old tractor but was too proud to tell anyone.'

The thing that most puzzled Robbie was why the whole family seemed to think the sun shone from Ezra's backside. He was an out-and-out rogue, but they couldn't seem to see it. 'You really are a piece of work, aren't you? You lie to everyone to make them do your dirty work for you.'

'As far as I can see, being honest hasn't done Rachel much good,' spat out Ezra. 'Fine for you to preach — look at you, you've had an easy life. It's written all over you. Rachel is about to lose this place. All her life the powers that be have let her down. They didn't even see to it that her kids got an education, just because they weren't perfect. Don't you dare preach to me about lying! I wanted those boys to feel that they'd contributed in some way, been useful and done something positive to help their mother.' His eyes bored into Robbie's. 'Rachel isn't some smart shyster who knows how to play the system. You won't find any plasma screen TVs in her home, and where's the kids' smartphones, eh? Sure, I'm not bloody Snow White, I took a gamble to try to help my cousin and it backfired. My fault, not theirs. Mea culpa.' He held out his hands to Robbie, as if for the cuffs. 'Take me in if you want, but leave this family alone. The horse has gone back to its owner, the pigs will be on their way home tomorrow, all having been fed and looked after . . . and a couple of cans of fuel? Well, I'll pay for those. You'd do better to look for the man who was prepared to pay top dollar to cause grief to those farmers and waste your precious time when you have better things to be spending it on.'

This unexpected outburst took Robbie aback. And there was some truth in it. Suddenly the whole thing seemed thoroughly petty. Why *were* they chasing their tails with this crap when they had a psycho and a gunman running riot in the town?

Wait a minute. Guns! That was why. He hadn't asked about the guns.

'One last question. Did your man ask you to steal any guns? Only the money here,' he picked up the envelope, 'seems rather excessive for the job you did.'

Ezra frowned. 'Guns? What guns?'

No one spoke. After a while, Robbie said, 'Don't leave here, Mr Lorimer. We will have more questions for you.'

'And Rachel? What are you going to tell her?' Ezra asked.

'Nothing tonight. I suggest you have a nice family chat this evening and do some explaining before we are forced to do it ourselves. Goodnight, Mr Lorimer, and thank you for your time.' Robbie took an evidence bag from his pocket and slipped the envelope into it. 'Evidence, sir. We'll notify you about it in due course.'

Outside, he heaved a sigh of relief. 'That went well. I don't think.'

Charlie exhaled. 'I just want to get away from here.'

'Me too. Let's bugger off.'

As they drove back across the darkened fen, Charlie said, 'There's one thing that really bothers me, Rob.'

'Only one?' Robbie's head was full of questions.

'The description that Ezra gave of the man who paid him to carry out those thefts . . . it sounds to me just like Alistair Ashcroft.'

Robbie closed his eyes. With everything else that was going on, he'd not made the connection. But Charlie was right. Okay, a thousand other men looked like that too, but nevertheless, Ashcroft was one of them. He leaned forward. 'Constable? Can you put your foot down when we get to the main road?'

Their driver nodded, the car surged forward, and they made the rest of the journey on blue lights.

CHAPTER EIGHTEEN

Jackman listened to Robbie and Charlie relate their interview with Ezra. When they had finished, he sat in silence, looking into space while they glanced at each other.

'So you're saying this mystery man who allegedly holds a grudge against Clay Bullimore and farmers Beaton and Dewsbury is a dead ringer for Ashcroft?'

'According to the last sightings we had of him, sir, although that was a while ago now,' said Charlie.

'It crossed our minds that he might've arranged them as a diversion, something to keep us dancing all over the county while he gets on with . . . whatever he's planning to do.' Robbie shook his head. 'We got nothing to suggest that Ezra was involved in the gun thefts, but he's a real oddball, sir. He just doesn't seem to add up, does he, Charlie?'

'No, he doesn't,' Charlie said. 'I'd really like to do some more background checks on Ezra Lorimer, sir. We know he was suspected of handling stolen goods, but I'd like to dig deeper.'

'Tomorrow, Charlie. It's getting late. You and Robbie get off home and grab a few hours' sleep. Ezra can wait until the morning.' He paused. 'Just one thing. Did you show him the photograph of Ashcroft?'

'Charlie didn't come up with the thought until we were almost back here, sir,' said Robbie. 'I'll go back first thing and see if he can ID Ashcroft as his man.'

Jackman was tempted to go out there himself, but he wanted to see Laura. He had already had to postpone their meal out with Sam to the following night. They were both understanding but it made Jackman sad. He had made this big decision and had wanted to celebrate it with her. As usual, work had got in the way.

'Okay, Robbie, but I'd do it really early if I were you, just in case he decides to take himself off.'

'You got it, boss. I'll be up with the lark.' About to leave, Robbie paused. 'It makes sense, doesn't it? Ashcroft playing with a family of innocents like them.'

'Perfect sense,' said Jackman. 'He'd enjoy the game.'

After they had gone, Jackman rang Laura. Sam had stayed at her apartment with her until forensics had finished. When they heard that he would be working late, they had grabbed a fish-and-chip supper.

'Sam didn't want me to be alone after what had happened earlier, bless him,' said Laura. 'So we went back and spent some time sorting out a few more of the things I wanted to take. Until we get the mill set up, I'm going to be using a clinic room at Greenborough Hospital for appointments with clients. I'm just about to drive over to Cartoft — or should I call it home?'

'Sounds good, doesn't it?' said Jackman, softly.

'*Very* good, darling.'

'I'm leaving now too, so I'll see you there.'

Jackman ended the call and stood up. Just one more thing to do. He needed to know how Kevin was. He had refused to go to hospital, despite all their efforts to persuade him.

Kevin answered his phone on the second ring. 'DI Jackman, sir. Is everything okay?'

'We are just shutting up shop for the night. I'm worried about you, Kevin.'

'I'm shaken, sir, but that's to be expected. Alan will be home soon. He had a late call and got held up, but he's found a colleague to cover for him.' He gave a hollow laugh. 'He'll be starting to think I'm doing this on purpose.'

'Don't underestimate the shock you've had, Kevin.' Jackman knew Kevin would object to what he had to say next. 'I'd like you to take a few days off. You are due to start with us next week, but we can postpone it for a while. Have you somewhere you could go that's away from here? You need some down-time and a bit of distance, Kevin.'

Kevin's silence seemed to last forever, until Jackman began to wonder if he was still there. Finally, he said, 'I must keep working, sir. I can't be hiding away. We all know what we sign up for and we just have to deal with it. What's more, I'm starting to think that the sniper is using me to set up his targets. If we are clever, we might be able to use that to our advantage. Twice I've been within shouting distance of him, so maybe *you* should be watching *me*?'

Jackman frowned. Kevin's tone was far too matter of fact. He was young, inexperienced, and had just seen two men shot dead right in front of him, as well as discovering the body of a third. Kevin was no hard-arsed soldier honed for combat. He was a sensitive and compassionate copper.

'I applaud your dedication, Kevin, but I really think you've suffered enough in the last few days and I want you to take some time out. Look, I'll ring you tomorrow morning and we'll talk again. I'd rather not have to pull rank on you, so think about what I've said and talk to Alan. Alright?'

Sounding unconvinced, Kevin said he would. Despite his words, Jackman suspected he'd see him at work the next day. He only hoped the boy wouldn't suffer for it later.

He ended the call, picked up his jacket and left.

* * *

At around one in the morning, Marie's phone rang. She struggled to rouse herself, afraid it would be yet another death. It took her a few moments to realise that it was Esther Lorimer speaking.

Esther's words tumbled out. 'You said to ring you. If I thought of anything odd, you told me to ring.'

'Esther, yes, that's right. Now, is something wrong? Are you alright?'

'I don't know why he did these things, Sergeant Evans, but he must have a good reason. Ezra cares about us. He wouldn't hurt us or get us into trouble, I'm sure, but . . .' her voice tailed off.

'Tell me what's worrying you, Esther. I'll help if I can.' Marie was wide awake now. 'Has Ezra done something else?'

'You need to talk to Paul, Sergeant. I overheard him and Levi talking about something Ezra asked Paul to do. I don't know what it was, they shut up when they saw me, but now Paul is shit scared. I thought I'd have it out with Ezra but he doesn't want to talk to me, he won't even open his door.'

I bet he won't. 'Listen, Esther, you leave this to me, okay? I'll be there first thing and we'll try to sort it out, I promise. You just try to get some sleep. It's nearly half one in the morning, you know. I'll see you tomorrow — and, Esther, don't tell anyone, okay?'

Esther hung up. Marie sat for a while, wondering whether to wake Gary and tell him about the call. They could do nothing tonight, so she decided it would keep until breakfast. She lay back down and closed her eyes. What was Ezra asking Paul to do that was so frightening?

Only one thing came to mind. Guns. Stolen ones.

She recalled being told that Paul was volatile and prone to outbursts of temper, and she pictured the shattered door. Someone sure took their temper out on that, as well as Kenneth Harcourt's old gun cabinet. It had been reduced to kindling. Had Ezra deceived Paul with some cock-and-bull story, just like he had Noah and Jacob?

Marie lay awake, staring into the darkness. Everything rested on whether Ezra recognised the photo of Ashcroft, and whether he'd been responsible for stealing those guns. If that proved to be the case, then a rather frightening theory began to materialise. One by one, the pieces of the jigsaw slotted into place. It was just a hypothesis, but it was also just about possible. Wanting to cause mayhem and keep the police busy, Ashcroft picks on Ezra, who makes use of his crazy family to earn himself some money. He also pays Ezra to get one — possibly two — of the brothers to steal him a gun. A gun that he then passes on to the man he has hired to assassinate certain designated targets. Marie let out a soft groan. But that man is evolving into a very dangerous killer in his own right, and Ashcroft has a renegade on his hands. He would certainly not have accounted for that in his vengeful plan. If she was right, then she and Jackman could be right in the middle of a deadly situation, caught in the crossfire between two ruthless killers, each one out to better the other. She shuddered. She'd ring Jackman at first light and throw this theory at him, so they could bring Ezra in for questioning as soon as possible. He could be the key to finding Alistair Ashcroft.

Aware that she would need her wits about her in the days to come, Marie tried to sleep. But Alistair Ashcroft had taken that from her too.

* * *

Another person experiencing a sleepless night was Kenneth Harcourt. Eventually, with a mumbled assurance to his wife, he gave up.

Half an hour later he was in his office at the gun club. For the whole of the preceding day he had been going through membership records and asking the staff about any members or prospective members who might have given them cause for concern. Now, at three in the morning, he was leafing through his diary, hunting for any mention of his old friend Arthur Barnes.

Harcourt was an inveterate note maker and keeper of diaries. He kept everything — pieces of paper, memos and torn-off scraps on which he'd recorded telephone numbers.

In his head was a vague memory of something that had happened a couple of months ago that could help the police enquiry. It involved Arthur. He had been a brilliant armourer. Usually efficient and meticulous, his turbulent home life sometimes caused him to behave irrationally. Knowing of his heroic past and his fraught relationship with his wife, Harcourt forgave him the occasional lapse.

He found what he was looking for. A brief note made six weeks earlier. Arthur had had an altercation with one of the newer members. It was nothing major but had rattled Arthur to the extent of calling the man an irritating piece of shit. In the note he'd made, Harcourt had registered amusement at Arthur's outburst, nevertheless he had scribbled the name down so that he could check this man out at some point. And here it was. Ralph Renwick. He recalled checking the man's credentials and finding nothing amiss, but had he actually talked to him?

Harcourt sighed. With his darling daughter still occupying fifty percent of his thoughts at any given moment, it wasn't surprising he forgot things. He tried to recall this Renwick. Arthur had described him as upper class, and his voice and his clothes did indeed speak of breeding. He had a rather supercilious air, a know-it-all attitude which had got under Arthur's skin. Apparently, Renwick had questioned Arthur's knowledge about a weapon and its handling. The discussion had descended into an altercation. Harcourt couldn't recall seeing Renwick at the club after that.

He got up from his desk and went to the register. All members signed in and out every time they visited. Any guns issued out that were club property were recorded by their new temporary armourer, a woman named Jacqui Hampshire. Harcourt hoped she would take up the post on a permanent basis, for she was meticulous with the stocks and really knew her stuff, having been part of a British shooting team for several years.

He scanned the register, going back six weeks, but there was no mention of Renwick. Harcourt returned to his office and looked up the man's contact number, made a note of it and put it in his pocket. As soon as the day began, he would ring DI Jackman. What if there was more to this altercation than Arthur had said? And why had Renwick subsequently avoided the gun club? Prior to the argument, he had attended regularly and, as far as Harcourt could recall, was becoming a pretty proficient target shooter.

Alarm bells rang in Harcourt's head. A picture formed in his mind of Renwick talking to their receptionist and picking up some leaflets from the display rack on the foyer desk. The one he was most interested in was a club that had recently opened a new range somewhere north of Lincoln. It was a very professional outfit with two clubs in Lincolnshire. They had recently taken on a retired army firearms training officer and now offered *Sniper Experience Days*.

Harcourt hurried to the foyer and picked up the leaflet. Sniper Experience Days. Oh shit! He read the blurb. He'd heard about these and they were very popular, even though they cost around three hundred pounds a day. Participants would travel by 4x4 to a remote part of the North York Moors where you could get a taste of firing such weapons as AK-47s and take part in mock hostage situations. The events also offered long-distance target shooting in open countryside with a trained instructor, and, if you were good enough, there were even advanced courses. A sentence from the leaflet stuck in his brain: 850 metre long-range target shooting with a steel-core Cyclone 308 military sniper rifle. No previous experience necessary.

Harcourt felt dizzy. He looked at his watch — five a.m. Should he phone now? He drew in a breath. To hell with it! He found DI Jackman's mobile number in his contacts and hit dial.

* * *

For the third time in two hours, Rosie awoke to the sound of fretting babies. She staggered out of bed, vaguely wondering if it were a twin thing, the fact that they started crying at exactly the same time.

With a groan, Max pushed the duvet aside. 'You stay here, flower. I've got it.'

Gratefully she climbed back into bed and sank into a troubled half-sleep. She was exhausted. This could not go on.

Half an hour later, having worked his magic, Max returned carrying two mugs of tea. All was quiet.

Rosie hauled herself up. 'Boy, do I need this.'

Max smiled sleepily at her. 'They are still pretty poorly, but they are improving. Another day and I think they'll have turned the corner.'

'That's good. Poor little mites. Earache is horrible and they can't tell us, can they?'

'Oh, they have their ways. Like yelling their heads off.' Max grinned.

'True.' She turned to Max. 'Darling, we need to talk.'

Max lost his smile. 'That sounds ominous.'

'It's serious, Max. We've done our best to be both coppers and parents but the fact is, I'm just not coping.' Rosie closed her eyes in relief. At last, she'd come out with it.

'What are you saying, Rosie?' asked Max, quietly.

'If you agree, I'd like to become a full-time mum, and I want you to go back to work — full-time. At the moment I spend my whole working day worrying about you and the children. You are the best dad in the world, and you have more of a way with the twins than I do, but I can't do both anymore.'

For a while Max said nothing. He took her hand in his. 'Are you sure about this?'

'Totally. No question. I'll go in today and ask Jackman to put the wheels in motion. When my shift finishes tonight, that will be that. My place is here, Max, at home with the twins.'

Max let out a whistle. 'That came out of left field.' His grip on her hand tightened. 'I do understand, though, Rosie, really.'

She smiled at him. Why did she feel like crying? 'I love you, Mr Cohen.'

'I'm pretty smitten myself, Mrs C.' He leant over and kissed her cheek, not quite scalding her with tea. 'Even if you do come out with some stunners sometimes.'

'I think it's this ear problem that brought it home to me. I was supposed to be tracing candidates for our shooter, and all I could think about was Jessica and Tim. I wasn't doing my job properly, and with things as they are at present, that means I'm letting the team down.'

'If I go back, I'll worry too, kiddo.'

'I'm not doubting that, Max, but you're able to compartmentalise. I can't. I know it will mean a drastic drop in income, but my career can go on hold until the kids are older. Then, a few years down the line, perhaps we'll think again.'

'We'll cope. If it's what you really want,' Max smiled at her, 'then I'll not object.'

Rosie sipped her tea. 'Then that's sorted. And do feel free to pass on any tips on how to calm a screaming twin.'

'One day, flower, I'll write a book on it.'

'We'll make a fortune.' She snuggled against him. 'Quick cuddle, then I'll get ready for my last day at work. I've a feeling I'm going to be really on the ball for once.'

'The team will miss you, Rosie.'

'I'm not going away forever, and they will know I'm doing it in everyone's best interests. If I'm not functioning properly, it could be dangerous, and I couldn't live with the consequences.'

* * *

Harcourt had just called, ridding Jackman of all hope of getting any more sleep. Was this Renwick the shooter? It certainly looked that way. He too had heard about these Sniper Experience Days, in fact a couple of their own firearms officers had gone on one and had raved about it for weeks.

He got out of bed, careful not to disturb Laura, and went downstairs. He rang the CID office and got the detective on night shift. 'Bob? Do me favour and run a name through the PNC for me, would you? Ralph Renwick. He's local by all accounts, but I don't have an address for him yet.'

A sleepy voice repeated the name and said he'd get back as soon as.

Jackman rubbed his hands. This could be their first real lead to the sniper. If they could identify this guy, and also get something from the enigmatic Ezra Lorimer, they might just make some headway with tracking Ashcroft.

He didn't have long to wait. 'Nothing on a Ralph Renwick, sir. I've checked the local phone book as well, but there are no Renwicks listed. It's too early to contact DVLC or the DHSS, so I'm afraid I've drawn a blank.'

'Thanks for trying.' Jackman hung up. As he had expected. It convinced him all the more that Kenneth Harcourt had unknowingly been training up their shooter for bigger things. Although it was still very early, Jackman decided to shower and get ready for work. As he made his way back up the stairs, his mobile rang.

'You're up early, Marie.'

'Sorry, boss, but I need to tell you something that happened in the early hours of this morning.'

'I've got some news for you too. It's evidently been an eventful night. You first, Marie.'

'Esther Lorimer rang me, sir. She overheard part of a conversation between her brothers Paul and Levi. She said it sounded as if Ezra had asked Paul to do something for him and it had scared him badly. The only thing I could think of was the gun thefts.'

Jackman considered that. 'It's perfectly possible, isn't it? We need to get out there with Robbie. He said he'd be heading off in time to arrive by seven a.m. We need to go with him. You haven't rung and told him about this yet?'

'No, sir. I wanted you to know first.'

'Ring him now, and we'll tie up at the station, okay?'

'We'll be there. Gary's already in the shower — but, sir? What about your news?'

'Ah, yes, well, Kenneth Harcourt recalled a bit of a dust-up between Arthur Barnes and one of the club members, a man named Ralph Renwick. This guy was apparently very interested in one of these specialised once-in-a-lifetime experience days.'

'Like wing-walking? Or driving an F1 racing car?'

'Like picking up an AK-47 and being a sniper for a day.'

'Holy shit! Oops, sorry, boss.'

'No apology necessary, Marie. I wholly concur. The problem is, he's not known to us and we have no address for him, so we need to start a serious search. Ten-to-one, he's our shooter. I'll get Rosie and Charlie on that as soon as they get in. Meanwhile, we hit the Lorimers.'

'See you at the factory.' Marie ended the call.

Laura was sitting up in bed. 'What's the time?'

'Too early for you to be up yet, but I have to go, I'm afraid. We need to beard a lion in his den, preferably while he's still half asleep.' Jackman pulled clean clothes from his wardrobe. 'But tonight, we all go out. One way or another, I want us to have our celebratory meal.'

'Don't make promises you can't keep. And don't forget, lions have sharp claws.' Laura held her arms out to him. 'One kiss, before you slip into action mode, Detective Inspector?'

'Now there's an offer I can't refuse.'

He leant down and kissed her, lightly at first. After a moment, he pulled away, breathless. 'Laura Archer, you are a very difficult woman to leave.'

'Then you better not leave me, had you?'

'Never. Except for work. Now I'm off for a cold shower.'

'Shall I join you?'

'Then I'll never get away! I'll lock the bathroom door.'

'Spoilsport.'

Jackman's smile stayed with him until he was ready to leave. Then the whole horrible situation flooded back. 'I'm off now!' he called up the stairs. 'Come down and lock the doors, Laura. And ring me later, promise?'

He waited until he heard her footsteps. 'I love you,' he called to the closed door.

'Ditto!' He heard a key turn in the lock.

Jackman gazed out across the endless fields.

Are you out there, Alistair Ashcroft?

CHAPTER NINETEEN

This time Rachel Lorimer was incandescent with rage, but anticipating this reaction, Jackman had made a PC drag a magistrate out of bed and issue a search warrant for the whole place, and the motorhome.

'Did Ezra talk to you last night, Mrs Lorimer?' Robbie asked urgently. 'He had something very important to tell you.'

'What are you talking about? I never even saw Ezra last night!' Rachel was almost jumping up and down in her fury.

'Rachel! Calm down.' Marie stepped forward. 'This really is important. Ezra promised to speak to you. There was something he wanted you to know about before we came knocking on your door.' She looked intently at Rachel. 'He's done something that could get your sons into a lot of hot water. Do you understand?'

Rachel's expression was stony. 'And what has he done exactly?'

'First, we need to see him. Do you want to come with us?' Marie asked.

'Too right I do,' Rachel said through gritted teeth.

Two uniformed officers were already stationed outside the motorhome.

Jackman stepped forward and rapped hard on the door. 'Ezra Lorimer! Police! Open up please.'

Getting no answer, Robbie walked around to the front and tried the driver's door. 'Locked, sir. And there's a screen pulled down over the windows.'

Jackman went to call out again but Rachel Lorimer got there first. 'Cousin Ezra! Get yourself out here this minute!'

Silence. A pigeon flapped its wings. Ezra too had flown.

'Break in!' Jackman called out to one of the police constables.

The lock was easily cracked, and Jackman wrenched the door back.

Marie peered inside. No sign of Ezra Lorimer. His clothes were still there, and nothing appeared to have been taken, but the man himself was gone.

'We need to talk, Rachel. Can you get the family together?' Marie looked at her rather sadly. 'Your cousin has caused your sons a lot of damage, and you need to know the truth.'

Rachel turned her back and stalked towards the farmhouse, yelling out her children's names, her face set and grim.

It took around ten minutes for them to assemble — in varying stages of undress but all with the same expression on their faces — sheer terror.

Rachel sat, ram-rod straight in an old armchair, and looked at each of her children in turn. 'So, which one of you bunch of blockheads is going to tell me what's been going on?'

'Let me speak first.' Jackman stepped forward. 'We need to explain a few things before you start apportioning blame. These young people have been conned by your cousin into believing that what he told them to do would benefit you.'

Heads nodded frantically at this.

'Explain.'

As Jackman told her, Rachel's anger slowly dissipated and an expression of intense hurt began to spread across her face. When Jackman had finished, she sighed and said, 'I still cannot believe that he took them all in like that.' She stared at them incredulously. 'How could you be so gullible? Jacob I can understand, but as for the rest of you . . . Even *you*, Levi?'

'I believed him, Ma.'

Gillian, Levi's young wife, said softly, 'You made him welcome here, Mother. You said he was good to us. Why should we doubt him? It's no wonder my Levi believed him.'

Levi's mouth dropped open. He stared at his wife in awe.

Rachel appeared to deflate. She said nothing.

'I suggest that everyone goes and gets dressed,' said Jackman. 'Rachel, we have to talk about Ezra. Is that okay with you?'

She nodded.

'And don't leave here,' Jackman said to the departing family members. 'I'm afraid you'll have to ring your place of work, Levi. We need to talk to you all individually and it could take some time.'

No one argued, all of them obviously thankful to escape the heavily charged atmosphere of that room.

'Have you any idea where Ezra has gone?' asked Marie.

'None whatsoever, and as my car is still where he left it last night, I'm not sure *how* he went either.'

'The boys have a Land Rover, don't they? Maybe he took that.'

Rachel went over to the window. 'All our cars are still here.' She turned to Marie and Jackman, frowning. 'Why are you so interested in what my boys have done? Its small stuff, isn't it, compared to what you have going on in the town. Come on. What's really going on?'

Jackman said, 'We think Ezra might be one of the few people who is able to identify a killer we're after. We have to find him.'

'I see.' Rachel sat back down. 'Okay, what do you want to know?'

'Tell us everything you know about Ezra. Even the smallest detail could help us.' Jackman and Marie sat facing her.

'We were great friends when we were small, and I mean very small — toddlers really. Then his family moved away but we kept in touch. Ezra was always kind to me. He remembered Christmas and birthdays when no one else did, and always sent a card. We wrote, detectives. I know people don't do that very often now, but every month, I'd get a letter, and I'd reply. Things have been tough, money-wise, we have no mobile phones and a long call on the phone is a luxury. For the price of a stamp, I kept up my friendship with my cousin.'

Marie guessed that there hadn't been many people who'd been good to Rachel along the way.

'Did he visit often?' asked Jackman.

'Never. This was the first proper visit in decades. That's why we were so pleased to see him. It lifted my heart, it did, to finally see him in the flesh.'

Marie took out her pocket book. 'Is this his address, Rachel?'

She looked at it. 'No. That's his old address, he hasn't been there for years.' She stood up. 'I'll get it for you.'

A few moments later she returned with a scrap of paper. 'This is it. Forty Coldharbour, Windy Ridge Park, Kirkhamby, near Hull. It's a static caravan park, or so he told me.'

Marie thanked her. At a swift look from Jackman, she called it in to the station, asking the local officers to call there, and keep calling, in case he returned home.

'You say you didn't see him last night, Rachel. Why was that?' Marie asked.

She frowned. 'Actually, it was odd, now you mention it. He'd done a big shop for me but when you lot turned up, he left everything in the car. Esther and Noah unloaded it in case anything spoiled. He'd brought the makings of a lovely dinner, so I cooked it, but he didn't come to eat. I sent Esther over, but she said he never opened the door.'

'Was she sure he was in there?' asked Jackman.

'Oh yes. She heard him moving about. He called out that he had things to do and he was tired. And that was that.'

'What time was that?'

'Around half ten. It was too late to eat really, but after all the malarkey with that horse, and coppers all over the place, we needed food.' She glowered at Jackman. 'Thanks to you, I ended up with indigestion.'

Jackman stood up. 'We need to talk to the family, Rachel, but we are fully aware that they've been tricked. The worst part of it is that we suspect guns were stolen on Ezra's say-so, and that will be impossible to overlook. Nevertheless, we'll do our best for your kids, I promise.'

Outside, Jackman took a long breath of fresh air. 'That was bloody unpleasant. Damned Ezra. He's really damaged that family.'

Marie didn't answer. She was thinking about Rachel and Ezra the toddlers. About how close they were and how he never forgot a birthday. Then he pays a rare visit and causes mayhem through his wish to provide for the family and help them. And now, leaving the family to pick up the pieces, he does a runner.

'Marie? Earth calling!' Jackman was staring at her.

'Sorry, boss. I'm just trying to make sense of Ezra Lorimer.'

'You'd have to put a week aside for that one. Meanwhile, we need to find out exactly what he asked Paul to do.'

She shook her head to clear it. 'Yes, of course. I suggest we talk to Levi first. Paul can be, well, a bit mercurial.'

They didn't have to wait many minutes for Levi to emerge, still tousle-haired but now dressed. In his jeans and denim shirt he looked like a giant naughty schoolboy. 'I got to tell you everything, don't I?'

Jackman nodded. 'Afraid so, Levi, and if you tell us of your own free will, it will be better for you.'

'Come into the kitchen. Ma's over at the static talking to Esther.'

They sat around the old pine table. Marie wondered how many secrets and arguments this table had been privy to over the years.

Levi began. 'Ezra told Paul and me that he was here because of something very serious, and we weren't to tell a soul, especially Ma.'

Here we go, thought Marie. What pile of shit did he dish out to these two?

'He said he was here to settle an old family debt. Someone owed our father big-time. If we helped him out, he would be able to give us a lot of money to help Ma.' Levi looked thoroughly miserable. 'I know I ain't very bright. I got a good job and I does it well, but it don't require too much brainpower, just strong muscles, and I don't get bored doing the same thing over and over. Ezra's the clever one, so I believed what he said.'

'What did he want you to do?' asked Jackman.

'Steal a gun. Said the man who'd got hold of it had something to do with our father's death. He said he couldn't say much more right then, but if we got that gun away from this man, we'd be saving lives, and we'd be very well paid for doing it.'

'Saving lives?' asked Marie.

Levi nodded solemnly. 'He said the man was going to sell it to someone who wanted to kill lots of people. If we got the gun first, he couldn't sell it, could he? We'd be heroes.'

All to obtain a rifle for Alistair Ashcroft's sniper. Marie shook her head.

'You tried the gun club but that was too difficult, so you broke into the man's house. I think you got carried away, didn't you? You found the gun that Ezra asked for, but you took two more, isn't that right?' Jackman said sternly.

Levi looked down at the scratched tabletop. 'Paul isn't good at following orders. He does what he wants and sod the rest of 'em. And he lost his temper with the gun cupboard 'cause he couldn't get into the metal one. I had to drag him away. Anyway, he took an old shotgun that he swore had belonged to our granddad and a target gun because it looked cool, like one from an action comic.'

'Did you tell Ezra about these other guns, Levi?' asked Marie, guessing what the answer would be.

'No way! We gave him the one he wanted, that scary rifle, and Paul hid the other two.'

'Where are they?' Jackman asked.

'In the root veg store. They're all wrapped up safe like. I'll show you, shall I?'

Jackman nodded. 'Hand them in, and it will be a hundred times better for you.'

Five minutes later they were holding Kenneth Harcourt's precious heirloom, the Dickson boxlock ejector, along with his target rifle. Both had been oiled and cleaned, were carefully wrapped and were undamaged.

'Good lad,' said Jackman. 'We'll take these now. Hopefully the owner will be understanding.'

Levi stared at him with wide eyes. 'What's going to happen to us? I don't know what Ma will do without us to support her. We only just get by on me and Paul's wages. It'll kill her if we get put away.'

'I'm not sure yet, Levi, but try not to worry too much. Ezra is to blame for everything, and if I get my way it'll be him who pays, not you.' He frowned. 'Even so, you committed a serious offence so you'll have to come down to the station and make a statement. I'm sure you'll never do anything like that again, will you. Am I right?'

'Never! It was totally stupid.' Levi sniffed, looking as if he were about to burst into tears. 'People say we're morons — well, maybe they're right.'

Marie shook her head. 'You were taken in by a conman, Levi, and you did it to help your ma. That's not being a moron, okay? I'm not saying that what you did was a good thing, but I do understand why you did it.'

Looking somewhat placated, Levi went out, saying he needed to talk to Paul who had apparently gone into meltdown. His place was taken by Robbie and Gary, who had been trying their best to calm Paul down. They had not been successful. 'The kid's like an animal, sir. Totally freaked out. I can't imagine how he holds down a job.'

'Charlie Button had him eating out of his hand last night,' Marie commented. 'Shame he wasn't in in time to join us.' She was just about to say something else when her phone rang.

'DS Marie Evans.' She listened, ended it and stood rooted to the spot.

'Marie?' It was Jackman. She heard him as if from a distance. 'Whatever's the matter?'

'That was the Hull police. They effected an entry into Ezra Lorimer's static. He's dead.'

'What? You mean he went home last night and killed himself?' Jackman sounded incredulous.

'No, sir. Ezra Lorimer has been dead for weeks, maybe longer.'

No one spoke, then Robbie said, 'Then who . . . ?'

More pieces from Marie's jigsaw puzzle suddenly slotted into place. She turned to Robbie. 'You won't believe this, but I think last night you and Charlie spent a pleasant half hour in a motorhome, talking to Alistair Ashcroft.'

Jackman closed his eyes. 'Of course! Rachel hadn't seen Ezra for decades, maybe not since they were kids. They kept in contact by letter. Ashcroft killed Ezra and took his place. He made use of this poor family simply to give us grief.'

'And to steal a sniper rifle for him,' added Marie.

'And make us look like fools,' added Gary.

'I think he was even more subtle,' muttered Robbie. 'He had them steal six pigs. Six. Why six? The team. That's what the villains call us, isn't it? Pigs?'

'And the horse too,' Jackman mused. 'Bullimore told me that Nimbus is a direct descendent of my Glory, my own beautiful horse that I rode as a youngster. Ashcroft's showing me just how much he knows about me and my history.'

'But what about the diesel?' Gary looked puzzled. 'Can't think of any message there, can you?'

'Not off the top of my head.' Marie gave a shrug. 'But who knows? That twisted mind of his may have concocted something.'

Jackman straightened up. 'Well, now we've assimilated that little bombshell, let's get the motorhome sealed up and forensics down here. He's been in there for weeks, there has to be some evidence left behind.' He paused. 'Second thoughts, get it collected and taken back to the prof's lab for a thorough sweep. Marie? You know Rachel Lorimer. You'd better let her know about her cousin. And if you can, find out how such a sharp woman was deceived by an imposter.'

Marie sighed. 'Leave it to me, boss.' Poor Rachel. Yet another of Alistair Ashcroft's casualties.

Nonetheless, they were a bit closer now. And the Lorimers would be left in peace.

Marie went back to the farmhouse and looked in through the window. She could see Rachel, moving around inside the kitchen. 'Rachel!' she called. 'Can I come in? I'm afraid I've got some bad news for you.'

CHAPTER TWENTY

Charlie put down the phone and let out a loud whistle. 'Rosie, listen to this!'

He hurried over to her workstation, eager to impart this latest bit of news. 'That was Marie, ringing from the Lorimer place. Ezra Lorimer, the guy Robbie and I talked to last night in his motorhome — well, he was most likely Alistair Ashcroft in disguise. Hull police have found the real Ezra dead in his home.' Charlie's eyes were wide with excitement. 'Now Ashcroft is missing again.'

Rosie swivelled round in her chair. 'So he's been living with the Lorimer family, posing as their cousin, for weeks? That's unbelievable. How come they didn't realise he was an imposter?'

'Marie said the younger members of the family had never met him, and Rachel hadn't seen him since they were kids. Apparently they kept in touch by monthly letters. There's no technology out there at the farm.' He frowned. 'And we all know how Ashcroft likes to take his time and do his homework. He probably befriended the real Ezra and got him to reveal all sorts of things about himself and the family before he killed him.'

'He's certainly a bloody good actor and mimic. I'm betting he could impersonate the real Ezra's accent to a tee,' Rosie said. 'And from what witnesses say, he's quite charismatic.'

Charlie shook his head, 'He had me fooled. And to think, we've had a photo of him on the office wall for the last six months. I should have seen who it was.'

'Robbie was taken in too, so it must have been a great disguise.'

Charlie went back to his desk. Marie had asked him to find out whether any vehicles had been stolen last night from anywhere in the vicinity of Hawkers Fen. As the motorhome was still there and all the Lorimer cars accounted for, they were wondering how he got away.

As Charlie checked the logs from the night before, the realisation hit him afresh. He had been within touching distance of a brutal psychotic killer! He recalled snippets of their conversation. At one point he'd said to the supposed Ezra that getting the family into trouble hadn't been one of his best moves. How Ashcroft must have laughed at that.

'You alright, Charlie?' Rosie called out.

'I sat there spouting off like a prat to the man we are moving heaven and earth to catch, and I didn't even know. What kind of a detective does that make me?'

'A human one? Don't beat yourself up, Charlie. He fooled everyone, including Ezra's own family. He's been *living* with them for weeks, and even Rachel didn't know he was a fraud.' She went over to him and ruffled his hair affectionately. 'Come on, Charlie. He's a pro. Just be thankful that you walked away from him unharmed, both of you. That's a miracle in itself!'

He sighed. 'I still feel like an idiot.'

'Well, don't.' She grinned at him. 'Just think. We've unsettled him, which is a starter. He'll not be able to use the Lorimer boys anymore, and he's lost his little hideaway in Hawker's Fen. They are all steps in the right direction.'

'As long as it doesn't make him even madder and he ups his game. We have enough to worry about with the sniper.'

He shook his head, trying to dispel the image of that caravan and himself, sitting opposite a killer. 'I'd better get on.' He frowned. 'I wonder . . .'

'What?' asked Rosie.

'The fake Ezra had been to the supermarket to collect shopping for the family. That's why we had to wait so long for him. I was thinking about the CCTV cameras at the shop. If we could get a really good picture of him disguised as Ezra and put it out in the local media, we could get a few reports of sightings, which might lead us to where he is based.' He scratched his head. 'I mean, he has to have somewhere to live and operate from, other than that old motorhome.'

'Fair point. Why not ring Marie and ask her at which supermarket he shopped.' Rosie looked at Charlie hopefully. 'I suppose it would be too much to ask, but might he have used a credit card?'

Charlie gave a little grunt. 'Far too much, Rosie. But we can't assume anything, can we? If we can find a picture of him at the tills, then we can soon check with their receipts and find out how he paid.' He picked up his phone. 'I'll do as you say and ring the sarge.'

'Ask her what he bought as well,' added Rosie. 'It makes it easier when going through the till receipts if you can tie in the goods that were purchased.'

Charlie picked up the phone.

'Good thinking, Charlie,' Marie said, 'but Jackman was one step ahead of you. He's already got uniform checking that out. He used the big new Aldi on the trading estate, and he paid cash. Rachel said he left the receipt in one of the shopping bags. He spent over a hundred pounds. It was enough to feed the family for a week and included all sorts of goodies.' Marie gave a sigh. 'He's an enigma all right. The family all say how kind he was, how generous.'

'Probably part of his con act,' grumbled Charlie. 'I can't believe he has a soft and fluffy side, can you?' There was a silence. 'Sorry, Sarge,' Charlie said. 'For a moment I forgot about your run-in with—'

She stopped him. 'It's alright, Charlie. *I've* not forgotten, and that's what counts. I'll not let what he did fade from my memory until I have my cuffs on him.'

'I hope I'm there to see that, Sarge.' Charlie ended the call. Back to the drawing board. 'How exactly did Ashcroft leave Hawker's Fen?' he mused.

'Are they sure he did leave?' Rosie's voice cut through his thoughts. 'You did say it was a godforsaken spot, so what if he holed up somewhere to wait for the flak to settle?'

She was right. Uniform would have checked with the few neighbours, but there were old disused barns, deserted pumping stations and all manner of decrepit outbuildings scattered about that area. They'd never be able to search them all. 'I'd better start with the stolen vehicles, but you could well have a point, our Rosie, in which case I'm wasting my time.'

Half an hour later he discovered that he hadn't wasted his time at all.

'Listen up, Rosie,' he called excitedly. 'A motorbike was stolen a week ago from a house out on Thatcher's Fen, which is the nearest place to Hawker's Fen. A tall rough-looking man was seen riding it away. The witness said the thief clearly knew his way around bikes and navigated those dangerous fen lanes like a TT racer.'

'Sounds promising,' Rosie said. 'Alistair Ashcroft used a powerful bike last time, didn't he?'

'He must have nicked it and hidden it, ready for an emergency getaway,' Charlie said.

He rang Marie again.

'We are just about to leave, Charlie, but I'll pass that on to Jackman. It makes perfect sense. I'd say you've hit the nail, wouldn't you? Nice one!'

Charlie still felt ridiculously pleased when either the sarge or the boss praised him, just like he had when he was a rookie detective. He desperately wanted to be part of the team but through no one's fault, he always felt like the junior and the least important part of it. Maybe that would change when Kevin joined them. For once he wouldn't be the new boy. He looked at Rosie. 'You okay?'

Rosie looked up. To his surprise, he saw that she was crying.

'Whatever's wrong?' He hurried over and perched on the edge of her workstation, looking down at her anxiously.

She sniffed. 'I really love you guys.'

'And we love you too, Rosie, but why are you crying?'

'I meant to tell Jackman first, but . . . Oh, Charlie, I'm leaving the team. Today is my last day.'

The tears fell unchecked now.

'But why?' Charlie said. 'You and Max are doing brilliantly.'

'We're not,' she snuffled. 'That's the problem. I need to be a proper mum for the twins and right now, that's not happening. They're babies, they need me at home, not off somewhere chasing a serial killer. So Max will be coming back full-time while I look after the kids.'

Charlie was secretly delighted that his oppo, Max, would be back permanently, but Rosie was a big part of their team too.

'I don't know what to say, Rosie. It won't be the same without you, but I'm sure you are doing the right thing.' He put his arm around her shoulders. 'It can't have been an easy decision.'

'Once I'd faced up to it, it was very easy indeed. I have no choice.' She paused. 'Sorry to offload all that on you, Charlie.' She smiled faintly.

He squeezed her shoulder. 'Maybe when the kids are older, we'll get you back?'

'We'll just have to see what life throws at us.'

Charlie straightened up. 'Well, I need coffee. What about you?'

Rosie nodded. 'Heaven knows what the boss will say.'

Charlie smiled at her. 'You know exactly what he'll say. He loves his family too and he'll understand. He'll just be sad to lose you, like we all will.'

* * *

Jackman said little on the drive back to the station. They had two very different, but equally dangerous killers in Saltern-le-Fen, and he was anxious that by spending so much time on Ashcroft, they could be provoking their sharpshooter. He had warned them, via Kevin Stoner, to pay attention and they had ignored him, keeping their sights firmly fixed on Ashcroft. They could be making a fatal mistake.

Once again, Jackman was overwhelmed by indecision, unsure of his next move. It seemed to him that whatever he did it would end in disaster. He glanced across to Marie, who was concentrating on the road ahead.

His phone rang, startling him out of his negative frame of mind.

'Rowan, it's Ruth Crooke here. I need you to know that there was no way we could keep a lid on the crisis we are facing. The press have picked up the fact that there's a gunman loose in our area and I need to make a statement within the hour.'

'It was inevitable, ma'am. You couldn't have hidden something of this magnitude for long.'

'I'm sorry I couldn't buy you a little more time, but there it is. We have assistance arriving today from the surrounding divisions and other county forces. The public need to see a reassuring police presence on the streets to forestall any panic. We have the manpower now, and specialist tactical firearms units from all over. We will do whatever it takes to stop this individual, in whatever manner is appropriate.'

Jackman felt an unexpected surge of relief and his resolve flooded back. If the gunman wanted attention, he was going to get it, big style, leaving him free to concentrate on Ashcroft. He said as much to the superintendent.

'It could drive him underground, Rowan. Police crawling all over the town could seriously upset his plans, but, yes, Ashcroft is your priority now. I'll give you all the help I can.'

"I'm a patient man," Ashcroft had said. *Well, so am I.* Jackman's eyes glinted, steely in the silver-grey light of the fens. 'It's all I think of, Ruth. Day and night. This time I intend to catch him.'

Eyes on the road, Marie's jaw set. 'I'll drink to that,' she muttered softly.

Her phone rang. 'Would you get that, sir?' she asked him.

He took the phone from her and put it on loudspeaker. 'Jackman here. Marie is driving.'

'Ah, good.'

'Gary. Is there a problem?'

'I tried your phone, sir, but you were engaged. There has been a development here. Forensics did a preliminary sweep of Ezra Lorimer's motorhome prior to taking it away and they found a letter. It's addressed to you.'

'Ah!' breathed Jackman, 'Confirmation that the imposter is Ashcroft. Who else would leave me a note?'

'We haven't touched it, sir. What would you like me to do with it? Forensics have bagged it.'

Jackman knew that according to the regulations it shouldn't be touched, but this was Ashcroft. There could be no time to lose. 'We are almost back at the station. Can you have a word with the uniform in charge there, beg if you must, and get someone to fast forward it to my office? And, please, don't remind me about protocol.'

'Understood, boss. I'll deal with it immediately.' Gary ended the call.

'Contact?' Marie said.

'Looks that way. I wonder what little aphorism he'll have for us this time. We've already had *forever in my thoughts* and *lest we forget*.'

'I reckon that he'll be wanting to engage with us, don't you? Especially since this gunman is trying to steal his thunder.'

Jackman frowned. 'We don't actually know if he is aware of that, do we?'

'True, but he'll find out soon enough if this guy decides to pick off more victims than Ashcroft asked him to.'

As they drove in through the station security gates, Jackman felt a thrill of anticipation. This was what he had been waiting for. He swallowed hard. What would the message say?

CHAPTER TWENTY-ONE

After a terrible night, full of images of William tied to the stake that even vodka and his lovely Alan could not dispel, Kevin Stoner had decided that there was no way he could take time off work. If he moped around at home, he'd probably go mad. He needed to keep busy, because the second he allowed his mind to wander, his thoughts returned to that stark image. William had been killed so callously, so deliberately. Life had never seemed so fragile to Kevin as it did right now. He'd seen terrible things, but he'd never get over the coldness in the shooter's voice.

In a moment of weakness, he'd even phoned his father and poured out his heart to him. As always, the diocesan bishop's deep reassuring tones had calmed him somewhat, but they could not assuage the pain of what had been done. Most of all, he wondered why the gunman had picked him, of all of them, to witness his crimes and act as his messenger. He wasn't even out of uniform yet.

And so he had gone to work. His sergeant hadn't been pleased to see him when he'd turned up for duty as usual. It took an award-winning performance and a timely reminder of how stretched they were to convince the man that he was fit for work.

Now he was on his way to his first job of the day, at the Fenside Gun Club, where he was to talk to Kenneth Harcourt, the owner. Clearly, he had been rather too convincing, because an officer who had just been involved in witnessing a serious shooting should really not have been dispatched to a gun club. Worse still, his temporary crewmate for the day was an officer called Ernie Teal. Teal was not well liked, to put it mildly. The police love acronyms, so he was known in the mess room as a BONGO — Books On, Never Goes Out.

Kevin chose to drive. Teal liked that arrangement, it meant he could stuff his face with food for the duration of the trip.

'Do you ever stop eating?' asked Kevin testily. He hated noisy eaters and was amazed at just how many sound effects Teal could generate in the process of devouring a Mars bar.

'I need the energy. Never know what we'll be facing next, do we?'

All Teal was likely to face was a blast of excess calories and a sugar rush.

It was a long and irritating journey, and by the time they arrived, Kevin was pissed off. His last few days in uniform and he had to spend one of them with Ernie Teal, proof indeed that there was no God.

'Look, why don't you wait here? It doesn't need two to show this guy a photograph and take a few notes. I've got it covered.'

Nodding happily, Teal produced a Curly Wurly from his jacket pocket and looked at it lovingly.

Kevin almost tripped in his eagerness to get out of the car.

Harcourt was waiting for him in the foyer, hand outstretched. 'This is very good of you, Officer. I'm sure someone could have emailed this picture to me, rather than drag you out when you are so busy.'

'DI Jackman wanted us to see you personally, sir. My name is Kevin Stoner.' He showed Harcourt his ID. 'He wanted you to see a photo of a man called Alistair Ashcroft. It's a still from a video clip taken on a smartphone but it's a good likeness. Have you ever seen him around here? Also, DI Jackman wondered if your CCTV might have picked up an image of this Ralph Renwick you spoke of?'

'Regarding the CCTV, that was one of the first things I thought of, but we don't keep them longer than the standard thirty-one days. Renwick stopped coming some time ago, so that was a non-starter.' He frowned. 'I even went through some video footage we took at a big open day we held, but he didn't feature there either.'

Kevin handed him the photograph of Ashcroft. 'And this man? Do you know if he's ever been here?'

Harcourt stared long and hard at the photograph. 'He's certainly not a member, and I'm pretty sure I've never seen him before, although there is something slightly familiar about him.'

'We have posted flyers all over Saltern-le-Fen. You might have seen one of them.'

Harcourt frowned. 'I don't recall seeing them, but then, I do get rather distracted sometimes.'

Kevin knew about Harcourt's young daughter so he didn't press him. 'No matter, sir. Perhaps I could leave the picture with you and ask you to show it to your staff? There's just a chance someone may have seen him at some point.'

'Why do you think this man would have come here, Officer?' asked Harcourt.

'We believe he is the man who orchestrated the theft of the guns from your home, sir.'

'Good Lord!' Harcourt stared again at the picture. 'But I thought this Renwick was the gunman? I don't understand.'

Kevin lowered his voice. 'It's complicated, sir, but we believe that Ashcroft hired the gunman, who is possibly Renwick, to kill certain people for him.'

'And he used my gun to do it.' Harcourt sighed. 'This is atrocious.'

'I agree, sir,' said Kevin, with feeling.

Suddenly Kevin had had enough of guns. 'Please do ring DI Jackman if anyone does recognise the photograph. And thank you for your time, sir. I must get back now.'

'I'll walk out with you.' Harcourt opened the front door for him. 'I appreciate your visit.'

'No trouble, sir.' Kevin shook his hand again and returned to the car. He was not looking forward to the trip back to the station. He found Teal leaning against the side of the vehicle, chucking sweet wrappers in through the open window. Kevin groaned.

'We're done here,' he said briskly. 'Get in.'

Teal hauled himself into the car and belched.

Barely restraining his temper, Kevin started up and accelerated forward with a jerk. At the junction with the main road, he braked and waited impatiently for a big slow-moving 4x4 to pass before pulling out.

Kevin wasn't generally so irritated by things, not even by Teal, and he began to wonder if he should have taken DI Jackman's advice and had a few days off.

While he pondered, he heard a crack. The windshield shattered. He stared at it blankly for a few seconds, unable to work out what had happened. Then he turned to his crewmate.

Ernie Teal, chocolate bar still in hand, stared sightlessly at the crazed windscreen, a neat hole oozing blood in the centre of his forehead.

Kevin scrambled from the car, the policeman in him wanted to identify that 4x4. The other part was desperate to get away from the horror in the seat beside him.

He hit the orange panic button on his radio and yelled, 'Officer down!' After that, everything became a blur. He was vaguely aware of people running towards him, of shouting, and then, as if from a great distance, he heard Harcourt's voice, asking him if he was injured.

Kevin tried to speak but no sound came out.

He knew he was now sitting on the ground with his back against the police car, and that Harcourt was talking to him, but he was incapable of movement or speech.

All he could see was a splintered windscreen, and Ernie Teal's dead hand clasping a brightly coloured chocolate bar.

* * *

Jackman read the letter from Ashcroft for the third time.

My dear Jackman. Well, it was fun while it lasted. I enjoyed being Ezra enormously. There is something empowering about assuming a false identity. Wearing a mask enables you to act out of character. It frees you from yourself.

You are an intelligent man and will no doubt have figured out my bit of mischief regarding the six pigs and Glory's descendent. The oil theft probably had you guessing, but incredible as it may seem, that one was a simple act of charity. Rachel really could not afford fuel, and Ezra would have helped her. The fact that those sweet, deluded boys messed it up was just unfortunate.

So, what now, you will be thinking.

We shall have our moment, my friend, for in the end it all comes down to you and me. Naturally these sorts of games inevitably incur a certain amount of collateral damage. Oh, and the inimitable Marie. I owe her for bringing such a dramatic halt to my last adventure in Saltern. Tell Marie I am so looking forward to seeing her again. Perhaps this time I can return the compliment. Not that I haven't been seeing a lot of both of you recently. Despite the lovely Laura, I still think you would make a handsome couple. Enough! I have work to do, so prepare yourself, Inspector Jackman, and expect the unexpected!

Yours always,
Alistair

Jackman shivered when he read the bit about Laura. Maybe it was time for her to take a short vacation, somewhere far from Saltern-le-Fen. Not that she'd go, although Ashcroft's invasion of her consulting rooms had scared her badly.

He heard a sharp rap on his door.

Marie burst in. 'The shooter, sir! He's killed a police officer! PC Ernie Teal, shot dead. Guess who was sitting next to him in the squad car?'

Kevin Stoner.

'I don't think I know Teal, do I?' He said slowly, trying to assimilate this latest bolt from the blue.

'He is, er, *was*, not universally liked, sir, considered the laziest copper in the division, but even so . . .' She shook her head.

Jackman was up and on his feet. The loss of a colleague always hit everyone hard, demoralising the whole station. Ashcroft would have been aware of that. With a single bullet, he had destroyed two lives. Kevin Stoner would never be the same again. 'We better get out there.'

Marie held up a set of car keys. 'I've already grabbed a vehicle. Shall I drive?'

Jackman nodded absently. Just before receiving the letter from Ashcroft, he'd had a sobbing Rosie in his office. She was clearly devastated at leaving them when they had such a desperately serious case running. But she wasn't coping and that could jeopardise the safety of their team. With a heavy heart, he had agreed to stand her down as unfit for duty, but at least he would get Max back full-time, so it wasn't as if they would be two down. Even so, Rosie had skills that no one else in the team possessed. They would miss her.

When he told her, Marie was of the same opinion. It had been a tough choice, but neither of them thought she had made the wrong decision. And her job would be there for her if and when she decided to come back.

Marie said, 'He's crossed a line, hasn't he? Killing a police officer.'

'He crossed the line as soon as he started killing.' All at once, Jackman was overcome with exhaustion. 'We have to stop him. And we have to find this gunman. If we get hold of him, he could lead us to Ashcroft. I'm betting he wouldn't go down alone.'

'We know from what he said to Kevin that he has little regard for Ashcroft. He'll give us all he knows. The thing is,

Ashcroft is clever, he might well have just fed him lies and told him nothing that could help us.'

'I'd expect nothing less, but sometimes the smallest slip can provide the key to the whole thing.'

Marie pulled onto the long, straight drove that led to the gun club and put her foot down. 'At least we can rule out Bethany Gadd, our retired police sharpshooter. Kevin said that the sniper was definitely male.' She glanced at Jackman. 'We won't be getting our new detective next week, will we, sir? That poor guy has been through hell these last few days. It'll take some coming back from.'

'Kevin Stoner should never have come back to work so soon, never!' Jackman said.

'And what would you have done, sir? I seem to recall a certain DI fighting to stay on the case when his whole family was being targeted. He's a damn good police officer and would no more be able to sit at home and watch *Antiques Roadshow* than you or me.'

'I wasn't in deep shock, and that young man is,' Jackman said gravely. 'This time he has no say in it. He's going to be off for a good long while, and under the proper medical care. We'll do a situation report when we get there, and I'll phone the FMO with my opinion.'

As they approached the lane to the club, they found a police road block. Uniform were turning back all traffic into the area. A white-faced constable told them that the incident had taken place right at the junction between the lane and the club entrance gate. Ahead, emergency vehicles were lined up along the road, blue lights flashing silently.

'Luckily there is a rear exit from the Fenside, even though it's little more than a rough track. Everyone has been taken inside to get their statement before they can leave.' The PC waved them through. 'The crime scene is cordoned off and we are already checking for bullet casings. You can't drive in, so I suggest you park and walk in along the footpath. Alternatively, there's the track that goes to the back of the club. An officer further down will direct you, Sergeant Evans.'

Marie thanked him. 'Shall we walk in, sir?'

Jackman nodded. It would make it easier to get away.

Kenneth Harcourt met them at the door. Already haggard, he now looked like the walking dead. His face was gaunt, the eyes hollow and the mouth slack. 'I was talking to PC Stoner just seconds before it happened. He was on his way out. Then . . . then . . .'

Jackman touched his arm. 'It's okay, sir. Just take your time. Why don't you go inside and get yourself a drink? We need to speak to our colleague and assess the situation, and then we'll come and find you.'

Harcourt nodded mutely, turned and like a somnambulist, trudged back towards the open doors of the foyer.

'He's on the brink too, unless I'm very much mistaken,' Marie said.

Once again, they found Kevin in the back of an ambulance, but this time the paramedics looked much more concerned. One of them, whom Jackman recognised, took him aside. 'He won't allow us to take him to hospital until he's spoken to you. He's very agitated, keeps asking for you.'

Jackman took a deep breath and stepped up into the ambulance.

Kevin looked up at him from haunted eyes. 'Sir! I'm so sorry. I should have listened! I should have done things differently! Oh, why didn't I?' The words tumbled from him in a torrent. 'I'm so very sorry.'

'Hey! Hindsight is a wonderful thing!' Jackman said. 'And if it's any consolation, my sergeant has just reminded me that we'd both have acted just as you have. So, it's not your fault, understand?' He didn't like the look of Kevin at all. He needed professional help. Jackman immediately thought of Laura. 'Listen, Kevin, I need to make a quick call then I'll be right back, okay?'

He went to where Marie waited. 'I'm going to get Laura to meet the ambulance at the hospital. I'll ring her and alert her to the problem, then if you'd find out where they will be taking him and let her know, I'll go back in with Kevin.'

Having phoned Laura, he returned to the young officer, wondering what to say to him. What approach would he himself respond to best?

'Right, Constable. Are you up to giving me a sitrep?'

Kevin blinked a few times, then exhaled. 'Yes, sir. I think so.'

'Good man! Now, Harcourt said that you were just leaving. You were driving?'

'Yes, sir.' He took a shaky breath, but the policeman in him was beginning to gain the upper hand. 'I stopped at the junction with the lane to allow a dark blue 4x4 to pass by.' He closed his eyes. 'I think it was a Jeep, a Grand Cherokee, and it had tinted windows. I did notice that.'

'Excellent, Kevin. And then?'

'My windscreen shattered, sir. The frame stayed intact, but the glass was crazed and I couldn't see out.'

Having had little experience of drive-by shootings, Jackman assumed that a handgun must have been used, unless . . . could there have been two occupants in the car? 'Kevin, before the screen went, did you see the vehicle's driver? Did you notice if he was alone?'

Kevin hung his head. 'Didn't look, sir. The fact is, I was pissed off at Ernie.' He gulped. 'Teal wasn't easy to work with, he was a couch potato in a uniform, but still, he didn't deserve to die. He had a family, sir. And my last words to him were not very friendly.'

Jackman smiled gently. 'I'm sure a lot of the other guys would have been much harsher than you, Kevin. You aren't known for slagging people off, and from what Marie tells me, Teal did nothing to win friends in the workplace. That's tough on hardworking cops who want to get on with the job and see it through.' He paused. 'But you are sure you saw nothing of the driver?'

Kevin didn't answer, and Jackman noticed that he was shivering, 'Okay, lad. Enough for today. We need to get you checked over. I'll see you later. Meanwhile you'll have the pleasure of meeting my lovely other half, Laura.'

* * *

Rory and his team were trying to keep on top of the "every-day" deaths as well as the priority cases such as suspected murder. He was lucky that it was a large facility, but then he was expected to cover a massive area, plus the fact that he was a very fine pathologist often opened doors in budgetary terms.

Today he was working in Rory's Retreat, the name his technicians used for the room used entirely for forensic cases. To avoid cross-contamination, the entrance was situated in a different part of the building, and it had a special UV-C lighting unit that eradicated DNA and bacteria. Rory spent a lot of time in that room.

'By George! I've got it!'

Spike looked up from his work. 'Got what?'

'Dear boy, that's your cue to call out, "by George, he's got it." Have you no culture at all?'

Spike grinned. 'Okaaay . . .'

'The perfect murder.' Rory almost purred the words.

It was a game they had been playing for several years — how to commit murder, outwit the police *and* the forensic examiner and get away with it.

'Okay, Prof. Hit me with it.'

Rory laid down his scalpel and adopted his finest tutorial pose. 'First, I have to admit that it will all depend on your victim having a certain, well, medical problem, but neverthe-less, I believe it's impossible to trace.' He smiled benignly at Spike. 'A fatal overdose of potassium!'

Spike frowned. 'But you'd need to bring the levels up to about seven or eight, and for it to be fatal you'd have to inject it. We'd find the puncture wound.'

'Not if it were injected into the victim's haemorrhoids! No pathologist in the world is going to check old Farmer

Giles for needle marks! And don't forget, when the body dies it produces large amounts of potassium, so who would know about it?'

Spike roared with laughter. 'One tiny problem! Your victim would have to be buck naked with their arse in the air, and not see you coming at them with a syringe in your hand! Sounds a tad tricky to me!'

Rory waved dismissively. 'Oh, there are a few wrinkles to be ironed out, but nothing insurmountable. Good, isn't it?'

'The best yet,' admitted Spike. 'And it would be even better if you had a bent GP in your pocket. Then you could get them to prescribe something like Spironolactone prior to your murder, that would reduce the excretion of potassium, and if he'd suggested a potassium supplement like Sando-K to build up the potassium levels anyway, you'd be on your way.'

'Good thinking, my evil-minded little friend. And to continue that theory, as the supplement is water soluble, we could get our fatal dose of potassium from dissolving the remainder of the tablets and injecting them! Ta-da! Job done!'

'In retrospect,' said Spike thoughtfully, 'I think using a GP is too risky. They could be a weak link since they'd probably crack in a police interview. Safer to just nick the potassium from A&E. They carry plenty of the stuff.'

'Smart boy. Just remind me never to upset you.' Rory looked down at the body of William the street dweller, and all his humour left him. 'But it's a lot less trouble to deliver a shot to the head, isn't it?'

'Another kind of perfect murder, I suppose,' said Spike. 'Certainly not undetectable but very effective.'

Their musings were interrupted by a message broadcast over the intercom. 'Professor Wilkinson, sorry to interrupt, sir, but forensics are requested to attend another shooting.'

'Location?'

'The Fenside Gun Club at Saltern Fenbank, sir.'

Rory groaned. 'Cancel what I said about putting my money on DI Galena in the Body Count derby.'

'I've warned you about gambling before, Prof,' Spike said. 'Do you want me to take this one?'

'We'll go together, Spike. You can do all the work and I'll just look pretty.'

Spike threw him an amused glance. 'Right. I'll get my equipment together while you go and powder your nose.'

'I swear you get more impudent every day!'

Surrounded by death, day in, day out, this banter was their way of coping. Rory and Spike had built up a good rapport during their time together and Rory would miss the other half of their double act. Would his next technician have a sense of humour?

CHAPTER TWENTY-TWO

Back at the gun club's foyer, Kenneth Harcourt had rallied somewhat. He had taken Jackman's suggestion of a drink seriously. Jackman had been thinking more along the lines of hot sweet tea, but the glass of Scotch in Harcourt's hand seemed to be doing the trick.

'Before I forget, DI Jackman, I can confirm that Arthur Barnes did own the handgun he had with him when he was killed. He said he didn't like leaving guns anywhere near his wife, so he kept his own guns here in the armoury. They are listed in his records, all licensed.'

'But the Ruger is missing?' added Marie.

Harcourt nodded. 'It is.'

'Are you up to answering a few questions, Mr Harcourt?' asked Jackman. They took seats away from the entrance. 'Did you see the car that stopped in front of our police vehicle?'

'Yes, but I only took a cursory glance. I wondered if it was one of our regulars arriving.'

'Colour? Make?'

'Dark blue, and I think it was a Cherokee 4x4.'

'Did you see the driver, Mr Harcourt?' Jackman asked.

'I'm afraid not. I did see the front window opening, then moments later I heard the gunshot. I ran towards the police car, but the 4x4 sped away, too quickly for me to get the licence number.' He pulled a face. 'I'm sorry. It all happened so fast.'

'It was definitely the front driver's window that you saw open?' asked Marie.

'Oh yes, absolutely.'

'That means the driver fired the shot, so it had to be a handgun. No one could drive and aim a rifle,' Jackman said. 'Must have packed a punch to go through safety glass and kill with such accuracy.'

'It was a powerful handgun for sure. I know that kind of report,' Harcourt said. 'A real *Dirty Harry* type of weapon. As to range, it was just a few metres away. Something like a Smith and Wesson Magnum has awesome muzzle energy. A single bullet from one of those could easily kill.'

'He's got himself a bit of an arsenal then,' Marie said.

'I remember that Ralph Renwick was interested in all sorts of guns.' Harcourt looked at Jackman. 'I rang a couple of places that host these sniper courses, but no one had booked in under that name.'

'If you could give us the names and locations of these other clubs, we'll have our officers call round with photos of the man we think is behind all this. It's a million-to-one chance that he'd show up personally, but it's just possible he met Renwick at a venue such as this.' Marie didn't hold out too much hope, but it was worth a try. 'Another thing, sir. I was wondering how our suspect knew that you had a sniper rifle. Who was aware of its existence?'

'Other than family, only Arthur. That makes me think that as Arthur was killed by your suspect, he most likely had dealings with him, and must have spoken about it.' He frowned. 'Although I can't think why.'

They heard a vehicle pull up at the entrance.

Jackman stood up. 'We have to go, sir. Forensics have arrived. Don't forget, if anyone here has seen the man in the photograph PC Stoner gave you, or Ralph Renwick for that matter, ring us immediately on our personal numbers.'

'And tell everyone to steer clear. Neither of them is to be approached at any cost,' added Marie.

They made their way down to the stricken police car, where Rory and Spike were just setting down their aluminium briefcases. Marie was pleased to see that the ambulance had gone, meaning Kevin would soon be under the care of Laura Archer.

Rory stood back and allowed Spike to take the lead again. He wore an uncharacteristically serious expression. 'I'm sorry for your loss. He was one of your own, wasn't he?'

'He was,' said Jackman gravely. 'And unless I'm mistaken, he died simply to put another nail in Kevin Stoner's coffin — his career in the police force, and possibly his sanity.'

Rory raised an eyebrow. 'But why is this Ashcroft creature trying to destroy our Kevin? He's such a sweet boy.'

'I wish we knew. It's just one of a dozen unknowns that surround Ashcroft and his motives for doing things,' Jackman said.

'He's certainly an enigma, I admit that much.' Rory pushed up his glasses, which had slipped down the bridge of his nose. 'Now, while I have your attention, I had the tox report back on Arthur Barnes, plus I did a little research on his past medical history. He had been on a serious drug regime, both to cope with pain from his original injury while still in service, and later for depression and a variety of stress-related problems. He continued to collect his meds from the pharmacy in East Street, even after he hit the streets, but,' he paused, 'we found he'd stopped taking all but the painkillers. There were large doses of analgesics in his system but no trace of the anti-depressants.'

'There were no tablets in his bag or on his person, were there?' asked Marie.

'Probably sold them to get money for food,' Jackman said sombrely. 'Could coming off these particular drugs cause paranoia, Rory?'

'Undoubtedly. And a whole lot of other nasty symptoms, especially if you just stop cold.'

Marie felt a pang of sorrow for the dead man. He had gone from war hero to abused husband and had finished up on the streets, killed while being used as a pawn in a madman's evil game.

She'd had her fill of the dead and really didn't want to look at Teal's body. But he was, after all, another victim of the investigation they were working, and she ought to see the scene for herself.

Ernie Teal looked almost comic. Poor Teal. If only he hadn't had that chocolate bar clutched in his hand.

Spike was bending over the policeman, checking the head wound. He looked up when she approached. 'We won't be able to tell you anything that isn't patently obvious, Sergeant Evans, not until we've located the bullet. Even then, I doubt whether I'd be able to tell you what kind of gun was used, other than it was a powerful and lethal pistol and the gunman was a very good shot. If you can track down the gun and we can find the bullet, then we can make a match. Otherwise . . .' He shrugged.

'It's alright, Spike,' she said. 'I wasn't looking for answers. As you say, it's patently obvious what happened. I'm more interested in finding the car that the killer used than knowing the make of gun.'

Marie walked back towards Jackman, wondering if anyone had spotted the blue 4x4 on the security cameras yet. She knew that an attention drawn had been issued immediately after the incident occurred, but she hadn't heard of any sightings. There was a good chance they'd find the vehicle nose down in a drainage ditch in some godforsaken part of the fen, while the killer had driven off in a completely different vehicle.

Suddenly the enormity of trying to find a faceless killer in a big rural county seemed almost too much to cope with. Unless something went seriously wrong with his plans, Ashcroft had the upper hand all the way.

'We will get him, Marie.' She hadn't even realised that Jackman was standing next to her.

'You've been using that bloody crystal ball again, haven't you, sir?'

'No need. It's written all over your face.' He gave her shoulder a gentle squeeze. 'There's nothing we can do here. Uniform have just told me that none of the club members saw anything that might be of help to us. Most were on the ranges, wearing ear defenders, and didn't see or hear a thing. After all, gunshots are the norm here, so where better to carry out a shooting? The only person to notice the car, other than Kevin Stoner, was Kenneth Harcourt.' He looked at the police car and the gaggle of white suited forensic technicians around it. 'Ella Jarvis has already taken all the photos required, so Rory is arranging for PC Teal to be taken to the morgue.'

Marie nodded. 'Have you spoken to Ruth yet?'

'Briefly. She is making a second announcement to the media, and I'll see her directly afterwards. By the way, when she said she was drawing in help from the around the county, she wasn't joking. From what the commander here tells me, the whole town is crawling with police.'

Marie said nothing. She was coming to believe that all the policemen in the country wouldn't stop Ashcroft and his devious machinations.

Jackman looked at her, head to one side. 'Come on, my friend. Where is my DS Glass Half Full? We've been here before, haven't we? Endless night, groping in the dark, and then we get a break. Someone, somewhere, will see or hear something, notice an anomaly and put two and two together. It *will* happen.' This new, positive Jackman continued to amaze her.

'You're right, sir. It was just a bit of a jolt, seeing Ernie Teal like that. He had no clue when he came out here that it would be his last journey. There was not a trace of shock or horror on his face. It was as if someone just switched him off.'

They walked back down the path towards their vehicle. 'Want me to drive?' asked Jackman.

'I'm fine, boss, honestly. I'm over it now, back on track again.' She slid into the driver's seat. 'Tell me more about the letter Ashcroft sent you. I didn't get a chance to see it for myself before we dashed out.'

Jackman could recite that letter word for word. 'He's so confident. It's like he's some kind of pack leader and we are a bunch of little kids, running around playing some stupid game of his invention.' He drew in a long breath. 'But I didn't like the reference to Laura not being around.'

'Do you think there's a direct threat to Laura, boss? Because if there is . . .'

'I know. I do know, Marie, but for some reason I think it's just another one of his games, more sowing seeds of fear in my mind to unsettle me.'

'Can you take that risk? Can you be certain it's just a game?' Marie knew that she herself was on Ashcroft's hit list, and at times almost welcomed the thought of a final showdown. But Laura! That beautiful, gentle woman with the cornflower-blue eyes and blonde hair. Unthinkable. The woman Jackman loved. Ashcroft mustn't hurt her.

'I'm certain that's not on his agenda. He could easily have killed her, or taken her, when he broke into her consulting rooms.' Jackman looked at her. 'He told me to expect the unexpected. Taking Laura would be too obvious.'

Marie hoped he was right. 'So, what nasty twisted scenario has he planned for us next, I wonder?' she mused.

They fell silent, and it lasted all the way back to the station.

* * *

Alistair Ashcroft entered the church and immediately a sense of peace descended over him. He breathed out and in the silence emptied his mind of the clamour, the voices that hammered at his brain every minute of every day.

He sank into a pew and leaned forward, head bowed, as if in prayer.

'Hello, David. Good to see you, my son.'

The priest stood at the altar, scraping a small puddle of dried candle wax from the base of one of the ornate candlesticks.

Alistair lifted his head, muttered an 'amen,' and smiled innocently at the older man.

'And you, Father? Are you well?' Ashcroft did sincerity very well. As Ezra Lorimer he had positively excelled himself. They had loved him, every one of them. He was sorry it was over — he'd enjoyed having them all eating out of his hand.

The priest was speaking to him, telling him about a new group he was hoping to get off the ground, a weekly get-to-gether in which lost souls could speak candidly to their fellow-sufferers about whatever troubled them.

Ashcroft was sure he'd get a good response, mostly because of the tea and cake, though he didn't say so to the priest. Troubled souls don't share their demons that easily. He wished the priest every success, and even offered to help out.

Father Malone beamed down at the man in the pew. 'You're a good person, David. I would be delighted if you would be generous enough to give me some of your time. God will reward you, you can be sure of that.'

Alistair smiled modestly. 'What's the point of life if you can't spare a little of the time that God gave you to help others? I'd be happy to assist.'

And he would. He always enjoyed being among lost souls, especially the truly damaged ones, they were so malleable. It would be a real tonic. He stared up at the massive cross suspended above the chancel. He had an idea this troublesome priest would come in useful one day.

He bowed his head again and the priest moved away to allow his charitable friend David some private time with his God.

God, of course, was some way from Ashcroft's thoughts. He was taking advantage of the peace and quiet to work out the timing of his next move in the tournament between him and the police force — or DI Jackman and DS Evans, to be more precise.

It was a wonder to him, considering the complexity of his various machinations, that he was still way ahead of the game. It came down to basics, didn't it, in the end? Build a good solid foundation, do your research and go from there. At least his father had taught him that much. The bastard had built his business empire from nothing, simply through knowing how to play the game. Ashcroft had two things to thank his father for — his business acumen, and his death. After his father had driven off the road and killed himself, Ashcroft junior had inherited a small fortune, thanks to which he was free to pursue his games.

He took a lungful of the dank, incense-laden air. Back to business. He had to ensure he got the timing right for this next act of the play. He would have to ensure that his trusty "employee" was in place, ready to take up his role.

Ashcroft smiled darkly. He was sure that he would be agreeable. After all, it was in his best interests to comply, and if he were to refuse, Ashcroft would kill him. Simple. There were plenty of others only too happy to take him up on such a lucrative offer.

CHAPTER TWENTY-THREE

Having spent twenty gruelling minutes in her office, Jackman and his superintendent went down to the incident room, where every available officer had gathered for an extraordinary meeting.

Knowing the efficiency of the station grapevine, and the gravity of what had occurred, it was doubtful that there was anyone who hadn't heard what had happened to Ernie Teal. However, it was expected that Ruth would make a formal announcement to her officers. She had told Jackman that she wanted to dispel any rumours that might have spread.

'We have released the news of the death of a serving police officer, but withheld his name until the family and his friends have had time to grieve in private. The public have been asked to be aware of the danger posed by this gunman and as far as possible to stay indoors. I have endeavoured to avert wholesale panic by assuring them that this man has specific targets. He is not a spree killer who will massacre random victims.' She looked around the room. 'Although this hasn't been broadcast, we believe he is actually a hired gun being used by Ashcroft. There has also been some speculation that he is a loose cannon and may turn out to have an agenda of his own.'

When she had finished, Jackman took the lead, giving a progress report on the sniper and Alistair Ashcroft.

'I've just heard from uniform that the 4x4 Jeep Cherokee, which had been stolen, has been found abandoned and burnt out. No surprise there. There was a CCTV camera at the gun club, but the police vehicle obstructed its line of sight, and there are no cameras on the route he used, so,' he raised his hands, 'we've drawn a blank with that line of enquiry.'

'How about the owner of the vehicle, sir?' asked Gary Pritchard. 'Was there CCTV where it was stolen from?'

'It was taken from a quiet cul-de-sac in one of the Saltern villages, Gary. No one saw or heard anything, and there is no coverage out there.'

'Private domestic cameras?' asked Robbie.

'Uniform have already spoken to the neighbours,' said Jackman. 'It seems to be a very untroubled community, mainly retired people, and no one has cameras. I think we are wasting our time continuing along that path. We need to step up our efforts in the search for Ashcroft. So far we are assuming he stole a motorcycle from a nearby village, concealed it, probably somewhere at the Lorimer place, and then took off when we began to show an interest in Ezra Lorimer. By then we had already begun to suspect that Ezra was in fact Ashcroft in disguise.'

'We heard from Humberside police that he killed the real Ezra, sir. How did he murder him?' asked Rosie Cohen.

Jackman understood Rosie's interest. During the original case, one of Ashcroft's nightmare murder scenes had sent her into freefall and she had been signed off duties for weeks.

Marie answered in his stead. 'In a manner most unusual for Ashcroft, who as you will all remember from last time, usually devised horrendous methods for dispatching his victims. Ezra had his throat cut. Their report said it appeared he had been drinking with someone in his caravan. There was no sign of a fight, and they believe he must have been attacked from behind while enjoying a glass of whisky. When forensics get their reports through, they will send us a copy.'

Jackman continued. 'We suspect that Ezra Lorimer had outlived his usefulness, so Ashcroft simply terminated him. If you think back, Ashcroft always felt he had a divine right to act as judge, jury and executioner regarding people he considered to have escaped judgement. He believed that he was righting wrongs. But Ezra had done nothing wrong, he was simply Ashcroft's ticket to insert himself into the Lorimer family.'

'And once there, he used the innocent, gullible sons to steal a rifle and cause various other annoying disruptions in the area,' concluded Marie.

'Now he has finished with Ezra, the question remains as to whether he will adopt a new persona, or will he move forward as himself? Our last clear picture of him is almost a year old, and we don't know how much his appearance might have changed in that time.'

'Also, he was injured in the collision with my motor-bike,' Marie said. 'We have no idea if he has scars now or, possibly, a limp. He didn't seem impaired in any way, did he, Robbie? Charlie?'

They shook their heads. 'No, Sarge,' said Robbie. 'Nothing we noticed.'

'I want you two to try to recall anything, anything at all, about the man you believed to be Ezra that might help us track our killer.' Jackman looked from one to the other of them. 'And no beating yourselves up for not realising it wasn't the real Ezra. Ashcroft is a consummate actor, and if he could fool Ezra's own relatives, you lads didn't stand a chance.'

'Still feel like a plank,' muttered Charlie Button.

'Well, don't. Stop feeling angry at yourself and channel your energies into catching the bastard.' Jackman stared at the gathered officers. 'Look, I know it's tough. "Officer down" are the two words we most dread hearing, but also spare a thought for PC Kevin Stoner. He has been taken to Greenborough Hospital. His parents are with him, and he is being temporarily cared for there. What we don't know is why he in particular has been chosen to witness three shootings at close range, and to be first on scene at the initial death — that of Christopher Keyes. If any of you, as his friends and colleagues, can help us with that, any suggestion, even if it's tenuous as hell, please come and speak to one of the team, okay?'

'How is he, sir?' asked PC Stacey Smith.

'We don't know, Stacey. You all know what trauma like that can do. He's a tough kid but I guess only time will tell. He is being counselled by the force psychologist, Laura Archer, and she'll update me as to his progress.' He paused. 'This is not going to be easy, I know, but I need every one of you to try put aside what has happened and get out there and find the sniper and Alistair Ashcroft. They are both right here in this town and probably hiding in plain sight, especially in Ashcroft's case. Find them for our dead colleague, and for heaven's sake, find them before we lose any more of our number.'

He watched them file out or return to their desks. He had asked a lot of a station that had just lost one of their officers, but he had no choice.

'Coffee, boss?' Marie asked.

'Please, and as strong as that crappy machine can make it.'

As Marie headed for the vending machine, Robbie approached him.

'Er, when you said if we think of something, no matter how small . . .'

'Spit it out, lad.'

'It came to me when you were asking us to consider whatever we recall about our meeting with the fake Ezra. Sir, he was wearing a very expensive cologne. I mean he wasn't drenched, but I caught a hint of it, and I recognised it immediately.'

'Come into the office, Robbie, but go get Marie first. I want her to hear this too.'

A few minutes later, clutching mugs of hot coffee, they mulled over what Robbie had told them.

'Why on earth, when you are disguised as a rough, country man like Ezra Lorimer, would you wear an expensive fragrance?' asked Marie. 'Ashcroft doesn't make slip-ups like that, so why would he do it?'

'That's one for the psychologists,' murmured Jackman. 'Pity Laura is tied up at present.'

Marie looked over her drink at him. 'You could ring Sam Page, boss. He's helped us out before.'

'I might just do that. What did you say it was called, Robbie?'

'It's one of Penhaligon's Portrait range, sir. It's called Terrible Teddy. I have a friend who wears it.'

Marie snorted. 'Bloody funny name for a cologne.'

Jackman had seen the collection in Harrods. It was made by a company who had a royal warrant and a reputation for quality, having been established way back in the 1800s. It also cost a small fortune. 'As far as I remember, all the fragrances represent a member of the aristocracy. Is that right, Rob?'

'Yes, sir. I forget what my friend told me about it, but I think it could be why Ashcroft likes it so much.' He pulled out his smartphone and tapped in the name. 'Oh yeah, he'd like this alright. Listen. *Teddy was a smooth operator who lived for the thrill of the chase.*'

'And it's expensive?' Marie asked. 'How expensive exactly?'

Robbie searched again. 'Eau de parfum just under two hundred pounds. So I'd say very.'

Marie let out a low whistle. 'Hell fire! And Ashcroft was wearing it in a crappy, falling to bits motorhome? Why?' She frowned, then added, 'And if he's so bloody clever, why hand us a potentially major clue on a plate?'

Jackman picked up his phone, found Sam Page's number and put the question to him.

Sam was silent for a while. 'Hmm. It would be my guess that he wanted to retain just a little of himself even while acting as someone else. He needed to remind the world at large what a powerful man he is. He would know that none of the Lorimer family would recognise the scent, and it made him feel superior. Plus, as we know, he is a megalomaniac. As far as he is concerned, anyone else who happens to smell it couldn't possibly be clever enough either to recognise it or realise the implications.'

Jackman thanked Sam and said he would contact him again later, after he'd ascertained how Laura was getting on with Kevin Stoner. Their meal might have to be postponed yet again. Sam said he understood completely and hung up.

'One thing's for certain, sir.' Robbie looked almost fierce. 'If I meet him again, in whatever role he assumes next, and get the slightest whiff of Terrible Teddy, he's dead meat.'

'What you found is important, Robbie. It could help identify him. And the best thing is that it's not something you can grab a bottle of in Superdrug. It's a statement perfume and something very few people could afford.' At last, something concrete. 'If it were cheaper, I'd get hold of a bottle and give every officer in the station a whiff, just in case they find themselves in his company.'

'Can't see Ruth Crooke's budget extending to cologne from Harrods, can you?' said Marie.

'Don't worry. I'll pinch my friend's bottle. I'll tell him he's assisting with a murder enquiry and I promise you, he can afford to replace it.' Robbie grinned. 'He lives and works in Peterborough. I'll ring him and tell him I need it as a matter of urgency. He can courier it here, no problem.'

'He'll do that? Wow, I'm impressed,' Jackman said.

'He owns a national courier and parcel delivery company, so if he can't, no one can.'

Marie smiled at him. 'You're a star. And I'm dying to find out what two hundred quid's worth of scent smells like.'

'According to the blurb, it's incense, leather and Ambroxan, whatever that is.'

'Haven't a clue,' Jackman said.

'It says here it's a kind of musky, amber odour, but I'd think the strongest tone would be the incense.'

Marie started to speak, then stopped, looking hesitant. Jackman noticed. 'What are you thinking, Marie?'

She swallowed. 'I've just had a flashback to my crash. I thought Ashcroft was going to kill me. He stood over me, and before he kicked hell out of me, he just stared down at me. He was hurting and full of hate and frustration, but I remember now: in those few seconds, I smelt blood, and sweat, and motorbike fuel . . . and aftershave. It was like a hint of the stuff they burn in churches. Incense.'

'So even back then he was wearing it,' whispered Jackman. 'It's his signature! He will always wear it.' He turned to Robbie. 'Ring your friend. Tell him this really is a matter of urgency and to please send it. I will pay for delivery. And well done for remembering, Rob. Excellent work, Detective.'

'Thanks, boss, I'm on it.' And he was. Robbie looked up from his phone, smiling. 'Sorted. He's going to pick it up immediately and a motorbike will be on its way to us within the hour.'

Jackman exhaled. 'Fantastic. It's a start, isn't it?'

'It is,' said Marie, her eyes shining with resolve. 'And this time, he's ours.'

* * *

Laura Archer remained with Kevin throughout his hospital assessment. Initially his blood pressure and heart rate had been perilously elevated, but they soon returned to near normal as the initial shock began to fade. He would be kept in for observation and to prepare him for the inevitable results of being witness to so much trauma.

At first, he had been stunned, then he experienced an hour or so of denial, insisting he was perfectly well and should be allowed to get back to his job. Listening to him one would have thought that nothing out of the ordinary had happened, or that he didn't care.

Laura knew different, of course. He was going through the process. After a further hour he confessed to feeling a terrible helplessness — why hadn't he been able to do anything to prevent Ernie being killed. This very quickly turned into anger, first at himself and then Alistair Ashcroft. And then he broke down.

Laura sat with him, her gentle voice explaining that everything he was going through was natural and a normal reaction to such a traumatic event. He should allow his emotions to express themselves and he should give himself time to move through the stages.

'Human beings are remarkably good at coping with traumatic experiences, so long as they understand what is happening to them.' She smiled at him. 'Don't beat yourself up, Kevin. Everything that happened, every time, was out of your control.'

'I feel bad that I was mean to him — maybe not outwardly, but I could have been kinder. I mean, he might have had a reason for behaving like he did. Maybe he had a problem?'

'But if he never told you, how would you know?' Laura said.

'But I never asked, did I? I could have made the effort to find out if there was something in his life that was affecting him, but I didn't.' He shook his head. 'Just like all the others, I believed he was nothing but a lazy slob.'

'Well, maybe he was, but no matter what he was or wasn't, he was an innocent victim of a very bad man.'

Kevin sighed. 'Like Christopher, Barney and William.'

'Like anyone who is unlucky enough to come to the attention of that psychopath.' Laura saw Kevin's father and mother looking anxiously in their direction. They had gone to the hospital cafeteria while the psychiatric team interviewed Kevin and were now hoping to spend a little time with their son. 'Are you happy for me to go and make a couple of phone calls, Kevin? I won't be long. Your parents are here and they'd like to see you. Are you happy with that?'

Kevin nodded.

She stood up and beckoned to them. Laura had never met a bishop before and found him remarkably sympathetic.

He would be good for Kevin. He seemed to have just the right amount of empathy without indulging in histrionics. On the other hand, Kevin's mother, Penny, was so anxious that she looked as if she needed help herself. Laura hoped this would pass because right now, Kevin needed calm reassurance, not a mother who was a sobbing, emotional mess.

But after a few words of reassurance, Penny gathered herself together, 'Of course, of course. It was such terrible news to receive, and seeing him like this . . .' She shuddered. 'I'm so sorry, but don't worry, we'll be there for him.'

Outside, Laura sat down on a bench in a small paved area close to the entrance. She needed a few moments on her own, away from all the anguish and heartbreak that Ashcroft was so good at causing. It took her several minutes to realise that a light rain had started to fall, and she was getting wet.

She went back inside and, looking for somewhere quiet to sit, made her way to the hospital faith room. She sat down in front of a large, brightly coloured mural. It depicted a pastoral scene with rolling hills, small copses of trees and fields of corn. A bright sun shone in a cloudless azure sky. She could almost hear birdsong and the chirrup of crickets.

For a while she immersed herself in that scene, felt the warmth of the sun on her skin, smelt the clover and the grass beneath her feet. She listened to skylarks, and a gentle breeze ruffled her hair. Peace.

After a while she allowed herself to think about Alistair Ashcroft.

On the last occasion on which he had terrorised Saltern-le-Fen, she had seen the results of his handiwork first hand. The memory of what he did would stay with her forever. She had also watched him devastate the lives of those who were trying to stop him. She reminded herself that Ashcroft was not omnipotent. One day, he would be brought to justice. Meanwhile the trail of wreckage, the shattered lives he was leaving in his wake, was mounting every day. Even she had not been spared. His invasion of her sacred space had affected her much more deeply than she admitted to Jackman.

Laura believed that Ashcroft was driven forward by his belief in his own omnipotence. He would make an interesting subject for study — once he was safely behind bars.

She was so deep in thought that she didn't hear the door click, followed by the sound of footsteps.

'I knew I'd find you here.'

She gasped, spun round.

'Sorry! I didn't mean to startle you. I didn't want to disturb you in case you were praying.'

'Sam!' Her heart stopped racing. 'I was miles away, and I certainly wasn't praying.'

Sam sat down next to her. 'Jackman told me what happened. I called in on young Kevin Stoner and his father told me you had stepped out for a while.' He looked around the faith room. 'This is where I would come too, if it was raining and I couldn't sit outside.'

They sat together in silence for a while, until Laura whispered, 'He's an enigma, isn't he? He isn't conforming to the usual model. I would have thought that by now, he would have begun to devolve, become more chaotic, even sloppy. Think of the dramatic mood swings he exhibited just before the police almost caught him that last time. I would have put money on them escalating but he seems even more controlled than before.'

'I wonder,' said Sam, 'if he uses the periods between his killing episodes to step out of himself completely and become a different person for a while. Adopting another persona might enable him to regroup in some way.'

Laura nodded slowly. 'We know he had various existences before. In most of them, he was a charitable, altruistic person. People who knew him at those times loved and admired him. He even passed himself off as a psychological counsellor at one point, I seem to remember.'

'From what we know from his file, that's how he rolls. I think he likes to be in the company of needy, damaged, vulnerable people,' mused Sam. 'He becomes their support and mentor, and he revels in the adoration they show him.'

'All of that would support his self-belief and make him stronger. Unwittingly, they are feeding his psychosis. Then, when he is recharged, he starts killing again. God.'

'If he wasn't so dangerous, I'd admire his patience.' Sam grimaced. 'But as it is, he just scares me.'

'You aren't alone, Sam. I keep remembering that he promised to meet me in person. The thought terrifies me.'

'I haven't forgotten, my dear young friend. And it's one reason I'm here. You shouldn't be wandering around alone, should you?' Sam said sternly. 'There are police patrolling the hospital but they can't watch everyone. I know you can't let Ashcroft rule your life, but as you said yourself, he marked your card. Even if it was just an empty threat, you have to take it seriously.'

Laura felt a rush of affection for her old friend. She slipped her arm through his. 'I can't think about that too deeply, Sam, or I'd never step out of the door. I won't let that monster imprison me. If he preys on weaknesses, then I'm damned if I'm going to be weak.'

'Just be careful. Discretion, and all that?' Sam patted her hand. 'You are a precious commodity, Laura Archer — and I'm not the only one who thinks so.'

There was a silence for a moment or two. 'I cannot begin to understand what Jackman is going through at present,' Laura said. 'I don't mean just worrying over me, it's everything. His old nemesis Ashcroft, another maniac with a gun who has now turned to killing police officers, everyone he loves or cares about under threat, and the responsibility for a town's safety, all on his shoulders. How long can he keep this up, Sam?'

He turned to her and said, 'I believe he will, Laura — until Ashcroft and his hired gun are safely behind bars or in the morgue. His adrenalin is pumping and he's in fight mode. He'll see this through, I know it. It's the aftermath that worries me, but we'll deal with that when the time comes.'

'And that nightmare? I know it still bothers him.'

'Let's hope that with everything else he has to deal with, the memory of that dream will fade. He's not a fanciful man, is he? Jackman doesn't believe in omens and portents. It was simply terrifyingly real, and it was about Marie and the man who killed his sister-in-law, so obviously it will have affected him. That's totally understandable.'

Sam sounded so certain that Laura felt her spirits lift. She recalled how Jackman suddenly seemed to change. It was as if he had shifted his whole game and brought a different attitude to bear on the situation. She said as much to Sam.

'You know as well as I do that he's developed a coping mechanism and it's working.' Sam smiled. 'Now, young lady, are you going to do as Uncle Sam says, and not go dashing off alone anymore?'

She nodded. 'I'll be careful, I promise.'

'That's not quite the same thing.' He looked at her over the rim of his spectacles.

'No, I mean it, Sam. I won't underestimate Ashcroft's threat, but life has to go on.'

'Just remember, it's the only one you have. Don't throw it away.' He stood up. 'Right. Sermon over. Let's get back to Kevin, eh?'

CHAPTER TWENTY-FOUR

This was truly hilarious. A mess room full of strapping, macho blokes, all spraying expensive men's cologne on their wrists and discussing it with utter seriousness. Priceless! Robbie wished he had the courage to video it on his smartphone.

Once the room was reeking of "Terrible Teddy," Robbie took the precious bottle and walked through to Control, where he treated all the officers there to a whiff. It took around half an hour to seek out most of the men and women who were likely to be out on the streets and have a chance of crossing Ashcroft's path. He even sprayed a little onto a handkerchief and allowed the dog handler to offer it to his canine partner. The German Shepherd merely coughed, unimpressed.

He returned to the CID room, sat down at his desk and stared at the distinctive bottle. Smaller things than this had led to the capture of criminals in the past. One thing was for sure: when this case was finally over, he never wanted to smell that perfume again.

Charlie Button called out to him from the other side of the office. 'Boss wants us in his office, mate. He said to bring a chair and your notebook.'

Robbie picked up his notepad and took his chair to Jackman's office. Marie and Gary were already there, and

Charlie and Rosie were gathering up chairs. What was this all about?

As soon as everyone was seated, Jackman began. 'Ruth Crooke and I agree that there is little point in us wasting time trying to track the sniper. We already have highly trained uniformed officers out there asking questions and following up leads, so they can carry on. We are going to do what we set out to do in the first place, hunt for Alistair Ashcroft.' He picked up a sheet of paper. 'To this end, I have had Rosie trawl through the last investigation and pull out any addresses or locations that he was connected to, even slightly, and list them. We'll work in pairs and visit each place, then widen the search to anywhere else that might be connected or in some way attractive to him. We'll go armed with a new set of photos that Orac has produced in IT. She has aged him slightly, and made subtle changes in each picture, in the hopes that even if he's disguised, one of them may bear some resemblance to his real self. We'll talk to anyone who will listen and show them the pictures.'

Robbie was relieved that they were going to be doing something concrete, even if it did remind him of being back in uniform and doing house-to-house enquiries. Robbie was determined to be the one to find Ashcroft. The man had made a fool of him, and Robbie Melton couldn't be doing with that.

'To start with, we'll tackle the estate agent who handled the properties Ashcroft got rid of around a year ago. He may have been back since, either buying or selling — or renting of course. If that fails, as I suspect it will, we try all the other estate agents and letting companies in Saltern and the surrounding area. He has to have a base. You take that, Gary and Rosie.' He stared at the list again. 'Robbie and Charlie, I want you to check out his old solicitor, paying particular attention to the properties that were in his possession, just in case he didn't sell them all before he disappeared. There was also a woman who had business dealings with him pertaining to the sale of his properties. Her name was Philippa, or Pip

Courtney. Ashcroft deceived her badly, and I doubt that she now harbours the fond feelings that she had for him then, but she saw a lot of him. She would recognise him if she saw him, I'm certain of that.'

'And me, boss?' asked Marie.

'We are going to church.'

'To confess our sins?' Marie grinned at him.

'Could do that as well if you like, but, no. To see if Ashcroft has made an appearance in any of them. If you remember, last time he used a lot of biblical quotes and references and we deduced that he liked to frequent churches. He was also known to attend meetings and volunteer for charity work, all church-based. Maybe he's trying something like that now.'

'It's a good cover, hiding under the petticoats of religious do-gooders. He's got such a silver tongue, he'd have them all eating out of his hand in no time.' Marie scowled.

'Exactly,' Robbie said somewhat bitterly. 'You only have to think how he deceived the Lorimer family — and us — to know how damned good he is.'

'And let's not forget that missing motorbike, the one he got away from Hawkers Fen on. Did he ditch it? Store it somewhere? Give it away? Or sell it? Ears and eyes open, guys,' Jackman said.

They were just about to leave when Jackman stopped them. He looked at Rosie, smiled, and said, 'There is one other thing that you should know.'

Listening, Robbie wasn't surprised to hear that Rosie was leaving. He had been amazed at how she and Max had coped thus far. It was a sensible decision, but he would miss her a lot. He had always admired her dogged tenacity. Like a terrier, she never let anything go.

They all crowded around, wishing her well. There were hugs. Tears were shed. Then Jackman told them that they would have a proper send-off later, but right now they were too busy chasing a certain psychopath.

Robbie looked across to Charlie. 'Ready?'

Charlie nodded. 'Ready.'

'And I want you wearing Kevlar vests whenever you are out on the streets,' Jackman added. 'Ruth has arranged for CID officers, as well as uniformed officers, to have these for the duration of this situation. They are stab and ballistic resistant but only to handgun standard. They won't stop a sniper's bullet, I'm afraid, but we know our assassin uses a handgun too, so it's worth wearing one, okay?'

'Oh hell, I hate those things,' Marie muttered.

'Think yourself lucky you aren't having to wear the heavier kit, you know, the one the Armed Response Units and the firearms officers have to use. And no excuses, Marie Evans. You of all people should protect yourself as much as possible. After all, you and I are at the top of his list, aren't we?'

Pulling a face, Marie reluctantly agreed.

'We've only got an hour and a half before the four o'clock meeting, so do what you can this afternoon and crack straight on in the morning, okay?'

They all nodded, gathered up their chairs and left the office.

Back in the CID room, Robbie took Rosie aside. 'You don't have to go out this afternoon, you know. Jackman will understand. These are your last few hours here. Do you want to spend them traipsing around estate agents knowing there's a sniper on the loose? You could make a whole lot of enquiries by phone.'

She smiled at him. 'Thanks for caring, Robbie, but until I hand over my warrant card, I'm a police officer. And why the hell would I want to stay here on my own while you lot are having fun hunting killers?'

He threw up his hands. 'I give in. Just be careful, okay?'

He'd done his best to dissuade her, feeling he owed it to Max, but Rosie was clearly having none of it. 'Let's go and grab one of those new vests then, shall we?' he said.

* * *

Gary could not believe the change that had come over the town. Saltern-le-Fen was no metropolis, being smaller even than Greenborough, but it was a bustling market town, whose twice-weekly farmers' market attracted locals and visitors alike. Now it was practically deserted, and the few shoppers who were out hurried along the streets, heads down, keeping close to the shop fronts.

'This is weird,' whispered Rosie.

'Ruth Crooke's warning has hit home, I'd say.' Gary looked around. 'There are more police on the streets than civilians.'

'Can't blame them, I must say.' She checked her list for the address of the first estate agent. 'No one knows where or when the gunman will strike again.'

'Not sure *he'd* agree with you.' Gary indicated to a man, clearly drunk, staggering around the deserted market square, shouting, 'You want me? Come and fucking get me, arsehole! Hiding in the fucking shadows! Bloody coward!'

Before Gary even had a chance to move, two uniformed officers materialised from nowhere and escorted him away.

'He's got a point,' muttered Rosie. 'It is a cowardly thing to do, shoot someone.' They walked on. 'That's something that bothers me about all this. Think back to the horrific scenarios, the slow, terrible deaths that Ashcroft's evil mind concocted for his original victims. Why has he changed his MO so radically this time around and hired a shooter?'

Gary thought about this. 'Maybe it's because last time he was enacting just retribution, as he saw it. Now it's a vendetta against the police — well, the boss and the sarge to be exact — so execution-style deaths are more appropriate, and for that you need an expert.'

'I just find it hard to equate such an impersonal method with Alistair Ashcroft.'

Gary shrugged. 'Well, we know he likes guns. After all, he did shoot Jackman and try to shoot Marie, didn't he?'

'True. And maybe he likes the power of sending out a minion to kill in his name.' Rosie stopped and double-checked the list. 'Millgate and Forshore. Let's talk to them.'

It didn't take long to realise that they were wasting their time. The manager was more concerned that the spate of murders would bring house prices down and affect his business. 'Cancellations! That's all I've had. No one wants to go viewing houses in a town that's being terrorised. In two years, Saltern will be a ghost town, you mark my words.'

Rosie had showed him the photographs of Ashcroft in his many possible guises, but Millgate just shook his head. 'I've had no one that looks even vaguely like that in here.' He passed the pictures to two rather miserable looking young men, who agreed that they hadn't seen him either.

They gave up. Outside, Gary said, 'I've a feeling this is a taste of things to come. Who's next?'

'The new one down Galleon Alley — er, Galleon Homes. They're relatively new and as far as I can remember, they mainly do long-term lets.' Rosie led the way down a narrow, cobbled lane with shops on either side.

At least this time they were greeted with an expectant smile, a definite improvement on Millgate. Introducing himself and Rosie, Gary learnt that the agent was called Ronnie Beasley and he was pretty much a one-man band. With just one assistant, who was out doing a valuation, he handled most of the transactions personally.

'Can't be too negative about this situation, can we?' said Beasley. 'Things have a habit of flaring up and then dying down and becoming yesterday's news. People will always want houses or places to rent.'

Gary commended his positive attitude. 'Any chance this man has been in, sir, possibly wanting to rent somewhere?'

Beasley stared at the pictures, before pausing at one of Orac's computer-generated likenesses. 'There's something about this one that rings bells.'

Gary held his breath. He felt Rosie tense beside him.

'He may not look exactly like that. These are just approximations,' Gary said hopefully. 'Do you think you've seen him?'

Beasley frowned. 'Yes. About six weeks, two months ago, a man who looked something like this came in looking for a property to rent. I remember he was very particular about his requirements and money didn't seem to be a concern. Sadly, I didn't have anything that suited him.'

'Sir?' Rosie leaned forward. 'How did he differ from this picture? Could you describe him for us?'

'He had very short hair. I think they call it a fade. Fuller on top then fades to a close-cut back and sides, and it was a sandy blond colour. I thought then that it was really a cut for a younger man, but still, it suited him.' He gave them a slightly apologetic smile. 'I notice these kinds of things because my wife is a men's hairdresser.'

'Height and age? At a guess,' asked Gary.

'About my height, but age . . . I'm not good with ages.' Beasley paused. 'Possibly in his forties? Casually dressed, but he had that look of money about him, if you know what I mean.'

Rosie took a handkerchief from her pocket. 'This is a long shot, sir. I don't suppose you remember if he was wearing a fragrance that smelt like this?'

Beasley looked apologetic. 'There I can't help you, officers. I have no sense of smell.'

Gary swore under his breath. Just our luck. We get a possible ID, a guy who was up close and personal with our mark, but he can't smell anything.

'If it helps, he looked the kind of man to wear something classy, even if it was just to go to the golf club for drinks.'

Or the gun club? 'Would you have his name on record, sir?' Gary said. 'And a contact number?'

'I'll look for you, but when we had exhausted all the houses I had on my books, he told me not to worry, he'd have to look elsewhere. He did say he'd call in again at a later date should he be unlucky and need to rethink his criteria.'

Beasley went to a filing cabinet and thumbed through a series of folders. 'Ah, well. I made a note of his name and what he required, but there's no number, I'm afraid.'

He returned to the desk and handed Gary a sheet of paper.

'Richard Reeves,' Gary murmured. 'Right.' He skimmed through the list. 'He was very specific, wasn't he, sir? Detached property, double garage, three bedrooms, quiet location with no near neighbours, and within a five-mile radius of the town centre.'

'That's right, Officers. He said he would be alone here for a while, then his family would be joining him a little later. He said they had dogs and he didn't want close neighbours in case the animals disturbed anyone.' Beasley frowned. 'Can I see those pictures again, please?'

Rosie handed them to him.

'Yes, that's definitely him. It's just the hair that's different. The thing that gives him away are the eyes.' He thumbed through the other pictures. 'It's the same with all of these photos. You can change everything about that face to make it look different, but apart from changing the iris colour, you can't alter those eyes. They are oddly almond shaped. I thought it was unusual at the time.'

Gary stared at them. Beasley was right. Then he recalled a snippet of information about Alistair Ashcroft from the original case. The special school that he had attended had suspected him of suffering from a genetic disorder called Fragile X Syndrome, something that often shows itself in a long narrow face with large ears and almond-shaped eyes. Alistair had not exhibited all those physical differences, but his eyes were large and almond shaped.

He shivered. Ashcroft had been right here, looking for a new lair.

'Can we take this list, sir? You can rest assured, he won't be back.'

'Please do, and I must say, I'm afraid to ask why you want to find him.' Beasley looked at them anxiously.

Rosie flashed him a reassuring smile. 'We just need to talk to him about an ongoing investigation, sir, that's all.'

But Beasley wasn't to be reassured so easily. 'Has he got something to do with this gunman?'

Gary intervened. 'Please don't worry about it, sir. We just think he might be able to help with another case we are working on. Tell me, what was your impression of him?'

'Bit of a toff. Well-off, well spoken, obviously well-educated, had a sense of humour as I recall, but was rather intense and very picky about what sort of property he was looking for.'

Gary nodded. 'Well, thank you for your time, sir. You've been most helpful.' He handed him a card. 'And if you should see him again, please ring us immediately.'

Beasley nodded. 'I hope you find him, Officers.'

As they left, Gary saw him quickly flip the sign on the door to Closed. Beasley wasn't taking any chances.

'Now we know the kind of property he was looking for, we can see if any of the other agents had a similar request,' Rosie said. For a moment she looked excited, then her face fell. 'Well, you can. We'll never get around all of them before the shift ends or they close, and then, well, it's all over for me.'

'And I'm very glad it is, Rosie. Time for you to be a mum and not miss those precious early years. And don't worry about us. We'll catch the bugger for you!'

'You'd better.' She took a slow breath. 'And look out for my Max, won't you, Gary? Until this is over, I'll worry myself sick every time he goes out of the door.'

'Of course I will.' Gary was serious now. 'We all will. This team is special, we look out for each other, you know that.'

Rosie looked as if she was about to cry again, then she sniffed and said, 'Okay, Gazza, let's check that big letting agent just off the market square. With what Beasley told us we have a better chance now.'

'Lead on.'

CHAPTER TWENTY-FIVE

'I had no idea there were so many churches in Saltern,' said Marie. She had already ticked off three non-starters from Rosie's list. 'Next one is the Church of Our Lady of Sorrows. It's Catholic, isn't it?'

'The biggest and most ornate. I can see something like that appealing to his over-inflated ego, can't you?' Jackman said. 'And it's only a few minutes' walk from here.'

Marie kept looking around her, constantly checking the tops of buildings — upstairs windows, flat roofs, any place that a sniper might choose to conceal himself. It was a strange feeling, knowing that at any given moment, you could be in the crosshairs of a rifle sight. She'd had stark confirmation of how fast things could happen when she saw Ernie Teal sitting in the police car, dead. One second he was considering a nice chocolate bar, the next he was gone. In the time it had taken for a windshield to shatter, a life had shattered too.

Jackman glanced at her. 'You okay, Marie?'

'As good as I can be, knowing a killer is out there and both our names are on his to-do list.' She turned to him. 'But I have no intention of hiding under my office desk until this is over, so I'll bloody well take my chances.'

Jackman chuckled. 'Spoken like a true Evans!'

'So, how are we going to tackle this lot of bible bashers?'

'With tact, if you can recall what that is, Sergeant.' He was still smiling when his mobile rang. 'Jackman.'

Marie waited. From Jackman's expression it obviously wasn't another death. She looked at him enquiringly.

'Gary. He says to check out photo number four. They've had a positive ID on a man who resembles that one but with shorter, sandy-coloured hair.'

'Brilliant! That's a step forward — but hang on a minute. Suppose he changed his appearance for every estate agent?'

'Gary also said the witness referred to the eyes. They are quite distinctive.'

Marie remembered those eyes vividly. They had stared into hers, full of hate and loathing. She swallowed. 'They are, aren't they? I wonder why neither Robbie nor Charlie noticed that when they spoke to "Ezra?"'

'They weren't expecting anyone other than Rachel Lorimer's cousin. There was no earthly reason to think the man they spoke to was anyone other than who he claimed to be. Plus, I swear even I wouldn't have recognised him in the clever make-up and that old facial scar, with the wig and beard, and I've met him face to face — unfortunately.' Jackman grimaced. 'At least we know how he is working.'

The doors to the big church stood open. Larger than the others, Marie found it rather austere. Their footsteps echoed on the flagstones. Other than an old couple sitting close together in the Lady Chapel, the place seemed empty. They looked around hopefully.

'Father Malone is in the vestry,' the woman said.

Jackman thanked her and led the way towards a door to the left of the chancel.

The layout was different from the church she had attended as a girl. The Methodist chapel had been plain and simple. This one seemed designed to impress.

Jackman knocked on the vestry door

'Come.' Father Malone was a tall, heavy man with a balding head surrounded by a halo of curly ginger hair that grew to meet a tight ginger beard.

'Come in, come in. How can I help you two lovely people?'

Jackman held up his warrant card, as did Marie.

'Oh no, Brendan's not in trouble again, is he?' A cloud spread over his face. 'That boy! What is it this time? Petty theft again? I did say I didn't want to press charges, but . . .'

'No, sir,' Jackman stopped the flow. 'We've come to talk to you about a quite different matter.'

The priest pointed to two hard chairs. 'Then please sit.'

Jackman explained who they were looking for and asked if anyone new had started visiting the church recently, possibly someone who'd expressed interest in helping with charitable activities. 'He's well-educated, Father, and quite charismatic.'

'No, Detectives, I can't say I've seen anyone like that. There have been very few new worshippers of late.'

Marie showed him the photographs, although she didn't believe they would be of any help.

The priest looked through them and handed them back. 'I can't say I've ever seen this man, I'm sorry.'

Jackman gave him his card and a copy of one of the original pictures of Ashcroft. He asked the priest to hang onto it, and if he ever saw the man to ring him immediately.

'I wish I could have helped you, Detectives, but only one man has been kind enough to offer his help in the past few months. He doesn't look like that, and I wouldn't say he's charismatic at all.' He gave a little laugh. 'Far from it, he's quite taciturn in fact.'

Jackman's eyes narrowed. 'What does he look like, Father?'

'Working-class man, a bit rough around the edges. Though he does have, er, strong opinions about things, so maybe I'm wrong in thinking he's not educated.'

'How long has he been coming here?' asked Marie.

'Only a week or two, and not regularly. His name is David.'

'What does he look like, Father? As in hair colour for instance.' Jackman looked edgy.

'He always wears a hat, so I can't tell you about his hair, but his clothes are pretty well worn, almost scruffy. It took a while to get him to talk, but he's a very kind man at heart.'

'A hat, in church?' commented Jackman.

'Not everyone conforms to tradition, Detective. And in these days of diminishing congregations, I welcome them with open arms no matter what they are wearing.'

Marie took the photos from Jackman and selected the fourth. 'You're sure nothing about this likeness reminds you of David? Take another look, Father. Take each feature in turn and look really hard.'

The priest covered part of the face with his hand and stared at the picture. The silence was palpable. Finally, he gave a little sniff. 'Funnily enough, there is something about those dark eyes. David has very dark eyes.'

Glancing quickly at her, Jackman said, 'When did you see him last, Father?'

Father Malone looked at his watch. 'About four hours ago.'

'Here?' Marie exclaimed.

'Well, yes. Where else?' The priest looked puzzled, 'He comes to pray.'

Oh right. Of course. Pray for whom exactly? For Ernie Teal? For Kevin Stoner maybe? Marie almost snorted in disgust.

'What do you know about this David?' asked Jackman. 'Anything at all you can think of.'

Father Malone lifted his hands in resignation. 'Very little, Detective. I'm here to listen. I don't pry into people's lives and rarely ask questions, unless it's about someone's faith.'

'So he's told you nothing about his personal life?' Marie said.

'If he did, I couldn't tell you, surely you know that.' His expression was reproachful.

'We are not talking about the confession, Father, just day-to-day chat, things he might tell anyone,' Jackman said.

The priest looked thoughtful. 'He told me he had no family in Saltern, which made me think he was taking advantage of the seasonal work around here. But then his hands were smooth and clean. They looked too soft for a manual worker. He did say he was a very private man and that being in this church calmed all the thoughts that sometimes threatened to overwhelm him.' He frowned. 'This is purely supposition, but I wouldn't be surprised if he suffers from some kind of mental illness.'

It was all Marie could do not to explode. If only this man knew the extent of Ashcroft's psychological problems.

Coolly, Jackman said, 'What makes you think that?'

'I felt that, deep inside he was harbouring a terrible anger. Talking to him, you could sometimes sense it bubbling up, then calming again. And he is careful about what he says. I've seen that before in people who are grieving and don't know how to handle the mood swings. Maybe he'll tell me one day.'

And maybe he won't. Marie said, 'Father? Do you happen to have CCTV here?'

'Only at the front door. We had a young tearaway get in with a spray can a while back. I had to get a professional company in to clean up after him.'

'And how many doors are there here?' she asked.

'Apart from the main door, there's the South Aisle door and the vestry door, which leads to my house.'

'Does David use one of those?'

'Actually, no. He comes in the main entrance.'

Jackman's look seemed to say, could we be that lucky?

She nodded. 'Father, we need to see this morning's footage.'

The priest went to a cupboard in the corner of the room. Inside was a small wireless CCTV monitor. 'Gift from one of our more generous parishioners. I can view everything from my mobile phone if I wish.' He picked up a mouse and began scrolling through that morning's footage. 'Ah, got it.' He stood back to let them see a figure approaching the main door.

The man had dark, rather scruffy clothes, heavy trainers and was wearing a baggy brown driver's cap. Marie would never have believed that this could be Ashcroft — until he glanced up and looked directly at the camera.

Marie watched while an insidious, knowing smile passed across his face and was gone. Suddenly she could smell petrol, blood, and incense. Without a doubt, "David" was Alistair Ashcroft, and he had sat quietly in this church while his hired gun robbed PC Ernie Teal of life.

For a moment, Marie thought she was going to be sick. Jackman touched her arm. 'You okay?'

Swallowing bile, she struggled to collect herself, vaguely aware of the priest staring at her. 'Yeah. Just give me a moment.'

Jackman was speaking to him. 'Father, we believe that David is really Alistair Ashcroft, a wanted man. He is a very dangerous killer and we have to find him.'

The priest bowed his head, crossed himself and murmured a few words under his breath. He looked up. 'But he offered to help me with a new meeting group, somewhere those who are troubled can come to talk about their problems. You say he's a murderer, but why would such a man offer to help with charitable work?'

'I'm afraid he's done this before, Father. He makes himself out to be a saint with a listening ear, and vulnerable people love him, but all the time he's gloating over their misery. Father, he's evil.' Jackman's voice was hard.

'That's a very strong word, Detective. It's generally reserved for the Antichrist.'

'This man caused the death of a close family member.' Jackman sounded angry now. 'I know what I'm talking about.'

Marie looked at him in surprise.

'I'm sorry, Father. That was wrong of me. Nevertheless, I cannot emphasise strongly enough just how dangerous this man is. Now, did he say when he would be back?'

'Friday, at ten, to help me prepare for the meeting. Other than that, he has no strict schedule. He comes and goes.'

That was days away, they couldn't just wait around until then. 'There will be police watching the church from now on, Father.' Marie was back on track. 'Naturally, if we haven't caught him, we will be waiting for him on Friday morning, but we need to find him way sooner than that. And we'll need access to that CCTV footage. Is that okay with you?'

'Of course. I'll give you the password, and to make it easier, you can download an app that lets you view it remotely.'

There was nothing more the priest could tell them, so after leaving their cards, along with instructions on what to do if he should turn up again, they hastened back to the station.

As they walked, Jackman barked orders into his phone. He wanted Our Lady of Sorrows placed under round-the-clock surveillance.

This was a recent sighting, the closest they had been to Ashcroft other than in his guise of Ezra Lorimer. So he was definitely based locally. Now, if Gary and Rosie could just get a bite from one of the estate agents . . .

Marie quickened her pace.

* * *

Rachel Lorimer was still angry, but now she was angry at herself for having been taken in, and furious at the man who had killed her cousin. Although they didn't see each other, over the years, she and Ezra had maintained their bond. Yes, he had been a bit of a rogue but he was kind to her. Now he was dead, her family in tatters.

Of all her children, only Jacob seemed to accept what had happened, but even he was downcast, grieving for his lost horse. Esther had locked herself in her caravan and refused to come out. Noah was in a deep depression, fantasising about being thrown into some police dungeon and never released. Levi was terrified that their actions would result in a criminal charge and then his job would be in jeopardy. And Paul, well, Paul had driven off after the police left, and they hadn't seen him since.

Now, as evening approached, Rachel began to wonder where he had gone. He wasn't stable at the best of times, but an upset such as this could result in serious problems. He had a terrible temper and although he had never actually hurt anyone, she feared that one day, pushed too far, he could be a danger to himself and others.

She stood at the kitchen sink, peeling potatoes and staring out of the window, looking for signs of Paul's return. Gillian, Levi's wife, sat at the pine table, slicing runner beans. Today, Rachel had seen a different side to their meek Gillian, and she looked at the girl with a new respect. Levi needed support.

Levi entered, laid a dead rabbit on the table and said, 'Want me to skin it, Ma? It's a plump little devil, make a tasty pie.'

'Later, boy. Go hang it in the root store and try not to let Jacob see. You know how it upsets him. Right now, I've got another job for you.'

Rachel watched him hurry off. She suspected she would get little backchat from any of her family for a while. When he was back, she asked if he knew where Paul was. 'No lies now, that's all finished and done with. Just give me a straight answer.'

He looked her in the eyes. 'No, Ma, I don't.'

She accepted his words. She knew when the boys were lying, and now Levi was being straight with her. 'Alright. Go and get the others and bring them here — and no refusals, especially from Esther.'

Again he scuttled off, and Rachel felt a surge of love for her poor family of overgrown children. Despite the risks involved in bearing so many, Rachel had done what her husband wanted and given him a big family. But he had died, and she was left to carry the burden.

One by one, they drifted in and sat down at the table. Rachel pointed at the one empty chair. 'Do any of you have the slightest idea where Paul might be?'

They all shook their heads. Then Jacob raised his hand, hesitantly.

'Do you know where he is, son?'

'I think he is looking for the man who killed Uncle Ezra and who lied to us.'

Rachel sighed. The thought had crossed her mind as well. 'Does Paul know where that man might be?'

Jacob screwed up his face. 'I don't know, but when he does find him, he'll kill him. I heard him say that just before he drove off.' He smiled at his mother. 'That's good, isn't it?'

She closed her eyes. 'No, son. You can't just kill people, even if they are bad. The law has to deal with them. Paul might get himself into trouble.'

'Oh,' said Jacob, sounding disappointed. It seemed he couldn't stand to see an animal killed but wiping out the man who had deceived them was something else. 'Shame.'

Now Rachel was worried. 'Levi, you have to find Paul and stop him.'

Levi, who had been slouching over the table, drew himself up. 'Yes, Ma. But where do I look?'

'You know your brother better than any of us. You know where he goes, who he meets. Just look for him.'

'I'll go with you.' Gillian put down her paring knife and stood up. 'Two sets of eyes are better than one.'

Rachel saw a look of admiration and relief on Levi's face. 'Is that okay, Ma?'

She nodded. 'Just bring him home.' She paused. 'And, son, be careful, and watch that woman of yours, alright? The town is not a good place to be right now.'

Jacob stood up. 'I'll go too, Ma. Levi might need me.'

They all looked at the youngest Lorimer in amazement. It was the first time in many years that he had even acknowledged Levi's existence.

For his part, Levi seemed ready to burst into tears. 'Can Jacob come too?'

Rachel smiled at her sons. 'I'm sorry, Levi. I know he would be a great help to you, but night is falling and I really need him here to protect the rest of us. Do you understand? Both of you?'

Levi nodded. Jacob said, 'I understand, Ma. And don't worry, I will protect you all.'

It was all Rachel could do not to cry. Were her two warring boys really talking again? Maybe some good would come out of this mess after all.

CHAPTER TWENTY-SIX

'Look, guys, we can't work twenty-four/seven.' Jackman surveyed the room. No one had gone home. They had had a brief catch up and learnt that Robbie and Charlie had had no luck at all with the solicitor. There had been no contact of any kind from Ashcroft since the day he disappeared. All his transactions had been closed, all his properties disposed of, and all his monies moved out to an unknown destination. End of story.

'I suggest you all get off home and be ready to start early tomorrow. We now have some leads and the net is closing in. We are restricting his movements and shutting off some of the places that he retreats to. We also have an up-to-date description and a CCTV shot of him. We are in a better position than before, so tomorrow we tighten the net further, and if all else fails, he has an appointment at the church on Friday.' He looked at each one of them in turn, trying to impress on them the seriousness of the threat Ashcroft posed. 'Watch your backs. Stay vigilant every moment. Trust no one, and ring in at the slightest hint of something being wrong. Got it?'

There was general a murmur of agreement, and Gary said, 'And the same goes for you, boss.'

Jackman nodded. 'I'm not going to underestimate this man, believe me. Now get home.' He stopped, looked at Rosie. 'And don't worry. This is not goodbye. Once this horrible case is over, we'll give you the best send-off ever, I promise.'

Rosie smiled rather sadly. 'I'll hold you to that, sir. Go careful, all of you, I couldn't bear it if—'

Jackman held up his hand. 'You think of yourself and your little ones. And even though you won't be here, keep your policeman's head on, Rosie, and stay watchful. Treat everyone with caution until this psycho is locked up, understand?'

'I won't need telling twice, sir, believe me.'

They all stood up. Each of them hugged Rosie, gathered up their things and filed out.

Jackman felt a rush of emotion. How lucky he was to have such a loyal team. He promised himself that they would come through this unscathed. He had to get to Ashcroft, before he got to them.

* * *

Kenneth Harcourt had earned himself something of a name in the shooting world. His club, the Fenside, was considered one of the best in the region. Deciding to use that to his advantage, he rang the two biggest rival clubs, both of whom hosted Sniper Experience Days. He had spoken to them before, trying to discover if Ralph Renwick had booked a place on a course in the last month or so. This time he was asking for lists of all their members and the guests who had booked on those courses.

He knew both owners pretty well and decided to tell them exactly why he was making this request. He and his club had been targeted, and he needed their help. The police would be making the same request, but friend to friend, he hoped they would help him.

Within half an hour, he had two lists giving the names of all the people who had taken part in the Sniper Days.

Both clubs had strict membership requirements. No one with a criminal conviction could join, and everyone using the club's weapons had to produce a valid passport or driver's licence. Those using their own guns had to supply shotgun and firearms certificates. Everything was photocopied and kept on file, including a photo.

Harcourt had become obsessed with finding the man who had shot and killed first his friend Arthur and now, at the entrance to his property, a police officer. He considered everything this killer did as a personal affront. To add insult to injury, he was using Harcourt's own gun to carry out his murderous attacks.

He scanned the pictures eagerly, hoping for a glimpse of someone he recognised, particularly Ralph Renwick. No one seemed to fit the bill. Dejected, he tossed the papers onto his desk. Then he thought again and picked them up. They were of no use to him, but maybe there was a face on one of those lists that meant something to the police? Harcourt picked up the phone and rang the mobile number for the detective inspector called Jackman.

* * *

Soon, Jackman was staring at the lists Kenneth Harcourt had sent. He had no idea what this Ralph Renwick looked like, but nevertheless, he checked them carefully in case a face cropped up that was known to them. Many of the images were typical passport mugshots, and far from clear. Then, on the last page, a face caught his attention. He realised that he hadn't been looking for Ashcroft, he had been looking for the shooter, using the estate agent's description. But the face staring out at Jackman was that of Alistair Ashcroft, he was sure of it. Ashcroft in one of his many disguises.

His mind went into overdrive. Ashcroft on a sniper course?

Jackman groaned out loud. Oh, sweet Lord, there was no deranged gunman! They'd been looking for two killers when there was only one! He closed his eyes and put his head in his hands. What had the gunman said to Kevin? *Tell him not to get side-tracked with his old adversary, because I'm just as dangerous.* What was he saying? That he had changed, become a different kind of killer? A new adversary? Jackman exhaled. He needed to talk to Laura.

He hurried downstairs to find the duty sergeant. He briefly told him he suspected that the shooter could be Ashcroft, then had him circulate the message. He daren't risk anyone underestimating the man they'd thought was a hired gun.

Next, he made one of his very rare trips down to the basement to visit Orac, the High Priestess of the IT department. It was a standing joke that Orla Cracken, aka Orac, terrified Jackman. It wasn't so much her white blonde Mohican haircut but the mirror contact lenses she wore that Jackman found so disturbing. He generally sent Marie to talk to her, but tonight it was down to him. He set his jaw and made for the stairs.

He found Orac alone in her hi-tech domain. He wondered if she ever went home. Did she even have one? Besides the fact that she lived and breathed computing, he also knew that she had a secret, something to do with her past, which she had once revealed to Marie. For once, Marie had refused to share it with him, saying she didn't betray confidences. So not only was Orac exceptionally brilliant, but she was mysterious too.

'You must be in rather desperate need, Detective Inspector Jackman, to risk venturing unaccompanied into my lair.' Those metallic eyes betrayed nothing, but he knew she was teasing him.

'You know me so well, Orac. Yes, I do need your help.' He handed her the photo of the man he suspected to be Ashcroft. 'We believe we have a match for one of those likenesses you produced. Do you think you'd be able to play with this driving licence photo and see if it is the same man?'

'Of course. Would you like me to ring your mobile tonight when I have something for you?'

'If it's not too much trouble,' he said politely.

'Oh, anything for you, Inspector.'

She did it every time. Orac had made him blush. No matter how hard he tried to act the professional, he always finished up like a tongue-tied schoolboy. He murmured another thank-you and scuttled away, calling himself names as he went.

Outside the building, he rang Marie. 'I'm on my way to meet Laura, so she can give me her opinion. I'll ring you later with an update and we can discuss it.' He paused. 'Second thoughts, I had promised to take Laura and Sam out tonight for something to eat, a bit of a celebration, even if it's not the most appropriate of times. Why don't you and Gary drive over to Greenborough and join us? A Greenborough restaurant will be a damned sight safer than any of Saltern's at the moment.'

Marie asked where they should meet them.

'DI Nikki Galena recommended an Italian place close to the market. It's called Mario's. Do you know it?'

'I'll find it. You know me, boss. I can sniff out food at five hundred paces. What's the celebration anyway?'

'Tell you when we see you.' Jackman ended the call and hastened to his car. He couldn't wait to get Laura and Sam's opinions on his theory.

A&E was still very busy when he arrived at the hospital. Through the crowds of waiting patients, he glimpsed Laura, talking to one of the hospital psychologists. He made his way over to her.

'Kevin is just being discharged. His mother and father are taking him home with them for a couple of days, after which his partner Alan has arranged to take some leave. He'll move in for a while to keep an eye on him.' She gave Jackman a relieved smile. 'He'll survive. He just needs some time away from the job. I've volunteered to keep some regular slots free for him. Talking it through will be a big part of his recovery.'

'As long as nothing else happens.' Jackman had not wanted to sound so negative, but the words had slipped out. So far no one had come up with a plausible reason for Ashcroft selecting Kevin as witness to the various horrors he'd devised, and Jackman had an awful feeling that he wasn't finished with him yet.

'We can't allow ourselves to think like that,' Laura said, in gentle reproof. 'Being on sick leave will get him away from the sharp end for a while. I've suggested that he and Alan go away for a few days, maybe get some sea air. I can't see Ashcroft traipsing around the country after him, can you?'

He couldn't. Ashcroft was far too busy in Saltern to go trotting off to the seaside. 'You're right, but I can't help worrying about him. He came too close to a complete breakdown this time, and I'd hate to see such a promising young man leave the force because of that twisted bastard Ashcroft.'

He took her arm and led her to a quiet corner where several wheelchairs were parked. 'I badly need to talk to you and Sam about a new development regarding Ashcroft, and I hope you don't mind, but I've asked Marie and Gary to join us at Mario's.'

Laura smiled. 'That's wonderful. I haven't had a chance to chat to Marie for ages.' She hesitated. 'You haven't changed your mind, have you — about us?'

Jackman kissed her cheek. 'No, Laura Archer, I have not! Now, I'd like to speak to Kevin before he leaves, then we'll find Sam and get over to the restaurant.'

Laura went to fetch Sam. Jackman found Kevin sitting alone in a cubicle. 'Sir! It's really kind of you to come back. I feel much better now. Just really shaky.'

'I'm glad to hear that, Kevin. I came to see you because I don't want you to worry about your transfer to CID. After you've had a break and feel strong enough to jump back in the deep end, your new job will be waiting for you. Just don't rush it. You will have to be assessed anyway, so chill for a while.' He grinned. 'And take advantage of Laura's offer. She's a damned good psychologist, apart from being a great human being. She will help you.'

'I know, sir. And I promise to see her regularly.' Kevin hesitated. 'I do realise that this will take a lot of getting over. It's bound to have an effect.'

'Good man.' A nurse carrying a clipboard came bustling into the cubicle. 'Time I went, Kevin. You take care, okay?'

The difference that just a couple of hours had made was remarkable. Kevin Stoner would make it back to the Force. He'd be a changed man certainly, but that wouldn't stop him being a fine detective.

Jackman saw Laura waving to him from the far end of the emergency ward, where she stood waiting with Sam. He took a deep breath. It was going to be a momentous evening.

My life's partner. His heart skipped a beat. He still couldn't quite believe that she was prepared to share her life with him — him, with all his flaws, his failings. It seemed too good to be true, yet it was real.

'Ready?' Laura asked.

'Ready.'

* * *

In the static caravan that he shared with Jacob, Noah was busy carving a piece of wood. Supposed to be a heron, it wasn't coming out right. He wasn't concentrating, that was the problem.

Jacob was playing patience and talking softly to himself.

Noah was tempted to ask him the reason for his sudden change of heart regarding their eldest brother, Levi, but he decided to leave well alone. It was a mystery what went on in Jacob's head.

'I wonder where Paul went,' Jacob said suddenly. 'I mean, I know he's looking for that man, but where?'

Noah shrugged. 'Who knows? He could be anywhere.'

'Why did he make us do all those things, Noah? Why did he lie? That posh man really loved that horse of his. That's a bad thing to do, taking something someone loves. Will we go to hell, Noah?'

'Ma says no. We were just gullible, whatever that means. Anyhow, it weren't our fault. Some people are just bad, Jacob. I hope they catch him and lock him up where he can't hurt people anymore.' Noah felt his anger rising again. He hated being made a fool of.

'Well, I hope Paul finds him, don't you?' Jacob shuffled his cards then began building little card houses out of them.

'He could get in very serious trouble if he does — I mean, if he hurts him.' He frowned. 'Then Ma would be all upset and angry again.'

Jacob pulled a face. 'Oh, that's not good at all.'

'No, it's not.'

Jacob suddenly looked like a small boy. 'Noah, I didn't tell Ma everything. Should I?'

Noah turned cold. 'Depends what it was. Tell me, then we'll decide afterwards.'

'Should I tell her about the gun Paul had with him?'

Noah closed his eyes. Oh shit! 'His air rifle, you mean?'

'No, it was a little gun.' Jacob pointed two fingers at his brother. 'Bang! bang.'

'Where did he get a gun like that from?'

Jacob flinched. 'Don't yell at me! I don't know!'

'Sorry! Sorry! I'm just frightened. It's just . . . I never knew Paul had one of those.' Noah stood up and began to pace.

'So? What about telling Ma?'

'Let me think, okay?' Noah didn't know what to do. It seemed to him that whatever he did his mother would be livid. What did she used to say? Something about rocks and hard places. He came to a sudden decision.

'Noah?' Jacob was staring at him expectantly.

'We have to tell her. She'll never forgive us if we don't.' Noah opened the door. 'Come on.'

Slowly, reluctantly, Jacob followed him. Noah recalled another of his mother's expressions — "a lamb to the slaughter." He knew what that one meant alright.

CHAPTER TWENTY-SEVEN

The meal had been a good idea. While his friends relaxed, Jackman decided to get the work stuff out of the way before explaining the reason for this sudden celebration.

Both Laura and Sam agreed there was a strong possibility that Ashcroft was following the pattern of many serial killers and was beginning to alter and refine his MO to accommodate new circumstances.

'His original crusade, aimed at making those poor people pay for what he saw as their transgressions, is done with,' Sam said. 'Now he simply wants revenge. The compulsion to kill is just as strong, and he still uses the same kind of signature that he used before — the photos and messages — but he no longer has to match the punishment to the crime.'

Laura added, 'He has chosen a different method — assassination using a gun — and has adopted a different persona. He's no longer the avenging dark angel, he's a hunter, and you, Jackman, and you, Marie, are the prey.'

'And all the others are collateral damage, as far as he is concerned.' Jackman nodded thoughtfully. 'Including an entire town that he's reduced to a state of abject terror.'

'He's probably loving it, the bastard,' muttered Marie.

'Without a doubt,' said Sam. 'Serial killers crave attention.'

'He must have been planning it for a long time,' Laura said. 'Ever since you foiled his previous activities.'

'The patient man.' Jackman sighed.

Everyone was quiet for a while, then Gary said, 'How will the fact that we've brought a halt to his game with the Lorimers and are now watching his precious church affect him?'

'He doesn't yet know for certain that we have pinpointed the very church he uses, but he might well have his suspicions. He seems to spend a lot of time looking at us through a camera lens, so he could even have seen us checking out the different churches,' said Marie.

'He's very clever,' Laura said, 'so he will probably have factored that possibility into his plans.'

'Over to Plan B,' said Sam, unfolding his serviette and placing it across his lap.

Jackman poured everyone a glass of water. It should have been champagne tonight, but they all needed to keep their heads clear.

As he replaced the bottle on the table, his phone rang.

'Bugger!' said Marie. 'What now?'

They watched his face as he listened to the duty sergeant.

He ended the call and turned to them. 'Shots were fired in Saltern a short while ago. Uniform and a tactical firearms unit were close by.'

Marie groaned. 'And?'

'All under control. It seems a group of gang members from the Carborough Estate here in Greenborough went hunting for a rival drug dealer. Things went pear-shaped and some little scrote pulled a gun, but they hadn't taken into consideration the huge numbers of police on the streets. No one hurt, three thugs banged up and a drug dealer's address raided. Pretty good collar, I'd say.'

The relief on everyone's faces was almost comical.

Before anyone could speak, two waitresses arrived, carrying steaming plates of food. Jackman sniffed the aroma appreciatively. This was just what they needed right now.

When everyone had their respective dishes in front of them, Marie turned to Jackman. 'Okay, boss. You've made us wait half the bloody evening — now cough! What's this all about? What are we celebrating?'

Jackman grinned, glanced at Laura and said, 'Laura has agreed to move in with me permanently, we're now partners, officially.' As he told them, he looked quickly around the group, and saw nothing but delight on their faces. No one warned them to be careful, no one said they should wait. They were all united in their determination not to allow Ashcroft to blight their lives and their expectations for the future.

'Best thing I've heard in ages,' said Gary, beaming.

'I'll second that!' Marie reached across the table and squeezed Laura's hand. 'I'm so happy for you.'

For a moment Jackman's sadness for Marie and her lost love came over him again. He felt quite guilty, being so happy with Laura when Marie was still alone. Gary was a great lodger and an enormous help, but he was no life partner. Shaking off the feeling, he said, 'Tell them about our plans for the mill, Laura.'

'Oh yes! The builders have already done a brilliant job making it safe and it's all plumbed in, wired up. The ground floor will make a fantastic consultation room.'

They chatted on, relaxing for the first time in ages. Jackman watched his friends enjoy themselves. For a precious couple of hours, it was as if Ashcroft didn't exist.

Then someone splashed a drop of tomato pasta sauce on the tablecloth. Scarlet on white. Marie's white blouse and the spreading blood stain.

All the horror of the nightmare came flooding back. It was as if Ashcroft himself had walked into the restaurant — a warning to never, ever let his guard down.

Laura took his hand and gave it a reassuring squeeze. Only she had noticed.

He whispered, 'Sorry.'

She smiled rather anxiously, then steered the conversation to the important topic of what to have for dessert.

Not long afterwards they were ready to leave. It would be another early start tomorrow. Jackman paid the bill. It was a pity that he and Laura couldn't drive home together but they had each brought their own car.

They said their goodnights. 'I'm in the hospital car park,' said Laura, 'and so is Sam. It's only a five-minute walk away. You get back to Mill Corner and Sam will walk me to my car, won't you, Sam?'

Sam nodded. 'My pleasure. And listen everyone, as soon as this is over, you must all come to mine for dinner — and get a taxi, because there will be champagne in the fridge! This wonderful news needs a follow-up party.'

'Sounds great,' said Marie, echoed by Gary.

Jackman beamed at Laura. 'It's a date. How about yo—?'

A loud crack ripped through the night and Sam Page collapsed.

'Get down!' Jackman screamed.

They threw themselves onto the pavement and rolled into the shelter of a row of parked cars.

Jackman crawled over to Sam, pulled him into the cover of a shop doorway and did a swift evaluation. 'Marie! Ambulance!'

'Sam!' Laura crawled into the doorway and sank down next to her dear friend. 'Oh, Sam!' Tears ran down her cheeks.

Jackman held both hands over Sam's wound and pressed hard. The blood seeped through his fingers, but Sam was alive.

Already he was beginning to wonder about Ashcroft's game. After all, thus far he had always been fatally accurate, every time. So why just wound Sam?

'Ambulance on its way!' shouted Marie.

'Okay. Just stay where you are, you two. Sam might not have been the prime target. He's hurt, but he's alive.'

Jackman continued to do his best for Sam, willing the twos and blues to get there fast. Sam didn't have age on his side. Jackman remembered Laura telling him that he'd had some kind of heart problem, and from the amount of blood, Jackman was pretty sure that the bullet had damaged a major blood vessel. They needed help or they'd lose him.

Laura was devastated. Jackman had always known how fond she was of her old mentor, but she was reacting as if it was her own father lying wounded on the ground. But of course. Sam Page *was* a father-figure to her. She'd lost her dad at a very young age, and since her days at university, Sam had been there to guide and look out for her.

Sam was regaining consciousness and starting to move.

'Stay still, Sam. You'll be fine. Just keep still until the paramedics get here.'

'What happ . . . ?' Sam groaned.

'Laura, keep talking to him. I need him to stay still because of this bleeding.'

She stroked her mentor's hair. 'It's alright, Sam, we're here. Just lie still, the ambulance is on its way.'

'Marie? Gary?' called Jackman. 'Any idea where the shot came from?'

'Negative,' Gary called back.

'Too dark to see,' added Marie.

'Just stay down. Don't forget, he's a patient man. It could be you he really wants.'

'I think he's done exactly what he wanted to do, sir. He'll be long gone.' Marie sounded angry. 'How's Sam?'

'I'll be a good deal happier when the ambulance gets here.' It was odd that no one else had seen what happened, but he supposed they were off the main road and the restaurant was busy. 'At last!'

Blue lights flashed from the end of the street, which was suddenly filled with people, noise, activity.

Uniformed officers from Greenborough Station were first on the scene, closely followed by two paramedics. Jackman had never been so pleased to see an ambulance in his whole life.

Even though he was inclined to agree with Marie that Ashcroft was already miles away, he still was wary. He was especially concerned for Laura and Marie. Their old adversary could easily bide his time and then strike again.

Jackman handed the scene over to the Greenborough officers, who set about cordoning it off. Laura found him and took his hand. 'Sam's stable, but they are blue-lighting him to A&E. The medics told me the bullet has nicked the brachial artery, which is why he was bleeding so profusely. They need to get it sorted very quickly, or . . .' Her voice shook. Regaining control, she said, 'Luckily the hospital is only minutes away. I'll follow them there.'

'Of course. I'll come with you.' He looked around for Gary and Marie and found them talking to the Greenborough crew. 'Could I ask if one of you would drive my car back to the nick and leave it there for me?' he said. 'I'll go to the hospital with Laura and we'll take her car home.'

'No problem, boss,' said Marie, taking his keys from him. She sighed, looking around her, evidently still searching the dark buildings and black windows for signs of a gun barrel. 'I hope Sam is okay. Tell him we're thinking of him.'

He nodded. 'Of course, I will.'

Gary took Marie's arm. 'Come on, Sarge. Nothing more for us here.'

Jackman turned away. Yet again, that bastard Ashcroft had managed to ruin something beautiful. The man was like a cancer, a malignant evil, stealing beauty and replacing it with something vile. This had to end soon, or Ashcroft would destroy them all.

He wanted to howl in frustration. Just let him make one mistake, he said to himself, one tiny mistake.

* * *

Not far away, another man echoed Jackman's howl. That, too, was silent, sealed off by the gag around Paul Lorimer's mouth. Even though he knew it was hopeless, he strained against the ropes that held him fast to the chair.

How could he have been such a fool? Believing he was hunting down the imposter, he had charged into the lion's den, straight into a trap.

He had often been to the camper van and chatted with the man he believed to be Ezra, over a coffee or a beer. On one occasion he had noticed some letters lying on the table, addressed to Ezra at 7 Abbey Lane, Saltern-le-Fen. But didn't Ezra live near Hull? Puzzled, he made a note of the address.

So, when the false Ezra disappeared, Paul had a good idea where to look for him. He even knew how he had made his escape. About a week before it all happened, he'd seen a motorcycle concealed beneath an old tarpaulin in one of the old outbuildings that they never used. He had recognised it as belonging to a bloke who lived in neighbouring Thatcher's Fen. He'd worked on the engine a couple of times to earn a few extra pounds for Ma's pot. At the time he believed that one of his brothers had stolen it and, reluctant to bring Ma's wrath down on their heads, he held his peace and waited to see what would happen.

He had found it earlier that evening, concealed in the back garden of 7 Abbey Lane. He went to take a closer look.

At that moment a sack was pulled roughly over his head and something struck him squarely on the back of his skull.

Now he was a prisoner.

Paul's anger turned to worry, and then to fear. Why was this man keeping him prisoner? What did he have planned for him?

A tear slid silently from his eye. Some hero he'd turned out to be.

* * *

Rachel Lorimer listened to what Jacob had to say and then sent the two boys back to their caravan. She had been remarkably calm with them.

Paul with a gun and that vile temper of his. Not a good combination.

Rachel weighed up her options, of which there appeared to be three. It was late and there was a very good chance that Paul wouldn't find the imposter anyway. So, option one was that she could just wait for him to come slinking back, tail between his legs, and confront him then about the weapon. Number two was that she could go and look for him herself, but Levi and Gillian were already combing the streets for a sighting of his car. If they found him, they would be sure to bring him home immediately. That left option three, phone Marie Evans.

And if she chose the last one, what then? Paul would be hunted down by an armed unit. Frightened, stupid and with a temper that flared up out of nowhere, Paul could end up dead, shot by a police marksman. Things were bad enough for her already, without losing her son.

Rachel sank down at the kitchen table and put her head in her hands. She felt very old. How on earth had Paul got hold of a gun? And a handgun at that? She could only think it had something to do with the men and women he sometimes worked with on the farms. Most of the migrants were hardworking people but there was a small core of hardened criminals among them. Maybe one of those had asked Paul to hide a weapon for them.

Rachel shook her head. The kids had always been a trial but now they were grown she no longer knew how to deal with them. There was no one to turn to anymore. There would be no more letters from Ezra, no more cards and no one to share her problems with.

Rachel Lorimer was on her own, struggling with a family that was fast getting out of control. All because of one man — someone she didn't even know!

Finally, Rachel stood up and went to the telephone.

CHAPTER TWENTY-EIGHT

Alistair Ashcroft smiled down at the young man, whose face was scarlet with rage and the effort of struggling against his bonds. He shook his head. 'Look, Paul, I understand why you're so angry with me, but you have to see things my way.'

The look he received was murderous. However, Ashcroft was a patient man, so he dragged another chair across the room and sat facing Paul Lorimer.

'The first thing you should know is that you have been lied to by the police. They have told you a whole pack of untruths about me, and because we were friends once, I want you to know the real truth.' He leaned forward, all sincerity. 'The most important thing for you to know is that Ezra and I were close. I loved him like a brother, and I did not kill him.'

Paul was still struggling, but more feebly now.

'Sit still, boy, and listen. If you stay calm and quiet, I'll remove the gag, and if you listen and let me tell you what really happened, I'll untie you and let you go. Deal? What do you lose by just listening? Nothing, right? Think about it, Paul. I didn't have to stay here, did I? I could have gone anywhere, back to where I came from, but I didn't.' He laughed softly. 'I left those letters for you to see. They say you're not very bright, but I disagree, and you've proved me right by finding me when half the police force couldn't do so. That's why I knew I could trust you to help me.' He looked at Paul and raised his eyebrows. 'So? Can I remove the gag?'

He waited.

Paul nodded. Ashcroft moved around to the back of the chair and loosened the gag, which slipped down around the boy's neck. 'Better?'

Paul coughed, then muttered something. The main thing was that he didn't scream. Ashcroft returned to his chair.

'You must have realised you were my favourite. Your brothers are great but I always thought you were special. I'm sorry I lied to get you to help me, like with the gun for instance, but I didn't dare tell the truth. Imagine if I'd told poor Jacob. It would have been a disaster. You are the only one I can really trust.'

'Who are you?' croaked Paul.

'My name is Ralph Renwick, and Ezra was very dear to me. But,' he looked sadly at Paul, 'he got himself involved in some very dodgy deals back in Hull. I tried to warn him but by then he was in too deep. He upset some seriously nasty people and he feared for his life. Sadly, he was right to do so.'

'So *they* killed him? Not you?'

'They did, Paul.'

Paul looked unconvinced. 'But why did you come here? Why pretend to be Ezra?'

'Well, to keep it short, Ezra told me all about your family and how much he cared about you all. He also said you weren't managing very well and that he was worried for your safety. The man he was frightened of lived in Saltern-le-Fen and knew where you lived. I wanted to protect you but also find the man who killed Ezra. That's why I needed the gun that you and Levi stole for me.' He allowed Paul to digest this information. 'And I'm very sorry I had to hit you earlier, but you would never have listened if I'd just tried to talk to you, isn't that right?'

Paul shook his head. 'I wanted to kill you.'

'I know, I know, son. But now you have the truth, and I'm glad. I know you struggle with your temper, Paul, but you are far brighter than the others. I know you will understand that what I'm telling you makes sense. For Ezra's sake, I need to find that man before he gets to your ma and the rest of the family.'

'But why did you have to kill all those other people? I don't understand.'

'You think I killed them?' Ashcroft looked suitably horrified. 'Ezra's killer must have been watching. He stole that gun from me, Paul. After all your efforts, I never even had the chance to use it.'

'So, you are innocent?'

'Of everything, apart from deceiving you boys. And I only did that to help you in the long run. Oh, Paul, I do so wish I had been the real Ezra. I felt so at home with you all. I mean, I treated you well, didn't I? Bought you food and drink? Be fair — would I have done that if I didn't care for you?'

'I guess not.'

That was all he wanted to hear. The bait had been taken.

'Then I'll untie you, we'll have a drink together and I'll answer all your questions, okay?'

Nodding, Paul gave a wan smile.

Alistair Ashcroft smiled back at him. 'Then I need a favour from you, if you're willing? If you do this for me, you will earn yourself and your ma more money than you've ever seen.' He took out a wallet and opened it. 'This is just a little down payment.' He peeled off six fifty-pound notes and pushed them into Paul's pocket. 'You get the rest later. And it's money for nothing, trust me.'

He had watched the boy's eyes glint as he took out the money and knew it had clinched the deal. He untied Paul and gently massaged his wrists and ankles. 'Okay, my friend, you are now my second in command. We have a reconnaissance operation to carry out. But,' he gave Paul a knowing wink, 'they say an army marches on its stomach, so we'll eat first. Then we need to do something about your appearance if we are to move around unnoticed.'

'But the town is full of police, and—'

'Half of them are looking for you, and the rest are looking for me.' Ashcroft gave a contemptuous laugh. 'Fear not, young soldier! For one thing, we are not going into town, and with a couple of simple additions to your clothes, you will be able to walk right past them, believe me.' His laughter faded. 'I want to thank you, Paul, for helping me. As far as I am concerned, catching the man who killed your uncle, my dearest friend, is the most important thing in the whole world. And the only way I can do it is to convince that detective Jackman of my innocence. You understand, don't you?'

Paul looked at him gravely. 'Yes, Ralph, I understand now. Just tell me what I have to do.'

* * *

Marie and Gary finally got home, after what Gary called "a night to remember." Marie was just endeavouring to shut the car door quietly when her mobile rang.

What now? It was late, and a call at this hour did not bode well. She prayed it was not bad news about Sam Page. Cursing softly, she took her phone from her pocket and stared at the display. Unknown number.

Tentatively, she answered. 'Marie Evans.'

'I need your help.'

'Rachel! What's wrong?'

'It's Paul, Marie. He's gone looking for the man who impersonated my Ezra. He said he was going to kill him.'

Marie knew what it must have taken for Rachel Lorimer to pick up that phone. 'Listen, Rachel, I'm really pleased that you rang me, but don't worry yourself too much. We have half the Fenland Constabulary out looking for that man, and if we can't find him, how will Paul?' *Unless he knows something that we don't.*

'I know that, but just . . . if he did find him, there's something you really need to know.'

Rachel Lorimer paused. Marie waited.

'He has a gun.'

Marie closed her eyes. Had Saltern-le-Fen suddenly turned into bloody Dodge City? Did everyone tote a gun nowadays? 'Do you mean his air rifle?' She recalled that all bar one of the Lorimers used them to keep the rats down.

'No. Jacob saw it. He said it was a pistol.'

'Where on earth . . . ?'

'I don't know! I'm just scared for him, and I don't want you lot shooting him either!' Rachel sounded almost hysterical, which was unlike her.

'Calm down, Rachel, we won't shoot him.' *Unless he does something really stupid.* 'But — and this is important — does Paul know where this man might be?'

'I don't think so. I mean, why would he?'

'Maybe he gave him an indication, when he was acting as Ezra?'

'I doubt it, and you know my kids, Marie. You don't drop hints to them, not one of them will catch on.' She paused for a moment then added, 'I sent my Levi and Gillian to Saltern to look for him and bring him home.'

What to say? Marie certainly didn't want to give Rachel the unvarnished truth, that the streets were alive with police officers, some heavily armed, all hyped up and looking for Ashcroft. The tension out there was palpable, nerves were stretched to their limit. It was not a good place to wander around at night, especially carrying a gun.

'Look, I know you have to do whatever you have to, Marie. But he's not a bad boy. He's just angry and hurt . . . If you can, please help him.'

'Of course I will. I'll do everything in my power. Now, does either Levi or Gillian have a mobile phone? Can you contact them and ask them to come home? They would be safer with you.'

'We can't afford them mobile things. We don't have nice fat police salaries, like you, Marie Evans.'

'Sorry, Rachel, I didn't think.'

Rachel Lorimer didn't deign to respond. 'I just want my kids back safe.'

'I'm going to ring the duty sergeant right now, Rachel, and ask him to tell his guys to look out for Levi and Gillian.'

'Good. And Paul?'

'The same goes for him. Let's just hope he doesn't wave that gun around. I'll tell uniform that he's not a threat, but to be careful not to frighten him. It's the best I can do.'

'That's all I can ask.' There was a rustling of paper. 'Now here's Levi and Paul's car numbers. Levi has an old Vauxhall and Paul drives a Renault.'

Marie wrote down the licence numbers, make and colour of the cars. It wasn't a big town, and with so many people keeping off the streets, uniform should find them without too much trouble. It was Paul's reaction if approached that worried Marie. 'I've got your number. I'll ring you if I have any news — and, Rachel? You call me if any or all of them come home, no matter what the time, okay?'

Marie ended the call, and hurried inside the house.

Gary was boiling the kettle for a cup of tea. 'I don't even want to ask what that was about.'

Marie raised her eyes to the ceiling. 'Oh, nothing much. Paul Lorimer has turned into Roy Rogers and has gone after Ashcroft with a pistol. Levi's organised a posse to fetch him back, and his ma wants us to find them all and send them home. That family!' She shook her head. 'But I'll have to ring the station and report it. I can see the headlines now — police gun down poor deprived kid with learning difficulties. The public will love it.'

'And are you going to tell Jackman?' asked Gary, taking milk from the fridge.

'I have to. And I'll get the latest on Sam at the same time.' Her expression darkened. 'That gunshot is still ringing in my ears, how about you?'

'I'm trying not to think about it. It was such a good evening up until then. I was totally relaxed — then, bang!' He shuddered. 'I can say it now, Marie — I was scared. Really scared.'

'You weren't alone, Gary. I was shitting myself. Ashcroft promised to take me out one day, and I thought that day had come.'

Gary handed her a mug of tea. 'Make your calls, before we frighten the life out of each other.'

Marie smiled at him. 'Thanks for being here, Gary. I think I might have fallen apart if I were on my own. At least we can buoy each other up, can't we?'

He grinned at her. 'That's what mates are for. And it works both ways. I may be a man but that doesn't mean I don't need a bit of support.' He pointed to the phone. 'Ring it in, before Wyatt Earp Junior starts cleaning up the town.'

* * *

Sam Page was being assessed prior to surgery and Jackman and Laura had been asked to wait outside. Jackman had got them coffee, which tasted even worse than the stuff the station provided.

Despite his attempts to persuade her to go home, Laura had insisted on staying. 'It's all my fault, Rowan. I should never have got him involved. I knew how dangerous Ashcroft was and yet I still asked Sam to come and stay with me after the apartment was broken into.'

Jackman had never seen her so distressed. 'Sam was aware of the danger,' he said gently, 'and he came to you, didn't he? You didn't force him. I reckon he'd have been pretty hurt if you hadn't turned to him, don't you think?'

Laura didn't reply.

'If anyone's to blame, it's me,' Jackman said. 'I let my guard down tonight, and no one should know better than me that you never do that with Ashcroft on the loose. Just because we were out of Saltern, I allowed myself to believe that we were safe for a few hours. I just wanted everyone to take a breather and enjoy themselves, remind them that there's a life away from mayhem and murder.'

Laura took his hand. 'There's really only one person to blame, isn't there? It's not your fault, and nor is it mine.'

'The main thing is that Sam is still alive.' That still puzzled him. *Why* was Sam not dead? Unlike Christopher, Barney, William and Ernie.

'Thank the Lord,' whispered Laura. 'He's been like a father to me over the years, always there to talk me through the tough cases or just to discuss interesting ones. I'm not sure what I would have done if he had been killed.'

Jackman wondered that too. When they had talked about families in the past, Laura had always steered the conversation away from herself. It had soon become clear that it was a subject to avoid. 'What happened to your real father? Don't tell me if you'd rather not.'

'He died,' she said simply, 'far too young.'

Not wanting to push her, Jackman assumed it must have been cancer or something like that. 'That's rough on a kid,' he said softly.

'He went to work one day — he was a consultant psychologist too, you know — and he never came home.'

'It's alright, darling. You don't need to say any more.'

'I was always going to tell you one day,' Laura said softly. 'It's no secret, it just hurts, so I try not to think about it. You see, a patient he was treating pushed him out of a window and he fell to his death. He was thirty-eight.'

Jackman closed his eyes. 'I'm so sorry!'

'That's why I became a psychologist too, to continue his work caring for the damaged people that need help so badly. A few years later, Mum married again and moved abroad. I never really took to my stepfather, so I was pretty much on my own after it happened.'

Jackman didn't know what to say. He'd often wondered how people coped with such situations, when someone close to you is suddenly erased. And of course, it had happened to his brother James. When his beautiful wife went out one day and didn't return, James had fallen apart.

Laura squeezed his hand. 'It's alright, honestly. I should have told you ages ago.'

Before he could respond, a nurse beckoned to them. 'You can go back in for a while, but we will be prepping him for theatre shortly.'

Sam was conscious but heavily sedated. Even so, he smiled when he saw Laura. 'Sleepy,' he murmured. 'Very sleepy.'

'How's the pain, Sam?' asked Jackman.

'Pain?'

'Ah, they've given you some of the strong stuff then?'

'Feel wonderful,' burbled Sam, and closed his eyes.

The nurse checked the monitors. 'I suggest you go and get some rest now. He's booked for theatre quite soon and afterwards he'll be taken to Intensive Care. The bullet damaged the brachial artery, and we have a vascular surgeon coming in to operate on him. It's a complicated procedure, and we'll need to monitor his heart very carefully as he's had cardiac problems in the past.'

'I'd rather stay,' said Laura.

'I'm afraid you won't be able to see him, probably until tomorrow lunchtime at the earliest. You can leave your number and we'll ring you should there be any cause for concern.'

Jackman put his arm around her. 'You need some sleep, Laura, and so do I. He's in safe hands.'

Laura hesitated, then nodded. 'You're right. But I'll drop you off at the station early in the morning and come straight back here.'

He was happy with that. He was also happy that a number of uniformed officers were in attendance at the hospital. Sam would not be left alone anywhere the public had access. He didn't think Ashcroft would be back, but they were taking no chances.

As they drove home, Laura suddenly said, 'Ashcroft never intended to kill him, did he? It was a message for you.' She laid her hand on his leg. 'Sam's wound is in the identical spot where he shot you.'

He nodded. 'Except I was lucky. It was a smaller-calibre bullet and it missed the artery.'

So he had been right to wonder. Ashcroft never missed his mark and he hadn't this time either. As Laura said, he was just reminding Jackman what he was capable of.

CHAPTER TWENTY-NINE

Uniform located Levi and Gillian at around one in the morning and sent them straight back to Hawker's Fen. They had no luck with Paul, or his car, and by morning, Rachel Lorimer was not the only one to be worried.

Jackman tried not to imagine the worst, but it wasn't easy. Paul Lorimer was a vulnerable adult. He'd always been a loose cannon, always had a short fuse, and now he was carrying a lethal weapon.

Jackman was in the office waiting for Ruth Crooke to arrive so that he could give her a report on the previous night's events. Laura had told him that Sam had pulled through the operation and was being closely monitored. It was a huge relief, but he worried about Laura being at the hospital on her own. Unbeknownst to her he had contacted DI Nikki Galena and explained the situation. Nikki had immediately made sure that her uniforms on duty at Greenborough Hospital were watching Laura as well as Sam Page. The knowledge made Jackman feel a little easier.

During the original investigation and before he and Marie were injured, Jackman had felt some compassion for the terribly damaged little boy who had become a psychotic killer. Now, all that he felt was frustration and the urgency of stopping him. All empathy had gone. Jackman noticed that he was having deeply emotional thoughts and was sometimes overwhelmed by his fear for his colleagues and the dreadful burden of responsibility for their safety. Then there were the recurring flashbacks from that nightmare. Trying to staunch the bleeding from Sam's gunshot wound was traumatic enough, without having to contend with the notion that he was actually working on Marie.

Jackman checked his watch. Ruth would be here soon. That bloody nightmare. Why hadn't it faded by now? In fact it seemed to return with increasing force every time it came into his mind. He kept telling himself it was just a bad dream. They did sometimes stay with you. Indeed, he could still recall some of his dreams from childhood — both good and bad. He knew it was no portent of doom, Jackman was far too hardboiled for that kind of rubbish, but he wanted it gone. Every time it came back, it stole his reason for just a few seconds, but those seconds could be vital if he needed to deal with some emergency.

With a vicious swing of his forearm, Jackman swept the reports from his desk. Not content with disrupting his waking life, Ashcroft had even invaded his sodding dreams!

Releasing his anger seemed to have helped. As he knelt and gathered the papers up, he felt the positive Jackman return. Come on, he told himself, we're turning the screw. We are making it difficult for anyone to move freely in the town, and that had to include Ashcroft. And there would be no let up. When Ruth was told of Sam's injuries, still more troops would be drafted in to Saltern-le-Fen, he was sure. If he and Marie really were the objects of Ashcroft's attention, and were going nowhere, then Ashcroft would be forced to remain too, and suffer the consequences of trying to work in a town that looked as if martial law had been declared. 'Good,' murmured Jackman out loud. 'Now you feel the heat for a change, Alistair Ashcroft.'

* * *

In fact, Alistair Ashcroft was feeling very pleased at how things had turned out. His little experiment had worked far better than even he had anticipated. Almost from the beginning he had singled out Paul from the other Lorimer boys and if Paul had not come looking for him, he would have gone to him. He had an important role for the youngster.

Ashcroft was no fool. He could see it was becoming increasingly difficult to operate freely in Saltern, but it didn't matter. He was tiring of this game. It was so one-sided. He had expected more of the Fenland Constabulary's finest.

He had stayed awake into the early hours of the morning, trying to analyse why he felt the way he did and had come to no conclusion. After all, this was no crusade, fuelled by a deep longing to right a wrong, like last time. The satisfaction each death had brought him then seemed hard to replicate this time around. Something was lacking. Maybe it was time to move on. He would get rid of his two pathetic opponents and disappear.

Now he had Paul Lorimer to do his bidding, everything was in place. He could bring it all to a close, today if he wanted, or tomorrow at the latest. He was a patient man, but the waiting was over. This was Jackman and Marie's last twenty-four hours.

'Paul, my friend, when you have finished eating, I'm going to lay out our plan of action and we'll see what you think of it.'

* * *

Rachel Lorimer sounded both relieved and angry.

'Paul's safe, Marie. He phoned us. He's in Greenborough. He went on a bender and has apparently been sleeping it off in some bedsit belonging to someone he knows from work. He's coming home as soon as he's got the alcohol out of his system and is fit to drive.'

For some reason, Marie wasn't totally convinced. 'Did you ask him about the gun?'

'He said that Jacob is telling fairy stories. He admits he did say he would kill the fake Ezra if he found him, but he never had a gun. He told me to tell Jacob to stop fibbing and getting him into trouble. I told him he didn't need Jacob, he had gotten himself into quite enough trouble all on his own.'

Rachel seemed content with Paul's explanation. But . . . Marie's doubts remained. 'When he gets home, please ring me. I'd like to talk to him, okay?'

'Of course, and I'm sorry to have caused a lot of fuss for nothing.'

'We were as worried as you, Rachel. I'm just pleased that you've heard from him. Uh, did he sound okay? Other than the hangover?'

'Absolutely fine. He said he was sorry. He's not used to strong alcohol. He pretty well never drinks, so I think it hit him hard. Serve him right, young fool! I won't let him forget this in a hurry, believe me.'

Rachel hung up, leaving Marie undecided whether to breathe a sigh of relief or worry even more. She went to see if Jackman was back from the super's office.

She found him in the corridor talking to Robbie and Max. She immediately knew from their faces that something was wrong. She hurried towards them, almost frightened to ask what it was.

Jackman's expression was grim. 'Laura just rang me. Sam's taken a turn for the worse. Ruth Crooke is on her way to the hospital now. He has no family, and he's been a huge help to us in the past, so she thought it appropriate.'

'Do you want to go?' Marie asked immediately. 'You must want to be with Laura.'

'She's going to text me if his condition deteriorates further. Meanwhile, we have a possible lead to Ashcroft. Robbie and Max are just heading out to see if it's viable.'

'It sounds kosher, Sarge. Where we are going is only twenty miles from here, so we'll report in as soon as, okay?' Max said.

It was good to hear his familiar Cockney voice again. She watched them hurry off. 'I've just heard from Rachel

Lorimer, sir. She says Paul rang her. Apparently he got hammered and had been sleeping it off at a mate's house in Greenborough.'

'One less problem to worry about,' Jackman said.

'If it's true,' she retorted.

'You think otherwise, Marie?'

She frowned. 'It doesn't quite fit with what we know about Paul Lorimer, sir. Like the fact that he rarely drinks. And how did he get to Greenborough if he was drunk?'

'Anyone can drown their sorrows if they are upset or pissed off enough. And if he doesn't drink much, well, it would hit him like a runaway train.' He looked at her thoughtfully. 'And maybe his mate drove his car there for him? Who knows? Or maybe he went straight to Greenborough when he couldn't find Ashcroft here?'

'I know. I've told myself all that, but it still niggles. I can't see him giving up that easily if he was seeing red over the fake Ezra.'

'I see. Well, I know those "niggles" of yours, so if you're having one now, keep in touch with Rachel Lorimer until you know he's actually home and safe.'

'I've already planned to do that.' Marie shrugged. 'I'm probably fretting over nothing but I won't be happy until I see or talk to him myself.' She gathered her thoughts. 'So, what is this lead?'

On their way to his office, Jackman said, 'There's another thing we have to thank Kenneth Harcourt for. He's been talking to two other gun clubs, both of whom conduct Sniper Experience Days, and one of them put him on to their firearms training officer, who's ex-army. Harcourt asked him if he'd had anyone on a course in the last few months who had been cause for concern in any way. The guy said not especially, but did get back to Harcourt a bit later saying that there was one man that he had found a bit disturbing.'

They went into Jackman's office.

'And . . . the man in question is the one who from his driving licence photo resembles Ashcroft.' Jackman picked up a scribbled memo. 'Listen to this. "This particular guy was intense, really so. Most applicants for this course are armchair heroes, acting out some video game. Some are adrenaline junkies, some want to go a step further than Paintball, and others want a taster of army life to see if it's for them. This guy didn't fit into any category I've ever come across before."' Jackman looked up. 'It sounded worth sending Rob and Charlie to ask a few more questions.'

'I'll say. I look forward to their call.' Her face fell. 'But I'm not looking forward to a call from Greenborough Hospital. Are you sure you don't want to go, boss? I can hold the fort here.'

'Thanks, Marie, but with the super off site, I'll hang on a bit longer. I'll ring Laura shortly and keep you posted on how Sam's doing. Meanwhile, I suggest we just keep busy.'

Marie returned to her desk. She wanted to ask forensics if they had found any interesting evidence on the jacket that she had pulled off the little scrote who had placed a wreath on her motorbike.

'Ah, telepathy! I was about to ring you, dear heart,' Rory said. 'Although not about that rather manky jacket. Now, let me see . . . it's here somewhere.'

Marie could hear him rummaging through papers.

'Here we are,' said Rory. 'There was nothing of significance that could lead to identifying the owner, but there was an inordinate amount of animal fur, hair and other assorted detritus on it. I'm not talking about a moggie or a pet pooch here, this was sheep's wool, cow, donkey and pig hairs, apart from a hefty dose of chicken shit. Regular young farmer, he was.'

'One of the Lorimers,' murmured Marie. 'It has to be.' In retrospect, the more she thought about the retreating figure that she had pursued down her road, the more she believed it could have been Noah. If only she had seen his face! She'd seen one of those jackets in his caravan, but it could have belonged to Jacob. Not that it really mattered anymore. Ashcroft had moved on considerably since then. 'Thanks, Rory. So, what were you going to ring me about?'

'Well, we found the bullet that killed your colleague, Ernie Teal, buried deep in his brain, and although my talented young Spike told you it was doubtful that he would be able to identify the gun, the dear boy underestimated his own talents. It was an S&W 500 cartridge. You are almost certainly looking for a Smith and Wesson Model 500, one of the most powerful handguns in the world and most definitely capable of killing with a single shot. It has as much firepower as a rifle.'

Marie groaned. 'Just what I needed to hear, Rory. Bad enough having a psycho wandering the streets, but with one of those tucked in his underpants . . . It doesn't bear thinking about.'

'Well, I for one can think of better things to keep in one's boxers.' Rory giggled.

Laughing, Marie thanked him and hung up. Where had Ashcroft got a revolver like that? Since talking to Kenneth Harcourt, she had a new appreciation of the financial value of weapons.

She stood up. She had better pass this on to Jackman. Then it came to her that she'd forgotten to ring her mother. Marie pulled out her mobile and called Rhiannon.

As she waited for her to answer, Marie had a sudden longing to just throw a few things into a bag, fill up the bike and take off for Wales. The thought of the solitude of the mountains brought a lump to her throat.

'Sorry, darling. I'm doing the prescription run for the wrinklies this morning and the signal's bad in this place.' He mother's voice came and went with the poor signal strength. 'I'll find a better spot and ring you back.'

A few moments later she was back on the line. 'Better? I'm in between the two valleys and it's usually okay here.'

'Much better, Mum. I just wanted you to know that I'm alright, just overworked, and it was too late to ring last night.'

'It's never too late. But I know how busy you are.' There was a pause and her mother said, 'You have no idea how much I worry about you, Marie. There was a breaking news flash on the BBC earlier. It said a police officer had been killed in Lincolnshire. It was your killer's handiwork, wasn't it?'

'You know I can't say, but as you are rarely wrong about anything . . .'

'Was he a colleague?'

'I hardly knew him, but it makes no difference, he was one of us, and the whole force is hurting.'

'This might sound hard, my darling, but don't let it distract you or make you angry. Keep a cool head and think clearly. You're a fine detective, so don't let this evil man make you emotional, because I'm sure that's his plan.'

'Oh yes, Mum, he knows how to cause chaos alright.' She thought of Sam Page, another innocent victim, hanging somewhere between life and death. It was all collateral damage to Ashcroft.

'If only it were possible, I would drive right now to your misty fens, gather you up and bring you home.' Her mum had a catch in her voice.

'There's nothing I would rather do, and that's the truth, Mum.'

They both sighed. 'But that won't happen,' her mother said. She lowered her voice. 'I'll be praying for you, for all of you. Try to stay safe, my angel, and look after that lovely Jackman.'

'Oh yes, I'll do that, I promise.'

After a few more comforting words, Marie ended the call, promising herself that as soon as this was over, she would take some leave and bugger off to Wales.

She was already making plans for the care of her cat when she heard Jackman calling. 'Got five minutes, Marie?'

'On my way. Shall I bring coffee?'

'Mind reader!'

Jackman looked a lot less sombre. 'Sam's out of the woods. He's still being monitored very carefully but the crisis has passed. Laura said that barring anything unforeseen, he'll pull through.' Jackman looked almost elated. 'You know, I had no idea just how much Laura thought of that old chap. She was totally grief-stricken. And he was standing right next to her. It was bad enough for us, but Laura's not law enforcement. She'd never experienced anything like it before. Anyway, she's over the moon that he's recovering now, and I've got DI Nikki Galena's troops keeping a close eye on her as well as Sam.'

'Smart move, sir.' She told him about what Rory had said, and about the handgun.

'I really do not like all this weaponry he's got hold of.' Jackman's face creased into a frown. 'I just pray that Ashcroft doesn't have some kind of major finale planned.'

'Like a mass shooting?' asked Marie. She imagined shopping centres, fleeing crowds.

Jackman just nodded. 'Except that he'd know it would mean his own death. Our tactical units would take him out, no question.'

'And he did say it would come down to the three of us in the end, didn't he?' Marie said.

Jackman's desk phone rang. Max's Cockney accent filled the room — Jackman had switched on loudspeaker.

'Quick update, boss. This is good, better than we hoped. That training officer has fingered Ashcroft for certain. He's coming back with us to make a full statement — Rob and me thought you'd like to hear what he has to say — but right now we are checking another bit of interesting info.'

Jackman glanced at Marie, whispering, 'Better and better.'

'The security here is as tight as a duck's backside, and I don't reckon matey-boy Ashcroft was aware of exactly how tight it was. They have hidden cameras all over the shop, and our firearms officer here, whose name is Nicholas Benfield, reckons he's got some really tasty snaps of our Alistair,' he paused, '*and* his car.'

Marie leant forward.

'Can't wait to meet this man,' said Jackman, 'and see his rogue's gallery.'

'As soon as we've gathered everything up, we'll be on our way, boss. See you travelling time plus twenty.'

Jackman hung up. 'We are inching ever closer, aren't we?'

'"By strength and guile, we'll get him." Now where did that come from?'

'It's the motto for the Special Boat Services, the special forces unit that Barney, aka Arthur Barnes belonged to,' Jackman said.

'Well, it seemed fitting. This is one interview I do not want to miss.'

'Neither shall you.' Jackman smiled. 'Thank heavens this gun club is not too far away. I can't wait to get this man's opinion of Ashcroft's skill as a sniper, can you?'

'Can I ever!'

* * *

'Well done! I'm proud of you.' Ashcroft nodded. 'Beautifully executed, and the perfect precursor to your next performance.'

Paul looked at him blankly. 'Long words and me don't get on, Mr Renwick. Best stick to the short ones.'

'Call me Ralphie, Paul. All my friends do — except for poor Ezra, he called me Toff because he said I was posh and loaded.'

'If you're that rich, why didn't you bail Uncle Ezra out when he got tied up with these bad people?' ventured Paul.

'Because the kind of debt he ran up was beyond even me.' Ashcroft's tone was one of sadness and regret. It was tiring, really. Even for this little beetle-brained idiot, he needed to put on a convincing performance. 'I'm well-off, I agree, but not as loaded as your uncle believed. I would have moved heaven and earth for Ezra, and it hurts me every day to know that I failed him but,' he raised his hands, 'what could I do?' He sighed loudly, then allowed his smile to slowly return.

'But back to you, Paul. You did well, very well. Now we need to practise your next call.' He paused. 'This is the one that will earn you some serious money, my young friend.'

The young man stared at him, a look of deep concentration on his worried face. 'Tell me again, Mr Renwick, er, Ralphie, why I'm doing this. Apart from the money.'

Somehow Ashcroft maintained that smile. God! This idiot was trying even his patience. 'Of course, Paul. It's important that you fully understand.' He took a deep breath. 'I'm a wanted man. The police now know that I'm not Ezra but they believe that I killed him and took his place. Even worse, they think I'm this maniac who is going around shooting people. So, even though I am completely innocent, I'm wanted for murder.' He stared hard at Paul. 'I've taken a huge risk by staying to try and sort this out. I could have just fled, couldn't I?'

Paul nodded slowly. 'Yes. Yes, you could.'

'Exactly, but I didn't. Mainly because I've become very attached to you and your family, and I also want to stop these terrible shootings and clear my name. The police have no idea who I am, or what I look like. I certainly don't look like the man you thought was Ezra, do I?'

Paul grinned. 'No way.'

'So you see, I could easily have run away. Now, the fact is, I can't just go to the police. If I walk into that police station, I will never come out. They will never believe me. Meaning I need a way to talk privately to DI Jackman and DS Evans. They seem to be the only ones who might listen to me, but I dare not take the chance of ringing them and suggesting we meet.' He looked at Paul. 'Are you with me so far?' Paul nodded. 'Man to man, Paul, you've met them and talked to them. I trust your judgement. They are decent people, aren't they?'

After a while, Paul nodded again. 'Yes, I think they are straight. They care about Ma, and they were good with us, considering the trouble you got us into.' There was a slight accusatory edge to his words.

'Something I will always bitterly regret, but regarding the present situation, you will help me? I'm innocent, Paul, and as I told you before, my last hope is to convince Jackman and Evans of this. I need to get them on their own, away from all those other police officers, and I need your help to make that happen. There is no other way.'

'One phone call, one trip out with you, and then I go home?'

'With enough money in your pocket to feed your family for a year.'

Solemnly, Paul held out his hand to Alistair Ashcroft. 'Deal.'

* * *

An hour and a half later, Paul Lorimer sat alone in the big old house, fingering the fifty-pound notes in his pocket and wondering what to do. He had a full stomach, had been out with Renwick to visit the place he'd chosen for his rendez-vous with the two detectives, and now, if he wanted, he could up and run. He wasn't locked in. Renwick trusted him. He would be out for several hours, he said, so Paul was to watch television and relax. They would run through the second phone call he was to make and as soon as the meeting was over, he would be free to go home with the rest of the money. One more call, one small job, and that would be the end of it.

For the twentieth time, Paul took out the money and stared at it. Even this was more than he'd ever had before, but Renwick had said there was more to come. No, it was worth waiting. Still, he was anxious. The biggest problem was getting this next bit right. He knew what he was like. If the smallest thing went wrong, his temper would flare up and he would lose it. And then he'd lose everything.

CHAPTER THIRTY

Even if he hadn't been wearing camouflage pants and a khaki T-shirt, Nick Benfield couldn't have been anything other than "army". He was tall, muscular, and clearly worked out a lot. His fair hair was cut close to the scalp, and he had what Jackman could only think of as a tough, weathered baby face.

'If it's alright with you, we'll do this in an interview room and tape what you have to say. It'll make life easier for us, should what you have to say turn out to be admissible evidence.' Without waiting for an answer, Jackman led the way to interview room four, followed by Benfield and an excited Marie.

Introductions over with, Jackman said, 'Can you tell us everything you know about this man?' He pointed to a photo that lay on the table, one of Orac's better representations of Alistair Ashcroft. 'For the tape, I am showing Mr Benfield a likeness of Alistair Ashcroft.'

'The name I knew him by was Gavin Archer. He became a regular visitor to the gun club around two months ago. After about three weeks he signed up for the Sniper Experience.' Nick briefly paused. 'As I told the other detectives, he was different to most of the people we get on that particular course. He was, well, so *into* it. He was intense about absolutely everything. For most participants it's a fun experience, a bit of excitement, playing at being a fighting soldier for a day. Not so with Gavin. No fun there. He made every aspect of it a deeply serious undertaking. I was very uncomfortable teaching him, DI Jackman. I've had a thousand squaddies pass through my training sessions, some of them real tough cookies. There's been a few weirdos too, but no one made me feel like Gavin Archer did. It takes a lot to ruffle me, but he managed it, and how.'

'What sort of a shot was he, Nick?' asked Marie.

'First class. One of the best novices I've had on the range. The guy was a natural. You'd only have to tell him something once. When he first started, he said he was worried about eye dominance. Now, most beginners haven't even heard of that, let alone its possible effect on the shot. He was such an eager student, I should've liked him, but I didn't.'

'From what you say, it appears he did have some knowledge of guns, even though he said he was a beginner,' Jackman said.

'I'd say so, yes.'

'We believe that prior to joining your club he was a member of the Fenside Gun Club here in Saltern. Would that seem right to you?'

Nick nodded. 'It would answer several questions about his ability. And Harcourt's club is a good one. I spent some time there years back. He has a good crew.'

'You heard that the armourer was shot and killed?' Marie asked.

Nick looked angry. 'I did, and ever since I have been asking myself whether I trained the man who pulled the trigger on Arthur Barnes and those other men.'

Jackman said, 'If he hadn't gone to you, he would have gone somewhere else. You have no reason to blame yourself at all. He was a killer with a plan. He used you and your club like he's used so many others. The main thing is that you could be instrumental in us catching him. You have given us new up-to-date footage of him and you've provided us with

273

a vehicle registration number. Robbie and Max are checking that out right now. That's a big thing, Nick.'

Nick Benfield didn't look totally appeased by Jackman's words. 'Training soldiers — getting them ready for battle — is one thing. Teaching some psycho the tricks of the trade is another. It makes you sick to your stomach.'

That was how Ashcroft worked, using and manipulating people to get what he wanted.

'Listen.' Nick Benfield leaned forward across the table. 'I'm not sure if this will help, but the man I knew as Archer became close buddies with another club member. I'm pretty sure they met up outside the club, but I certainly saw them in the café together several times. Thing is, this other man — his name is Larry Turner by the way — is not only a gun collector, he is in one of your tactical firearms teams.'

'He's a copper?' Marie said, horrified.

'And a pretty obsessive collector of small arms. I heard he owns around thirty or more weapons.' Nick looked from one to the other. 'He's a nice bloke, I always liked him, so I couldn't see why he was so pally with Archer.'

'Because that's what Archer, or Ashcroft as he really is, wanted. Police officer or not, Ashcroft charmed him.' Jackman wrote down the name. 'Is he still a serving officer, Nick?'

'I think so. He hasn't been to the club for a while, but I can get you his address if that'd help?'

Marie stood up. 'It's okay. I'll get someone to run it through our computer right now.'

She went to the door, called to a constable and gave him the name. Jackman's mind was doing overtime. A police marksman. What better choice for a buddy? How long had Ashcroft been planning this? And was it all just to get back at Marie and him? It was beyond reason.

'There's one more thing, Inspector.'

Nick's voice tore him from his reverie.

'At the same time as Archer, or whoever he is, was with us, a handgun was stolen. We had a good idea who had taken it, but we had no proof. We'd had a bit of trouble with a young chap who was a right big mouth. He'd been given a two-day ticket for the Sniper Experience, won it in a competition or something like that, but he was disruptive and we asked him to leave after the first day. He raised Cain and I threw him out. Afterwards we discovered a gun had gone missing. We assumed it was him, but maybe . . .'

'Maybe someone else took advantage of the furore,' Marie said.

'Could be.'

'Nick, was it a Smith and Wesson Model 500 revolver?' Jackman asked.

'How the hell . . . ?'

Jackman and Marie shared a glance. 'Now we know where he got it,' Jackman said. He returned his gaze to Nick Benfield. 'Ashcroft stole it, not your young troublemaker.'

'That's a mighty powerful weapon!'

'We know. It's already killed a police officer,' murmured Marie.

'Jesus!' Nick whistled softly. 'What is this guy?'

'He's a master deceiver, Nick,' Jackman said. 'Hellbent on destruction. One last question. I know this may sound odd, but did you ever notice him wearing a particular cologne?'

'Yeah, I did, as a matter of fact. Most guys doing these courses finish up all sweaty but this Archer always smelt good.'

'Thanks for that, you've just confirmed another link.' Jackman stopped the tape and stood up. 'Your help has been really invaluable. If you think of anything else, here's my card. Did you come in with Robbie and Max, or did you bring your own car?'

'I came with your detectives.'

'Then we'll get a car to take you back.' Jackman held out his hand. 'Thank you again. It's very much appreciated.'

While Marie organised transport for Nick Benfield, Jackman hurried back upstairs to the CID room.

'Boss! We're on the right track.' Max looked as if he was on something. 'We reckon he's still using the same car as when he was posing as Gavin Archer. Oh, and the real Archer is a long-term patient in the Grange Nursing Home in Fenchester. He was mugged and sustained a head injury that left him on life support for a while. He's a single man with no relatives, debilitating brain damage and no recollection of the mugging. Now, although it was thought nothing was stolen in the attack, I suspect his driving licence was nicked and Ashcroft used it as ID to get him into the gun club.'

Robbie hurried over to join them. He too was barely able to curb his excitement. 'We've just picked up the car being used a few days ago in the Calder Road area. We lost it when it went off round the back doubles, but we have civilians checking the data from all the ANPR cameras coming into and going out of Saltern. If we can pinpoint a road or location he uses regularly we can concentrate our search in that area.'

'Good work. Maybe the tide is turning for us.'

The two young detectives went back to their desks, while Jackman returned to his office to look at the CCTV footage that Nick Benfield had made available from the sniper course. He saw at once that the man calling himself Gavin Archer was Ashcroft.

When Marie joined him, Jackman was watching a separate film, one made to advertise the courses. Ashcroft, unaware of being filmed, was lying stretched out full-length in long grass, wearing a black polo top and black cargo pants, his sniper rifle on a tripod and pointing to a target that was so far away it was almost out of sight.

'Now that is called focus,' muttered Marie, seeing the look of total concentration on his face.

'Remember what his old teacher said about him during the last case. Even as a boy, Ashcroft could do anything he put his mind to, and excel at it.' He gave a short laugh. 'Although I suspect being a serial killer wasn't something the teacher had in mind.'

Marie sat down. 'I just saw the super's car fighting its way through the press cameras by the car park.'

'Well, I'd better bring her up to speed. At least we have something positive for once.'

Just as he was about to leave, Max appeared at his door. 'Boss, we've got a bit of a problem with the police firearms chap, Larry Turner.'

'Come in, Max.' Jackman returned to his desk. 'Problem?'

'Thing is, he's been on sick leave for quite a few weeks now — stress, they say — and because of his job, he's been rested.' Max looked at his pocket book. 'Welfare did a domiciliary visit recently and he wouldn't even let them in. He called out that he was really poorly and that his sister was coming to collect him and take him back with her to Weymouth.'

'Is this going where I think it is?' asked Jackman.

'Probably. HR has no contact address for his sister, and now he's off the radar.'

Jackman swore under his breath. 'Where does this guy live?'

'Hartley Eaudyke, three miles outside Saltern. Small house on the main road into the village. It's called Snipedale.'

'Most appropriate, I'm sure. Fancy a ride, Max? And you, Marie?'

They stood up. 'Aren't you coming, boss?' Marie asked.

He shook his head. 'I'd better report in to Ruth, but ring me if you find anything of interest, okay?'

Marie gave a little salute. 'Will do. Go and grab a vehicle, Max, I'll be right with you.'

'On my way, Sarge.' He turned in the doorway and grinned at her. 'I'm glad to be back.'

'We are too, mate. Now bugger off and get that car.'

* * *

Needing to get away from his idiot acolyte, Ashcroft found a small café in Saltern's only shopping precinct, from where he watched the police moving to and fro. How he hated that boy Paul and his evil temper, stupidity and childishness. He hated having to go over every single thing again and again before it sank in. Ashcroft stared into his cup. This whole business had become tiresome. Why, even his old nemesis had disappointed him. He had expected so much more of their game — twists and turns and hair-raising moments, but there had been no reaction at all from them. He needed a new challenge, because clearly Jackman wasn't up to it.

He drank his insipid coffee, wondering where it had all gone wrong. His expectations had clearly been too high. Best to end it and start afresh elsewhere. It would not be the epic conclusion he had been looking forward to, but it would be satisfying enough. Then he'd move on.

He downed the rest of his drink and stood up. It hadn't been all bad. In fact, the journey had been edifying and rather enjoyable. His new skill with deadly weapons gave him a massive advantage, and he had confirmed his talent as a chameleon. If nothing else, it had shown him that there was nothing in this world he couldn't do.

So, what next?

He left the café and strode back to the car park. Time to dispense with Jackman and his Marie, and kiss goodbye to Saltern-le-Fen.

CHAPTER THIRTY-ONE

Larry Turner's house looked neglected, uncared for. Weeds were fast overtaking the plants in the front garden, and the small lawn was long overdue for a cut. Marie had a bad feeling about it.

'I get the feeling we're going to draw a blank, don't you, Sarge?' Max said. 'Doesn't look the kind of place where someone would keep a valuable gun collection, does it?'

Marie agreed. It was a small, old-style semi-detached house just off the main road into Hartley Eaudyke. With a little more care, it could have been as attractive as the adjoining house, which certainly put Larry Turner's to shame.

Max rang the doorbell and waited. After a while he bent down and looked through the letterbox, then turned to Marie. 'There's been some kind of disturbance. Stuff all over the floor and a broken table lamp.'

'I'll go round the back.' Marie ran around the side of the house, through a low gate and into the back garden. She tried the back door and the French windows, but all were locked. She peered in but could see no further signs of anything being amiss. She glanced up to the bedroom windows and saw that one was slightly ajar. No way could she get inside that way.

Then she noticed a shadowy figure behind the curtains of the house next door. 'It's okay, we're the police,' she called out, and held up her warrant card. 'Could you come out and talk to us, please?'

A few moments later an elderly lady stood on the other side of the fence. 'Can I see that warrant card properly? And what do you want?'

The accent was a local one and she was obviously not a trusting sort of person. In fact, she looked downright hostile.

'I'm Detective Sergeant Marie Evans. My colleague, DC Max Cohen and I are trying to find Mr Turner.'

'Haven't seen him in weeks, and not a word to me to say he was going anywhere.' The old lady looked put out. 'I know he's been poorly, but there are such things as good manners, *and* he'd promised to feed my Henry this week so I could have a few days with me sister in Skeggie. Had to cancel, and she ain't best pleased.'

'Oh dear. I'm sorry to hear that. I suppose you don't hold a key for him, do you?' Marie asked.

'Oh no. We gets along fine, but he's a private man and he wouldn't go handing keys out. Says he's got things in the house that's under lock and key and it's best they stays that way. Things to do with his work with you lot, I suppose.'

'Probably,' said Marie vaguely. 'You didn't hear anything like the sounds of a fight before he went, did you?'

The woman shook her head. 'No, but I does have me TV up loud, on account of me hearing aid playing up. Anyway, he was a quiet man. I've never heard no raised voices, even when he had his friend around.'

'His friend?'

'Tall, well-spoken man used to call recently. Very polite, he were. Said he went target shooting with Larry.'

Marie pulled a copy of the latest picture of Alistair Ashcroft from her pocket and handed it over the fence. 'Is this the man?'

The old lady squinted at it. 'That's him, only his hair was different. Same eyes though. Yes, that's the fella.' She passed the photo back.

As Marie took it from her, she saw Max walking round the side passageway. 'This lady here says that Ashcroft was visiting Larry, but he's been away for weeks.'

'With his sister in Weymouth?' asked Max.

'Weymouth?' the neighbour stared at him. 'He never mentioned no Weymouth. I thought his sister was abroad, teaching English in some Belgium college.'

'Really?' Max looked at Marie. 'Time to effect an entry, as they say. What d'you think?'

'Agreed. Thanks, Mrs, er — you've been a great help.'

They went back round to the front. 'I've already checked the windows, and this is too tough to shoulder in,' Max said, pushing at the door.

'I'll ring and get an enforcer brought over,' Marie said.

While they waited, to Marie's surprise the next-door neighbour appeared carrying two mugs of tea. 'I watch them cop dramas on the telly, so I know you'll be wanting this. If you want sugar, I'll go and get it. My name's Betty, by the way.'

'This is great, thanks, Betty.' Marie smiled at her. 'Tell me, what sort of man is Larry, other than private?'

'Hard to say.' Betty's brow creased in concentration, 'He's not your typical yellowbelly,' she said, using the local term for people born and bred in Lincolnshire. 'Really does keep himself to himself. Never once seen a lady friend visit, and he doesn't go down to the local for a pint with the lads. Tell you the truth, I'd be a bit worried about him if he was my boy.'

'And how often did the man in the photo visit, Betty?' Marie asked.

'Quite a bit over the last month. I was pleased to see Larry had a friend at last, but then he got ill. I think it's what you call a nervous breakdown. Anyway, after that the friend came less often.' She shrugged. 'And that's it, really.'

It was ten minutes before the vehicle with the enforcer arrived. They stared at the as yet unopened door. 'I hate this bit,' Max said.

Marie knew what he meant. It was a feeling she should have got used to after so many years in the job, but probably no one did. Excitement at what you might find yet also fear of the same thing.

With a crack of rending wood, the enforcer broke through.

Max went in first, with Marie at his heels. They moved from room to room but nothing seemed out of place, other than the things lying on the hall floor.

'Bit odd, wouldn't you say, Sarge?' Max looked puzzled. 'I'd be expecting to see more upheaval.'

Marie looked around, trying to get a feel for what Larry Turner was like. The house gave little away. There were a few photos, all related to work, mostly of Turner and his mates in uniform, toting their rifles. There were some medals in a case and a few highly polished trophies, and a pretty impressive sound system and record deck, but other than that and some shooting magazines, the place was almost bare. And it was an exclusively male domain, with nothing about it indicating a woman's touch, no attempt to make the place a home.

They avoided disturbing the things in the hall, just in case this turned out to be a crime scene, and started up the stairs.

Marie was almost certain that they were going to find the mortal remains of authorised firearms officer, PC Larry Turner. Yet that kind of discovery was usually preceded by the unforgettable stench of decaying flesh. This house smelt a little musty, as any would if it had been locked up for some time, but other than that she smelt nothing. So why this sense of foreboding? She kept thinking about the way the real Ezra Lorimer had been callously terminated when his usefulness ended. Surely it would have been the same with this man? With every step, her trepidation mounted.

Max had slowed down too. Glancing at him, Marie guessed he felt as she did.

They reached a short landing with three doors leading off it, each one firmly shut. Max took a determined breath and opened the first.

Marie looked into a small family bathroom. It was clean, functional, and tiled to the ceiling in silvery faux marble high gloss tiles. There was a white bath and a shower cubicle, basin and toilet. On the windowsill was a china toothbrush holder with a single brush and the usual toothpaste. Towels still hung over the heated towel rail. All pristine. She'd been in hotel bathrooms less immaculate.

Max pulled the door closed, and with a glance at her opened the second door.

What was intended as the guest bedroom was being used as Larry's study and gun-room. Along one wall was a desk with a laptop and a letter rack and, rather incongruously, a retro design Mathmos lava lamp.

'Rocket Telstar,' Max crooned. 'My favourite!'

Marie shook her head. 'Well, I learn something new about you every day, Max Cohen.' She turned her attention to the rest of the room, basically gun cabinets and a workbench with cans of oil, soft cloths and a variety of other tins and bottles.

The bad thing about it was that the cabinet doors were all wide open, and there were some very conspicuous gaps in the rows of guns.

'Blood.' Max pointed to a stain on the carpet, close to one of the cabinets. 'I thought it was spilt oil but it's blood alright.'

It looked as though she had been right to be concerned. 'We'll finish our sweep, then ring this in. We'll need forensics. And we'll need to check how many guns are licensed under his name to know how many, and which, are missing.' She ran her eyes over the room again but saw nothing else by way of evidence.

'Okay, last room coming up,' said Max and swallowed.

Marie stepped forward and pushed the door open.

For a moment nothing she saw computed. Then she smelt it.

'Oh, dear Lord! What has he done this time?'

Max slipped in past her and stopped in his tracks. 'Fuckin' hell!'

'Ring Jackman, now, Max! Tell him we have another victim and we need Rory here, pronto.'

She closed her eyes but the scene remained, seared into the back of her eyelids.

It had to be Larry Turner, but only forensics would tell her that.

The body lay on the bed in a recumbent position, reminding her of pictures she'd seen of mummified Egyptian pharaohs, except the bandages had been replaced by heavy duty clingfilm, the wide stuff that they used for packing furniture for transport.

From what she could make out, the victim had been stripped, and then wrapped into a tight cocoon. From the amount of blood within the "package", she guessed that this person had met the same end as Ezra Lorimer. It — he — looked like a giant side of meat ready for the freezer.

Because of the wrapping, very little smell had leaked out into the atmosphere but Marie could see that in places fluids were starting to seep onto the bed linen. If he'd been left much longer, the smell would have been unbearable.

Marie thanked God she hadn't made forensics her career. 'Imagine having to deal with this abomination.' As soon as the words were out, she hated herself for them. This "abomination" was another living, feeling human being who'd fallen foul of Alistair Ashcroft's twisted mind. Another police officer.

Max touched her shoulder. 'Jackman's on his way, Sarge, and he's asked for a priority on forensics.' He stared at the bed and its occupant. 'If only I was religious. I feel I should be saying a prayer for that poor guy.'

Marie turned to go. 'We've seen enough.'

* * *

Alistair Ashcroft hurried away from the church. The voices and the clamour were becoming hard to bear and he'd been planning to spend a little time in the quiet of the old building. But, as he had turned into the road, he'd seen more people milling about by the foyer than usual, and warning bells had rung. There were no uniforms in sight but he had a strong feeling that Jackman had put two and two together regarding the church.

He gritted his teeth. Now where to go? There was no time to drive out to one of his wild places on the marsh, he had too much to do.

He got into his car and drove to a small car park that looked out over the river. It was never busy, being too far away from the shops and the town centre, and today it was almost empty.

It would have to do.

He paid for an hour, locked the car and found a narrow footpath that ran down to some old disused moorings. Occasionally a lone fisherman would try his luck there, but today there was no one in sight. Ashcroft sank down onto a low seat that the fishermen used and stared at the greenish murky water of the river. This was what he needed — quiet and solitude. Some peace in which to unravel the twisted, tangled mess of his thoughts.

Some of these involved Paul Lorimer. The urge to kill that stupid boy was almost more than he could bear, but he needed him for his plan. And he needed to fulfil that plan — to gaze upon the lifeless bodies of Rowan Jackman and his Marie — before he could leave this dead-and-alive hole forever.

By the time he stood up again, some thirty minutes later, the last detail of his plan was in place and he felt almost serene. He ought to know by now that these temporary malfunctions in his thought processes were to be expected. After all, the stupidity of those with whom he came in contact was sometimes more than he could bear. Even Jackman had turned out to be a disappointment. At least his frustration was slightly appeased by the thought of the strain he had subjected the entire Saltern police force to. Most satisfying of all had been his relentless harassment of that young PC. He had chosen Kevin Stoner having noted his compassion towards the street people of Saltern, plus the fact that he was homosexual and therefore more vulnerable. Ashcroft had no real sense of what he subjected others to, being entirely without empathy himself. Like a feral child, he'd had no family to model himself on.

I'm the invisible man, Ashcroft said to himself, and so I'm invulnerable. He laughed. Poor Jackman and poor Marie. Soon, they would be paying the price for proving such unworthy opponents.

By midnight, Alistair Ashcroft would be on his way to a new life, a new campaign.

He started his car. Now for Paul Lorimer. Ashcroft turned off the engine again. It had come to him to wonder what made him so particularly angry towards that stupid boy. He thought of Paul tied to that chair, powerless and trembling in fear, fear of the unknown, dread of the coming pain and humiliation. Himself as a child. How he'd hated that weak and feeble boy!

Well, he was that child no longer. He had moulded himself into a new man, someone unique. And he would show his uniqueness by sparing the life of Paul Lorimer, who was least worthy of being spared.

CHAPTER THIRTY-TWO

Robbie Melton waved the printouts from the vehicle checks. 'We've picked up the car, sir, on several different occasions. We can pretty well pinpoint the direction he travels in. He always heads towards the east side of town. Uniform have upped their presence in all the residential roads within a one-mile radius of where he was last caught on camera.'

Soon he would be face to face with Ashcroft again. Jackman felt it in his bones. There was no doubt that they were drawing closer. Their arch enemy had made a crucial mistake in not realising that the Sniper Experience gun club had so many CCTV cameras. Then there was his grotesque killing of Larry Turner. The neighbour had verified that Larry's new "friend" drove a car of the same make and col-our as the one recorded on those CCTV cameras. Unless he had changed it very recently, it would only be a matter of time before he went through either a police traffic camera or past an eagle-eyed bobby or PCSO, then every traffic car in the area would be after him, blue lights flashing and sirens blazing.

Robbie lowered his voice. 'I knew Larry Turner, boss. A couple of years before I transferred here, I went on a firearms course and Larry was on it too. He was a good guy. He was dead keen to get into the national team, the target shooting championships and all that. He was pretty obsessive about it, but I guess we all have to have a passion, don't we?'

'Not sure what mine is,' murmured Jackman. *Other than Laura Archer.*

'I reckon it's policing for you, sir. Oh, and horses.'

'Horses I can go with, but not the policing part.'

Robbie intuited what he was referring to. 'Ashcroft can't keep himself hidden for much longer, sir. Our guys on the streets are looking at everyone sideways now, including any iffy-looking women, if you know what I mean.'

Jackman went back to his office. All his bravado of a few moments ago evaporated as soon as he was alone. Doubts flooded in. Was Ashcroft becoming disorganised? Would this mean they had a better chance of catching him, or would he instead become a desperate and dangerous loose cannon? And what then?

This was no good. In order to give himself something to do, he rang Kevin.

'Jackman here. Just checking on how you are.'

Kevin said that he was still shaken but felt much better. His parents were treating him like a five-year-old with the measles, but he was kind of enjoying it. In a few days, he and Alan were driving down to Cornwall for a week in a friend's holiday cottage. 'Sun, sea, and vodka, sir. Along with Cornish pasties, Alan reckons that should cure anything.'

Greatly relieved, Jackman phoned Laura, who answered almost immediately. 'Sweetheart! I was just going to ring you, Sam's recovering, and they're no longer concerned about him. Isn't that fantastic? And Ruth Crooke was amazing. She's organised a private room under a false name for security. Will you be okay if I stay with him, darling? They've offered me a temporary bed here for the night.'

Actually, Jackman didn't want her out of his sight, but being with Sam under heavy police guard would be a damn sight safer than being with him. 'Just keep in touch, won't you?' he said. 'And if anything bothers you—'

Laura interrupted him. He wasn't to worry, she was taking no chances at all.

'Boss?' Marie stuck her head around his door. 'We're back. Rory is busy at the crime scene, and he said to tell you he'd rather you didn't send him any more like this one. Even he felt queasy.'

'I'm not surprised.' Jackman grimaced. He shook his head to rid it of the memory of that corpse, wrapped like a parcel in clingfilm. 'Now, have you heard from Rachel Lorimer about her son? Is he home yet?'

'Rang her just now, sir. She's much more relaxed. He's not back yet but she said he'd rung home. He said he'd gone looking for Ashcroft again, but he'd be home by nightfall if he had no luck.'

Jackman frowned. This wasn't good news.

'One thing does bother me, boss. When I spoke to Jacob about the horse theft and the other stuff, he told me he never lied. He said his ma had told him to always tell the truth and shame the devil. He's a simple-minded kid, and I think if he said Paul had a gun, then he did have one.'

'If he's roaming the streets of Saltern hunting for Ashcroft, why haven't any of our foot soldiers picked him up? Every unit out there has his description,' Jackman said.

'What's he up to?' murmured Marie.

'I dread to think, but I don't believe his story about getting rat-arsed, do you?'

'You know I don't, sir.'

Jackman smiled, then his expression became serious. 'Paul Lorimer needs to be found before nightfall.'

* * *

The man he knew as Ralph Renwick sat back in his chair and slowly applauded. 'Well done! As near perfect as we could expect from you, young man.'

He was taking the piss, surely? Suddenly Paul had the urge to reach out and strangle this man.

'Now, all we have to do is go over the timing again.'

Paul gave a sigh. He knew the times for goodness sake! 'Do we have to, Ralph? I've got it all in my head, honestly.'

'Once more.'

For the first time, Paul looked this man directly in the eyes. They were heavy-lidded like those of a cat, and as cold. Suddenly he was afraid. 'Sure, sure. Let's do it.'

'Good. Now listen to me very carefully.' Ralph Renwick ran through the times, while Paul repeated them.

'Finally.' Renwick bent down and whispered in his ear. 'Your acting was very good, but just to give it an edge, remember this. If you mess up, get even one word out of place, this is what will happen to your ma.' Renwick leaned closer until Paul could feel his breath on his cheek and whispered in his ear.

Paul gasped. 'I won't let you down! I won't!'

'No, you won't. Because ruin my plans and I'll ruin your mother, and maybe that pretty sister of yours too.'

Paul's voice cracked. 'I won't get it wrong. I promise!'

Renwick stood up abruptly, the smile back in place, but the eyes just as hard. 'Then this is yours.' He pushed a thick envelope into Paul's hands. 'Put on the best show of your life, and then go home and forget everything, understand? There is enough money there to wipe the last few days from your memory forever. Is that clear?'

All Paul could do was nod, bewildered. Understanding nothing.

* * *

As the shadows lengthened across the fen at close of day, Rachel Lorimer made her way to her daughter's caravan.

As ever, Rachel wondered at the way the girl lived, surrounded by heaps of clutter, but by now she'd accepted that Esther wouldn't change.

'Is there anything you need to tell me, girl?' she asked softly.

Esther lowered her head.

'You gave Paul a gun, didn't you?'

Esther shook her head slowly. 'Didn't give it. He took it.'

'I see.' She gave her only daughter a sad smile. 'It's alright, Esther. I just needed to know.' She endeavoured to widen the smile. 'And one other thing — a certain item that belonged to your grandfather. Do you have it somewhere in this, er . . . ?' She waved an arm around.

Esther looked up. 'Are you mad at me, Ma?'

'No, girl, I'm not mad at you.' She paused for a moment, Esther watching. 'There is something I want you to do for me — for all of us. It's to do with your brother Paul.'

'Sure, Ma. What do you want me to do?'

'Good girl. Now, I've heard from Paul, and it's like this . . .'

* * *

There was an unusual atmosphere in the station that evening. Though their shift had finished some time ago, only now were the team beginning to drift off home. The first to go had been Max, wanting to get back to Rosie and the children, but the others almost had to be thrown out.

Now, even though there seemed little point in staying, Jackman, Marie and Gary sat on, listening to the reports coming in from the streets of Saltern-le-Fen.

The uniformed officers had narrowed the search for Ashcroft's base to an area roughly half a mile wide. They were now out in force, knocking on doors and requesting to look in outbuildings and garages to try to locate the black Peugeot car that they now knew Ashcroft drove. Every police man and woman had the licence number branded in their memory.

Jackman stretched and yawned. 'I think it's time we called it a day, or we'll feel like rubbish tomorrow. There's little we can do here, other than wait.'

'Or in your case, pace up and down. Do you realise you're wearing a track in your office carpet?' Marie said.

It was true. He felt uncommonly edgy and seemed incapable of sitting down for any length of time.

'Jackman, I know this sounds a bit dramatic, but would you like to stay over with us tonight?' Marie looked at him anxiously. 'You said Laura is staying with Sam at the hospital, and Ashcroft knows exactly where you live, doesn't he? I don't think you are safe there alone.'

'I second that, sir,' added Gary. 'I've been thinking that if he's realising that the net is tightening, he might want to end the whole thing while he still has the chance.'

'I've got a sofa bed. It won't take a minute to make it up,' Marie said. 'We'd feel a lot happier.'

It was tempting. Ashcroft had already visited Mill Corner twice.

'Please, Jackman?'

He wanted to say yes. 'I appreciate your offer, really I do, but . . .' How could he tell her he was half hoping to find Ashcroft lurking in his carport?

'One night, sir. I've got toiletries and shaving gear that you can borrow,' Gary said.

Before Jackman could answer, his mobile rang. It was an unknown number and it took a few moments to realise who was speaking. He switched the loudspeaker on. 'Calm down, Paul. Now start again, but slowly.'

'He's got Ma! That man what I thought was Uncle Ezra! You have to help her, you have to!' Paul sounded so frantic it was hard to make out the words.

'Tell me what you know, Paul. Where has he taken your mother? Do you know that?'

'I did it wrong!' Paul was crying now. 'He said he'd hurt her, and Esther too, if I got it wrong, and I messed up!'

'Got what wrong?' asked Jackman.

'Phone calls! I had to make calls, and I got the times wrong. Now he's taken Ma.'

'Where are you? We'll come and get you.' Jackman spoke calmly.

'You can't. He'll be back soon and if he sees you here, he'll kill her, I know he will.'

'Tell me where you are, Paul.' He scribbled a note and held it out to Gary. *Get location of this call!* Gary hurried out.

'He's here! I'll try to ring back.' The line went dead.

For a moment Jackman stared at his phone, then he sprang into action. 'Marie! Ring Rachel Lorimer, now!'

Marie pulled out her mobile, rang the number and switched the loudspeaker on. 'Hi, Levi. Can I speak to Rachel, please? It's DS Evans, and it's urgent.'

'She's not here, Sergeant. She went out to talk to Esther earlier on, but when I went over to her van, neither of them was there. I'm getting real worried about them.'

Jackman's heart sank. So, Ashcroft hadn't finished with the Lorimers after all. Marie asked Levi exactly what time he realised that she had gone, and he said it must have been over thirty minutes before. 'And her car's not here, Sergeant. But she never goes out at night. She hates driving these lanes in the dark, scares her rigid.'

'Levi, please ring me if she comes back — immediately, okay? Meanwhile we'll do what we can. You and the rest of the family stay put and an officer will be with you shortly.' Marie ended the call, just as Gary came back in.

'Can't specify an address, but the nearest tower gives us a general location of the area where uniform are searching for Ashcroft's car.' Gary handed Jackman a list of six road names.

'Inform the duty sergeant of the situation, Gary. Ask him to keep the police presence low key, but to keep their eyes peeled for any signs of trouble, or sightings of Rachel Lorimer or her old 4x4.'

'Got you, boss.'

As Gary turned to go, Marie said, 'And ask for a crew to get out to the Lorimer place ASAP. See if they can get a more accurate time for when Rachel left, and get them to keep an eye on those boys. We have no idea how they will react with the mother and sister missing.'

Jackman followed the tracks in his carpet, pacing. What to do?

With a grunt, he sank down into his chair and pointed to the one on the opposite side of his desk. 'Sit, Marie. We need to assess what we really know, and how to proceed.'

Marie shook her head. 'Very little. Just some garbled story from a young man who is behaving totally out of character.'

'If he was acting, I'd be very surprised,' Jackman countered. 'And if he's telling the truth, we have two women in mortal danger. And don't forget, they are off the radar at present.'

'Okay, let's assume he's telling the truth. Do we think Ashcroft actually abducted them? Or possibly lured them away from the farm?'

He thought for a moment, 'I'd say the second option, he lured them. He'd know he couldn't take his car. He could have phoned Rachel and told her that Paul was in trouble or hurt and she needed to come immediately.'

Marie nodded slowly. 'That's quite feasible. Plus, if she hates driving at night, she might well have taken Esther with her.' She pulled a face. 'But then, why not tell the family? She only had to say she was going to collect their brother and none of them would have been worried about her.'

'Oh, you know Ashcroft, Marie! He could have invented a dozen plausible reasons for not telling anyone.'

'Very true, but Rachel Lorimer is a law unto herself. She does only what she wants to, always has.'

'Then maybe Ashcroft knew that, and tried a different method, like using Paul himself.'

'He did say he'd been told to make phone calls, didn't he?' Marie paused, thinking. 'So, bottom line, we go with Ashcroft having Rachel and Esther?'

'We can't afford not to, can we? We just have to hope that either uniform spot something, or Paul manages to ring us back.'

A few minutes later, Gary returned. 'The sergeant understands the situation and has put out an attention drawn to

Rachel and her daughter, with the order to proceed in that area with extreme caution.' He turned to Marie. 'And two officers are on their way to the Lorimer Farm as we speak.' He looked from her to Jackman. 'Do you think we should call the team back in?'

Jackman shook his head. 'No, not yet. There's nothing they can do at the moment. It's a waiting game, I'm afraid. Gary, would you be up for going out and meeting those PCs at the Lorimer place? You know what the Lorimer boys are like. A couple of coppers with no prior dealings with them could inadvertently upset young Jacob causing Noah to flare up.'

'Of course,' Gary said immediately. 'That's a good point, and I'll keep in touch in case they hear anything from the mother.'

Marie followed Gary out, off to get her and Jackman a drink.

Jackman was left alone with his thoughts. Completely out of the blue, he recalled a man named Tyler Cane. Many years ago, he had worked with this rather enigmatic detective, who had held some very unorthodox and "unpolicemanlike" views. Cane believed firmly in karma, and he and Jackman would sometimes talk well into the night, pitting his rather unworldly ideas against Jackman's materialistic ones. In particular, Jackman recalled Tyler Cane's method of dealing with fear. He could hear him now:

We coppers love an acronym, Jackman, so use this one. FEAR: False Evidence Appearing Real. Most of our fears are just a collection of perspectives and self-defence mechanisms dinned into us as kids in order to keep us safe. We go on to inherit fear from others as we proceed through life, but it's something other people teach us. Don't allow your fears to control you, Jackman. See things for what they really are. Recognise them, understand them and they won't have power over you.'

Tyler Cane had died in a high-speed car crash aged thirty-one, leaving Jackman a priceless legacy of positive thoughts. How amazing that he had thought of him now, just when he needed wise counsel.

Marie came back with a mug of tea. 'No coffee. My mum says we should drink more tea than coffee, and it's supposed to be good for shock, so here you are.'

As she raised her mug, Jackman's mobile rang.

They gave each other a long look. Jackman answered.

This time Paul Lorimer sounded as if he were speaking with a gun pointed at his head. Maybe he was.

'Ralph Renwick wants to speak to you and Sergeant Evans. Alone. It has to be both of you.'

Jackman gritted his teeth. So this was it. The showdown.

'He says if you bring anyone else, or have any form of backup with you, there will be dire consequences.'

Paul had to be reading those words, he wouldn't have a clue about "dire consequences."

'He also says that if you don't meet him, he will hurt people, lots of them, until you agree to listen to him.'

Jackman heard a distinct tremor in his voice. 'I'm listening, Paul. Is he there with you now? Can I talk to Mr, er, Renwick?'

Pause. 'He's not here.'

Jackman didn't believe him for a moment. 'Okay, Paul. Where does he want to meet us?'

'He said you would know where. And if you don't, that pretty PC Stoner certainly would. Bad things have happened there.'

Jackman glanced at Marie. The waste ground behind the railway line.

'One hour, or innocent blood will flow. It's your choice, DI Jackman.'

The line crackled, then went silent.

Jackman lifted his desk phone and asked for immediate triangulation on the last call to his mobile. They waited in silence.

'He's still in that original area. It's walking distance from there to the river and the waste ground.'

'Right.' Unnaturally calm, Marie sat and sipped her tea. 'It seems right, is what I mean. After all this time, all the horrible damage and destruction he's caused, it's right that it should come down to the three of us.'

Jackman stared at her. 'Jesus, Marie! Are you honestly thinking of meeting him? On his terms? We'd be mowed down in an instant. Look at the firepower he has.'

'But wait,' she said. 'He won't just shoot us as soon as he sees us. It's not his way. He will be compelled to tell us just how powerful he is, and what failures we are. Unless he does that, he'll feel that his mission, or whatever it is, has not been fulfilled.'

Jackman was impressed. 'When did you get a degree in psychology?'

'When I last spent some time with your Laura.'

'But what do we do? We can't risk him spotting any backup. If he really does have hostages, and I believe he does, it will be their death sentence.'

'There will be no other vehicles, and no firearms squad. There will be just us.' Marie put down her empty mug. 'Oh, and one other. The best sniper we have. They will be concealed in the back of our own vehicle. We walk away from the car and keep Ashcroft's attention on us. The sniper slips out as soon as it's safe to do so and finds a vantage point with a clear line of sight to Ashcroft. One threatening move and they'll finish him.'

It could work, but by God it was risky. He closed his eyes. Risky, but it would be worth it to put an end to Alistair Ashcroft's reign of terror.

His eyes snapped open. 'Okay. We'll do it.' He picked up the phone and called the super. 'Ruth, I need the very best marksman we have, and one of the most agile. No six-foot six beefcake, please, this one needs to be a veritable lethal shadow, right? We have under an hour and we have to do this exactly as I say, or innocent people will die. If we do this right, it ends tonight.'

After he'd replaced the phone he jumped up. 'Go and get us two of the best Kevlar vests you can rake up. I'll find a car that will suit our purpose best. See you downstairs in ten.' He stopped in the doorway and looked at her, his eyes bright. 'You and me, Marie. That's how he wanted it, and that's what he'll get.'

'You and me, Jackman. Let's go.'

* * *

'You excelled yourself, Paul. You've earned your money. I had intended you to do another small job with me, but I've changed my mind. Stay here for another half an hour after I've gone, then go home. Your car is in the double garage. Lock it up again when you leave and put the keys on the kitchen table.'

Renwick was dressed entirely in black. Black shirt, black trousers and boots, and a heavy black body-armour vest. On the floor beside him was a helmet. Paul had seen a dozen men like this on the way here, patrolling the streets.

When they had gone to the rendezvous site to check it out, Renwick had dressed them both in hi-vis jackets with an official-looking logo on the back. With yellow hard hats, they looked for all the world like construction workers from the other side of the river, or Highway Maintenance men. Renwick had said that the best place to hide was in plain sight and no one, not even the police, had looked twice at them when they walked by. At the time, Paul had found it exciting, like being in an action movie. He rather liked being a second in command, although Ralph Renwick's changes of mood were hard to keep up with. Now Renwick was a police firearms officer. Paul had to hand it to him, he was in plain sight alright. Now he understood exactly what that meant.

'If things go well, Paul, it will be partly down to you, so thank you. I might not see you again, but I will get justice for your uncle.'

For a moment Paul thought that Renwick was going to hug him. He mumbled something and backed away.

Renwick picked up his helmet. 'I've a few more things to collect, and then I'll be leaving. Remember. Thirty minutes, then get out of here. Understand?'

Paul nodded. 'I understand.'

'Goodbye, Paul Lorimer. Have a nice life.'

CHAPTER THIRTY-THREE

Despite Marie's protests, Jackman insisted on driving. To her relief, he kept to the speed limit. Slowly the adrenalin was starting to pump through his veins. As they approached the deserted area that had once been a meeting place for mountain bikers and kids on skateboards, the enormity of what they were doing started to hit home.

'Marie, I . . . I wanted to say . . .' he struggled to find the words. 'I could never have asked for a better partner.'

'And I found a boss that I'd walk to ends of the earth for, so no regrets, Jackman.'

'You two are a right barrel of laughs,' said a muffled voice from the back of the Dacia estate. 'The tears are blurring my night-vision optics. And before you start writing your wills, have a little faith, will you? Remember who's with you.'

'Sorry, Bert, we're not belittling your prowess,' Jackman said softly, 'but it had to be said.'

He was glad the super had arranged for Roberta Gleeson to be their sniper. Not only was she a crack shot, she was also lithe, wiry and incredibly fit. Which she might have to be. Before they left the station, he had made sure they had the right vehicle. If luck was on their side, they would get out of the car and walk away from it, then, under cover of darkness, Bert would slip out undetected. However, if Ashcroft suspected a trick, he would lock the car. He could do that with no problem, because the boot lid on a Dacia operated with a key and was not on the central locking system. Bert would still be able to get out with ease. And, finally, he had disconnected the interior lights. The last thing he wanted was Bert opening the door and a light coming on!

He'd done all he could, and now it was crunch time. 'Good luck, everybody,' he whispered. 'Let's get the bastard.'

Jackman took a deep breath and turned into the waste ground. He needed to find a spot in heavy shadow to give Bert the best chance of a swift and undetectable exit from the vehicle.

'Over there, sir.' Marie pointed to where a single light glowed in the darkness. It was coming from the old storeroom that the dossers used to sleep in.

In the headlight beams he made out a thick clump of wild elder shrubs growing close to a broken-down fence. He pulled up close to it and left the headlights on for a few moments. He opened his door and Marie did the same. They paused, gathering themselves, then Jackman whispered, 'Here we go,' and slammed the door shut. He heard Marie do the same, and then a whispered voice said, 'Extraction complete.'

Bert had used the darkness behind the headlights, and made her move out of the vehicle, closing the door at the same time as Marie, and slipping into the bushes.

'Lock the car!'

The sound of Ashcroft's voice made him shudder, and then he steeled himself. He had been waiting so long for this moment. He pressed the button on the ignition key and heard the locks click.

'Good. Now walk towards the building, very slowly, and with your hands in the air.'

Jackman couldn't quite place where the voice was coming from, but it wasn't very far away. The last thing he wanted was to be in an enclosed space. That could be fatal for them both. Their guardian angel would have no clear line of fire and they would be dead meat. Somehow, he would have to prevent them having to go inside. But as it was, he didn't need to.

'Stop there. Are you wearing wires?'

'No.'

'Jackman. Take off your jacket and your protective vest.'

For a moment, Jackman hesitated but in the end he removed them, holding the vest up in one hand.

'Drop it. Then open your shirt.'

Gritting his teeth against a retort, he let the jacket go and unbuttoned his shirt, exposing his chest. 'No wires. Satisfied?'

'Want me to do the same?' Marie called out. 'I'm more than happy to.' She stripped off the Kevlar vest, undid the top three buttons of her blouse and pulled them wide. 'No wires, Alistair Ashcroft.'

'Enough! Do up your blouse, now!'

'Ooh, touchy.'

'Shut up,' Ashcroft growled.

'Sorry, I'm sure.'

Jackman flashed her a warning glance. He admired her courage, but didn't want her taunts to trigger one of his personality swings. Even so, he took the opportunity to try and locate where Ashcroft was standing. He desperately wanted to know what kind of gun was trained on him. It was obvious that Ashcroft had set up a light source of some kind in the doorway of the storeroom, probably a battery-powered lantern. This allowed him to see them while he remained in darkness.

'I assume that there is a large force of armed policemen waiting up on the main road. I'm sure you didn't just decide to drop in on me unaccompanied,' Ashcroft said, his tone even.

'For the sake of Rachel and Esther Lorimer, that's exactly what we did, Ashcroft. There is no one with us, no one waiting at the gate, nor anyone punting up the river for that matter. You said alone, so here we are.' He spread his hands and threw the car keys towards the sound of Ashcroft's voice. 'Check the car if you like. You'll find it's not full of gun-toting coppers.'

At least it isn't now. He thanked the Lord that Bert had decamped so quickly, and although there really were no cars at the gates, Ruth Crooke had put Saltern in lockdown with roadblocks at every intersection.

'Where are Rachel and Esther, Ashcroft?' called out Marie. Their voices echoed in the deserted strip of land.

'Good question.'

Jackman wasn't certain, but he thought he had seen the slightest movement in the shadows slightly to the left of the storeroom. That was also the place the voice was coming from. He tried to recall what was there. A few trees, some bushes and some piles of debris from another abandoned storeroom. Suddenly he was mighty glad that Bert had powerful night vision scopes on her gun.

'Where are they?' Marie's voice was hard as nails.

'Mmm. Now, let me think . . .'

'Why don't you get out here and face us! We've come alone, unarmed and unprotected. You, on the other hand, hold all the cards, yet you still skulk in the shadows. Coward!' Marie seemed to have no fear at all.

'Ashcroft!' Jackman called out. 'She's right. Come out and face us like a man.'

'And have a police sniper take me out? I don't think so.'

'There is no fucking sniper! God, you saw us arrive! Look around you. No cars, no backup of any kind, just us, Ashcroft.' Jackman told himself not to plead.

'Forgive me if I don't trust you, but you see there's a lot of cover here, and with a decent rifle, even from a great distance — well, I should know, shouldn't I?'

The hint of amusement in his voice made Jackman want to rush screaming at the shadows where the killer was concealed and throttle him with his bare hands. Instead, he said,

'Then just tell us where those women are and let me ring it in, so that someone can pick them up. Please, Ashcroft, at least keep that side of the bargain.'

'I don't recall any bargain,' said Ashcroft quietly.

It had always been a possibility that he had already killed Rachel and Esther, but somehow Jackman had not believed it. Now he wasn't so certain. He looked across to Marie, but this time she remained silent.

With a loud exasperated sigh, Jackman said, 'Okay, Alistair, have it your way. Get it over with, whatever you have planned, because this is going nowhere, is it? You must want to talk or you wouldn't have set such an elaborate trap for us, you'd have just picked us off in the street, like those other poor innocents.'

Now there was a definite movement. A dark figure stepped from the shadows. In a moment of incomprehension, Jackman thought it was Bert, showing herself for some reason, then he realised that it was Ashcroft in a black firearm officer's uniform, complete with helmet and handgun. Clothes that must have been taken from Larry Turner's house.

'Innocents? You think?' Ashcroft sneered.

'Yes, I do,' Jackman replied. 'You've torn that family to shreds, and for what?'

'The answer is standing right in front of me. To get to you, of course. And let's be honest, Jackman, Ezra Lorimer is no great loss. As for the family, well.' He laughed. 'You did meet them, didn't you? Those kids should have been drowned at birth!'

'Is that right? Well, thanks for that!'

Jackman and Marie spun round to see Paul Lorimer standing just a few feet from them.

'How in hell's name . . . ?' Marie gasped. 'Paul! Get out of here!'

But Paul was going nowhere, he stood full square, facing down Ashcroft.

'Well, well. If it isn't little Paulie. You're even more stupid than I thought. You've made a big mistake coming here, and after I'd so generously spared your life. I even paid you. Dear, dear. So few brains, you're positively dangerous.'

'Oh, I'm dangerous alright, and you are evil!' snarled Paul, and pulled a gun from his jeans' waistband. 'For Ezra!'

Before anyone could do or say anything, he had fired a shot at Ashcroft.

The kid's aim had been true, but the shot had hit the body armour.

The force of it sent Ashcroft staggering backwards, but that didn't prevent him firing his own weapon, and with a grunt, Paul fell to the ground.

The next few seconds seemed to pass in a blur. Jackman heard Marie scream out, 'Bastard!' and throw herself down beside the young man. Two shots rang out. He was pretty sure it was two, and finally the most bloodcurdling scream he could ever remember hearing. It echoed all over the waste ground and rose up into the night like the howl of some infernal hound.

He spun around to see Roberta Gleeson sprint past him towards Ashcroft, and two figures in dark clothes, standing shoulder to shoulder a little behind and to his left. When he looked again, there was only one, and she was now running towards her fallen son.

'Rachel?'

'Paul! My Paul!'

He looked ahead to see Bert standing over the writhing figure of Ashcroft, her gun muzzle just a few inches from his head. 'Sir! Paramedics required!'

'I've already called them!' Marie shouted back, who was now cradling Paul in her arms. 'For this boy, not that evil bastard! Let him die!'

First, Jackman went to Marie. 'Is he . . . ?'

'Still alive, but . . .'

Rachel appeared at Marie's side, crooning to her son, 'My brave, brave baby! Don't you worry about anything, Ma's here and she has you now, my beautiful boy.'

Marie stared up at Jackman, tears welling up.

Already, the sirens could be heard in the distance.

'I called them just before all this happened,' whispered Rachel Lorimer, her attention all on her son. 'You are a hero, my Paul. I'm so proud of you.'

'Am I, Ma?' He smiled up at her weakly.

'I'm here, my darling, and I'll never let you go.'

Jackman knew that her words were now falling on deaf ears. He had seen where the bullet had entered the lad's chest. Scarlet blood pumped across his white T-shirt, and in that moment, Jackman knew his nightmare would never return.

Marie took his hand. 'Leave them now,' she said through her tears. 'We have someone else to pay attention to.'

They marched across to where Alistair Ashcroft still writhed on the filthy ground, blood gushing from both his legs.

'They just appeared in front of me,' said Bert, shakily, her weapon still trained on Ashcroft's head. 'Just as I was going to take my shot! I'd have killed them if I'd tried to get a shot away. It was them who shot him, sir. They kneecapped him.'

Alistair Ashcroft's face was contorted in agony. He looked down at his legs.

'You just killed a kid,' Marie said.

Ashcroft drew back his lips in a sneer. 'Good.'

'Bert, can you close your eyes for two seconds?' Marie turned to Jackman. 'You did not see this.'

She swung her leg back and launched a kick at one of Ashcroft's shattered knees.

Another howl rose into the night and lingered there, mingling with the sound of approaching two-tones.

'That's for Harvey. Now we're quits.'

Marie Evans turned her back on the screaming man and walked away.

Jackman looked at Bert and shrugged. 'Long story. I'll tell you some time. Just don't ask her who Harvey is, will you?'

EPILOGUE

'Guess what, sir? For once we have some good news to give to Kenneth Harcourt.' Robbie Melton smiled happily.

Jackman and Marie looked up from their undiminishing pile of reports. Jackman closed the file he'd been working on. 'Okay, spill the beans. Don't just stand there grinning.'

'I was down talking to the duty sergeant at the front desk and this young bloke walks in. Says he wants to confess to a crime. Well, I was all ears, naturally.'

'Hurry up, Melton! What crime?' Marie asked impatiently.

'He's admitted to driving the car that killed Kirstie Harcourt. Chris Keyes was his best mate, so because he had been drinking and was starting a new job that week that had to have a clean driving licence, Chris took the flak. He told us that now his friend was dead he couldn't live with himself, knowing that everyone believed Chris had run a girl down and not stopped.'

'Well, I'm absolutely delighted to hear that,' said Marie. 'Kenneth Harcourt will finally be able to stop wondering what really happened.'

'And now someone has accepted the blame, perhaps he will be able to move on,' added Jackman.

'I was told he is selling the gun club,' said Marie, 'and his private collection.'

'I heard that too. He's probably had enough of guns and the heartbreak they cause.' Jackman remembered the look on Harcourt's face when he discovered that it was his gun that had killed his friend Arthur. 'We'll take a trip out this afternoon, Marie, and give him the news.'

'Oh, good and, please, this time can I ask him why his house is called Wits' End? Go on, let me.'

He laughed. 'Okay. If you must. But try to be tactful.'

It was a good feeling to be delivering positive news for once. He and Marie had spent a lot of time with Rachel Lorimer and her family recently. They had come away full of respect for the way she had managed all those years with no help. And then Ashcroft, in his guise as kind Uncle Ezra, had done such damage to them. Laura had offered to talk to them, especially Jacob, who was suffering from the loss of his brother, and it did seem to be helping.

'Boss? Would you have time to sit down with the rest of us and fill in a few gaps?' Robbie asked.

'Sure. Is the team all in the CID room now?'

'Yes, sir.'

'Then get everyone a drink,' he passed Robbie a handful of coins, 'and I'll be out in five.'

Jackman perched on the edge of Marie's desk and began. 'First, Sam Page is out of hospital and recovering well. He's staying with us at Mill Corner for a while until he can cope on his own. He sends his regards to you all.'

'He gave us a fright alright,' said Gary. 'Poor guy, what a shock. I'm really glad he's doing well.'

'And you'll be pleased to hear that Kevin Stoner will be joining us at the end of the month. He's another one recovering from damage Alistair Ashcroft inflicted.' Jackman looked at the assembled team. 'So? Loose ends?'

'What will happen to Ashcroft, sir?' asked Robbie.

'As you know, he's on remand until his trial, then it will be down to the judge and jury to decide.' He frowned. 'We have enough evidence to lock him up for life, but the question will be whether he's of sound mind. His defence might claim not guilty by reason of insanity, or possibly that he's guilty, but insane or mentally ill, which would mean he'd be committed to a psychiatric facility.'

'Is there a chance the jury will decide that he'd been perfectly in command of his faculties when he committed those atrocities? That he is simply an evil killer?' asked Charlie Button.

Jackman shrugged. 'There is a chance, of course. Then he would go to a Cat A maximum security prison, somewhere like Frankland or Wakefield.'

'Where he belongs, with the other monsters,' muttered Max. 'One thing's for sure, he won't be doing a runner, not with no kneecaps!'

'It's in the lap of the gods, isn't it, sir?' said Marie. 'Let's hope he comes up against a shit-hot prosecution lawyer out to make a name for themselves.'

'Plus one of those judges that would bring back hanging if they had half a chance,' added Max.

For once they were able to laugh at Ashcroft's expense. They had spent years with his presence hanging over them like the Sword of Damocles. And of all people, it was the crazy Lorimer family that had given them the freedom to joke again. Jackman looked at the team, relaxed and cheerful once more. 'Listen up, guys, you will all be wanting to know exactly what happened that night. There's been a lot of rumours going the rounds, I know, but Superintendent Crooke wanted to keep things under wraps until some of the trickier details had been sorted out.'

'About Paul Lorimer?' asked Robbie.

'And the part his mother and sister played in it.' Jackman got off the desk and brought a chair over to the group. 'This is where it gets a bit complicated. Ashcroft lured Paul to where he was staying by deliberately leaving a letter with an address where Paul would find it. Paul went to look for him in order to punish him for murdering Ezra, and Ashcroft ambushed him. He then spun Paul a whole web of lies about being best buddies with Ezra, swearing he wasn't responsible for his murder. Paul pretended to fall for his story. Ashcroft then offered him a lot of money to help him set up a "secret meeting" between him, Marie and I, ostensibly to clear his name. Paul suspected it was a crock of shit, but at this point he decided he could have the best of both worlds — keep the money and take revenge on Ashcroft for the damage he'd done to his family.'

'I thought he was a bit slow, but that took brains and cunning.' Gary looked puzzled.

'Rachel told me that he was academically challenged, sometimes childish, had anger issues and could be pretty unstable, but he wasn't stupid. Paul wasn't about to trust Ashcroft after the lies he'd told, but he was scared of him. Ashcroft made two mistakes with Paul. He underestimated him, and he had no idea that he had a mobile phone and a gun hidden in his car.'

'Sloppy.' Max smiled like the Cheshire cat.

'So, on Ashcroft's orders, Paul made the phone call to his mother saying he'd got drunk and was sleeping it off. Then, as soon as Ashcroft went out, Paul phoned her again on his hidden mobile — one she knew nothing about, incidentally — told her the truth, and explained what Ashcroft was planning.'

Gary exhaled. 'But wasn't Ashcroft going to kill him? I'm guessing Paul hadn't worked that one out.'

'Probably not, but what he did realise was that Ashcroft didn't want to talk to Marie and me at all, he wanted to kill us, and Paul wasn't going to let that happen. Then he realised he'd bitten off more than he could chew and so asked for his mother's help.'

'According to Rachel,' said Marie, 'Ashcroft had done enough damage without killing little Marie Evans and that boss of hers. She reckons he's alright, that Jackman — for a copper that is.'

They all laughed.

'So Paul made that desperate call to you, about Ashcroft abducting his mother, and it was all acting?' asked Charlie.

'Very good acting too. His life depended upon it. But he'd already told his ma where the meeting was to be and she enlisted Esther to help her.'

'So they loaded their guns and went to save you two,' Max spluttered. 'Blimey!'

'They had no idea we had a marksman with us. And Rachel had no idea that Paul would show up either.' Jackman sighed. 'Let alone get himself killed. The arrangement was that he would go straight home with the money.'

'What happened to that money, sir?' asked Robbie.

'There was no sign of it anywhere. We can only think he hid it,' Jackman said. Marie glanced at him.

'One thing bothers me, boss,' said Max. 'The guns they used. They only had airguns at the farm. They would have hurt the bugger, but not kneecapped him.'

Jackman nodded to Marie. 'Tell him, Marie.'

'I always wondered what Esther's problem was. As you know, every member of that family is fragile in one way or another, but she seemed so normal — other than being a bit of a hoarder.' Marie gave them a rather sad smile. 'Turns out she wasn't a hoarder, she stole things. That's why she lost her job and Rachel kept her at home. She stole her grandfather's shotgun and kept it hidden in her van for years, and she stole the handgun that Paul had.'

'Bloody hell! Where did she nick that from? Last I heard they don't sell them in Tesco!' Robbie exclaimed.

'It belonged to a chap who used to give her a lift home from work sometimes. He was a Russian working in a food processing plant close to town, not far from where Esther worked, and he lived out near Hawkers Fen. She took it from the glove compartment of his van.'

'And it was unlicensed of course, so he didn't dare report it,' added Gary.

'And luckily for Esther, even if he had guessed she was the thief, he was deported shortly after.'

'Jeez, it all happens out at Hawker's Fen, doesn't it?' said Charlie.

'So, what's going to happen to Rachel?' asked Max. 'I'm totally with her for taking a shotgun to that bastard, but you can't just go around shooting people. It's against the law.'

Jackman leaned back in his chair. 'Well, as you know, she's been interviewed. She can't claim self-defence because Ashcroft wasn't trying to kill her when she shot him, so I'm thinking she'll get a conviction, but certainly no custodial sentence. She was in possession of an unlicensed shotgun and she used it, but when you consider the situation, there are plenty of other circumstances to take into account. She'll be okay, I'm sure, and hopefully she'll get some help at last.'

'And Esther?' asked Charlie.

'Her air rifle needed no licence. And oddly, both guns have disappeared. Jacob tells me that immediately after Paul was shot, Esther brought them home on Rachel's orders, and gave them to Levi, who took them to his shed and sawed the barrels in half with his circular saw. He then threw them in the river.' Jackman gave a half-smile. 'Jacob was delighted with Levi for doing that, and his elder brother has really gone up in his estimation.'

'Guess that just about wraps it up, doesn't it?' said Robbie. 'Thanks, boss.'

'One small thing, but I think it's pretty important — you should like this, Robbie.' Jackman really did smile this time. 'Clay Bullimore, the man whose horse was stolen, is going to offer Jacob a permanent job at his stables. He reckons that a lad with his knowledge and understanding of horses will be a real asset. Oh, and he's beefed up security at the stables.'

'Brilliant,' said Robbie. 'Excellent result.'

'Excellent result all round, I'd say,' said Jackman. 'Now we can get on with our lives again.'

'It's really over,' Marie whispered.

Jackman sighed. 'Yes, this time it really is.'

* * *

Sometime around seven that evening, Jackman and Laura left Sam watching television and walked across to the mill. The transformation was impressive.

'Think you can work here?' Jackman asked.

'It's perfect. Being that little way from the house, means it won't intrude on our everyday life.' She gazed up at Jackman, eyes sparkling, 'I couldn't have wished for anything better. It's so peaceful here in the village.'

And it was. For the first time, Jackman could walk in his garden, breathe in the fresh fen air, and not look over his shoulder.

Emotion washed over him, and he reached for Laura's hand, clasping it tightly. 'We have a future, don't we, Laura? Now that he's gone.'

'Yes, of course, we do. It's like emerging from some terrible nightmare, some awful dark and dangerous place, and feeling the sun on your face again.'

He nodded.

'Speaking of nightmares, sweetheart?' Laura looked at him thoughtfully.

He leant forward and kissed her. 'What nightmares?'

* * *

That evening Marie rode her bike out to Hawker's Fen. Rachel greeted her with an offer of tea and the warmest smile she'd ever worn. Though her eyes were still puffy from the tears she'd shed over the loss of her boy, she also looked a little like Marie's team did, as if a fire had been rekindled within her.

Marie told her about Clay Bullimore's offer of a job for Jacob, and the tears fell again, this time for joy.

'I understand he'll be stable boy in charge of Nimbus's wellbeing, and he'll be able to ride him and everything. A proper paid job. Will he accept it, Rachel?'

'What do you think?' said Rachel, snuffling. 'It'll be the making of him.'

Marie sipped her tea, made in a pot with real leaves. Rachel permitted herself a single extravagance — proper tea. 'I'm sorry you have to go through all this legal stuff, Rachel, but Jackman is pulling every string he can to help you. We are right by you this time.'

Rachel nodded. 'You know, I'd have gone to prison for that wicked man. I should have aimed a whole lot higher than his knee.'

'Why did you send Esther home?'

'I didn't want her seeing Paul like that, and I didn't want her taken to the station and questioned. Not then. I knew it would have to happen, but not with her brother dying in front of her. I just told her to go home, give the guns to Levi and look after the family.'

'Her pellet hit his other knee dead centre and split his kneecap in half. The surgeon apparently said it was a chance in a million.'

'I always knew she was the best shot of the lot of them. That's why I took her with me.'

'The shotgun did a perfect job too, Rachel. I must say I wonder which of you fired that particular gun.' Marie looked at her knowingly. 'You said it was you, so I have to accept that, but . . . ?'

'More tea?'

'Thank you.' She smiled to herself. Rachel's reticence to answer confirmed Marie's belief that it had been Esther who'd fired the unlicensed shotgun, and Rachel's skilfulness that destroyed Ashcroft's knee with an airgun. She had just been trying to protect her daughter from a more serious charge.

Marie took a paper package from her jacket pocket and pushed it across the table. 'Our secret, Rachel. Don't tell a soul, you understand? Your boy wanted you to have this and in my opinion, he earned it, every penny.'

'Blood money,' sighed Rachel Lorimer, not touching it.

'No, this was his gift to you. He wanted to do something to support the family he loved. Take it. It doesn't belong to anyone else, it belonged to Paul, and I'm sure he was proud to have secured it for you. If he had come home like he was supposed to, he would have taken such pride in giving it to you.'

Rachel peeked inside the envelope and gasped. 'You're sure you won't get into trouble?'

'No one knows. Just us. As far as everyone else is concerned, he hid it, and no one knows where. End of story.'

Rachel Lorimer closed her eyes and sighed. 'End of story.' She picked up the envelope and put it in a drawer in her kitchen dresser.

'More tea, little Marie Evans?'

THE END

ALSO BY JOY ELLIS

JACKMAN & EVANS
Book 1: *The Murderer's Son*
Book 2: *Their Lost Daughters*
Book 3: *The Fourth Friend*
Book 4: *The Guilty Ones*
Book 5: *The Stolen Boys*
Book 6: *The Patient Man*

NIKKI GALENA SERIES
Book 1: *Crime on the Fens*
Book 2: *Shadow over the Fens*
Book 3: *Hunted on the Fens*
Book 4: *Killer on the Fens*
Book 5: *Stalker on the Fens*
Book 6: *Captive on the Fens*
Book 7: *Buried on the Fens*
Book 8: *Thieves on the Fens*
Book 9: *Fire on the Fens*
Book 10: *Darkness on the Fens*
Book 11: *Hidden on the Fens*

DETECTIVE MATT BALLARD
Book 1: *Beware the Past*
Book 2: *Five Bloody Hearts*

STANDALONES
Beware the Past
Guide Star

Join our mailing list to be the first to hear about
Joy Ellis's next mystery, coming soon!

www.joffebooks.com

Thank you for reading this book. If you enjoyed it please
leave feedback on Amazon or Goodreads, and if there is
anything we missed or you have a question about then
please get in touch. The author and publishing team
appreciate your feedback and time reading this book.